Other Works
by
Rivera Sun

Books, Poetry & Short Stories
Freedom Stories: volume one
The Imagine-a-nation of Lala Child

Theatrical Plays & Presentations
Jimmy/Joan
Stone Soup
The Imagine-a-nation of Lala Child
The Education of Lala Girl
The Emancipation of Lala
The Courage & The Calling
Sweet Angel Fire
Morning Dove

RISING SUN
PRESS WORKS

Steam Drills, Treadmills, and Shooting Stars

-a story of our times-

by

Rivera Sun

Steam Drills, Treadmills, and Shooting Stars

-a story of our times-

Copyright © 2013 by Rivera Sun.

Rising Sun Press Works
P.O. Box 1751, El Prado, NM 87529
www.risingsundancetheater.com

Library of Congress Control Number
2012947301
ISBN 978-0-9848132-2-3 paperback
ISBN 978-0-9848132-4-7 hardcover
ISBN 978-0-9848132-3-0 e-book
Sun, Rivera, 1982-
Steam Drills, Treadmills, and Shooting Stars

Grateful acknowledgment is made to the following for permission to reprint these documents: The Earth Charter Initiative for *The Earth Charter*; The United Nations for *The Universal Declaration of Human Rights*; Joanna Macy and Associates for *The Great Turning*

Photos by Steve DiBartolomeo

Dedicated to:
our children
and our children's children's children

and also to
my Papa
who fought the steam drills of his time

Thank you.

Table of Contents

Steam Drills, Treadmills, and Shooting Stars

-a story of our times-

CHAPTER ONE

· · · · ·

The Front Line of Birth & Death

It begins.

The world is sleeping. Solitude sinks down around the contours of the mountains. Silence dusts the city. Daybreak's bustle threatens to fling night back against the sky, but for now a quiet settles on the earth, quivering.

Two things happen:

A child breaks through his birth-waters and gasps for air.

Two lovers cry out together as their baby is conceived.

So it begins.

She is darkness tucked in darkness passing midnight through her legs. Her mother midwifes the laboring of the daughter.

"Push," the older woman says. "He's almost here."

Henrietta pushed so hard her soul slipped out her skin. Stars and light lanced the empty blanket of her body and threw her last vestiges of childhood up against the night. Memories of girlhood billowed softly and floated back. Henrietta's mother looked up. She was a veteran on the front line of birth and death. The head in her hands, her grandson's heartbeat in her fingertips, her daughter's insides pulsing out.

1

The descending parachute of the past threatened to shroud the future of her daughter.

"You can't go back," the mother stated. With one hand, she released the baby's crown and swept the past aside.

Henrietta screamed.

A shower of stars flung across the sky. The dawn of new life flooded in the room. The mother of the mother caught the babe one-handed.

So it begins.

Precarious, life is. A flying leap. A sweep of hand. A star flung across the night. A lucky catch in a whirling circus act.

The grandmother placed the infant in his mother's arms. Both were raw and wet from turning inside out. Smiles grew like sunrises across the dark skin of their faces. Daybreak hurled the city's nighttime stillness up into the sky.

So it begins.

On the same day, in another corner of the awakening world, a man murmured,

"I'm late."

"So?" his wife whispered back to him. "Even the sun doesn't always rise on time."

Her heart was quickening in the drumroll of desire. Pale pinks and rosy fleshes met and tumbled in the sunrise. Her blonde strands of hair laced with his short and stubby wheat stalks. Contours slid and shuddered against each other. An earthquake rippled through them. A little gem formed in the secret caverns of the woman. Trembling surfaces rose and gently fell with air and breath and life.

"Jack?" she breathed, catching his darting eyes in the sky

blue of her own. "I love you."

So it begins.

The full roundness of the day stroked its kiss across the world. The sun released the lip of earth and blazed in a proud moment of nakedness.

Then the sun slipped into a cloudy suit of gray. The promises of dawn snuffed out. Curling smoke pinched the sensual aromas from the world. The time of soot and smog and ordinary work arrived. The whole world groaned and went to work.

The new mother did not get up. She stayed naked in her newborn skin of motherhood. Her infant curled against her breast. The veteran mother -grandmother now- sprawled across a chair. All three, exhausted and wide-awake, watched the sun dive upward into the clouds.

"Such courage," the grandmother said to the sun, and to her grandson, and to her daughter, who was, today, a mother.

Such courage . . . so it all begins.

CHAPTER TWO

· · · · ·

Skyscraper Man

Jack Dalton stopped in his driveway. He stretched out of his car like a skyscraper-man that had shot up from the farmlands to become the city. It was as if he had grown so fast toward urban manhood that the stubbly wheat fields from harvests past still clung to his head in spikes. Brown and silvered from winter's aging, his hair complimented the shiny steel of his suit. His tie fluttered flag-like as Jack grabbed his briefcase and strode inside his house. He threw off his sunglasses and revealed the first frost lines of wrinkles hesitantly sprouting in the corners of his eyes. Those lines crisscrossed around the looming crossroads of his life, uncertain if they would curl with laughter or crease with frowns.

He pulled off his coat and laid it on the chair. His figure revealed the lines of an aging tower -not as old as the short brick historical buildings with smoking pipes that sat beneath the financial district, but also not as young and shiny as the impossible giants in the latest generation of construction. The honest blue of Jack's eyes reflected the sky in all its weathers. He was too old to bother with the cheery artificial tinting of today's windows.

Right now, they reflected an eye-rubbing sort of day.

It began that morning, just before his alarm rang out. An

image of a black man appeared, almost familiar, but elusive in his details as Jack struggled to catch sight of him between the veils of waking and dreaming. Later, in the drive-through line, as the box-voice jumbled up his order . . .

". . . double cafe-latte boiled black?"

"No! Just black coffee. Black! Got tha-?" Jack stopped mid-word. The man strode boldly out of dreams and through the line of cars in front of him. Jack squinted through the windshield, but the black man's features glinted away in the chromes and metals of the cars.

"Would you like a scone with that?" the teller crackled.

"No." Jack looked back. The man was gone. The drive-through kid gave him the scone anyway. Jack ate it absent-mindedly as he walked from the parking garage to the office elevator. A stream of suits poured out of the opening elevator doors. A weathered cap flashed by. Jack blinked. A cap?

"Going up?" a polite inquirer asked as Jack hesitated in the lobby. Jack didn't answer. The doors slid shut. A coarse weave shirt reflected in them. He spun. No one.

Then, while Jack was killing time as the coffee cooled and the computers warmed, his boss boomed out some meaningless morning greeting, and the man's pasty white face turned chocolate-colored-dark with shining eyes. Jack choked. The boss' face returned to its customary paleness. Jack excused himself and stepped into his private office. He sat staring out the window at the sea of glass-steel towers and wondered what the visage was trying to tell him.

Half a dozen times throughout his life a gut feeling had pounded him into unexpected action. The helpful, but cryptic

6

visions would delay him at the airport while his plane crashed without him on it. They would hint in numbered codes that snapped into place just in time for him to renegotiate a contract. He would dream a metaphor of the next day's meeting and end up saving the company millions of dollars.

Jack groaned. These visions sat uncomfortably in the modern world of facts and figures. He had said nothing about the previous one, a sun-shaped mark that appeared on his inner wrist and refused to go away until he convinced his bosses at Standard Coal -against all reasoning- to diversify their portfolios. But now, as the company struggled to maintain high profit margins amid environmental, economic, and political challenges, his bosses were making out like bandits on their green energy investments.

Jack shook his head. He could be wrong. Perhaps it was just a dream. A black man walking past the drive-through line was hardly usual. And the boss' face? Jack shrugged and chalked it up to shadows. He brushed aside the strangeness of the morning and hunkered down to daily business. The image would fade over time, he told himself.

At four o'clock, he bid the boss goodbye.

"Got to be home for my little girl!" he called out. He jetted from the office ignoring the looks of envy from the cubicle fathers who worked until six. He drove too fast on the freeway and arrived long before his daughter's softball buddies dropped her off.

Jack paced across the plush cream carpet into the living room as the image of the man returned to nag him. He loosened up his tie and remembered the man's big, coffee colored hands. Jack pulled the noose off his neck and tossed it onto the armrest of the couch. He unbuttoned his shirt cuffs and rolled them up along his white and freckled arms. The other man's arms had been thick with muscle. Jack kicked off his shoes and shoved them under the low table that held the family's collection of magazines, pens, old mugs, and pocket change. He shook the tension from his shoulders, feeling the silk and cotton fabric pull against his arms. The image returned, sharply defined: broad shoulders in a plain weave shirt, cap on head, lips verging on a smile. Jack cracked his neck and opened the buttons on his collar. He stared at his middle-age sags and sighed at the other image . . . the man had strength enough to bowl you over. Jack's belly leaned over his belt as he sat and laid his head back on the couch.

It was just a dream, Jack insisted, but his gut feelings screamed a red alert. He meticulously flipped through his mental files of recent interactions. Nothing. He combed through the catalogue of current iconic figures. Nothing. He scoured his memory for past encounters with black men. Nothing. He willed the visage to return and explain its presence in his life. Nothing.

Thirty years of dealing with these powerful, persistent messages had taught Jack one thing: the longer he ignored them, the stronger they became. The image of the black man pulsed with energy and a hint of warning. Alright, Jack grumbled silently, if this is the 'meet and greet' stage of the vision, let's hurry it up. He spoke out loud in the empty living room,

"Come on, introduce yourself. Let's get going." Jack

8

waited for a response. Nothing. He hadn't really expected anything. He shrugged and turned on the TV, watching commercials as his eyes sagged and his thoughts spun round. His breath slowed. He dozed.

*   *   *

"Dad?" Allie called out. No response. She dumped her school bag on the kitchen floor and released her unruly brown curls from her rubber band. Brown eyes peeked into the living room. Dad's eyelids were shut in the achy-after-work sort of way. The TV had been left chattering to itself.

Fluorescent yellow soccer socks stepped across the cream-colored carpet. Skinny legs and knobby knees tiptoed like a praying mantis toward the couch. She eased her shiny purple shorts down on the couch and tried not to breathe. The wooden couch frame bit into her butt like a blunt-nosed crocodile, but Allie wasn't budging. She might make it into the next program without the dreaded, but expected comment, *have you done your homework?*

Allie glanced at the awkward sprawl that sent Dad's limbs flying in every direction. That's the problem with couches, she thought; they never fit. Either they sucked you in like quicksand or they bounced you off like a fat man's belly. *Or,* Allie sighed (at eleven, either/or sentences were not monogamous relationships), they strangled the backs of your legs until your toes turned purple-prickly. The best thing you could do with a couch, in her opinion, was ride horseback on it until the grownups yelled at you. Or . . . jump on it.

9

Neither of which Allie intended to do. The leather couch had a long history of squealing on her. She sat still as a pill commercial began. Oh, good, Allie thought, those were always gray-achy people popping pills and turning happy overnight . . . and then the list of side effects . . . nothing that would wake up Dad when a certain somebody was glued to the TV instead of doing her homework.

But I'm not glued to the TV, Allie thought rebelliously. I'm glued to a crocodile couch.

She caught the giggle in her stomach. It wiggled. The leather tooted. Dad grunted. Allie froze. The side effects scrolled down the screen. Difficulty breathing. Heart palpitations. High blood pressure. Who needs pills when you've got Dad and homework to avoid? *Consult your regular physician*, the screen warned. *And now . . . another message from our sponsors!*

More commercials? Allie groaned. She willed the bleach lady to wash the laundry faster. She crossly sent the high-speed internet advertisers a psychic message to hurry up. She rolled her eyes while Mr. Shiny Tooth grinned and winked and flexed his "an-older-man-who-cleans-is-a-housewife's-dream" biceps. Then a coffee commercial jingle-jangled out,

"*It's a great day for waking up!*"

Dad sat up. Allie squeezed her eyes shut and waited for the descending homework guillotine.

"Who was John Henry?" he asked.

Allie cracked an eye to double-check that he was actually addressing her. His knees shot out from the couch in a triangle. His elbows constructed scaffolding to hold his chin on top of

10

his palms. His fingers stretched up along his cheeks and scratched his sideburns.

"John Henry," her father repeated, "who was he?"

"Is this a quiz?" she asked reluctantly.

Dad flopped back onto the couch. The crocodile snorted. Allie bumped up into the air and the beastly thing nipped her on the way back down.

"Ouch," she winced. Dad looked at her.

"Don't you have homework to do?"

Rats. She kicked the double-crossing crocodile couch and started to trudge away. Rules were rules. Some questions were commands.

Jack flipped the TV off and closed his eyes. He must have been dozing. The screen behind his eyes flashed arms and hammers and those brown-set eyes that suddenly had a name: John Henry.

"John Henry," he repeated.

"It's a song," said a voice in his ear.

Jack did a startled backflip inside his skin. Allie climbed over the back of the couch and lay stretched out on its spine. Jack breathed deeply.

"What honey?"

"John Henry is a song," Allie informed him, "about a black guy who built railroads. We studied it in music." The continued blankness on his face elicited an exasperated sigh. Allie mimicked her music teacher,

"The Ballad of John Henry is an excellent example for all budding ethno-musicologists. Based on an actual historic figure in the late 1800's, John Henry was most likely a prison laborer

11

who worked on the railroads. The legendary strength and stamina of the man were immortalized in a song recounting his steel driving competition with a steam drill."

Allie's tone broke into an enthusiastic rush and she pounded the couch between words.

"He was all like *swoosh-boom, swoosh-boom*! Fighting down the steam drill, which went *wha-bamm, wha-bamm*! It was going to put all the guys out of work, so John Henry had to fight it."

She sang out,

> *"John Henry said to the Captain,*
> *A man ain't nothing but a man,*
> *but before I let that steam drill beat me down,*
> *I'm gonna die with a hammer in my hand!"*

The lamp of Jack's memory flickered dimly,

"Didn't he die fighting the steam drill?"

"Well, yeah, but he kicked that steam drill's butt!" She plopped down on the couch in a motion suspiciously like jumping and asked,

"Hey, Dad, will you help me with my math?"

Jack was dragged out of sepia-toned thoughts and into the glossy world of textbooks as a fog of fifth grade math engulfed them both.

Neither heard the garage door rumbling, the car door thudding, or the click of heels until the side door banged its daily hello against the wall and smacked a kiss upon the familiar purse.

"Hi Mom," Allie mumbled.

"Hi honey," her mom replied. "How come you're still in

your suit?" That was meant for Dad, not Allie, so she didn't answer. Mom rolled right on with her monologue, "Has Allie been so bad that she's going to bed without supper or did you forget to feed her?"

They exchanged a look. Sheesh, Mom, can't you tell we're stuffed with fifth grade math?

"Well," she continued, "it wouldn't surprise me if it was a no-supper night. What a day!" Sarah ran her fingers through her blonde hair and rubbed her pregnant belly, reminiscing. "My morning sickness was followed by our little cherub here holding up a stack -a stack!- of school papers to sign -in the drop off zone! I'm late for work. Allie's freaking out. She can't go on that field trip *today* if I don't sign *now*. Cars are piling up. Parents glaring at me."

Jack's remote control turned her volume down. His mind switched channels . . . another homecoming played out on Jack's inner screen: a canvas tent, a pot of beans, a smile, and no words until the kisses finished.

" . . . I couldn't even tell the boss I'm pregnant, not until he gives me that raise, which he won't if I go on maternity leave."

Jack left the math and took her purse, briefcase, and coffee mug. He shushed her,

"No words until the-"

"Not now, Jack. I'm late for pre-natal yoga. Double check Allie's homework and don't microwave her dinner, okay?"

Jack nodded silently.

"I'll be home late. Pam is going through another crisis. She'll want to talk. God, how that woman talks!"

I love you, Sarah, he said, but his mute button was still on.

Slow down, his subtitles translated. *I love you, come be with us.*

"Allie? Nine o'clock equals bedtime, got it?"

"Yeah." (Sheesh, Mom, that's baby math.)

And then she was gone. Jack poked his toe through a hole in his sock and looked wistfully after his wife. She was a whistle-blowing, steam-rolling train on a tight schedule these days. The home station stopover never lasted more than a few minutes and she only returned from her final journey late at night.

"Dad? Can I watch TV now?"

"Not just yet, Allie." The garage door hadn't closed. Allie scooted across the hardwood floor of the kitchen in her fluorescent soccer socks. Jack told her to go change into regular clothes while he made dinner. She zipped up the stairs.

Jack pulled a pre-made pizza out of the freezer. If Sarah had been home, he would have taken them all out, or, better yet, made the pizza himself. But his heart just wasn't up for the effort tonight. He paused in front of the microwave, thought of pots of beans on woodstoves, and decided to use the convection oven. Jack spun the oven dial to 425° and slid the frozen pizza in. Then he climbed the stairs to complete his after-work transformation.

In the middle of swapping his pressed black pants for a comfortable old pair of blue jeans, he paused. He sat on the bed, looking down at his chest hairs, the freckles on his knees, and the faint scar left over from his childhood shenanigans. Outside the second story window, the streetlights traded places with the sunset. All over the country, men just like him were coming home and peeling off work clothes. Grimy coveralls

14

were getting kicked aside. Painters were shedding speckled-white shirts and pants. Brown uniforms of deliverymen were falling on the floor. The blues and blacks of off-duty police officers slid down around hairy ankles. One by one, the men sat down on the edge of their beds. Bellies sagged. Chest hairs curled. Hearts beat. Lungs expanded and whooshed out in sighs. Legs stretched out from the beds in shades of brown, tan, and cream. Blue and red blood veins pulsed within them all.

Jack sat naked on his bed with his long legs and lumpy knees, thinking of his too-busy wife, and staring out the window at suburbs full of houses and men. They pounded and sweated and argued and bickered, strutted, paraded, fought, and bullied, intimidated, manipulated, wheedled, coerced, labored and worked all day. In the solitude of their bedrooms, they stripped their efforts down to one sheer naked truth: *a man ain't nothing but a man.*

Jack paused in the ritual of undressing to wonder what made one man different from another. Why did one wear gold watches, while another sported dog tags? Why did he pull silk shirts over his head, when others shed threadbare cotton?

Jack shifted uncomfortably on the bed. Though he'd like to chalk up his success to his intelligence and hard work, he had a suspicion that he was just a lucky winner of a skeleton, born at the right time, to the right parents, growing wealthy and fat while other men worked their bones back into the dust.

Jack shrugged. There was nothing he could do about that. He pulled a tee shirt over his head and slipped a lie around his heart: some men were special, different, more deserving than other men, that's all. He stood up, put on his blue jeans, and left the naked honest brotherhood behind.

He sucked in his gut to button his pants and frowned. He needed to lose some weight. These blue jeans had taken him a month of Sundays to break in. Some men bought designer distressed jeans, but not him. It'd be a shame to start all over again just when this pair was getting cozy.

Jack padded barefoot down the carpeted stairs to check on the pre-made pizza roasting in the state-of-the-art oven. He slid his hand along marble countertops and tapped his fingers on dark mahogany chairs and lowered the kitchen lights to a comfortable glow. He flipped on the oven light and smiled at the sizzling cheese. A few more minutes left.

Wha-bamm! Wha-bamm!

Allie was steam drilling the couch seats.

"Allie," Jack called out, "what did you think about that John Henry song?"

She stopped pounding. The crocodile couch sighed in relief and uncurled its leather dents.

"It was cool."

"You didn't think it was sad?"

"Because he died? Nah, my music teacher said he had to die so history could live on."

Jack blinked and tried to understand that concept. All men die. History continues on. What difference would a few more years of John Henry's life have made?

"Didn't he have kids?" Jack asked his eleven-year old historical expert.

"One," she informed him and promptly began to barrel out

16

the lyrics of the ballad, making steel driving faces that did not match her high-pitched chirp,

> *"John Henry had a little baby!*
> *You could hold him in the palm of your hand!*
> *And the first words out of the poor boy's mouth were,*
> *'my daddy is a steel driving man!'"*

He cut her off before the next verse, asking,

"You don't think John Henry would have wanted to see his kid grow up?"

"That would have been sad," she replied, matter of fact. "He beat that steam drill, but people just brought faster ones. John Henry wouldn't have liked that. He liked doing things with his hands and singing while he worked. You can't do that anymore."

Jack tried to imagine singing in his office. He couldn't.

"I suppose that's true."

"Yeah, and John Henry liked real work."

The pizza puffed golden in the oven. Tomato smells wafted toward their noses. Jack frowned at her.

"What do you mean, real work? I do real work."

"You work in an office," she stated, as if that wasn't real work. He gave her a *Dad* look. She gave him a *Da-aad, you're such an idiot* look. He sent the *you're too young to know that look* look back at her. She rolled her eyes . . . crossways. Jack smiled. She hadn't mastered *that* expression yet. He pulled out the pizza and started slicing. Allie leaned hungrily on the table and explained the concept of 'real work' to the idiot who held her dinner hostage.

"Back then, people used to do real work like making bread

and furniture and houses and growing vegetables."

He put a slice of pizza on each plate and motioned to the table -not the TV- and pointed out that it was a lot easier to be a lawyer and pay someone to do the 'real work' of growing all the food she was eating tonight.

"Yeah, but imagine if we did it! I could pick the tomatoes, you could carry the baskets, Mom would be home to cook them, and we could all sing."

Jack smiled. Sometimes, despite her head full of unrealistic notions, his eleven-year old just melted his heart and looked too young to be shooting out *idiot* looks. Jack wanted to snapshot that moment and live inside its toasty tomato smell forever. Then Allie crammed an entire slice of pizza into her boa constrictor mouth. Jack sighed and surrendered to the inexorable growth of daughters.

*   *   *

Later, to the slosh-mumble of the dishwasher and Allie's god-knows-what upstairs, Jack hummed a tune with words he couldn't remember until his stomach gurgled and a belch bellowed out. He looked down. His version of put-away-the-leftovers grumbled in his gut. He grimaced. This had to change.

Out came the tennis shoes from a dusty spot beneath the bed. Blue jeans were exchanged for shorts and Jack found himself poised before the treadmill in the family room, trying to remember how to program it.

John Henry sat down on the arm of the recliner.

Jack jumped, but then decided to play it cool, as if ghosts just showed up in his family room all the time. He tilted his head in the barest of nods, treating the apparition like an old buddy who had just popped in from the locker room of folklore.

"Don't start on me," Jack warned him. "I know what you're thinking."

John Henry stared back steadily.

"It's all different now," he stated, pulling up his slipping shorts and trying to explain -not excuse- his flabbiness to this muscled laborer. "We got machines that make everything so easy," he said.

John Henry crossed his arms against his chest, but remained silent. Jack babbled nervously,

"Yup, we got everything so easy, we even have these machines to take the easy off of us!"

He stabbed the buttons. Two beeps. The treadmill creaked slowly into gear. Jack stepped on at a gentle walk. Go easy, he cautioned himself. John Henry watched, expressionless. Jack punched the buttons with one finger.

BEEP. He noted every jiggle on his torso as he quickened up his pace. The other man sat like wrought iron.

"I didn't always look like this, you know," Jack said. "When I was a kid, I was the fastest runner on the track team. My dad's folks had a farm. Sort of a gentleman farmer, I guess. We'd go out on the weekend-"

BEEP.

"-and a little jog like this? That was my Sunday drive back before I got a car. I'd cruise around looking cool 'n easy, looking for girls, or at them anyway." Jack looked straight

19

ahead and anything but cool and easy. Back then he didn't hardly break a sweat. Now his shirt formed a Y of dryness between the spreading damp spots. "If I wanted to *run*," Jack bragged, "well, that was different."

BEEP. BEEP.

"I'd go out to my Grandpop's fields and stretch out on the dirt roads and cow paths."

BEEP.

"I'd just fly!"

Thud-thud, his feet pounded.

"God, that was freedom. To have a-"

Huff-huff, his lungs heaved.

"-good strong body on a fine cool morning-"

Huff, he gasped.

"-and just fly through the back fields!"

His thoughts took off as his breath ran out. Yeah, that was freedom, glory-bound. No worries ahead, no problems behind. Just feet thwacking the earth, air pumping in and out, cheeks flushed, clean 'n honest sweat pouring off your back, and blood pounding you alive! Jack slowed the machine down. He had no stamina to keep up with his past. John Henry continued to watch him. When he had eased into a steady jog, Jack said,

"Wasn't so hard to run back then. I didn't want anything more than to be a farmer just like Grandpop. A few vegetables, a couple of chickens, but then . . . "

His voice trailed off, lost in what life had run into. He panted, doggedly pushing on. "You just got to keep going these days. You can't stop. Got that mortgage and the cars and the new baby on the way and the other one thinking about college

20

already." He was tired now, but his legs plodded on, one after another. "Got to keep your eye on the prize. God knows what that is." He punched at the buttons, but the machine kept rolling at a pace he couldn't sustain. He leaped off onto the treadmill's sides and leaned his brow down on the console. It beeped apologetically and slowed the belt down. Jack watched it whir by without him. His chest heaved, heavy.

"How did we get here? I wake up in a cold sweat in the middle of the night from a dream that's all true: the bills, Sarah upset, Allie in tears, and I just don't want to take another step, but I got to. I got to, for them." The machine stopped. He lifted his head as the red lights faded off.

"I just want to wake up in the sunshine with Sarah smiling and Allie running barefoot in a field. Is that too much to ask, John?" He looked up. The figure was gone. The sweat felt cold on his back. His voice sounded odd in the empty room.

CHAPTER THREE

. . . . .

An Instant Click of Indescribable Perfection

Henrietta stepped into the snapshot's frame. Her dark eyes swung toward the camera. They stared outward with such a knowing look that the photographer swore the woman had done the impossible and heard the shutter click before the sound was born.

Then she stepped out of the framework of possible and impossible and was gone. The photographer trembled as he reviewed the image. The crowd of protesters mobbed around him. Their soundless mouths flapped like forgotten doors. They chanted words he did not hear to unseen foes who were not listening either. The child and his mother were burning in his retina. Out of millions of photos snapped in shuttered moments, photographers pray to catch one image of indescribable perfection.

And here it was.

The still likeness of the woman looked out at the madness of the world and dared to hope. Her eyes were burning coals of stars. The babe nestled against his mother. Her bones etched defiance against the worldly sky. Her lips neither smiled nor frowned, but burst with things that needed to be said. The photographer sighed in satisfaction. All photos speak a thousand words. This one contained a library.

The photographer's silence exploded with the throbbing cries of protesters demanding justice for the ravaged mountains in the coalfields of West Virginia. Their ragged chants had all the rawness of a handwritten sign taped to a stick. She could not have heard the click, the photographer thought. Its quiet sound would have been tromped on by the bullhorn's hollow rasping and the drumbeats that cracked out from an overturned plastic bucket. The photographer looked around at the band of protesters groaning and rattling out this strange citizens' form of prayer.

We should compose our protests into symphonies, the photographer thought. Then, even if no one else will listen, at least we will have heard the music's beauty. He looked around again, but did not see the woman. The protestors swarmed past the photographer, parting around his stillness. He thought he saw a flash of darkness in the rippling mob of paler skins. He stood on tiptoe, but could not see her. He hooked his reporter from the stream of people and reeled him in. He showed him the digital image of the woman.

"Oh, her," the reporter said, flipping through his notes, "the black woman . . . that's Henrietta Owens."

CHAPTER FOUR

· · · · ·

The Bloodhound's Report

Jack creaked and cracked his way to work. His body protested every step. Coffee rebelled against its duty and refused to perform its perky task. Jack flopped into his chair, groaning,

"When you get to be my age . . . "

He snorted, hearing the echoes of his father and his father's father. He had always wondered why they'd wheezed and puffed their plodding ways across the field on his family's vacations at the farm.

"You have to run!" he had once called out as he sprinted past. "It gives you strength!" His lineage shook their heads. He circled back, asking, "Why don't you run? It's so free!" His father swung his heavy stride step by trudging step.

"I gave it up," he said, "long ago, for you."

Jack wondered if that meant his running or his freedom. Or both. Now that he was their age, Jack found a freedom given up was not so easily regained. He had sold the physical liberty of his youth for comfort and convenience. His body ached from the first attempt to get it back. He winced as he tried to rub the soreness from his thighs. His secretary popped her highlighted head into the room.

"Sir, Mr. Schwartz would like to see you."

"What the devil does he want?"

"I don't know, sir. Shall I ring the devil and find out?" Perkier than a cup of coffee, she could quip the whole office to attention in thirty seconds flat.

"No, Cathy, just send him in." Jack took a swig of lukewarm coffee, stretched, cracked, and tucked in his shirt. Schwartz entered head first, followed by his sloping shoulders and baggy, brown coat. Then, lastly, his tail end slid through the door. His hanging bloodhound face drooped into perpetual lines and folds. He sniffed and sat.

"Morning, Mr. Dalton."

Not good. Not bad. Just morning. Jack appreciated Walter Schwartz.

"Morning, Walter. What's stirring in the rank and file?" Schwartz swung his drooping eyelids upward,

"What isn't?" He smacked his chops and pulled his chin, entirely unconcerned. "We got the usual muttering in the unions. Got some middle management grumblings."

Jack wished he'd just get on with it, but Schwartz wasn't built for speed. He was a sniffer, not a sprinter. If he moved too fast, he'd miss the subtle scent of trouble brewing. Jack let him take his time.

"The kids think they'll be stuck in their jobs for the rest of their lives. The gramps think their jobs are vanishing. The middle pops don't have a clue what's happening in the layoffs, but they're praying it doesn't include them."

Schwartz forecast the company weather. He read the barometric pressures as they rose and fell. He was bored by all the sex scandals and revolutions because he saw them brewing from miles away.

"So what's rumbling, Walter?" Jack repeated. Something must have hit the man's radar.

"Oh, we got some turbulence."

"Inside or out?"

"Maybe both, sir."

Jack didn't like the sound of that. "What's the gripe?"

"Mountaintop removal."

"Oh that." Jack flicked it aside. The whole issue annoyed him like a hoary, old fly. It had been buzzing around for thirty years as the coal company tore up West Virginia. Everyone knew the issue had no teeth to nip at Standard Coal. It'd been trying since Jack first poked his peach-fuzz face in the company door. Whole mountains had vanished in his tenure here. Flattening Appalachia was as ordinary to Jack as shaving. They could whack the issue now and kill it, he supposed. But why bother? It would keel over on its own, wave its feet dramatically in the air, and that would be that. Jack laughed,

"Schwartz, we have a memo out on that already. We're stopping mountaintop removal."

The bloodhound flung his surprised jowls from side to side as Jack continued,

"Yes, we'll stop as soon as the coal is gone . . . or the mountains . . . whichever happens first."

They wheezed together at the old gag. The knolls and ridges over the seams of coal in the Appalachia Mountains stretched in little, uninspiring lumps across four states. A team of men, a couple of machines the size of gymnasiums, and some permits were all it took. They tore the tops off the mountains, threw the debris in the valleys, collected the coal, and then moved on to the next ridge, leaving acres of unstable rock and exposed ore behind them. It was a sandbox game for the big boys, but it left an acrid taste in one's mouth. Jack and Schwartz wore puckered lemon frowns upon their faces.

"What's the problem then, Schwartz?"

"The eco-freaks got a little lightning flashing in their clouds."

"Not another handsome, good-looking activist?" Jack rolled his eyes. The romantic ones were so much trouble. Then again, so were the sloppy blunderers and the dour brilliant ones. Schwartz nodded,

"Yep. There's this kid named Henr-"

Jack choked. Henry? *Henry?* He felt a pressure in the room, a sign of strength . . . and trouble.

"Stop him," Jack ordered.

"Her," Schwartz corrected.

"What?" Jack's vision of a black man vanished.

"Her. Henrietta Owens."

"Student?"

"No, a single mom, unemployed."

Great, Jack groaned, a young mother turned environmentalist. Pissed-off, laid-off trouble. He sighed up to the ceiling. Trouble arrived in so many forms: hordes of locusts, epidemic plagues, raging wars. On the scale of global politics and billion dollar businesses, *this* was a gnat.

"Why are you telling me this?" he asked Schwartz.

"She was in the local paper."

Oh, a buzzing gnat, Jack amended.

"She's inspiring the mountain folks," Schwartz told him.

Oh, a swarm of gnats, Jack grimaced.

"It's not a union issue, is it?" Jack asked.

"Nooo . . . " his sleuth answered slowly, "but it could become one."

Jack believed it. Unions held protests the same way churches held family outings. Neither group required much of a reason to organize a picnic or a picket line. The sun is shining? Let's picnic! The rain is pouring? Let's picket! Jack leaned back in his chair.

"Do you really think she could get the workers in behind her?"

"Don't know, but that photo's stirring up the mountain communities."

Jack drawled, "I thought we had them fairly dampened."

"Yep," Schwartz said, "but you know how those mountain folks are . . . burning coals of resentment for generations."

"She sparked them up again?"

"Yep."

"How?"

Jack and Schwartz had played this game so many times together: identify trouble, assess enemy, destroy. Schwartz hunkered into the meat of it.

"It was a photo in the local paper that started it. Now the protest organizers are having her go around to picnics, lunch lines, churches-"

"Whoa, whoa, whoa. We own those churches." Jack scowled. Coal was God in West Virginia. Everybody worshipped it. God's right hand men of Standard Coal employed the priests and wrote the sermons. 'Protest' wasn't in their Bible.

"Eh, there's been some, uh, special services," Schwartz told him. Time to clean the House of God, Jack thought. The mountains are getting to the priests. They were hired to pray for coal. Protecting mountains is the devil's work.

"Alright, Schwartz, who is she?"

"Nobody, sir. Poor. Black. Unwed welfare mother. The kid's father is doing time up at the prison. Classic."

Easy to discredit, Jack thought. She's just another sucker on the system. Still, she might prove tough and hardy. She had nothing to lose and nothing to do but fight. Jack knew the human machine. Push it down too far and it had no choice but to try to rise back up. He leaned his elbows on the desk, staring out the eleventh story window. He watched the sun glint off the towers of the city, the cars, and the people down below. We might have to raise her up a little, he thought. Give her better options: a house, a job, a car. Something she'd be loath to lose. Jack turned back to the conversation. As he did, he felt a bitter taste. Just the coffee, he rationalized.

But just behind the ordinary workplace, Jack didn't see the vision that was not quite visible through the office's practical facade. Above the skyscrapers of the city, the massive spirit of John Henry spanned the urban landscape, watching and waiting for Jack's awakening.

CHAPTER FIVE

. . . . .

Ripped Off Mountains

Henrietta Owens' records lay upended on Jack Dalton's desk. He picked through them for clues to who she was, but her life started in sentences that kept trailing off or stopping short. It was as if all her socks were missing proper matches: high school honors list, but no college education; a guy named Tyrell Johnson who took her to homecoming, but not to prom; an engagement notice, but no marriage; a birth certificate for a baby who lacked his father's last name. Jack stared out the window. Underneath the scanty lingerie of statistics that clothe our naked human lives, Henrietta Owens remained a mystery.

Henrietta's mother could have told him. She had single-handedly raised that girl on prayers, miracles, and a nurse's nightshift salary. Arellia Owens ministered to the young, the old, and the in-between. Recently, she had left the halls of hospitals and stepped into a new position as a notary public for the city, but she still continued to preside over human lives. She marked the records of birth and death, houses bought and sold, marriages begun and ended. She stamped the weight of official acceptance onto life's events with titles, deeds, and licenses, condensing whole lifetimes into the legal shorthand of our culture.

Arellia Owens would have pinned Jack Dalton with a

brown-eyed gaze and scolded him for attempting to understand a *person* through facts and figures. She would have told him that we are a lifetime of a trillion heartbeats, a symphony of emotions, and a churning force within the realms of spirit. We are myths still in the making with our prophecies scrawled across the heavens . . . and some trickster's rearranging them when no one's looking.

Arellia Owens knew that no one's life made sense on paper. You cannot condense a person into facts. Our thoughts and motivations stretch wider than the globe. Our bodies contain the footprints of eternity. We carry the thousand shades of earth within us. Beneath her precise camouflage of pressed shirts and skirts, Arellia, herself, wore fresh-broken fields and lighter sun-dried stretches. A hint of iron rusted in her cheeks. Steel hardened in the lines around her eyes. She knew why her daughter stood up for the mountains . . . but no statistic could explain that to Jack Dalton.

*　　*　　*

The first time Henrietta had seen the ripped off mountains with their topless gaping holes, she had ridden ten hours on a bus to bring her infant son to meet his father for the first time. The miles inched by as they approached the prison. The baby rode within her arms. Her heart hammered in her chest.

When they crested over the ridgeline, Henrietta gasped in visceral recognition. Acres of torn-up mountainsides filled her eyes. Strange gladness coursed within her bloodstream. Something was finally large enough, wide enough, awful enough to express the way her life had been ripped apart. Five hundred acres stripped barren could hardly describe the past year that she had gone through. The scraped off greenery of her life lay in jumbled piles of broken branches. Joyous peaks had been bulldozed flat. Injustice had left its scars. The machinery of law had pressed its tread marks on her heart. Her cheeks felt eroded from a flood of tears that had no web of roots to hold it back.

As the bus wound its way up to the prison, Henrietta looked at the pinched faces of the other passengers. Their expressions puckered from the acid that life had thrown into their eyes. She felt like shaking all the other wives and mothers and showing them what lay behind the ridge. *It's us*, she wanted them to know. Whole bodies ripped to shreds. Mountain ranges torn up by a system that hides its consequences in places that few people will ever see. Up and down the east coast, national parks, state forests, and wildlife refuges were kept pristine, but here, hidden from the public eye, were the coalfield ghettos of the mountains.

The rackety bus wheezed to a stop in front of the prison. Henrietta straightened up her spine. The driver told her the jail had been built on a stripped-out mine. Henrietta shuddered and stepped out onto an eerie flatness that had no business being in the mountains. The frostbitten lawn denied any chance to run or hide. The unnatural expanse spread all around the prison.

It's bigger than the White House lawn, Henrietta realized, or the Washington Mall. She tried to imagine Dr. King delivering his dreams here. She couldn't. This kind of lawn buried dreams beneath it. In the distance, she could see the prison cemetery for the deceased convicts that no one came to claim.

Inside, Henrietta gave the guards the visitation slip with Tyrell's number on it. She saw the orange first, the suit that grabs your eyes and conceals personhood beneath. Then Tyrell emerged within that orange, flesh and blood and real. Henrietta's breath ran out all at once. Fear's fingers released her lungs. Relief stung her eyes. Subconscious worries burst like bubbles as they rose to her awareness.

Tyrell had always been a sovereign man, a ruler of himself.

"But there are times," he had told her once, "when the world seems to lay claim to me. It tries to tell me what to do, think, how to act . . . but then I realize there is nothing but my own mind's defenses to let such notions in. I cast the traitorous thoughts out of me."

Then the justice system had cast its iron claws of law around his life and Henrietta feared that the fiber of her child's father would dissolve beneath the bars of others.

"You cannot exile a man from himself," Tyrell had said.

And now she saw that it was true. His eyes slid themselves around her. His smile shined for her. His face was scrubbed over with emotion. She held his baby up to meet him.

Pain and pleasure split him head to toe. A lightning strike could not have stunned him more. Henrietta looked up and saw a trembling twitch forewarn the threat of tears.

"I'm sorry," he said and his expression wrote unspoken volumes of apologies as he stared at the miracle of his son. The guard stared straight ahead, posed like a statue above the human drama.

"I sent you photos," she murmured, "with the letters?" He shook his head, receiving only now the image of his child.

"I got one postcard," he told her.

She had sent him dozens. It was her turn to blink back what could flood them both. He caught the frantic dams she constructed in her eyes.

"It's alright, love. It's better this way, in person. He looks like you," Tyrell said. His eyes leaped back and forth from child to mother, unable to choose which one he loved the most. Finally, he surrendered, because there is no *most* to loving.

*　　*　　*

If the photographer had captured Henrietta in that moment, Jack Dalton might have understood why she stood up for the mountains. They formed a line of hope in her battle against despair. They were forested landscape her family would one day walk in. Every fallen acre ripped a mountain from their future.

Arellia Owens, notary public, knew nothing could condense her daughter into facts. For a quarter of a century, Arellia had tried to attach that girl to the reality of traffic signals and busy streets. She had chased that dreaming child from the realms of myths and tried to weigh her down with common sense. Yet, as pragmatic as Arellia was, she also knew the world was more than just its surface. There are stories hidden behind the scenery, invisible tales that affect our lives. These stories reveal far more than documents. Arellia Owens would have told Jack

Dalton that all those dates and facts on slips of paper couldn't explain as much as a single story. Not when it was a love story. Not when told correctly.

*   *   *

It did not work to say, *we met on a street corner, Mamma,* as Henrietta initially tried to say. Some stories cannot squeeze into the corsets of the ordinary. The details of taxicabs and stoplights explained nothing to Arellia. Henrietta mentioned that the crowds parted. Arellia nodded. Her daughter blushed and confessed she couldn't move as he walked across the street. Arellia sighed. Henrietta told her the cars screeched silently to a halt and a flock of doves flew overhead. Arellia did not say they were only pigeons.

For years, Arellia had watched Henrietta's friends racing toward adulthood. The young girls' drying and tightening skins of childhood itched them all like crazy. Arellia consoled the other mothers as their daughters writhed and wriggled sexuality and womanhood into their bodies, leaving the snakeskin of childhood irrevocably behind. She watched Henrietta ceaselessly, wondering what was taking her so long.

Henrietta was waiting for the stars to fall exactly into place. She endured the itching that had sent her friends rubbing up against anything in their burning to remove it. In the invisible marketplace of matchmakers, Henrietta's soul laid stretched out on the scale. Her childhood still shone sweetly, but her coming womanhood pulsed powerfully beneath it.

The sounds of the matchmakers of our souls are nearly

impossible to hear. The bustling of our everyday cities drowns out their gossipy bantering. Had Henrietta paused as she strode down the cement sidewalk, she might even have caught a glimpse of the matchmakers' invisible marketplace. Such consternation rippled through it as they weighed her soul. Such lust gleamed in their beady eyes. Such a rare bargain! So strong! So beautiful! And who would have its equal?

Not the herders with those bellowing young bulls that thundered through the alleyways of high schools. Not farmers with those spud and turnip lads who made sturdy, unexciting husbands. Not fishermen with sleek and slippery young men. In the depths of oceans are creatures worthy of this woman, yes, but they must meet their loves in open waters, not on the fish scales of smelly markets.

Poor Henrietta, how she wandered through her daily life, dodging cars with blaring horns, and racing to catch the city buses. Behind the scenes, the matchmakers made bargains, filling jars with gold and spices, and cutting lengths of cloth for other dowry chests. Henrietta rode the humid subway to the grocery store while the matchmakers scoured endlessly to find the equal to Henrietta's soul.

In the end, he came from nowhere.

He walked into the city as if he had just tumbled down from the nighttime sky. Half a city block away from where Henrietta waited at a stoplight, he walked slowly up the sidewalk. The jostling and noise did not disturb him. He looked casually at the stands of fruit. The plumpest peaches, apricots, and nectarines held no interest. He preferred the thickness of a quiet night and the streaming milk of stars.

The lights changed place. Cars halted. Trucks roared forward. The pedestrian sign flashed walk. Henrietta lifted her foot to cross . . . and saw him.

From that moment, Henrietta wanted him and no one else. A strapping snorting stallion passed by unnoticed. A king's ransom of a man was utterly ignored. A scholar who knew ten thousand words for love felt them all die suddenly upon his lips. Pedestrians streamed across the crosswalk. Henrietta remained frozen on the curb.

The universe momentarily realigned around this man. The street swirled its blaring colors around this black hole at its center. He traveled carefully up the block, looking at each item in its turn: the butcher shop and its carcasses, the tendril of blood across the sidewalk, the corner of the wooden crate that soaked blood up toward a stack of rosy apples, the hand of the vendor's almond colored daughter -Henrietta's heart clutched her chest to breathlessness, but his eyes continued- the girl's bearded father, the passel of rascals that bumped against him and yelped away.

Steadily, he regarded each object in its turn and then moved on. He paused on the corner and nodded to the beggar king who owned it. He gave the mat of hair and rags a few words of dignity. Perhaps, Henrietta thought, that's all he had . . . but who walks around the city with empty pockets?

This man, her heartbeat answered, and all at once she trembled head to toe. Her snakeskin childhood dropped a connecting strand. Her womanhood tensed against the mesh that overlaid it. She didn't want to be a child in this city full of women. Not with this man who had not noticed her, who turned over almonds with his eyes and gently passed up peaches and would not finger any of the cheap jewelry that the vendors tried to hawk.

Henrietta sighed. This ripple of night in the broad boldness of day would pass her by. His scrutiny touched every nook and cranny of the market. He searched the rooftops above the flapping stripes of awnings. He paused between the vendors' booths and broke into the blackest alleyways with his eyes. He saw everything. Like the first ray of light stretching across the world, his gaze crept closer.

Henrietta, standing with one hand on the crosswalk sign, decided she might just die when his gaze passed over her. She drank up the sight of the man with the mournful thirst of one's last supper. She feasted on the bend of his head, the quietness that graced his movements, the gentle openness of his back, and the length of his leg as it stepped off the curb. She devoured every step he took across the crosswalk toward her. The lips of her thirsty eyes touched the corners of his.

He felt that surreptitious kiss of eyes and caught her gaze. The advancing ray of dawn froze. Time held still. The earth slowed in its orbit. The moon of his smile rose. Henrietta prayed for a miracle to halt the inevitable advance of this all-eclipsing moment, but the sun abandoned them in impatience and resumed its trek across the earth.

Coal black eyes and liquid midnight ones held their position as the street burst back into ruckus. The man stepped forward to the edge of the curb. His feet paused inches from Henrietta's. Trucks thundered past. Behind the veil of the ordinary, he sensed the scale that weighs our souls. He listened for the haggling of matchmakers. He heard them shush each other as they noticed him, so close to the treasure of their wares. He turned back to Henrietta.

"What are you doing up there?" he asked.

"Waiting," she replied.

He leaned against the corner stoplight, dark skin next to silver metal.

"For what?" he asked and his hand fell to touch the crest of her own.

"For you," she breathed.

He smiled. He stood up and took the measure of the marketplace behind the scene of taxicabs and delivery trucks. He saw the matchmakers' sour puckering expressions, clawing him with wordless questions, searching for his treasury. He shrugged. The vastness of the night weighs nothing -less than nothing- it has no measurement at all. All the stardust of its infinitude floats above a single grain of earth. Yet, here were the matchmakers waiting for him to place a price upon their scale.

They sniffed disdainfully.

He scorned them.

He was a prince whose realm held no value in their marketplace. Richness wrapped around him, but it was all worthless on their scales. They had no use for that which hangs across the heavens. Brass tacks they understood. The quiet light of distant stars had no equivalent in their currency. He held out his hand to Henrietta,

"You don't belong here," he said.

"No," she agreed. She tilted her head. The matchmakers

got up from their stalls and mumbled. He stepped up on the curb. Henrietta's soul slid off their scale. The matchmakers' mouths fell open. Henrietta turned her back on measurements and let the man of nothing take her hand.

He smiled, "I found what I came looking for."

Midnight and darkness know no separation. They do not buy each other's closeness. Henrietta had been waiting to find the union of her soul. Tyrell appeared with nothing but freedom in his pocket and offered all of it to her.

*   *   *

This story wasn't in the pile of records Jack Dalton searched. He couldn't find the silver key to understanding Henrietta Owens. A mystery of mysteries was hurtling toward Jack Dalton fueled by the passion of her love. Her infant was in her arms. His father locked in jail. Her life was ripped as raw and open as the mountains all around her. If Henrietta Owens screamed out her heartbreak, those flattened mountains screamed right back. She loved them. Not one mountain lied and said it would be alright. She screamed and they made her voice into a thousand voices.

Had Jack Dalton asked Arellia Owens for advice, she would have simply told him,

"Run."

CHAPTER SIX

· · · · ·

Shhh-clink

Jack smoldered in his air-conditioned car. He slammed his horn to let off steam. It didn't help. The cars nosed each other's rumps. His air vents breathed exhaust. His radio refused cooperation. Rush hour choked its smoggy yellow thickness close.

I should have taken that last exit, Jack lamented, now there's no escape. Jack inched forward with the stalling traffic, antsy from a day behind the desk, ready to explode out from his car, Henrietta Owens badgering his memory.

She wasn't a protestor, not exactly.

. . . nor an activist

. . . nor an organizer.

She was a mother.

. . . who showed up one day

. . . and ended up in the paper.

The movement asked her to be a spokesperson.

. . . a figurehead

. . . a speaker.

Henrietta Owens had agreed. She'd never organized a march, though she subsequently inspired several. She'd never negotiated with police, though she seemed to walk right through blockades. She'd never been arrested. How is this possible? Jack wondered. He couldn't be more surprised if she walked on water and smelled of roses.

He anonymously called the police departments throughout the region. They all spoke highly of her: "very polite", "a nice young woman", "never gives us problems". Something was going on. He had his secretary call them back.

" . . . and tell them you're with Standard Coal," he ordered. Standard Coal who handed out the 'standard' Christmas bonuses. The responses straightened out immediately: "oh, she's a rabble-rouser", "a problem, yes, but we're handling it", and "no respect for law". Something's going on, Jack thought, gnawing at the issue in his mind. Man to man, they all spoke highly of her. Position to professional position, a whole list of epithets emerged. Jack couldn't pin her character amidst all the duck and dodging.

Jack found himself staring into taillights and remembering the photo with her eyes. Dark eyes, black and thick with depth. She pinned you with them without intending to and pierced your soul with scrutiny.

Jack honked his frustration at the unwitting car in front of him. He loosened up his collar. The sun burned through the windshield. A horn behind him bellowed. He glanced in the rearview mirror.

"Whaa-at?!" Jack spun around. He frantically rubbed his eyes. He glanced at the oblivious drivers to either side of him. No one else saw it.

A row of convicts was shuffling up the highway, wearing stripes and caps, leg irons; the whole nine yards. Jack flipped back to front. I'm hallucinating, he thought, it must be sunstroke. He cranked up the air conditioning. He unscrewed a plastic bottle and splashed water on his face.

An image of one man? A legend like John Henry? *That* he could rationalize . . . but an entire line of nineteenth century prisoners shuffling through a traffic jam in broad daylight? That was pushing it.

The convicts slid past him on the left.

Jack shut his eyes and counted breaths.

One . . . this isn't happening.

Two . . . this can't be real.

Three . . . are they still here?

He opened up his eyes.

Holy, holy, holy! His words failed him. He hit the gas, jumped up a car length, and slammed on the brakes behind another vehicle.

Shhh-clink. Shhh-clink. Shhh-clink.

The chains dragged steadily up and passed him again. Jack stared straight ahead, trying not to give the vision any notice. His eyes rolled toward the left. John Henry stared back at him.

Jack broke out in sweat. The smog tinted the man in sepia. He had a sledgehammer on his shoulder. John Henry kept his steady pace, passed Jack's car, and looked back.

Shhh-clink. Shhh-clink.

It went on for twenty minutes as the cars crept forward, stopped, and idled as the prisoners shuffled by. Jack kept glancing in the other cars, but not one other person gave any sign of seeing the chain gang trudging through the rows of vehicles. When the traffic snarl untangled, Jack shot free and barreled down the highway. His heart was hammering to the slow pulsing rhythm of their chain-linked steps: Shhh-clink. Shhh-clink. Shhh-clink.

CHAPTER SEVEN

. . . . .

Motherhood Today

"How was work, honey?" Sarah called out from her magazine as Jack staggered in limp-ragged. His single grunt appeased her split attention. For once, he was grateful for whatever glossy nothingness engrossed her. He cracked a beer. The sound caught her attention.

"That bad, huh?" She began an effort to avert a high-tempered evening. "Come on, no drinks before a kiss. What happened?"

No words before the kisses finish, he thought, but she was done with one little peck and returned to the magazine. He leaned against the counter.

"Nothing. Just traffic. It's hot for April."

"Use the air conditioner."

Jack suddenly realized where Allie learned the *you're an idiot* look. The tree that dropped that apple buried herself in the glossy world of her magazine where the husbands came home looking seductive, not sweaty, cross, and tired.

He took a drink. She flipped up the magazine. He choked.

"What is that?" he spat out.

"*Motherhood Today*," she mumbled. He grabbed it.

"Jack!" She tried to snatch it back. His remote control slid her volume down as she demanded the return of maternity wear and water births. Jack's head swam.

Henrietta Owens and her son were featured on the cover.

It took five minutes to read through the article twice. When he finished, Jack threw *Motherhood Today* across the kitchen with ferocity.

"What is your problem?" Sarah snapped. "You have something against this poor girl?" She had also read the article twice. "She lives in a tarpaper shanty in Appalachia where the water runs out red and lights on fire. The doctors told her *not* to breastfeed her baby. The toxins in breast milk are so high," Sarah shuddered, laying her hand across her chest, "they say making infant formula with the poisoned tap-water would be safer."

"I know what the medical professionals say," Jack growled. The Environmental Protection Agency required Standard Coal to dispense such useful information. He picked up Henrietta's crinkled picture and put it on the table. Sarah turned it around to face her. Jack watched her soften. His innards clenched. The article was sentimental brainwash. Well-written social-environmental propaganda. It was working on his pregnant wife. She lifted up the magazine and cradled it.

"Look at that poor little boy . . . and she's so young." Sarah spun around and her defiance hit Jack with a perfume of warnings.

"What are you doing?" he asked.

"Helping her." She rummaged in her purse and pulled out her checkbook, ready to make a donation to whoever worked to end mountaintop removal.

"Over my dead body," Jack warned her flatly.

"Oh, don't be dramatic," she said, disregarding him.

"I made that money–"

"–poisoning her baby," Sarah pointed out.

"You won't."

"I will."

His cellphone rang them to a stalemate.

"It's work. I have to go," he said.

"You just got home," she protested.

"I know. Sarah?" He tried to exact a promise of inaction, but his phone rang out demands. He answered it and grabbed his keys. No words. No kisses. He left.

By sunset, Sarah and her friends, yoga buddies, and soccer moms were pledging to Henrietta's cause.

CHAPTER EIGHT

· · · · ·

No Man's Holler

The weary bus sighed and stopped in the nighttime humidity of spring in Appalachia. The bus doors sucked the half-hearted air-conditioning back in and left Henrietta standing on the roadside. Her eyes closed against the uphill hike that waited before her. The strategy meeting for the mountaintop removal protests had left her exhausted. Count your blessings, she thought, and breathed to bolster up her will.

One . . . you're still alive . . . *breathe*

Two . . . you didn't get arrested . . . *breathe*

Three . . . your baby boy is waiting . . . *breathe*

She opened up her eyes to see dappled blues and darker blacks exchanging places in the treetops. She started up the road. Crickets cheered her on as she plodded up the road. She sighed.

The strategy meeting had been a disaster, fiery and defensive, full of flaring personalities and heated arguments.

"Hank," she had whispered halfway through, "you're my friend, but I got to tell you, I ain't sitting through six hour meetings. I can't. The bank closes at four. The last bus comes at seven. My baby's waiting for me at Wanda's. Just tell me what they decide."

He tried to defend the consensus process yet again, but followed Henrietta's exasperated look toward the meeting circle. Mild-mannered Louisa was patiently trying to cool the erupting volcanoes of temper as one of the out-of-town college activists butted heads with an indignant sixth generation Appalachian. Hank gave up and offered Henrietta a ride. She shook her head and said goodbye.

Henrietta was sore from the hard folding chairs and stiff bus seats. Her head ached from the arguments. She felt it now as she climbed the dark road up into the hollow. The bushes pressed in against the road, rustling and humid. The trees leaned overhead, stilling the night air. Henrietta loved the unrelenting flush of woods that now surrounded her. No Man's Holler was a forty-minute bus ride from the grocery store, thirty minutes further to the prison. Crawley's Slope was closer, but it was white and the prison guards lived there.

After her first visit to the prison with Jerome, Henrietta left the frozen city she grew up in and moved to No Man's Holler in the quiet days that lull right after Christmas. The new year found her stomping her feet and swearing over the tiny cabin's woodstove until she finally threw down the kindling, the matches, and her pride, and trudged five minutes through the snow to her neighbor's house. Wanda Nelson laughed her gracious fanny off at Henrietta, but she also picked up Jerome and carried him back over to the little cabin, where she taught her young city-girl neighbor how to build a fire.

A rumble down the road dragged her out of memories. She heard the truck before it turned the bend and caught her in its headlights. She let it. The uneven ruck-ruck-purr had revealed its identity as friendly.

"Rutherford Nelson!" she called out. "What can I give you to take me up to Wanda's?" Ford leaned his elbow on the roll-down window and motioned for her to hop in.

"Not a thing, Henrietta, not a thing."

She gave him a grateful smile nonetheless. When you got nothing else, a smile helps to pay your dues.

"You eat yet?" he asked considerately.

"No. You got something to eat?"

"No. Just wondering," he replied in the same tempo as his truck, ruck-ruck-purr.

"Shoot, why'd you ask me then?" she teased him. "That's like picking at an old scab 'til it bleeds. I'm hungry now."

Henrietta had picked up the language of the Nelson family bantering that rolled out in pie-dough dreams and someday cookies. Henrietta called it St. Tomorrow's Feast Day, the great celebration that would come without fail, with great style, with sumptuous delights . . . tomorrow. Ford Nelson pulled a hard right and said,

"Maybe Wanda'll fry you up some catfish. You had our catfish yet?"

"No," Henrietta answered with a smile, "I keep hearing about your big ole catfish, but I ain't tasted nothing that didn't look like kitten-fish to me."

They laughed as Ford turned onto the dirt road up to Wanda's. The night rumbled comfortably in cricket tones and the ruck-ruck-purring of the engine.

Ford glanced now and again at Henrietta as her eyes drooped steadily lower. He thought about asking if she was getting on alright, but decided to just let the girl rest. He'd hear plenty from Wanda sooner or later. Everybody in the hollow chewed and mulled on Henrietta when she wasn't looking. All winter long, since she'd first come . . .

*   *   *

"Ford? How long you think that girl gonna stay here?" his cousin Darrell had asked him a few weeks after Henrietta Owens had moved into Moses Nelson's old cabin. They were hunched over Ford's truck, breath steaming in the cold air. Darrell's shiny skin stretched taut over brown and leathered cheekbones. Ford answered as his oil-blackened hands coaxed the greasy auto part into working order,

"Dunno, Darrell. Her man up there's facing ten years for robbery." He swung his head into the engine of the pickup. Darrell leaned on the rim of the truck with the open hood above him. From a distance, it looked like he, too, had his elbows buried in the engine, cussing grease and ancient auto parts.

"We need more girls like Ms. Henri Owens. Smart. Honest." Darrell turned round and leaned his leanness on the side of the truck. He watched the crows flap across the snow-dusted trees, then spun back under the hood. His bright eyes gleamed with mischief.

"Too bad she's as good as married to that man, Ford, 'cause your boy needs to settle down."

A snort of acknowledgment erupted from the engine's innards. Ford extricated himself and mopped his hands and brow with the greasy rag. He squinted in the sunlight's brightness and then nodded at an approaching figure.

"Morning, Wanda."

"You two gabbing the birds out of the trees or just sitting there looking ugly?" Wanda teased. Her laugh jiggled in her pale yellow coat and her breath hung on the winter's air. Her face reflected Ford's in gentle browns and gracious lines, with the comfortable settling of age. Darrell stood his long limbs up as Ford slammed down the hood.

"Wanda? What you think of Ms. Henrietta Owens?" Darrell asked her. It was only fair to ask. Everything and everyone was fair cooking for a hungry hollow without much money, food, or news. If it was new, it was popped into gossip's mouth with the enthusiasm of fresh raspberries picked off the summer vine. If it was old, it was chomped on with the stingy determination of a miser with his gray and ancient piece of gum. Wanda took her time preparing up her special stash of Henrietta tidbits. Despite Henrietta being from a city and not a Nelson girl, Wanda felt the vines of kinship twisting round her loyalty already. She liked the girl and said as much,

"I think she can't cook for nothing, but she's real sweet and stronger than my daddy's moonshine."

The two men whistled. Moses Nelson's moonshine knocked men flat in a single punch. Local folklore told that great-great-great-who-cares-how-many-greats-ago   grandpa John invented the recipe on account of the white men who had tried to take the hollow. It ripped their innards out and sent them screaming from the place. His wife, Lucy Nelson, cooked it in her cornbread and fed it to their son. Every generation hence received hereditary dispensation from its wicked bite. Moses Nelson's moonshine might lick all lesser men, but it tickled sweet as spring water down Nelson throats. Wanda swore the men had just burned their gullets away, drinking all that firewater. Once, a potential in-law hinted that the recipe was probably getting weaker over time. The men chased him out of the hollow and informed their niece that her suitor was unfit to love a Nelson woman. An insult to their moonshine was a slur upon the family. Its legendary virility and strength were equal to their own. And, not to mention, it was also the secret elixir that made all their women beautiful. (The fact that moonshine brought out the beauty of a woman -any woman- was an undisputed truth.)

But now, a girl who was stronger than Moses Nelson's moonshine? Such a woman as Henrietta Owens was welcome in their hollow, Darrell concluded. He clapped his hands to warm them in the cold air. Ford stomped his feet. Wanda stuck her mittens in her armpits. Darrell blew on his fingers.

"You seen ole Thomas' boy? I think he's sweet on her," Darrel baited.

"Young Thomas best keep his fingers in his own honeypot and do right by that girl he's seeing now," Wanda warned. "Henrietta Owens is closer to my place than a fresh baked pie on the windowsill, and if that young tramp tries to lick her, I'll pull out my shotgun."

Ford laughed his easy rumble,

"Wanda, everybody knows you ain't never loaded that gun."

"What do I need to load it for? I'm gonna smack his head with it, is what I'm gonna do."

"I reckon that girl can take care of herself," Ford commented. Darrell's eyes widened as he imagined the moonshine strong girl in a fiery outrage.

"She got a tongue on her that can split firewood," Wanda gleefully added.

"That sharp?" Ford blinked. He'd only heard her sweet tones as he drove her up the road.

"Mmm-hmm, and precise." Wanda wasn't afraid to use a little exaggeration to build a line of defense around her young mother of a neighbor. Darrell caught the easy swing of banter, shaking his head back and forth in mock disbelief,

"Naw, Wanda, that girl is too young to be chopping anything, lil' baby-girl like that."

"Darrell Nelson, that baby-girl got a *baby-boy* in her arms. She ain't too young for nothing!" Wanda snorted. An easy laugh breezed through them all. She sighed; the afternoon was rolling on and she better too.

"Boys, you best stop snickering over things you're both getting too old to do. Don't you have some decent work to get at?"

Darrell leaned back against the old pick-up.

"Now Wanda, you said it yourself, I'm too old to be doing certain things," he teased. Wanda laughed and swung at him with a lazy hand before turning down the road shaking her head.

"Oh lord, Darrell, get on!"

* * *

The memory faded as Ford swung into the yard and shut off the trembling vehicle. Henrietta jerked awake.

"We're here," Ford told her. "I'll walk you in."

"Ain't no need-"

"Wanda may be getting lonesome for me."

Henrietta smiled. Ford would walk the chickens home at dusk, the old ladies down to church, and the children back from school. There weren't no arguing with his protectiveness, just thanking.

Wanda's door swung open with a flood of light that made them blink. Her voice called out,

"Don't be hanging out there in the dark. C'mon in. C'mon. Ford, you wanna come in for a bite?"

"Nah, Wanda, now that Henrietta's back safely, I'll just be rolling homeward. Evening."

Wanda motioned Henrietta in, shooed the mosquitos out, and waved goodbye to Ford with an economy of gesture.

"How's my boy, Wanda?"

"Sleeping like an angel. I asked myself, what did Henrietta Owens promise God to get a little boy like that, hmm? No fussing, nothing, all day long. Now, you ain't gonna wake him going down through the woods tonight, are you?"

"Well, I was-"

"-not gonna do nothing of the sort. I got my couch or the floor, but there ain't nothing wrong with neither. Lord, you'd wake him up crying, and then the whole holler'd be wondering; what is Henrietta Owens doing to that baby? Everybody knows he's the child of an angel."

Wanda was dishing out some supper with her sermons.

Henrietta smiled. Angels come in so many forms. Henrietta bowed her head and gave thanks for this one. She graced her food and added a special note for Tyrell. Even angels can get caught in prison cells, along with innocents and innocence and accidents and second chances.

Henrietta sighed. Tyrell was awarded a wrong time, wrong place conviction -apparently a common medal for a black man in this country. The men who pinned it on him thought; right man, right place, right color for the job. Tyrell was standing in the middle of a robbery, looking for a pen.

"What did you need a pen for?" the prosecutor had inquired.

"My wife wanted one," Tyrell answered, thinking of Henrietta with her engagement ring and shining eyes.

"You don't have a wife," the prosecutor spat and Tyrell no longer had an alibi. The checkout counter clerk testified before the jury. Tyrell was in the right place, at the right time, with the right height, weight, color. Tyrell couldn't identify any other suspect. He had been looking for a pen. Innocents and innocence were now stuck in a jailbird cage where justice locked them up.

Henrietta looked up from her prayer. Wanda had something in her lap and an odd expression on her face.

"What is it, Wanda?"

"Well, Arlene come by this afternoon all in a fluster, said I had to see something, but I had the baby in one hand and a diaper in the other and supper was boiling over, so I told her just to drop it there." She nodded toward the crooked straight-back chair that was retired to a catchall function by the door.

"She asked when you'd be back. I said I didn't know exactly, but I didn't have time for trading gossip. You know Arlene, she gave me that *look* and said to show you when you got home-"

Henrietta cut her off before she caught her breath.

"Show me what?"

Wanda slid *Motherhood Today* across the table.

"Sweet Jesus," Henrietta whispered as she read it.

"Honey, you're front page news," Wanda beamed.

"Did you read this?" Henrietta spluttered.

"I don't have my glasses."

"It says I live in a tarpaper shanty," Henrietta choked.

Wanda exploded, "That cabin got shingles on the roof except for one part of it is all!"

"It says we feed our babies formula made from poisoned tap water," Henrietta read.

"Uh! That ain't true. I get that baby *spring* water, bottled *spring* water to make that formula, just like y'all drink at home. We ain't stupid. We know that red water gonna kill us."

"It says I'm an environmental activist . . . a leader of mountaintop protection."

"Mmm-hmm, I think it means you're good-looking, front-cover quality."

"It says that I'm 'the emblem of a growing revolution against an entire system of repression, an iconic figure of motherhood protecting our children's future, a singer to pluck the heartstrings of humanity'."

"Honey, I don't care what it *says* you are," she tapped the photo of Henrietta with her baby, "it *means* you're famous."

It was too much for Henrietta. It was incomprehensible in

the midst of her weariness. It was utterly laughable. It made her want to cry. Henrietta gathered up her belongings, shaking her head as Wanda insisted again that she spend the night.

"No, no thank you, Wanda, but Jerome and I are gonna sleep at home tonight."

He stirred as she slipped her hands under him and lifted. He thought sleepily of crying, but smelled his mamma's mix of soap and sweat and sweetness and he snuggled in. Henrietta whispered out her thanks. Wanda tried to scrunch her booming voice into a hushed tightness, but it kept squeezing out around the edges,

"Oh Lord, *anytime,* you hear? Anytime! I just love that little boy like he was my own. You need a light?"

Henrietta shook her head and slipped between the walls of darkness.

It wasn't five minutes up and a little down and over to Henrietta's place. Her feet slid along a trail packed firm by generations of Nelson footsteps. Henrietta felt the breeze lift off the weariness of bus rides. Without the moon, darkness ran right up to her and locked her in embrace. Jerome's hand curled and uncurled against her breast. Her walking rocked him into slumber. The trees drew back their curtain as she reached a patch of clearing. Henrietta paused and sensed the hills falling down below her. The footpath skirted the clearing's top and when the trees resumed their places at the bottom, their uppermost branches barely scraped the height she stood at now. The stars pressed closer here. The wind could feel her contours without dodging all the branches. Henrietta moved toward the dark outline of a rock. With her purse, she whacked the grass for snakes, then sat and held Jerome beneath the stars. The cabin with its porch waited just beyond the clearing, but there was no sense in tossing sleeplessly where she couldn't see the shining canopy of heaven.

Jerome rode her breathing like a little boat upon the ocean's rise and fall. The crickets invited her heart to join their beat. The wind whistled polyrhythms, conducting full-leafed orchestras in whispered song.

A star shot out.

"Look at that!" she murmured to the sleeping child. "All these years, I've never seen one." Until she came to No Man's Holler, city lights had obscured her stars. Except for a few hours of intimacy with their depth and beauty, she'd never really known them, just mostly in myth and imagination.

Henrietta looked down at Jerome. Someday, too, her son would know his father. Not just through story, but in person. Not for brief visits, but held close for hours, sleeping against his chest. Henrietta wondered if her son would ever know what he had lost. Ten years stretched longer than the boy's entire childhood. It seemed too long a time to bear. She sighed and the child rode her longing. We're gonna make it, she promised her son, his father, and herself. Like a tiny boat shoved off into the ink of oceans, they would cross this vastness somehow. Henrietta had breathed a quarter century of breaths and beaten a billion heartbeats before a shooting star had crossed her nighttime sky.

"And now it has." She smiled and pulled the baby close into her thrill. He smelled of baking beans and innocence. In sleep, he sniffed the journey of her day. Not once in all her errand running had she brushed up against the shooting of her photo across the newsstands of America.

"Famous, huh?" she sighed. It would only be for a minute as a flash of guilt raced through the middle-class mothers of tomorrow; mothers who could afford subscriptions or the extra dollars at the checkout line to read the glossy painted news of motherhood. Henrietta tried to remember if she'd ever seen the publication. Probably. Her mother might have bought one. She shrugged. Legal documents were all Henrietta remembered reading above her growing womb.

She shook the thoughts away and looked back up at the sky. Shooting stars were supposed to be a sign, she thought, symbols of great portents . . . but good ones or bad? She searched her memory. Good. They must be good. It was the comets that foretold the cataclysmic prophecies.

Oh, that's just nonsense, she thought. There's not much difference between a comet and a shooting star. She rolled her eyes and rose against the cooling night. One's a burning ball traversing across our solar system. The other's just a little meteor going about its business as the earth swings along its orbit . . . and then the two collide. But still, she thought as she lingered on the clearing's edge, when human eyes catch sight of it, that falling meteor becomes a shooting star.

CHAPTER NINE

· · · · ·

Symbols & Portents

Arellia didn't like it.

"You stick your head out in front of something, it's bound to get blown off," she warned as she left a long-winded message on Henrietta's phone. "Don't be foolish. And call me right back or I'll think something's wrong and drive down there." She hung up.

Arellia frowned at the cover of *Motherhood Today*, pride and irritation alternating across her expression. The stoic midwife to the passages of birth and death, dispassionate, pragmatic, and practical, stared at the image of her daughter and wondered for the thousandth time; how could this girl have emerged from her? Only those dark eyes sparked immediate recognition in her mother. Yes, Arellia thought, she got those gritty jewels from me. They weigh her soul down just enough to keep a toe-tip on this earth.

What was that girl doing leading protests? She wasn't that kind of girl.

The orange streetlamp outside the window flickered on and glared. Arellia rose to shut her curtains on it, glancing up and down the block out of habit. She blinked. She opened the window and reached through the iron bars. Her fingers pinched a small object that was sitting on top of the air conditioner box. She drew her hand back with a white, delicate flower cluster. Baby's breath, Arellia noted, the kind of filler plant florists stick in bouquets. She almost threw it out, but stopped.

Baby's breath: a wildflower that grows in flurries across the meadows, spreading its tiny stars in a tangled web of greenery. Arellia looked back at the photo of her daughter and grandson. What was it Henrietta said just a few days ago?

"Oh, Mamma," she had breathed into the phone, "you just gotta come down here and see Jerome before he gets any bigger. He's sleeping right now, breathing in and out so soft." Her voice turned quietly fierce, "I'd do anything for that baby. *Anything.* Just to keep him breathing."

Arellia looked at the photographs along her bookshelves; Henrietta, tiny, no older than Jerome; Henrietta shyly walking up the steps to school; Henrietta with Arellia tight in a sudden hug; Henrietta with Tyrell, both caught in gentle laughter. Arellia fingered the cover photo of her daughter and her grandson.

Baby's breath. That changed everything. She carefully put the flower on top of the photo and called Henrietta again.

"Henrietta. It's your mamma." She paused. "Just . . . be careful. You start marching into police lines, you leave my grandson somewhere safe, you hear? Those police ain't gonna bat an eye at bashing you both, though Lord knows you're hardheaded enough to-" she broke off. "I didn't mean that, Henrietta. Just call me back, alright?"

She hung up feeling ancient. Slowly, she carried the photograph and baby's breath across the room and placed them on the bookshelf. She stood for a long silent moment, considering.

Arellia steered her life by omens, portents, and symbols; the proof of which lined the windowsills and countertops of her apartment. On the altar of her bookshelves lay the scarlet leaf that fell before her feet, the wheat penny that appeared on the sidewalk one day, the compass earring, the scrawl of someone's wisdom on a scrap of paper, and countless more. These became childhood lessons for Henrietta, who also learned to collect the fortune cookie slips that gave her good advice, the token coin that read *rest* and so she did, and the pencil that dropped from no one's desk to answer her exam correctly. From girlhood to adolescence, Henrietta placed her omens along the bookshelves with her mother's. Then one day, Henrietta had brought home the black curling feathers that foretold Tyrell's appearance in their lives.

Arellia shook her head as the past crowded up against the windows of the present. She stroked the one black feather that had remained upon her altar. She placed the photo and the baby's breath next to it and lit a candle. She stared into the flame and let the memories flicker in her.

*   *   *

When Henrietta showed her mother the feather omens, Arellia, heavy with premonition, had asked,

"What sort of downy bird is black?"

"Swans," Henrietta answered.

"Geese," her mother snapped, her hackles up against her

suspicions of a young man in flight, headed toward them. "Neither geese nor swans do well in inner cities."

"They can fly away," Henrietta pointed out.

Exactly, her mother thought, and they can carry you, my love, away with them.

"I think," Henrietta said, twirling one of the feathers from the handful, "this downy feather did not come from any bird that's been catalogued by scientists."

The day Henrietta brought Tyrell to meet her mamma Arellia froze with understanding. Henrietta had sensed the omens accurately: this young man was like no other kind of bird she'd ever seen.

"You'll sit down?" Arellia said, half question, half command. He answered by staying on his feet.

"Sometime," he responded sweetly in the same tone, half request, half command, "you must introduce me properly to your temple." His hand swept a gesture to the altars of the room, where the sacred texts of all traditions were held within the bookshelves' arms. Then he sat and made a place for Henrietta next to him on the couch.

Oh ho! Arellia thought. The subtle positioning begins! She loved him then, even as she scowled at the young man who intended to steal away her daughter. Arellia ruled her tiny apartment kingdom, but Tyrell bowed to no one but himself. With poised audacity he offered her a seat in her own chair, but since his motion was respectful, she warmed a degree toward him.

"Did your mother teach you such good manners?" she asked.

"A young man's manners are too immense a task for anyone's mother all alone," he answered, "a whole society must bend to thresh that harvest."

"Where are you from?" Arellia asked. She could not picture his origins in any region. He belonged neither to the roughness of the city, nor the simplicity of the countryside, the tension of the north, the languor of the south, the straightness of the plains, or the looseness of the west.

"I come from stardust," he teased and Henrietta laughed.

"No, tell Mamma the truth."

"There's truth and then there's truth," he said, "which would you prefer?"

The curtains lifted in an errant breeze. The bars behind them striped the room with shadows. Arellia choked on premonition. The black feathers on the bookshelf altar stirred. Swear to tell the truth, they warned, and the young prince of nothing told them,

"I come from nighttime darkness. I grew from the same stardust as the earth."

Pigeons streaked past the window behind Henrietta and Tyrell. Arellia felt the cool breeze brush her and saw the shadow of lines fall across Tyrell. She rose and shut the window.

"Where do you live now, Tyrell?" she asked.

"Here," he answered with a twinkle, drawing a happy breath of his aliveness, "where else can I be alive and living at this moment? Nowhere else on earth but here."

"What an address!" Henrietta laughed at him.

"I have no other," he replied.

"Where am I gonna send my love letters?" Henrietta teased.

"Here," he answered and put her hand upon his heart.

At that gesture, Arellia surrendered.

All her trappings, all the treasure of her home would not keep her daughter in it. All her motherly securities of locks and doors and official stamps of approval or disapproval would not keep Henrietta from this young man. Arellia sat down to begin the formal negotiations of territory. She asked him for his facts and figures. He traded her only truth.

Where do you live? she had asked him.

Here, he had honestly said.

What an address! his sweetheart laughed.

I have no other, he told them truthfully.

There's truth and then there's truth.

Tyrell currently lived at the Y.

"What do you do for work?" Arellia asked in her civil-snoopy mother sort of way.

"What would you say if I told you that I gather potential from the nebulae and possibilities from the galaxies? Or that I start small businesses of people's dreams and catch falling stars part-time?"

"Do you make a living doing that?" Arellia hid her smile under a pragmatic front.

"I'm alive, aren't I?"

"What brought you to this city?"

"I came looking for something," he answered. *And I found it,* his smile hinted.

"How old are you?" Arellia asked him, suddenly hankering for an anchor point of numbers.

"Too old to look so young, and younger than I feel."

Arellia pealed her great golden bell of laughter that broke all of the formality in the room. She had never heard a more truthful answer to a question regarding age.

"And how long will you be staying . . . tonight?" she specified. He breathed the relief of someone who has just convinced God he was an angel and could spend an eternity in heaven. He, too, let formality fall away and slid his fingers through Henrietta's. They shook ever so slightly and Arellia saw suddenly that he was born of earth, he had a mother, he ate, slept, shit, swore, and he desperately loved her daughter. She forgave his truthful evasions of her questions. She would learn the facts . . . one day. Henrietta caught her eye with a familiar gleam of begging.

"Would you like to stay for dinner?" Arellia invited, though she knew Henrietta had begged, *ask him to stay forever.* Tyrell answered both the mother's and daughter's silent and spoken questions at once,

"I'll stay until you throw me out among the stars!"

Arellia let him stay until one in the morning then firmly sent him home.

"Do you want a taxi?" she offered.

"No, I'm used to wandering at night."

She allowed Henrietta to see him out and when her girl returned Arellia caught a glimpse of anxious tears pooling in her rainy eyes.

"Oh, Mamma, do you like him?"

Arellia was tempted to tell Henrietta that she'd put him in the *pending* pile, but her baby child's last strands of childhood still clung to her, and Arellia touched them gently, feeling touched that her daughter loved her so and was searching anxiously for her mother's approval, one last time.

"Yes, Henrietta, I do," she answered.

What more can you give them as their adulthood ships off from your shores? She would not fight to keep her daughter tied to her, though she would have liked a more secure partner for her girl. For years, Arellia had relied on earth's solidity as she passed people from hand to hand, wiping newborn mucus from their eyes or closing their eyelids one last time. Arellia would have preferred a man of four walls and sturdy floors, but she knew the strong lines of her girl's face, the inky eyes that graced it, and the soul that pulsed beneath them. Henrietta walked a milky path of life. She ran across the melting, freezing ice flows. Her feet would always stand on nothing. She did not need security, Arellia thought. She needed freedom. Who better to offer that than a man who comes from nowhere, owns nothing, and lives only here, inside his heart and breath?

Tyrell's arrest broke the limits of her comprehension.

"He did what?!" Arellia shrieked when Henrietta had called her.

"*He* didn't do nothing, Mamma. The police arrested him for robbing a store."

"Where on earth are you? I'm coming."

"We're in West Virginia."

"Good Lord! Whatever possessed you to go there? Doesn't Tyrell have enough sense to get arrested in some decent state like Ohio?"

"Mamma," Henrietta said through gritted teeth, "if we were

still home in Ohio, Tyrell wouldn't have gotten arrested. He probably don't look anything like the real robber, except that he's black."

"Didn't you see the robber?"

"No, I wasn't there."

"Well, that's the first sensible thing that's come out of your mouth today."

"Mamma! Nobody knew there was gonna be a robbery at that market."

"Did they catch the guy yet?"

"No, Mamma, they caught Tyrell. The other guy's probably in Ohio by now."

"Jesus."

Both were silent as the implications hit them. Then Arellia snapped again,

"For the love of all that's holy, why are you in West Virginia?"

"Tyrell wanted to see the stars."

"We got stars in Ohio."

"No, Mamma, we've got streetlights in Ohio. We went camping up in the mountains."

"Camping?!"

Arellia added getting arrested to the list of horrible things that can happen in the wilderness to crazy daughters of sensible urban mothers who try to warn them about ax murderers and rapists and grizzly bears and landslides and lightning strikes and poison ivy and god-knows-what. If that young man wasn't under lock and key, she'd personally go down to West Virginia and smack him for doing this to her daughter.

"How could he get himself arrested?" she fumed to an exhausted, half-listening Henrietta.

"Mamma, he didn't mean to," she sighed. She heard Arellia draw in breath for what sounded like another tirade. "Look, I'll call you back," Henrietta said quickly and hung up. In Ohio, Henrietta's mamma exhaled her sentence into the silence of a dead telephone connection,

"Baby, I don't mean a word I say. Just tell me where you are, and what you need, and I'll be there as fast as I can." She cursed herself for not saying that at the get-go.

How in the name of all that's holy could he get himself arrested? Arellia fumed. Or, more accurately, how could they arrest a man whom Arellia knew would never rob the joy from a room, or the glee from a child, or the illusion of wealth from a forty-dollar sweepstakes ticket winner, let alone some boring cash register at a grocery store.

By that time, Henrietta had moved into an apartment with Tyrell. She was spared her mother's furious sweeping of her guiding symbols off her altar. She never saw her mother fling her faith against the wall.

Arellia lit a single candle on the bare altar of her life. In the wax she planted one black downy feather. Then she banished mysteries and portents from her world. There was no magic to their days of raising bail and filing papers. There was no misty romance to learning that his parents had thought him dead. Arellia gritted her teeth at his mother's cursing, then slammed the phone down and ended her connection to them forever. Oh yes, she smiled grimly; he came from a nowhere that was better than the somewhere that he left. A society taught him the manners his parents never did.

Seven months after the arrest, with their lives hanging in limbo, waiting for the trial with bated breaths and crossed fingers, a matchbox with a stork painted on it showed up on Arellia's desk. Arellia kept her suspicions to herself, but she studied her daughter, looking for a certain glow or a subtle swelling of the breasts. Two weeks later, Henrietta confirmed it: she was pregnant. Arellia Owens, notary public, pulled every trick she knew to keep Tyrell's case from opening. She was determined to get Tyrell and Henrietta's baby born before his father went to trial. When the proceedings began in Henrietta's last few weeks of pregnancy, Arellia even thought of inducing the labor. The case closed before she dared to try it. Jerome emerged from wombs and safe places on a cold November night, two days after his father was convicted. Arellia held her daughter as she cried over the beauty of their baby and the bitter timing of the sentence.

The stoic midwife on the frontline of birth and death was losing ground. Her tiny family was reeling. Arellia tried to tuck her daughter back underneath her wing. In mid-December, she found herself begging Henrietta to reconsider her decision to move closer to the prison in West Virginia.

"Stay here in Ohio. You can move back in with me. I can help you with Jerome."

But Arellia lost that battle, too. Just before Christmas, she surrendered and walked over to Henrietta and Tyrell's apartment to wrap up her daughter's life instead of presents. She meticulously curled silver tissue around Henrietta's omens one by one. She told Henrietta not to lose the paper; she'd need it to move back. Henrietta said she'd save the paper, but she did not promise her return. Arellia found her faith resurging in the face of desperation. She poured her benedictions onto every object that she packed. She incanted blessings into the silver tissues that wrapped around the symbols of her daughter's life. She looked for auspicious signs about the move.

"What's this?" she asked, picking up a robin's eggshell.

"Jerome," Henrietta answered, smiling at the infant in her arms. "I found that one day before we knew our baby even lived."

"Baby boy blue," Arellia breathed. Her eyes welled up and Henrietta knelt down beside her on the floor.

"Don't cry, Mamma," she began, but then gave up trying to stop the storm of tears and let her mother cry. Arellia was full of unspoken bird-egg words and fragile worries that might crack before their time. Henrietta picked up the little blue eggshell cup with one hand. Her son snuggled in her other arm. She caught her mother's tears as they came dripping off her chin. Her mother noticed and released an achy laugh.

"Come," Henrietta commanded. She stood up with the egg and Jerome and tilted her head at her mamma. "Get up." She handed the cup of tears to Arellia and opened up the window. December's early nightfall flooded in. "Turn around," she told her mother. "Throw those tears over your shoulder and out the window."

Arellia smiled and obeyed. She tossed the tears and Henrietta slammed the sash down after them.

"The darkness has a thirst for tears," she said. "It's

swallowed plenty of my own. Sometimes, I think the nighttime tears that fall are what become the morning dew."

Arellia held out her arms and wrapped Henrietta close.

"My daughter," she murmured to the thick net of curls. The baby blue egg hovered in her fingers above Jerome's head. She clung for a moment and then returned pragmatically to packing.

"Don't forget to call," she admonished as she tucked the egg in a little jewelry box, "and open a bank account right away. You know I'm going to help you." She wrapped protections around her daughter every way she could. "You send me pictures of my grandson. And I'm coming to visit." The rustling of the silver tissue paused around a tiny key. "What's this?"

"I don't know yet, Mamma. I found it in West Virginia when I took Jerome to meet Tyrell."

Arellia wrapped it up.

"Make sure the lock on your house works," she ordered. "Does it have a deadbolt?"

"Mamma, it's in the middle of nowhere. I don't even know if it has a doorknob."

"Put a rock on either side, one for in and out." She picked up another unfamiliar object. "What's this?"

Henrietta frowned at it.

"Dunno, Mamma, let me see it." The object was thinner than her baby's finger and darker black. "I never saw it before. It looks like a judge's hammer."

"Must be your new omen," Arellia said and wrapped it up with all the others. "Though if you ask me, I think it looks like a sledgehammer."

"Well, Mamma, I think that's what it's going to take to get some real justice in this world."

Arellia closed the box and froze. The sharp tone of striking steel rang out to notarize her daughter's words.

*   *   *

Night had fallen against the windows of the apartment. The candlewick pooled in soft wax. Arellia leaned against the bookshelf, lost in memories and thought. The phone shrieked. Arellia jumped. The flame flickered and flirted with the photo of Henrietta and Jerome. The phone shrilled again, insistent. Arellia dove for it.

"Henrietta?!"

It wasn't.

"Yes, Colleen," Arellia sighed into the receiver, "I've seen the article. Thank you, I think she looks beautiful, too. No, she does not live in a tarpaper shanty. Look, I can't talk right now. I'm expecting a call from Henrietta. Bye."

Arellia repeated this leap, lunge, and answer routine all night. Henrietta never called. Arellia bit down irritation and went to blow out the candle. She stared for a long moment at the image of her daughter's black eyes, the mirrors of her own. Then she left the candle burning and went to bed. All night, the tiny flame kept vigil for her daughter.

CHAPTER TEN

· · · · ·

Mr. NBC

What does one do in the morning when one wakes up as a national celebrity? Henrietta didn't know about anyone else, but she changed Jerome's foul smelling diaper, fed him, and then gathered her bag up for the two mile hike down to the gas station to buy more water. Isn't that what every celebrity who lives under blown off mountaintops that bleed toxic minerals into groundwater does?

The breeze slipped in and out the open cabin windows, lifting the yellow curtains and teasing last night's dream from where it slumbered in her memory. In the dream, Henrietta's life spread out like ice flows fracturing under changing climates and rising temperatures. The ice heaved and groaned beneath her feet. Tyrell was with her, dragging chains that left trails of rust and blood across the stark blue-white flag of the ice. Henrietta and Tyrell leapt on faith as the black frigid water seeped through the cracks. They tried to run, but Henrietta carried Jerome in her arms and Tyrell's chains kept tripping him. She grabbed Tyrell by the hand and lugged him back from the edge. Tyrell's eyes flew open and Henrietta felt a sudden, drowning weight. "Pull up the chains, Tyrell!" she cried as the rusty linkages dragged them all toward death. He struggled, one-handed. She clung to him, one-handed. The whole family slid closer to the black waters.

She woke gasping for air. The immediacy of life-saving actions and decisions pulsed in her heartbeat. Jerome kicked the blankets and the spring sun poured in the window onto them. She nursed him and got ready to fetch the water.

The wind tickled her as she closed her door on last night's dream and bounced down the trail with Jerome laughing at the motion. A woodpecker hammered a rapid succession of knocks that pounded through the forest. Squirrels defended their territories with death-defying chases through the canopy. Now and then, her footsteps paused as a slant of light caught a perfect sculpture of a spider web strung between the lower branches of the trees. The forest sweated out rich scents. The breeze slipped in and out of leaves and brushed its fingers across Henrietta's face.

The road was wider and went straighter down, but she was glad to scissor her legs through the narrow forest trails and half run, half fall down the mountainside. She hummed songs that had no names as Jerome rode his mother's roller-coaster descent. Two certainties came flying out of the tree line as Henrietta burst through the brushy ditch and climbed up onto the road.

One: it was spring.

Two: it was time for action.

No more snuggling under the covers while the snow tucked its blanket up against the house. No more lighting fires and staying by them all day. No more puttering around one's own business without a thought for what lay beyond the veil of falling snow.

It was spring. The tremendous rush of buds to blossoms to full-blown leaves trumpeted overhead. The animals came creeping out of burrows and dens, roaring hungrily for food and sex. Migrations of winged creatures culminated in the treetops. The forest floor erupted into ferns, grasses, and riots of wildflowers. Get out of bed! the earth hollered to its inhabitants. Now is the time to renew the stuff of life!

Sap flowed down the trunks of trees. Bees swarmed to nuzzle the earliest pollinating plants. Each bit of uncurling life infused its neighbors with frenetic resurrection. The bursting greenery sent Henrietta galloping down the road. Her legs stretched into a run that set Jerome to joyous shrieks. It's time for action, she agreed. If the ice flows are melting, the only thing to do is leap for higher ground.

The overhead bell tinkled as Henrietta swung in the glass door of the gas station.

"Mrs. Thompkin," Henrietta called out, "when are you gonna carry more than chips and candy bars in your variety store?"

That's what the locals called the two shelves at the gas station. They reserved the title of 'grocery store' for the place in the next hollow over.

"When folks can afford to buy it. The Charities of Mercy done run me out of business," Mrs. Thompkin complained. The sisters came once a month after church to pass out canned goods and cheese that never molded or tasted good. Mrs. Thompkin and Henrietta turned as they heard Ford Nelson's old pickup scrabbling on the gravel in the yard. Henrietta could see Wanda leaning out the passenger side.

"See," Wanda proclaimed, "I told you she was coming down the hill. Henrietta! You are harder to get ahold of than a grass snake. Don't you got a phone?"

"Battery ran out yesterday."

"Well, charge it, girl; they're calling *me!*"

"Who?" Henrietta asked mildly as she paid Mrs. Thompkin for her water. Wanda looked at her like she was deaf, dumb and blind, which, so far as national media was concerned, she was.

"Everybody! But mostly Hank and Patrick and Louisa."

Henrietta grinned. The core organizers of the mountaintop removal protest were bound to be going crazy over that article. She could bet they never dreamed the issue would peak like this. Wanda kept berating her as Ford filled up his tank.

"Henrietta, you got to get with the twenty-first century. Get yourself some Skype!"

Henrietta rolled her eyes and everybody laughed. "I've gotta get one of those phones, Wanda, like my mamma's got. You know, with the computer in it." Henrietta added technology to the list of goodies at St. Tomorrow's Feast Day.

"Shoot, you sneeze and you lose reception here," Mrs. Thompkin complained.

"Sides, girl," Wanda added, "you best get a *car* first. You can't be hauling water and that baby up the holler at the same time. He's gonna be growing, too."

Wanda's eyes narrowed as a vehicle turned round the bend, "Glory, I wonder who that is. Ford, you know that car?"

"Nuh, I don't."

Around the gas station, everyone's heads turned to watch as

national media rolled into their secret hollow.

*   *   *

"Ms. Owens," Mr. NBC began, "did you grow up in these parts?"

These parts . . . how colloquial, Henrietta thought, such a lovely verbal camouflage to fit the Appalachian backdrop. She opened up her mouth to speak, but he had just turned to address the camera,

"I'm here with Ms. Henrietta Owens, mother and activist." He turned back to Henrietta and held the microphone out like an order. She reluctantly obeyed.

"No, I was raised in Ohio, where my mother lives."

Hi Mom, she thought irreverently; look who's on TV. The man who operated the primary camera caught her grin. The second cameraman panned across Wanda's gleeful smile and the orange swatch of her faded red housedress. He swept past the morose frown of wiry Mrs. Thompkin whose blue bandana lassoed down her thick underbrush of hair and zoomed in on her husband's checked and collared shirt that choked the brown rolls of his neck up to meet his distrustful expression. He paused a moment on the bemused patience of Ford Nelson that held steady while tee shirts flicked in the background on the breeze-blown clothesline. Finally, the camera lingered on an antique car Mr. Thompkin had long since given up on fixing. Henrietta saw the cameraman filming the car and thought; oh lord, they'll think we actually drive around in that!

The mountaintop removal protest organizers had arrived

just after the NBC news team had unpacked their gear. Louisa fed Henrietta sound bytes, Patrick tried to get in the shot, and Hank made faces at the baby. Henrietta wished they'd brought a plan for Mr. NBC, who steadily ignored all three. They looked un-photogenic and far too much like real Americans. Well, except for Hank, who *was* Appalachian born and raised and wore his overalls without a shirt and the hillbilly label like a badge of honor, despite his cohorts' pleas.

"Hank, please, *hillbilly* is the only derogatory term still used in mainstream media without any public outcry," Patrick would try to reason with the headstrong younger man. "Do you have to go out of your way to reinforce old stereotypes?" Hank would just spit tobacco on the ground and grin. The news reporters always interviewed him. Today, however, they merely panned him with the rusting old gas station pumps, the pile of tires, and the other photogenic scenery, while Jerome chewed his mother's collar and stared as they shot close-ups of his eyes.

"So," continued Mr. NBC, "you came here to protest the mountaintop removal?"

"No, not exactly," Henrietta said as she pulled Jerome off her collar.

"You fell in love with the mountains?" Mr. Big Time News suggested.

"Uh, sort of."

Patrick and Louisa let out frustrated choked-up noises. Come on, Henrietta, they urged through gritted teeth, don't blow this!

"Wouldn't you like to take us round the hollow?" Mr. NBC suggested. Henrietta looked at him. What did he expect?

Fiddling? Tarpaper shacks? White folks?

"What do you want to see?" she asked, thinking of the tangle of tiny roads that threaded through the trees and slopes between everybody's houses. Children's plastic toys mixed with machinery, both left out to bleach in sun and rust in rain and rot in mud. Muddy pens enclosed a lonesome goat or two while the chickens free-ranged wherever they pleased and helped the wandering dogs pull apart the garbage bins until someone hollered out the window for them to 'git out of there!' Broken down cars served as local lawn ornaments and the yards were naturally landscaped jumbles of tall grasses bumping up over god-knows-what in the bushes while the dishevelment of constant wood chopping tumbled across the driveways. There wasn't much to see for primetime purposes.

"How about your home?" Mr. NBC suggested.

"Oh no." She wasn't going to take them into the constant losing battle against mildew, dust, and dirty dishes that creeps up when you have no army of cleaning services to fight for you. "How about the mountains?" she suggested. "Don't you want to see the mountains?" What was this interview about anyway?

Good girl, Henrietta, Louisa mouthed silently. Patrick cheered. Hank shot her a wink. Mr. NBC said,

"Sure," and gestured to his van.

"Oh, we can't go up the road," Henrietta told them. "The coal company's got it gated. We gotta walk up the back ridge." First Camera kept recording as she said, "They'd like to hide this from the world, but it's hard to hide a mountain, even one they've torn apart."

Golden, First Camera thought, a perfect video clip.

Henrietta shifted Jerome and asked Ford to bring the water up to the cabin. Hank, Louisa, and Patrick invited themselves on the hike up to the ridge. Wanda fanned against the rising heat and told them,

"I ain't walking up no ridge. It's too hot for springtime, I tell you. Anybody who don't believe in global warming is just plain stupid. Phew!" She waved them off and retired to the variety store, which, while it didn't even dream of air conditioning, at least kept its humble fan churning from the day snow melted to the first frost that chilled the autumn air.

Hank jetted up the trail. Patrick grumbled about spring chickens as he huffed his aging girth along. Henrietta tried to keep a steady pace for his sake. He had told her sometime back that his doctors were always on him about his health. Henrietta knew his *doctor* was a once a year occasion, but his wife nagged him constantly about heart rates, blood pressure, glucose levels, and the various lifestyle diseases she suspected that he had. His wife knew all about them from the TV prescription commercials. Patrick's social security didn't cover pills, and his retirement funds from the coal company were a pay-on-death-account (which, according to Patrick, was the only reason they hadn't killed him yet), so they made do with nagging and half-hearted attempts at health that, Patrick admitted probably kept him alive better than drugs anyway.

Louisa followed him up the trail, taking a mental species count as they wove between tall white basswoods, ashes, birches, and yellow buckeyes, tulip trees, and sugar maples. A narrow and pragmatic woman, her straight brown hair was pulled into a no-nonsense ponytail at the nape of her neck and her stocky legs comfortably extended out of khaki shorts. She hiked along in an easy stride built from many years of climbing up and down steep mountainsides collecting the data of the demise of this ancient ecosystem. Her grim work was etched permanently in the lines that crisscrossed her face, scarred by too many years of bad news from the coalfields of West Virginia.

The news team trio struggled and puffed up the hollow slopes with their cameras and gear. Mr. NBC's shiny shoes slipped on the silt of the trail as he tried to keep his trousers clean. First Camera trod along like a cheerful Sierra Club explorer. His counterpart grimaced like a fashion videographer caught in a foreign war assignment.

By the time they reached the ridge, everyone was hot and sweaty and the news team saved their lungs by interviewing the organizers. Patrick scratched his back against an accommodating tree and delivered an abbreviated history of labor protests, coal, and miners. Polish by descent and as native to the locale as Irish Hank, Patrick told the history of the area with the humor of one who's seen it all and lived to tell the tale. His youngest grandchildren believed him when he bellowed,

"I was here before the mountains and I'll be here after the coal company buries everyone else under them!"

He'd mined and gone on strike and been laid off and sued and gotten re-hired until the coal company finally retired him at an appropriate age, albeit without a pension. Patrick, glad to be alive, became a reckless rabble-rouser who raged and ranted at 'the hard-hearted tyrants of the Alleghany's'.

"Yes, sir," he exclaimed, "since 1600 we've had non-stop

unjust subjugation 'round these parts. First the Indians were killed or forced out. Then the coal mining started and all the blasting of the railroad tunnels . . . that's about when the Polish came in. We were all miners from the old country. They brought us in to break the Irish strikers' backs. Hah! There ain't a trick on this side of the ocean that hadn't already been perfected on the other. The Polish miners could smell a scoundrel ten miles away. We went straight to the Irish and stood by them. No, we weren't falling for the coal company's lies. Not yet. Not 'til we got naturalized -same with the Irish-and we all became Americans. Yep, in the name of patriotism and citizenship, the Irish and the Polish stood side by side and swore upon the red, white, and blue, then went into the pits and came out as black as Henrietta there.

"I tell you, this area's seen more than its fair share of awfulness. Back then there were the black slaves and prison laborers, too. There's a lot of folks of all colors buried in these hills. You can't take a piss in the woods without watering somebody's great-granddaddy. Sometimes we can use the sanctity of the family graveyards to protect the mountains from the coal company. There are laws to let folks lie in peace that sometimes even those tyrants can't uproot. Other times, though, they bring in the bulldozer and just toss the old graves down into the valley with the lifeblood of the mountains."

Patrick looked up at the canopy of trees as if in prayer for the poor souls who could no longer rest in peace. Then he put aside the mourning of old ancestral ghosts and continued the narrative of abuses the region had endured.

"See, when the coal company got done butchering the

unions and replacing unruly miners with machines, I guess the only mischief left was to rip the trees off the mountains that have been growing them for fifty-thousand years. Yep, for the past forty years mankind's been scraping down the work of millenniums. It's going to take another thousand years for anything to come back. Before long, I reckon you could see the pits from outer space. They'll look like big ole gray and ugly you're-not-welcome mats put out for the aliens."

Louisa finished counting trees and turned toward the cameramen.

"Patrick is simplifying his statistics." She crossed thin arms across her chest and sent shivers down their spines with the look on her face. "These mountains will *never* grow back. Never. Not in a thousand years, not in forty-thousand years." She swung the weight of her PhD into the conversation and quietly summarized the worst of the ecological horror stories.

"Reclamation is a phrase you'll hear a lot about. To the coal companies, it means restacking the excess dirt back on top of the mountain in a contour that looks vaguely like the original ridgeline. It's kind of like blowing your leg apart and piling the globs of bloody flesh back together into something that looks like a leg. It doesn't mean you can ever walk on it. The rocks are unstable and prone to erosion. The topsoil is gone. When the coal company replants the old minefields at all, it is with invasive species that compete with native trees and plants."

Louisa shook with infuriation. "The overfill dumps bury the headwaters of streams and let high levels of minerals taint the water runoff that flows into watersheds, poisoning people and aquatic life. The dust from the mines flies around on the air and settles onto everything. I cannot express to you the tragedy of this ecological holocaust in such a bio-diverse region. And that doesn't even begin to talk about the effects of the carbon emissions from coal itself-"

"Uh, thank you, ma'am," Mr. NBC tried to cut her off.

"-which are *the* major contributor to greenhouse gases, global warming, and climate change."

"Thank you," Mr. NBC said firmly.

"You're welcome," Louisa snapped. "I know the networks don't like the words *global warming*, but I can assure you, from a firm scientific perspective, it is not a hoax." She glared at the reporter in disgust.

Like the grease that spins the wheels and sends vehicles flying across the land, Louisa, without an official leadership role or title, ran the army of the protesters as much as anyone. She connected dots, foresaw problems, averted disasters, raised funds, and saw opportunities forming months ahead of manifestation. Patrick's retirement allowed him time to show up at all the meetings. Hank's sporadic employment cycles and youthful devil-may-care authenticity lent him local charisma and sway. The unlikely trio formed an alliance as tight as any and, despite themselves, all sorts of protests, marches, fundraising, and public education campaigns somehow got accomplished. Louisa made sure they always thanked the masses of volunteers and organizations that backed and supported their every effort.

"A protest is not a crusade," she told her two cohorts, "led by an impassioned king charging off with his knights behind him. In this day and age, a protest is a shifting mass of people who come together like currents in a swirling ocean."

"Huh," Patrick snorted. "That's why it feels like nothing ever changes. We're just specks of foam flung against the shores of hardened stone establishments."

"Don't forget," Louisa's achy smile stretched, "shorelines are formed by constant battering. Even granite erodes under the persistent efforts of water."

"Eventually," Hank sighed.

Today, Hank twanged his accent thick as molasses and eased the tension between Louisa and the reporter by telling the NBC news team the legend of No Man's Holler. The cameramen used professional aplomb to keep from chuckling along.

"No *man* could set foot here, see. Women were fine, but no full-grown men. The Indians had legends and stayed away. Even John Nelson -who had got past his master, the slave catchers, the dogs, seven rivers, and two mountain ranges- couldn't find his way into No Man's Holler, though he could hear his wife, Lucy, singing and crying for him to find her. He had to yell back from that ridgeline over there 'til she heard him and climbed up to meet him. We could see 'em in the moonlight, over in Crawley's Slope, where my folks were. They'd be dancing and, uh, other things, but John had to stay up there on that ridge all alone for twenty years until his son came of age. Then, because the holler had raised a man of its own, the witchery of the place was broken and John Nelson moved in with his family."

Henrietta wished Wanda were here to protest *that*. It sounded like utter fabrication, a local blend of ballad, bedtime stories, and exaggeration. Of course, Hank would have to come and listen to Wanda explain why all his folks in Crawley's Slope were born crazy. A war of truth and lies and heritage, old family lore and stereotypes was guaranteed to flare.

When they crested over the ridge, the reporters gaped. The organizers smirked sadly. Second Camera immediately began filming the expansive gray slides of shale and scars of rock. Henrietta said apologetically,

"It's hard to catch it all on film. Nothing can ever express the empty shock that hits your gut when you realize an entire mountain's *gone*."

First Camera had her framed against two hundred acres of ripped up grayness where a set of mountains used to peak. The green forests halted abruptly on the ridgeline precipices of the coalmine. No birds flew across the wasteland. No deer or squirrel treaded on it. It was dead. Empty. Ripped open.

"That's the coal," Henrietta pointed out the dark gash. Second Camera zoomed in. Jerome squirmed and Henrietta set him down in the grass.

"That's the machine that slices off the mountains." First Camera swooped down and caught Jerome frowning at the machine's motored growls in the distance. The shot slid to crumbling piles of bulldozed rocks and back to Henrietta, who pointed out,

"The coal company promises jobs and income for the local families. It takes six men to tear apart a mountain. Six."

First Camera kept steady on her sorrowful face, envisioning the Emmy award he'd receive for the documentary version. He crossed his mental fingers and prayed she'd turn his way. His foot nudged the baby who made a little sound. Henrietta looked sadly down. First Camera thanked all the Gods of Film. Henrietta continued,

"That flat spot used to be a valley. That one over there used to be a ridge like this one. At night, I sometimes think I hear the whole earth screaming."

She picked up Jerome. First Camera grabbed a close-up of their faces, nose to nose; their warmth, their closeness, the baby with his mamma's dark brown skin and cheekbones already showing their connection.

"I can't imagine what he's gonna think when he gets old enough to understand all this . . . "

Mr. NBC sensed a magic moment and slipped behind the cameraman. Henrietta's eyes searched for his and in the process found the camera. She looked straight into the lens. First Camera fell in love. Henrietta continued,

"Nor can I imagine what the nation is gonna think when it realizes what it's doing."

First Camera accepted his imaginary Emmy award with teary eyes and dedicated it all to her.

CHAPTER ELEVEN

. . . . .

Vital Signs

"Did you see it, Mamma?"

"Yes, Henrietta, I saw the interview."

"Well?"

Arellia paused a long time before answering. She could picture Henrietta in the grocery store, holding the cellphone against one ear while Jerome kicked in the cart.

"It's ridiculous," she exploded.

"The interview?"

"No, you living out there in the middle of nowhere without cellphone reception. How am I supposed to know you're alright?"

"Watch me on the evening news, Mamma."

"Very funny," Arellia snapped.

"So, what did you think of the interview?"

Again, Arellia paused, vacillating between truth and worry. She answered carefully,

"I thought of Joan of Arc."

"You think God's calling me?" Henrietta laughed.

"I think she's dead, Henrietta."

"Should I get some armor?"

"Quit making jokes and listen up." Arellia wasn't happy. "Nobody's messing around out there. Those protests have been going on for years. You think the coal company's just gonna shut down because you, Miss Henrietta Owens, showed up?"

Henrietta said nothing. Arellia warned her,

"They will roll their bulldozers over you. They will drop a mountainside on your head. They will lock you up and you won't ever see the light of day again-"

"Mamma!"

"Don't you *Mamma* me! I did not -I repeat- I did not raise my daughter up to become target practice for irate coal miners, *do you understand?* And I did not midwife your precious little boy into this world to let his crazy mamma put him in danger! You want to fight mountaintop removal, that's one thing, but they're gonna go after Jerome to get you to stop."

"Mamma! I am *not* putting Jerome into any danger."

"You are," Arellia said flatly. "Every word you speak out against the coal company-"

"This ain't about some little hills in Appalachia, Mamma. With all those carbon emissions and global warming, there won't be a world for your grandson to grow up in!"

Arellia frowned. "That's just as much nonsense as the lunatics who think climate change isn't real. There is gonna be a world when Jerome grows up."

"Yeah? And what about for his kids? And theirs?"

"Ain't your cross to carry, Henrietta."

"You don't believe that, Mamma. I know it."

Arellia said nothing.

"What do your signs say?" Henrietta pressed her.

Arellia remained silent.

"Mamma, don't pretend you're losing reception. Answer

the question."

Arellia cursed daughters who knew their mothers too well.

"What do your signs say?" Henrietta asked again.

Arellia's shelves were brimming. It seemed that signs were falling from the sky, one, two, three a day. In her purse. On the street. Left on top of the bill at the coffee shop.

"I don't know what they mean, Henrietta."

"Just tell me what they are."

"There's a lot of little figurines, acrobats and cowboys, warriors; the stuff kids play with, you know? A piece of an electric railroad set. A scrap of yellow lace. And . . ." Arellia hesitated.

"And what?"

"I found a diamond."

"A diamond," Henrietta repeated.

"I turned it over to the police."

"What'd you do that for?" Henrietta said, exasperated.

"Well, it wasn't mine," Arellia replied defensively. "It seemed like the right thing to do. It's somebody's diamond."

"A diamond, huh? They're made from coal," Henrietta pointed out.

"I'm aware," Arellia replied without humor. She knew all the symbolism of diamonds; they last forever, they're a girl's best friend, they're the toughest substance in the world. Despite all that, Arellia had no desire to see her daughter hardened by the incredible pressures of plate tectonics. She didn't have to stand up against the madness of this massive world. Arellia's eyes flicked along her bookcases.

"Oh, I also found a little globe," she confessed.

"Of the earth?" Henrietta asked.

"Yes."

"See?" Henrietta insisted softly. "I don't want to get mixed up in trouble, but trouble's at our door. If we don't get involved, all of us, and do something, the house is gonna burn down around our ears."

"Well, that would explain the firefighter's keychain," Arellia said. She tried to laugh, but it came out bitter.

"Mamma, you better tell me about all those signs."

Silence.

"Mamma, either you're gonna help me do this, or you're gonna throw me into the lions' den all alone."

Silence.

"Mamma?"

Arellia listened to the whispering of souls. She heard the thousand wing beats of God's angels passing by. She heard the rumors of the days to come. She heard the whirring coin toss on the fate of man. Arellia saw the martyrs riding by. She saw the heroes falling one by one. When the dust of visions settled, Henrietta was not among the fallen bodies. Jerome was not a casualty. Not for now. Not while the coin still spun above them. Very well, Arellia thought, they live . . . for now.

"Listen carefully, Henrietta." Arellia walked along her bookshelf, touching the symbols one by one. A tiny book without any letters. A racing man. A pamphlet on Jesus and the Resurrection. A heart-shaped watch that no longer ticked, frozen at the eleventh hour.

"There is a story that must be told," she said. "There's not much time. There's a hero who needs resurrecting. And there must be a revival of the human heart."

Henrietta was silent, listening.

"Do you understand?" Arellia asked.

"No," her daughter confessed.

"You will. You will."

There was more, but Arellia dared not say it. The running man was striped in black and white. She thought he was intended to be an African tribesman running, but to her it looked like prison stripes. And the last thing they needed was a jailbreak. They had trouble enough without that.

CHAPTER TWELVE

·····

Lions' Den

'Daniel in the lions' den.
Oh-oh, Daniel in the lions' den.
Oh-oh-ho, Daniel in the lions' den!"

The barbershop quartet serenaded Jack as he stormed toward the office in the sunset. The night guard in the polished lobby nodded politely and shut the door on the song. Jack rode the elevator up eleven moody stories, laying out the cold bare facts as the bell at chimed at every floor.

One: Standard Coal was raking in the profits - *bing!*
Two: Standard Coal was tearing off the mountaintops - *bing!*
Three: the mountains would never, ever, grow back - *bing!*
Four: exposed minerals washed into the groundwater - *bing!*
Five: so far, the nation ignored the hillbilly protests - *bing!*
Six: but now Henrietta Owens was going national - *bing!*
Seven: the woman had incredible charisma - *bing!*
Eight: charismatic activists spelled bad news for coal - *bing!*
Nine: people would put pressure on the politicians - *bing!*
Ten: environmental exemptions would be repealed - *bing!*
Eleven: and that would be the end of coal - *bingo!!!!!!*

Public relations should have killed that television interview before it started, Jack thought. It should never have made it to primetime news. He walked grimly into the darkened office for the second after-hours meeting the boss had called this week. The cubicles were empty. The conference room lights scowled out ferociously. Jack stepped through the door.

His boss ripped Henrietta's face apart.

Jack flinched. Thomas Shipley, CEO of Standard Coal, the Captain, as his associates called him, slammed the remnants of the *Motherhood Today* cover photo on the conference table. His scowl curdled the milky simper of the Head of the Public Relations department. He slashed the Marketing Director with pointed words that snarled out from between his teeth. His paw pounded on the table and demanded answers.

Around the room, steely faces battened down their hatches to weather out his storming. Lightning zapped at the heads that stuck out the most. When the Captain's raging electrical storm ran out, a breath of relief ran through the room. No one had been struck down or set on fire, or worse yet: fired.

Jack watched relief roll into revenge. The eyes started flicking, the whiskers twitching, the chops licking. Jack, the company's grins-and-guns ambassador, heard the tones of war.

One: build up the threat . . .

"this is a direct attack against the coal company!"

Two: call on patriotic values . . .

"we've served this country for over two hundred years!"

Three: demonize the enemy . . .

"low class, attention grabbing, teenage welfare mother!"

"That's not true."

Executive eyes swung in Jack's direction. Jack blinked. Had he spoken?

"What's . . . not . . . true?" the Captain snarled.

The pack around him rumbled in their throats, swearing allegiance in their little growls. Jack gulped. He must have spoken.

"Henrietta Owens is twenty-five," he pointed out.

The boss roared with laughter.

"Old enough to get a job, then!" he howled.

The others joined right in.

"Old enough to have sucked too long on the tax-payers!"

"Tabloid material," one sneered, passing on the affronting article.

"She should have buttoned up that blouse-"

"Ah, but baby's hungry," the third one tittered.

Something roared in Jack. Suddenly the room swam and he saw John Henry towering over the smirking suits and ties, staring down the insurrection of their viciousness.

"Sit down, Jack," the Captain ordered. Had he risen? He felt the claws of eyes dig into him as he realized he was towering, his hands upon the table, a fury thundering in his chest.

"Jack, Jack," the Captain purred, "don't let her get to you." He fingered her torn up image, "She's charming, really, in a third-world-country sort of way."

Jack shuddered as they chortled. He laced his hands together, long white fingers as pale as all the others in the room. He warned them,

"Don't get distracted by race. You look at that photo and

see a black woman. I can assure you; the women in this country see a mother with a baby. Period."

"Then thank god she isn't white," the Marketing Director snorted. "She'd have the Nobel Peace Prize by now."

Again, they roared with laughter, forgetting Jack and launching into war maneuvers. Out came the standard tactics of lambasting, discrediting, blacklisting, and threatening.

"She's *national*," the Head of Public Relations warned. Jack bristled at the snarl in the man's tone. He told himself to calm down, wondering why he felt so suddenly protective. Henrietta's crumpled eye upon the desk stared out accusingly at all of them. Her son lay separated from her.

"Foster care or child services," someone else suggested. "She's unfit to be a mother. God knows what can happen at a protest!"

Especially if we supply the rubber bullets and private agents, Jack thought grimly.

"No good," one of the lawyers pointed out. "She's got a mother who can raise the child."

"We just need to threaten her a little. Get her worried for the boy. She'll back off."

"No, she'll squeal while she's got the public's eye."

"It's volatile, boys," the Captain whistled, "extremely tricky. We can't ignore it. Can't address it. It's not like beating up the union. Those are men. They signed up for the fight."

"Good lord," Marketing exclaimed, "she'll have the mothers of the nation holding baby-stroller marches!"

"Protest as fashion!" Public Relations saw it coming.

" . . . as weight loss!" Marketing groaned. They suspected

the columnists were hard at work already. The Captain ordered,

"We need to nip this in the bud. Call the media and silence her. Do what it takes. If they won't shut her out, start a counter campaign. If that doesn't work, well, there are other methods."

The silence in the room made Jack's hair stand up. Everyone heard the hidden insinuation. A bullet, an accident, an illness, a heart attack; they'd used them all before. The Captain added plaintively,

"We can't have moms and children in the streets."

No, Jack snorted very quietly, *that* would change this country. The Captain finished with what sounded suspiciously like a suggestion,

"What if there was tear gas? No one likes to hear a child cry. No respectable mother would ever bring her child to a protest after that."

"We've never tear-gassed an infant," Marketing protested.

"No," the Captain drawled, "not yet."

He picked up the baby he had ripped from his mother's image. From the table, Henrietta's worried eyes looked out.

CHAPTER THIRTEEN

. . . . .

Steel-Driving Woman

"Allie, hurry up!" Sarah shouted up the stairs. Jack jerked his head up from the kitchen table. She ran a hand across his back. "You're up early," she said.

"No, late."

"Late for work?" she echoed as she ground the coffee.

"No . . . "

The grinder drowned out his words. It stopped.

"What was that?" Tap-tap. She measured the coffee into the maker.

"I'm-" Jack's courage failed him. The coffee maker gurgled and let off comforting aromas to buoy him against the words he had to say.

"Allie! Come on!" Sarah yelled and then turned to him, "Honey, your clothes look like you slept in them."

"I did," he muttered. Sarah stared at him. She'd been in bed when he got home. He'd watched his sleeping wife and traced the contours of her body with his eyes. He lingered on their growing child still inside her. Then he shut the door and went downstairs, full of red-eyed envy. Sleep was not an option. The meeting tossed and turned inside him even now.

"Oh, well, you better change up for work," Sarah said.

"I'm not going," he spit out flatly.

"What?!" the exclamation shot out of her. Jack could almost see the blonde hairs rising on her neck. Her hand sloshed the coffee slightly. "Oh, I see," she said as her mind raced to smooth out his comment, "the boss gave you the day off."

"No . . . "

She put the pot down too hard and wouldn't look at him. The daily papers were screaming with statistics of unemployment, poverty, lay-offs, and sluggish economies.

"He fired you?" she asked.

"No," he replied slowly. She spun around and her belly swung just a little slower. She closed her suit coat tight around their unborn child. Jack's head bent down toward the table in exhaustion. Sarah almost asked him what was wrong, but she grew fearful of the answer and brushed past him to yell again,

"Allie!" She turned toward the kitchen and Jack caught her hand.

"Sarah . . . " he trailed off. His eyes were red shot and tired. He looked old. Their baby bulged between them. "I'm not going back. I want to quit."

Her silence screamed a thousand questions, all variations of *why*. He couldn't tell her. She was used to excuses of confidentiality, but this time it was his failing courage more than anything else that silenced him. He couldn't tell his much-loved, cosseted, protected, pregnant wife that he'd spent most of the night discussing tear-gassing an infant as if it were a round of golf, no different than any normal after-work activity.

At midnight, Jack spent more three hours in a private meeting with the boss, weighing the ethics and effectiveness of murdering a mother and child. Would an accident work convincingly? Or did it need to be an irate coal miner who flew off the handle? Or maybe a murdered mother would make a more provocative martyr than JFK or Martin Luther King . . . how much would it cost to make the nation just forget her? They'd decided it was too risky for the moment . . . but only for the moment.

As he left, the Captain bid him goodbye and clapped him on the shoulder,

"Just like the old days, eh?"

Jack said nothing. In the old days, it was only union leaders they'd planned to murder.

He drove home in a stupor. He saw the carbon copies of the torn out checks his wife had written. He checked the recent call list on the phones. He swore. Henrietta's image was reaching beyond the usual protesting suspects. He'd know those faces in the tear gas. They might be Sarah, Allie, or any of their friends.

"I can't do what they're asking," he said.

She misunderstood and squeezed him,

"Of course you can. You can work a deal out with anyone." She tried to jolly him up with pride. "You're the fastest contract shooter in the East." He stared at her and wished his own professional insecurity were all he was grappling with. "Come on," she urged. "Where are your shoes? It's getting late." Her voice rang out a little loud.

"I'm not going," he repeated.

She froze. Her back was to him now, one hand on the wooden chair, the other on her lower back. Her hair shielded her face and she spoke tightly through its highlights.

"Of course you are, Jack. It's one thing to send a little donation to a worthy cause, but . . . Jack, you can't quit now. What about the baby? This house? Allie?" her voice stumbled over the list of one-word reasons and in between her shoulder blades that looked so tense he read the unspoken question; *what about me?*

"Sarah, come on, look at me."

She didn't want to. She'd never learned to mask her raw and fearful heart. She looked up at the ceiling as if in prayer. When she turned, her stressed expression hit Jack strongly. He reeled. He regained his footing and spoke very carefully.

"I have to do as a man is called to do . . . to have convictions and morality." Jack felt a familiar presence come up behind him, strong and solid. "I have to stand my ground and be a man, like John Henry-"

"Oh?" Sarah hissed. Fury was the defense she'd learned for protecting the vulnerable nature of her heart. "What about John Henry's wife, hmm? You ever think of her? And what about his baby, huh?"

She started gathering her things for work, flinging frustration, fear, and worry into her purse along with her cellphone, energy bar, and lipstick.

"Go ahead, be a man! Go be like John Henry . . . die for your convictions."

Her hand was on the door as she spat out,

"If you -or John Henry- were a *man*, you'd get yourself to work, hammer out a goddamn deal, and keep this roof over your children's heads. That's what you'd do." She hollered a final time, "Allie!" and then stormed out to the car.

Jack looked at the form of John Henry that had come up behind him a few moments ago. The man was staring off into time and space. Jack heard the clink of steel and caught sight of a determined woman swinging hammers with explosive force. In the kitchen, Allie flew by with a wind of song,

"John Henry had a little woman -Bye, Dad!- *Her name, it was Polly Ann."*

Allie's breeze wrapped around him as she hurtled out the door behind her mother, singing,

"When John Henry took sick and went to his bed,
Polly Ann drove steel like a man, lord, lord!"

"That's enough, Allie." Sarah slammed the house door, the car door, and then the gas as Jack and John exchanged a long look. The garage door rumbled. Jack rubbed his throbbing temples.

"Well, John," he began, "the song says she drove steel like a man. However, it never says what she drove it *into*."

John's chuckle rumbled up through his chest, his smile, and then crinkled out through his eyes. Humor is an intimate thing. John knew the bite of steel through solid rock. And a man? Well, a man ain't nothing but a man.

*   *   *

Long after Sarah's car turned the corner, Jack trudged upstairs to change out of his crumpled suit pants and wrinkled shirt. He peeled off his thin black socks and picked the lint out of his toes. He pulled on his blue jeans and tee shirt and went back downstairs to call the office.

"Cathy? Yes, Jack Dalton here. I won't be in today. Cancel anything on the calendar. What? No, I don't know when you should reschedule things. Goodbye."

His head was throbbing from lack of sleep and arguments. Sarah's words stung him. Her self-involved hypocrisy galled him. She could write checks to Henrietta Owens, but he was supposed to suck up his guilty conscience and go to work?

"Be a man?" he repeated bitterly, standing in the shiny kitchen. The cleaning service must have come yesterday. The counters were polished. The sink was scoured clean. Every gleaming surface hurt his eyes. He closed them.

Be a man. What was that supposed to mean? Go to work and plan a murder? Show up at the office so Sarah could enjoy her comforts and conveniences without looking at the nasty business that paid for it? Play the game of make-pretend that everything is hunky-dory here in suburbia then drive to work and do his *man's* job?

She didn't know what he did at work.

She didn't ask.

He wouldn't have told her if she had.

At least, not all of it.

She knew he wrote contracts. She knew he was a damn fine lawyer, one of the best. But she, like millions of other Americans, had no idea what went on in the fine print of his work. They heard of union strikes and unfair negotiations. They heard of EPA standards and environmental loopholes. They heard of rising corporate profits in times of plummeting employment. They could imagine the avaricious greed and power-lust that led to such callous decision-making.

They didn't know the cold rationality and precise legalese that allowed such things to happen. They didn't realize that someone had to write those binding agreements and legal documents.

For twenty years, that someone had been Jack.

Maybe he was getting soft, he thought. Maybe he was losing his edge. In his twenties, fresh out of Harvard, rolling cigars with the bosses, wearing expensive tailored suits, he had laughed scornfully at the tree-huggers and eco-freaks like Henrietta Owens. They'd been around as long as he had. Fanatics, he had called them. Sarah had a few friends like that. Jack remembered ripping them to conversational shreds at Christmas parties. He also recalled Sarah's infuriated elbow jabs to get him to shut up. Jack shrugged. Things change. Allie came along. Sarah stopped being as irrational as her radical friends. She let go of the activist work she was doing and those friendships had faded over the years.

Jack padded across the cream carpet and sat on the leather couch. Usually the company let the police handle the anti-coal activists . . . or left it to the West Virginians. Citizens could do vile things the police could never get away with. Standard Coal simply fed the local people lies through the churches, rhetoric through the radio, and misinformation through the local newspaper. They fanned fear of unemployment and then paid the police to stand aside as irate citizens crushed the protest.

It was an old trick.

It should have been easy to destroy Henrietta Owens. For chrissake, she was black in Appalachia. If there were anything the locals hated more than tree-huggers, Henrietta embodied all of them: a black, unmarried welfare mother from a city in another state. Even Jack knew he was culturally programmed to dislike her. She was poor, a sucker on the welfare system. She didn't pay taxes. She didn't contribute to society through the socially applauded manners of charities and volunteer work.

And yet, that photo had gotten to him. She was real. Her baby looked like her. If the newspapers rolled a sensational image of Henrietta Owens' body sprawled dead on the ground, he would know the full extent of what he had participated in. In ten years, when the six o'clock news ran a show commemorating her tragic death, Jack would look at her son and know exactly who had stolen his mother away from him. The boy would be the same age as Allie was now.

"*Be a man*. Hah!" Jack's laugh barked out. How many men, like him, used their wives' complicity to excuse immoral actions? They went to work and paid the bills. When asked what they did, they made evasive answers.

How many women, like Sarah, used their husbands to shield them from understanding the impacts of their daily choices? The labels at the grocery store don't tell you about international labor laws. Wives come home raving about 'those cheap peaches from down in Georgia' and never mind the illegal workers who picked them because their husbands destroyed the farm workers' union last month. Or how about the made-in-China sweatshops that sewed all the latest fashions? Or the poisonous, mountain-sized landfills in India that swallowed up old cellphones?

No honey, go to work. Be a man. Keep the roof over our

heads, food on the table, money in the bank account. How was work? Just say 'fine'. Don't tell me how you screwed those poor people over . . . again. Save that for the company retreats and brandy toasts with other *men.*

What did she expect of him? Jack fumed.

Double standards defined his home and work. Don't let Allie get a sniffle, but ignore the children with lung cancer in Appalachia. Check the water filter, but destroy the water reports from the coalfields. Pay attention to the bank accounts, but turn a blind eye to the economy in West Virginia. Give to charities, but ask for a raise while negotiating lower wages for everyone else. Be outraged about the quality of public schools, but advocate tax cuts for the rich.

Jack groaned. How could he *be a man* in this insanity? The way Sarah said it, to *be a man* meant destroying one's integrity, letting hate and animosity drive one's actions, and turning a blind eye to other people's suffering.

The way Jack meant, "I have to *be a man,*" involved quitting his job, losing his home, sending his daughter back to public school, telling Sarah she couldn't have her new clothes, that second car, or that new patio furniture she'd been eyeing lately. Sure, Jack had savings. They had plenty of money. But how long would it take to find a job with integrity? In this lousy economy, a lawyer with his reputation would have a thousand offers to continue the work he'd always done, but not many from the companies that struggled because they had integrity. And would a company with integrity even hire a man with his reputation?

"A man ain't nothing but a man," a low voice murmured.

Jack jumped a mile out of his skin.

John Henry leaned against the glass bookcase.

"Jesus, you scared me," Jack exclaimed. He studied the ghost. The man seemed easy and comfortable, as if he'd been walking between the realms of life and death for a long time.

"So," Jack said, "you talk?"

John Henry shrugged, "I talk plenty. Don't nobody listen." The man's voice was deep and rich. It filled his chest and sauntered out slowly.

"People don't ordinarily hear ghosts," Jack pointed out.

"People don't ordinarily listen to nothing. Seems it's got to be extra-ordinary for folks to listen up right," John said.

"Why are you here?" Jack sighed. His life was confusing enough without visions or ghosts that talked back.

"Why are you?" John answered with a question.

"How the hell do I know? I'm just a guy with a family to take care of."

"Me too," said John Henry.

"No, you're dead," Jack replied bluntly. He was too tired for courtesy.

"Don't change much. My family got a family and that family got a family too. Got to try to look out for them all," John stated.

"You know how it is, then," Jack said. "You saw Sarah pound me with her steel and anger."

"Mmm-hmm," John nodded slowly. "She just a-feared is all. Scared she gonna end up like my Polly."

"Yeah, well, I'm sure it wasn't a picnic for Polly Ann after you died," Jack said.

"Oh, she got by. Some days were harder than others. Other times, they was better'n if I had lived."

"How can you say that?"

"Man ain't nothing but a man, Jack Dalton," John Henry drawled out. "I weren't no sinner, but I weren't no saint. Maybe that's why I'm a ghost now, cause-"

They won't take me in heaven.
They won't take me in hell.
They won't take me back on earth no-how."

John chuckled away the last strains of his unexpected burst of song. Jack rubbed his tired eyes. The living room seemed to be blurring. The windows reflected a different interior than they usually did. Outside, the green lawns faded brown and the neighbor's garage turned into a brick building. John stood up as the living room disappeared.

"Don't be a-feared now," John said. "We just gonna visit Polly is all."

Jack shook his exhausted head and didn't bother trying to understand anything. The carpet sank away into a set of shabby floorboards and the cream walls of his living room faded into old wooden planks. Footsteps creaked in the ceiling above him and the tenement neighbors argued on the other side of the wall. Laundry flapped out a clothesline hung from a window.

The door of the apartment flew open. Polly Ann swept in carrying a huge basket of laundry. The woman was a wiry bundle of dynamite. She snapped the sheets and whirled them through the air as she folded them. Jack stared in fascination as this tiny magician of a woman performed her swirling sleights of hand. The white linens flashed, darted and disappeared.

117

Her hands were tough and calloused. Her arm muscles twisted around her bones and pressed against the brown fabric of her dress like it was a second skin.

"Momma?"

The whirl of linens plummeted at the voice. Polly Ann craned over her shoulder as a young boy limped into the room.

"Chile? What you done to yo'self?"

The boy sported a black eye, a bloody nose, and a split lip. All five feet and two inches of her curled with concern.

"Don't tell me you bin fightin'?!"

"Nuh, Momma, I-"

"You run inna some wagon or somethin'?"

"Nuh."

"Spit it out. And don't be leavin' no part out. I gonna know." She reached for the water bucket and a clean rag and began tending his cuts. He winced.

"Some boys come beat on me, say my daddy was a fool what got himself killed."

Polly Ann stiffened. She turned away from her son and rinsed the cloth. Her back was still to him when she said,

"Ain't no sense in fightin' over the truth."

Beside Jack, John Henry clenched every one of his muscles from toe to jaw. Jack almost laughed when he saw the little boy tense up in a perfect mirror of his father. Polly Ann knelt beside her child and gave him some tough loving with her brusque rag and honest words,

"There's a lot of folks bin fool 'nough to git themselves killed. In fact, every one of them that's not livin' now. So those boys got a certain truth. I got another truth. And I'm sure yo' daddy had a whole other truth of his own." She inspected his split lip and handed him the rag to blot it with. Then she rose with an efficiency of motion born of hard work and returned to snapping the laundry into folds.

"Wash yo' hands up and help me with this. Gotta get them down to Miz Watson 'fore supper."

The boy did as he was told. It slowed Polly Ann down to work with him, but she let him fumble for the edges of the sheets with patience, continuing to talk as they worked.

"If yo' daddy was alive, you know what he do?"

"Go beat them boys inna the ground!"

"Lawd no, chile," Polly Ann rolled her eyes. "He tell you to git smart and stay outta trouble."

She smiled at an old memory and Jack saw it echo in John. Polly Ann shook her head and said,

"Yo' daddy? He was mighty strong, but he weren't too smart or he wouldn't have fought that steam drill."

"Momma!" the boy protested, bristling to defend his champion of a father.

"What?" she said. "There's other things then bein' smart. Yo' daddy himself always be sayin' *man ain't nothing but a man.* Yo' daddy, he was stronger than any man alive and I loved him fo' it. But, lawd, he sho had a heap of pride 'bout it, too. The way he held his head got us in a pile of trouble. The time weren't ripe fo' proud negroes. Still ain't." Polly Ann's face turned sad and troubled. She dropped the last folded sheet in the basket and patted it. Then she pinned her son with her strong gaze and told him,

"You 'member, son, if you do something shameful, it

natural to feel ashamed, but there ain't one other thing 'bout you to be ashamed of."

She turned to the dishes in the sink and bent her fierce energy into them like a tornado that just couldn't stop moving. She handed the boy a cloth and motioned for him to dry and stack.

"Yo' daddy fought that steam drill in part 'cause he was proud of his strength. But the other part of the truth is that he fought it 'cause he was kind. Yes, yo' daddy, he was one part pride, three parts kindness. He looked at that drill and thought, oh lawd, this is the end of us. Yo' daddy looked around at all the other men who ain't got no hope of fightin' and outta kindness he stepped up to do what he could."

Polly Ann sighed now and leaned her worn hands on the edge of the sink. Her small back surrendered to the long day of work. Her son's worried eyes looked on anxiously, as she said,

"But it weren't enough. They just brought more steam drills."

"So it true then, Momma? My daddy done got himself killed fo' nothin'?"

John hovered so close. He wanted to take up her load and lift off her weariness. Jack felt a similar urge. But Polly Ann straightened up her back without either of the men's assistance.

"Chile, there's truth and then there's truth. You jus' gotta pick the one you like the most. I think yo' daddy didn't have no choice. He was too kind, and I wouldn't be tradin' one drop of that kindness fo' no Harvard degree or no fancy house. Oh lawd, there's plenty what did make that bargain. Yes, yes, plenty of folks gittin' rich by grinding other folks inna the dust."

"Someday, Momma, I gonna be rich *and* kind," the boy assured her. She laughed and stroked his head,

"You do that. But 'member, if this world makes you pick one way or the other . . . you 'member that yo' mamma done tole you she take a kind son over a rich one, any day."

John stepped close to her and laid his hand on her cheek. She kept looking at the boy, but her fingers stroked where John's hand had brushed.

"Son," she said, "you 'member something else, too. Yo' daddy ain't here, but that don't mean he ain't watchin' over you still."

Then she spun with force and scooped up the laundry, gesturing for the boy to follow. This all muscle, no nonsense woman had only so many moments for comfort in her days. She sliced her tenderness into rare delicacies and saved her moments of weakness for holidays that were far and few between. The shabby daylight slid into the gracious cloaking of dusk as she swept out the door. Jack and John turned . . .

. . . and returned to the cool, sunlight-filled living room with its glossy-covered books and digitally printed family photos on the walls. Jack's head swam with dizziness. He laid his hands on the cool leather of the couch. The dark face of the TV stared blankly at him. John Henry leaned against the bookcase.

"Alright, John, I've got some questions," Jack said.

"Maybe I've got some answers," John Henry replied, though his tone promised nothing. His eyes seemed only halfway in this place and time.

"Why did I see you on that chain gang?"

"'Cause I was."

"Why?"

"Pride."

"Pride isn't against the law."

"Was for negroes 'round 1870."

Jack crossed from behind the couch to stand next to John.

"Why did you fight that steam drill?"

"Had to."

"Why?"

"How come a man does anything? His spirit tells him to."

"I don't believe in spirits," Jack stated. John Henry's brown eyes leapt up. His muscles bunched. He drew back his fist and punched Jack. Jack flinched instinctively, but John Henry's fist flew right through him. Both men burst into unexpected laughter. Jack shook his head, ruefully.

"I take that back," he admitted.

"Good thing you not dead . . . that punch would have sent you flying back to life," John Henry boasted.

"I believe it," Jack replied. He thanked the heavens that the realms of life and death had spared him such an experience. The two men stood in silence with the uncomfortable feeling of entwined fates surrounding them. They looked at each other reluctantly, like two shipwrecked souls marooned in a lifeboat together.

"What do you think, John? Should I quit?"

"I ain't never quit nothing that I didn't finish right." John Henry told him sternly. "You got a mess in front of you. Fix it good. Then go."

"I can't take on-" Jack cut himself off. He was looking at a man who had single-handedly beaten a machine that was said to be unbeatable. He laid down his life and he still hadn't quit his work. His family had a family and that family had a family too. He was still looking out for them all.

Jack drew in a breath in front of the ghost and started counting his blessings from the tips of his growing toenails to the luxury of his healthy living wife, daughter, and the new child on its way. He was facing a dead man who had watched his wife and child struggle on through life without him.

Jack looked around at his world of machines that washed his dishes, cleaned his laundry, delivered his news and entertainment, shot his typewritten letters around the globe in seconds, warmed his coffee and baked his pizza, kept his beer fresh and cool, and delivered him instant communication. He thought beyond the house to his car, airplanes, road construction equipment, factories, and machines that tore coal from the mountains and turned it into electricity.

"John?" he asked. "Do you think what your son said was true? Did you die for nothing?"

The man crossed his arms on his chest and dipped his head down in thought. Jack regarded this legend before him, this super-human folk hero who was sung about by countless generations of people white and black, rich and poor alike. He was just a man.

Perhaps all legends are made of regular guys who just get up in the overwhelming ordinariness of their days and go to work, Jack thought. He had always imagined heroes to be born special, and certainly the stories about John Henry had accumulated extraordinary proportions over the years, but there were no rainbows shooting out of the man's fingertips or thunderclaps marking his words. He was too damn short to be a legend, Jack thought irreverently. The man before him was as boring as the guys who drove the bus and stocked the grocery shelves and delivered babies and wrote the news reports. He had lines in his face and callouses on his hands and his nose was bent slightly where someone had broken it. He pondered Jack's question with an expression so familiar, Jack scoured his mind to place it.

It was his own.

It was the look that came over Jack when he watched Allie sleeping and tried to figure out what was best. It was a father's worry that overwhelms his heart and creases age-lines into his face. Suddenly, Jack had to know: did John Henry die for nothing?

"John?" Jack queried softly. The other man looked up. Thought waxed his deep brown eyes with murky layers. His lips closed on half-formed answers. Jack's anxiety coursed inside his blood vessels. He had to know. "All these years, you said you've been watching over your family, seeing how this country's changed or hasn't changed. I have to know . . . do you think you died for nothing?"

John Henry's face twisted in an odd expression. Something like a smile curled.

"Don't know, Jack Dalton. It all depends on you."

CHAPTER FOURTEEN

. . . . .

The Revolutionary Table

Patrick, Louisa, Hank, Wanda, and Ford all crowded around the kitchen table in Henrietta's two-room cabin. Old Moses Nelson's mother gave birth to him on that table. Strong and sturdy, rugged as the ancient oak that formed its boards; the table's grains held a wildness within them, as if the gale storm that had felled the tree had etched itself through the rings.

Wanda placed her elbows on the table's edge. Her bosom leaned against her father's birth-stains. Wanda thought for the five thousandth time since childhood that the house would crumble around that table and it would stand alone among the other trees, solid as a rock and twice as hard to move.

Her brother Ford leaned way back in the tilting manner he had learned as a boy around that table. Patrick stood stoically beside it with one fist curled and waiting on the edge. Hank sat his fanny on the corner and put his feet up on a chair. Henrietta bounced Jerome upon her hip, stirring up Wanda's memories of the long lineage of aunts and mothers who had also paced that kitchen. Louisa carefully arranged and rearranged her thin and dirt-etched fingers on the tabletop.

"That *Motherhood Today* article has given us -and you- a chance to lay siege to coal using national attention," Louisa began. "That photo grabbed the heartstrings of the country."

"Yeah, but to keep them, we need a plan of action," Henrietta pointed out. "I can't just spew off at the mouth."

"'Course you can," Hank snorted. "You do it all the time."

Henrietta whacked him on the arm. He grinned. She relied on his ruthless honesty for sanity and he knew it. They'd been friends since Hank Crawley's guts (and a twenty dollar bet) had propelled him into No Man's Holler last winter, collecting signatures on yet another petition. Her last name stuck out on the page of scrawling Nelson signatures, and he struck up a friendly conversation.

"You have to give them the facts," Louisa said. "Bio-diversity loss, a million acres of irreparable damage, four thousand miles of streams destroyed, the carbon emissions from the coal itself-"

"I think she has to speak more about the injustice going on," Patrick interrupted. "I think she's got to call out those greedy bastards who've been screwing everybody over."

"Hey," Hank added, "if she's going to pluck those heartstrings, she could give us hillbillies a better reputation while she's at it."

"You're a fine one to talk," Patrick snapped. "When was the last time you shaved?"

"Get off my back, old man. You're the one with a hole in your shirt." Hank poked it. Patrick slapped his hand away.

"Enough," Louisa warned them. "Wanda? Ford? Would you like to say anything?" She graciously tried to include them in the conversation, though she felt their presence was inappropriate. Neither had been active in the movement before.

Wanda had just showed up at the door with Ford in tow. Henrietta had been fine with them staying, so Louisa tried to include them.

Two heads shook. Henrietta paused in her pacing. She didn't like that look on Wanda's face. Wanda wasn't happy about something. Henrietta shot her a questioning look. Wanda shrugged and folded her arms tightly across her chest. Henrietta waited five seconds. Wanda burst out,

"What you think Henrietta is, huh? Some dumb parrot for the same old lines everybody's tired of hearing? Statistics ain't keeping those mountains standing."

Louisa began to object, but Wanda cut her off. Henrietta groaned inwardly as she saw irritation zip across the thin biologist's face. Louisa was such a stickler for communication protocol.

"Mmm-hmm, y'all want folks to feel sorry for you, huh? Well, I don't. Don't need nobody's charity or pity. And injustice? Huh. Screaming for justice ain't done nothing in a thousand years 'cept make us all tired of screaming and getting screamed at."

"You were singing a different tune in the sixties," Patrick muttered. Wanda snorted.

"That was personal."

"Tap water running out red isn't personal?" Louisa argued.

"Ain't no protest gonna fix my tap water now," Wanda said defensively. "Sides," Wanda added, "I ain't getting jailed over no environmental hooplah."

Louisa bristled up to deliver a lecture on ecology. Henrietta cut in,

"Wanda! What if they told you that you couldn't live here anymore and just had to leave?"

"Over my dead body!" She slammed her hands down on the table that had raised her family. "Ain't nobody making me leave. We Nelson's own our land here. We ain't never sold it off like them white folks in the other hollers. We'd rather starve."

"Some did," Ford interjected softly, "back in the Depression."

"In a few more years," Louisa put in huffily, "you'll all start dying of cancer from the exposed minerals and the chemicals in the air. No use owning land if the mines over the next ridge start choking you to death with poisonous dust."

"And those mines won't be slowing, stopping, or shrinking," Patrick said, "only growing bigger each year. We'll all get swallowed up by pit mining machines or buried by the landslides."

"And it won't stop there," Hank put in his two cents. "Those mines will keep spreading until they run right up to the suburbs."

"Global warming from carbon emissions doesn't stop anywhere," Louisa said severely. "Coal is going to kill us all, one way or another."

"Might as well make a stand here, then," Hank declared. "It's as good a place as any." He posed dramatically. "If I die today, I fall in the hills that birthed me and lie alongside my forefathers."

"Son," Wanda glared at him, "you best get your scrawny white hide over the ridge if you're gonna do any dying. This holler's only good for killing black folks."

"Nobody's getting killed, Wanda," Henrietta said. She could almost see the hairs standing straight up on Wanda's back. Wanda twisted round in her chair and gave that young mother a *look*.

"Henrietta Owens, you're a real bright girl, but you don't know nothing about history. You stick your head out agitating like Dr. King and JFK and Gandhi, and you're gonna end up just like them. Dead. D-E-A-D. Dead. You got that?"

"Wanda, those mountains are the civil rights of our time!" Henrietta protested.

"Humph. Girl, you ain't even got half the rights that was promised to us in the sixties," Wanda retorted.

"Fine then, Wanda, I only got half as much to lose." Henrietta tensed her tougher-than-Moses-Nelson's-moonshine bristles, but Wanda was a Nelson, through and through, and that kind of spitfire wasn't gonna curl her hair any more than it already was. She shook her head.

"Henrietta, you are as stubborn as Buella's mule and I don't even try to talk sense with that ass." She glanced up at Henrietta's set face and rolled her eyes.

"There ain't but one thing I can do about someone as young and stupid as you," she spat at Henrietta.

"What's that?" Henrietta asked.

"Pray."

With that, Wanda folded her fingers together and bent her head.

"Uh, Wanda?" Hank began.

"Shut up, I'm praying," she snapped. One eye popped open

and looked around at them. "Y'all gonna send Henrietta up against the almighty coal company without getting your Savior on your side?"

No answer came from the table except for a few awkward looks. They tended to leave religion out of things . . . less trouble that way. Wanda sniffed at them,

"Y'all need a miracle and you ain't even asked nicely for it?" She shook her head and muttered, "Lord, what is the matter with these people? First thing I gotta pray for is some common sense." She glanced up from her hands. "Y'all can pray to whoever you feel like, but if you're putting that girl on the front line, I'm gonna get *my* Creator on her side." With that, she lowered her head to bend God's ear.

The long moment of silence was broken only by a cheeky squirrel's chatter. The organizers looked from one to the other and glanced a little guiltily at Henrietta. When everybody realized that this was no short conversation Wanda was having with God, each surrendered to their own private oasis of the spirit.

With a feeling of relief, Louisa quickly sought the quiet void from which the web of all creation springs. A moment of silence might clear the air of argument from the room . . . and from herself. Louisa quietly thanked Wanda for this reminder. As an organizer, she should have remembered how essential this time of centering was for any meeting. She breathed in and out and watched the ripples of her breathing shake the dewing beads of change throughout the universe. She called on pure potential to help humanity, envisioning a host of *what if's* and *it could be's* and *maybe we could's* swooping into every person's mind.

Patrick danced his awkward dance with spirit. He never prayed direct to God, but to an unseen angel whose wafting wing beats brushed against him from time to time. Like Jacob wrestling in the dark, Patrick's soul grappled with his angel's challenges. He was tried and tested and left counting his blessings for one more day of life. Patrick quietly listened for the angel's passing, hoping to grab it by the robe and ask for guidance.

Hank, who would surprise you if you peeled off his Appalachian overcoat, launched with gusto into prayer. He closed his eyes, bowed his head, and, in his mind, called upon the old Taoist sage, Lao-Tzu. He had a real affinity for the guy. Hank fancied himself a holler sage of sorts, a hermit in the mountains unless he got a hankering for life. Then he substituted mountain moonshine for Taoist wine and went in search of what pulls all holy men from high-horse hermitages: women. Yes, Hank had an affinity for Taoist philosophy and all its earthly forms of wisdom. He respectfully asked Lao-Tzu what course they could take to save the mountains and mankind.

In his mind, Hank saw the Old Sage stroke his beard and pull upon his ear.

"Nothing. Absolutely nothing."

Hank begged him for another answer. The wise one added,

"You must let everything take its course . . . and that, of course, might end up saving you."

Hank pulled his hair and asked for further illumination. The Sage drew an enormous breath to launch into a lecture.

131

Hank interrupted,

"I don't have a thousand years. Can you just give it to me as a sound byte?"

Lao-tzu scowled with the disgust of one who had already condensed a universe of operations into eighty-one short poetic verses and now this impudent young man wanted a haiku?

"Well, actually," Hank admitted, "even a single sentence is too long."

Lao-tzu's wrinkled eyes flew open in delight.

"Ah, yes! You understand!" He bowed to the bewildered Hank. "Words are wasted breath beside the infinite suchness of the wordless Tao," the Sage commented.

Hank groaned in utter confusion.

"So . . . what do we do?" the young man pleaded.

"Do nothing . . . and something comes from that." Lao-tzu handed Hank a sound byte on a platter and hoped the young man's American palate could appreciate its subtle meanings. Hank's skepticism twisted up his face. Lao-tzu sighed. "Go ask the Immortal Sisters for an answer."

Hank perked up at the mention of wisdom-laden ladies.

"Are they cute?" he asked.

"Gorgeous," Lao-tzu replied and gave the young man directions to the Celestial Heavens.

We could write volumes on Hank's journeys through the inner mysteries of the Immortal Sisters who teach the sagest of the sages everything they know, but we don't have a thousand years, so we'll skip to the important part: at long last, when the Sisters bid Hank a fond farewell, one of them graciously rephrased Lao-tzu's single esoteric sentence into a simple kiss.

Hank's blue eyes flew as wide open as the sky. The kiss popped the cherry of his spiritual virginity. He tumbled through the intercourse of yin and yang, male and female, night and day, and saw the world collapsing into nothing and then just as quickly springing back into a something-ness that formed and grew and lived and died by fractions of a moment.

His mind spiraled back to No Man's Holler and he sprawled on the table clutching a single shard of sanity. He had no idea how to save humanity, but the *why* of it clung sweetly to his lips. He burst from quiet and startled them all from their prayers.

"Holy smokes and Mother of God, y'all, we've got to turn this ship around! Extinction?! Hell, that's like an eternity without an orgasm! Imagine it: No sex! No chocolate! No moonlit madness! Are we insane?!"

He leapt up on the table and laid out mans' options with the deep bellow of an auctioneer.

"On the one hand . . . we can die in an agonizing process of extinction involving carbon emissions, ozone depletion, global warming, famine, war, nuclear fallout, disease, and societal collapse. On the other hand," his grin exploded across his freckled face, "we've got *women!* Beautiful, lusty, healthy women! And food! Bread and collards and ripe ole tomatoes and pecan pie and god-the-list-is-endless! Did I mention *dancing?* Next to women?"

He was crude and crass and utterly honest and impassioned. He was twenty-two and the whole world was one mad orgasmic organism ejaculating copulation: birds and bees and garden hoses and well pumps and break waters and tidal plunges and thunder spouts and pines exuding aphrodisiac aromas while the slugs were foregoing all genders in their passions and the flowers were making wild love with pistol penises and petal labia and little buzzing vibrator bees.

"We'd be mad to give this all up!" he shouted on the tabletop. "Men are crazy not to pit our every working, waking effort to keep humanity a part of all of this!"

He stared at the startled, upturned faces. The table's soapbox urged him on. He paced it searching for solutions.

"Something. Nothing. Something. Nothing." The words exploded from him. His hand pumped gestures in and out, female embracing male in a fluid expression of the universe of love until, finally, it came! Hank groaned in ecstasy; in the release of thought; in the solution to mankind's conundrum; in the simplicity of the primal act that creates us all.

"Love." He sank onto the table in collapse and rolled onto his back. Henrietta's bemused expression stared down at him as he said, "All we gotta do is learn to love."

The group consensus grunted, "Huh?"

Hank sprawled his youthful lusty worldly understanding out, "We gotta love so much that we'd do anything -*anything*- to keep on loving."

He tried to find the words to express the power of this simple concept. "Our lust for love, our lust to live; that is what propels this world around! Love is what has run the motor of the universe since time began. It got each of us where we are today."

He rolled upright and put his face in front of Patrick's.

"Old man, what sent you into those black mines way back

when?"

"A job," Patrick answered testily.

"What did you need a job for?" Hank asked.

"My wife-"

"What did you need a wife for?"

"I love her!" Patrick exclaimed indignantly.

"You mean you went into Hell each and every day because of *love*?" Hank gaped and laughed and smirked all at the same time. Patrick scratched his head.

"I guess, when you put it that way . . . "

"Yep. I do," Hank said. "This whole world is propelled by love. It's the fuel that got us where we are today, not coal or gas or oil." He rolled over to Henrietta and said directly to Jerome, "What got you here, little guy?"

"Love," Henrietta answered for him. And sometimes that's all that keeps us here, she added silently, glancing around her kitchen. Hank sprang up into a crouch.

"Everybody preaches morality and godliness. I say fuck it! Literally. It's the craving for unity that turns this world around each day. And if we don't want to miss out on all the action, we got to get our butts into gear, quit hanging around like a bunch of wallflowers, and love this world like she deserves!"

"Amen, son!" Wanda shouted out unexpectedly. Hank whirled to face his unlikely supporter who stood beside the birth-stains of her father and testified, "If y'all men treated me the way we been treating this earth, I wouldn't just walk out on you . . . I'd run your lousy, no-good, two-faced, lying, crazy, drugged-up asses off the face of this planet!" She slammed the table with her palm. It kicked back a shudder that jolted Hank.

Everyone jumped and saw a vision of a righteously inflamed Wanda scouring the earth of abusive men.

"I think Mother Earth will stand up for herself, Wanda," Louisa said. "She's doing it already; hurricanes, earthquakes, tsunamis, heat waves, droughts, floods. We can't count the rapidly increasing number of natural disasters that are sending us the message."

"Can't blame Mother Earth," Wanda sniffed. "It's self-defense."

"Yeah?" Patrick grumbled dourly. "That's what the coal companies say when you threaten their profits. Self-defense. Makes 'em feel justified in threatening your life."

"We are just talking about some interviews here," Louisa reminded him. "They'll probably spend most of it asking about Henrietta's romantic life."

"That oughta be a short conversation," Henrietta snorted. "I'll have plenty of time to talk about coal."

Patrick commented,

"That's where it gets life and death."

"Oh, living, dying, who cares?" Hank erupted in impatience. He threw his hands up and stated, "You live until you die. Don't y'all want to have some fun while we're at it?"

His grin spread from ear to ear. Hank Crawley, in and out of scrapes his whole life, was daring them to risk everything as if tackling the coal company was just a long rope swing into a pond, or a no-hands sled race down the steepest hollow slope, or borrowing the neighbor's car for a joyride when you're only ten.

Patrick, gray in head and stout in waist, reflected on his

earlier days railing full-force against injustice. Fun? Humph. He was too old to consider police with clubs, tear gas, or riot gear fun. But as he thought about those early days, he realized a gray cloud of seriousness and survival was coloring the pallor of his memories. He blinked at the bright sunshine of Hank's suggestion. Fun? He was older now, with nothing but retirement and death stretching out before him. His grimness began to lighten up. Fun, huh? Well, he had nothing to risk but his own last few years and heck, who knows, maybe another lifetime, if those Hindus turned out to have it right. Shoot, if that were true, he'd best risk it all right now! Next time the skies might not be so blue, nor the air breathable at all. Make it fun, huh? He'd be down there at the protest singing Yankee Doodle instead of chanting angry slogans. Lighten it all up! Yep, he decided, this time around, let's have some fun.

Louisa calculated risks. Pain and suffering clung to snapping rope swings and smashing sleds and reckless joyrides that rolled into ditches. Prudence learned to take the slow and cautious path so nobody got hurt. Too late for that, she thought, with melting icecaps flashing through her mind. Louisa looked at the long and winding road before them. She saw the sunset of the human species. She realized that, fun or not, there wasn't time to not take risks. They'd have to leap and pray.

Quiet Ford, who had sat listening through it all, started chuckling in his chair. All the gods, goddesses, angels, saints, and sages blessed his patient silent prayer with an epiphany,

"What do we got to lose except life itself?"

His words struck lightning into Louisa's tangled web of

thoughts. Suddenly electrified, illuminated, bursting with energetic understanding, she cried,

"Yes. Yes! YES! That's exactly it!"

No one remembered later if she leapt up in her hiking boots and thick wool socks or if that table itself hoisted her up onto its shoulder. Henrietta had long suspected it of revolutionary leanings. No chairs ever sat quite right beside it. The table flung them back, calling out for pacing and impassioned speeches, fist poundings and declarations of independence. Its wood had emerged from roots that had soaked up the blood of generations of mankind. It had grown its beams from the bones of natives, whites, and black people alike. It had breathed in the stench of fear and hate and love and lust and drunken moonlight serenades. It had caught the reverberations of the last wolf's howl and the final touch of Lenape Indian hands. The dust of coal was newly on its leaves when a wild storm had knocked it to the ground. Now Louisa stood on it and assailed them with a speech so patriotic it sounded un-American.

"We are citizens of this nation," she proclaimed, "but even beyond the invisible borders of our cities, states, and country, there is a supreme geo-political body that claims our foremost allegiance. Even as the city yields to state, and the state yields to national authority, so is there yet one more governing body that claims the highest ranking among all the nation-states of man." She hesitated, almost afraid to say it. Then Henrietta dared,

"The Earth."

It was a matchstick in a haystack of insurrection, a traitorous statement in the current notions of the United States of America. It was treason to the laws of the country of their births. They were on the verge of declaring themselves to be, first and foremost, citizens of the Earth.

Of course! Of course! Hank groaned. Why had he never seen it? Who else granted them their human rights to air, water, sleep, shelter? Certainly not the U.S. Government. What other nation, state, county, or city negotiated the crucial laws of space and gravity and tidal currents, and coordinated the sun and clouds in a constitution that made a mockery of international boundaries and interstate commerce clauses? What other geo-political body gave all people liberty with their lives and taxed them only for reverence and respect?

The group of six humans -no, seven, for while the youngest one knew nothing of the concept of America, he already lived and breathed his citizenship with Earth- sat slightly stunned and suddenly robbed of national identity by this revelation.

You are *my* people, the Earth had just declared. The Earth, herself, had called them round her table and knighted each of them as champions.

"Can you hear it?" Louisa whispered, for suddenly the whole forest trumpeted its leaves. The branches clacked sharply in the beat of snare drums. The fife of birdsong whistled out its tune. Patrick's face turned ashy gray. He whispered the most patriotic of all American declarations,

"*When in the course of human events it becomes necessary for one people to dissolve the political bonds which have connected them with another . . .*"

The Earth was singing her revolution. She was calling her brave men and courageous women to her defense.

" . . . *a decent respect to the opinions of mankind requires that he should declare the causes that impel them to separation,*" Patrick quoted.

"Not separation," Louisa said. "Reunion. I call for a declaration of our allegiance to our entire globe as our Earth calls now for the United States to end its abusive practices."

"Its *long train of abuses and usurpations, repeated injuries and Tyranny,*" Patrick recited, grumbling.

"Yeah," Hank added, "we're waging sneaky underhanded terrorism against the Earth."

"Whose citizens are you?" Louisa challenged them. "When the battle lines are drawn, where will you stand?"

The house shook now with a gust from the storming forest and Henrietta held Jerome close. The tension built in the atmosphere. The course of events swirled madly around the wildness of this table.

"*When in the course of human events,*" Patrick repeated, "*any form of government becomes destructive of the inalienable rights of man to life, liberty, and pursuit of happiness; it is the right of the people to alter or abolish it.*"

He paused as a tremble shuddered him.

"This is treason," he said.

Hank scoffed, "It's only treason 'til you win the revolution."

The wind thrashed around the cabin. Henrietta turned on the lights against the darkening world.

"We must decide," Louisa said, with the ring-lined planks of an ancient tree beneath her feet. "Are we puppets of a mad empire or citizens of the Earth?"

Henrietta sighed. She held Jerome tight against her as the

storm darkened the room.

"We must make the choice," Louisa insisted. The first crack of rain smacked onto the roof. "Without the life support of Earth, the principles of this country -justice, liberty, pursuit of happiness- all mean nothing!" The rain tapped drumbeats of revolution on the tin and tar. "If we want to be loyal to our country, we have to start by being loyal to all the people, plants, places, and animals that keep us all alive!"

A billion raindrops broke deafeningly against the roof. They thundered on the canopy of leaves, the forest floor, anything they could find. Their wild clapping overwhelmed the humans. Six hearts pounded madly. The seventh heartbeat pulsed against his mother's. The one lamp barely held off the dark blue shadows from the storm. Louisa's face shone gold and midnight as she turned toward them.

"It is all for one, and one for all, like the old stories of democracy. We must shift our table to be round and offer the entire world a seat. No longer can man be king of beasts, nor the lion, nor any other. We must recognize our perfect union, our true democracy with all of Earth."

She stood and the light strove to catch up with her as she towered and cried out to all that hammered at the cabin walls. The moment called her passions howling from her throat. Louisa, white and thin, with dark brown hair that hung straight around her enigmatic frame, called upon her bloodlines that stretched back to the first peoples of this continent, the colonists who later came, and the immigrants who followed them. She called upon the elements that had given the breath of life to all of them.

"Rain!" she cried, for water gave her blood its form. "Come sit at this table! Wind! Join us with your breath. Clouds! Draw close and trees as well! Gather round and grace us with your presence."

Louisa chanted out a list of names, calling the rocks, grasses, mountains, field mice, and tiny creeping insects through the storm. She welcomed microbes, parasites, worms, and spiders, lichens, ferns, mosses, reeds, and seaweeds. She called on sun and warmth, snow and ice, frosts and glaciers. She made room for all the aspects of the Earth.

Her wide-eyed listeners felt suddenly the immensity of this new democracy. No longer were they lonely rebels, seven small humans against the world. They had the allies of the elements, the support of all creatures great and small. The rain slowed and the Earth drew closer, listening. The trees hung their leaves down to hear the murmured words beneath them. The mice crept underneath the porch. Seven humans leaned in together.

"We must give voice to all that has no human languages to speak in," Louisa said. "Henrietta, you must speak not just for the mountains, but for the trees, the rain, and all the creatures. You must speak-" she touched Jerome's head, "-for all the human babies and the ones that are to come. Their fate hangs by the thread of your words."

Henrietta shivered. *There is a story that must be told.* It was just as her mamma had sensed. Arellia had received the sign, a book with nothing written in it. Earth's creatures used no written language.

"It is a web, see?" Louisa said and interlaced her fingers.

Jerome watched her cat's cradle fingers weaving in and out.

"Imagine all the people, animals, plants, and elements," Louisa invited them, " . . . imagine them like gossamer spider webs, strung out across the expanse of the Earth. Every issue, every field, every person is a part of this. Here, if we tug at this sticky spot of the dying Appalachian Mountains, the whole web puckers and wrinkles, but it's all too sticky with injustice. We've got to break the old web and build a new one that grows from the democracy of Earth, itself. Henrietta, do you understand?"

"Oh, yes." She touched the cross sections of Louisa's white and bony knuckles with the dark and light shadow play of her own. "Here, here, and here. I start to break the threads of fear that hold us back. Here, I slip the new connections and understandings into place. Here, I bring two hands together," she smiled at Louisa and laced her fingers into the other woman's.

Hank's slid out to join them.

"Not just two hands," he said, "all of them."

"And not through fear, but through hope," Patrick added, as his flesh and age came under theirs and lifted up their burden. "We're building a new citizenship with all of Earth. We're becoming true Americans."

"Well," came Ford's slow voice as he rose from his chair. His dark, earthy hand joined the pact, "I never thought today would lead me to become a citizen of the Earth, or foment a revolution, or hear anything like what's been said today." He paused and thought a moment, "But all my life I've protected things; women, children, men, small animals, and I guess now

mountains and the whole earth. It's like the old song says . . . "
His deep baritone drew breath to moan out,

"Are you a protector of the meek?"

"Yeeeeeesssss, Lord," Wanda's voice shot out of darkness, trilling the response.

"Are you a follower of the Lamb?"

"Yeeeeeessss, Lo-oh-ord!" she rocked as she sung the reply.

"A soldier of the cross?"

"Yes, Lord!" Wanda sang the last notes and fell to silence. The others felt the hairs rising on their arms as they sensed that God was listening. Ford's face lifted up in supplication and his voice fell into the cadence of prayer,

"We're being asked today to make some mighty difficult choices. Asked to take up sides and try to make a mess turn out right. Lord, I can only do my best and I ask forgiveness if You see any wrong-doing in my actions. I hope You won't, Lord, no, I hope You see that Your ole Ford here is just a protector of all Your creations, yes, and all these other folks are, too. I ask Your blessing, Lord, for them, and for me."

"Amen." Wanda's hand joined theirs and sealed the prayer. The rippling air currents settled in the kitchen. Hank slid off the table. Birds resumed their callings in the trees outside.

They all looked at Henrietta. The course of action hung on her. She would be marching front and center. She would become the face for the force that strode behind her. She would step into the targets of the powers that lined up against them.

"Do you know what we're getting into?" Patrick asked Henrietta. "I've been jailed and beaten for doing no worse than holding up a picket sign against the coal company."

"Yeah," Hank chortled like the devil, "this is like sticking your shining face right out in front of their cannons."

"There may be death threats," Louisa added pragmatically. Jerome leaned against Henrietta's chest, playing with the buttons on her blouse. She looked down thoughtfully at him.

"I've been thinking lots and praying," she glanced at them, shadowed and gray in the rainy evening light. "But when I pray, I just send my hope out like messages in bottles. I got no idea whose shore they're washing up on, because I feel like I'm floating in the middle of an inky dark ocean of my life without any rudder or sails."

A rush of emotion pressed up inside her; fear, loneliness, worry. The wind rattled against the loose shingles on the roof. Henrietta swallowed and continued,

"The truth is; every day, we risk dying just to live. Tyrell and I, we risked this baby's life just bringing him into the world. I don't need to start splitting the hairs of courage now. I been in equal danger of dying since the day that I was born. In fact, death may be the only promise I know is gonna be kept. That makes it real simple."

Henrietta looked a long time at her son.

"I can die trying to live," she said softly to him as if making a bargain on their future, "or we'll all just die."

"Or," Louisa gently pointed out, "you could just live."

"Well," Henrietta replied as she started to chuckle, "I guess that would be the point of all this, wouldn't it?"

She looked at Louisa, who started laughing with her. A ripple of relief ran through the room. The storm sent a drip-dropping patch of sunlight into the room as the clouds slipped over the hollow ridge.

"What do you say, Henri?" Hank asked, brimming with eagerness. "Do you want to jump out of the bushes and make faces at the coal company?"

Henrietta laid one hand on the table as if for strength. The grains of wood sent wild rhythms running through her bloodstream. The risk of living life at all pounded in her heart and made her willing to take a chance. She raised the strong lines of her face. Her eyes shone hot in the dusky twilight.

"Oh no," she said, soft and serious, "I'm gonna do much more than that. I'm going to have a heart to heart with every household in this nation. I'm gonna sit down at their TV dinners. I'm gonna serenade them on the radio. I'll swap secrets in their beauty parlors and shout headlines at the checkout counter. We got to wake this nation up and it'll take every alarm clock that we've got. The first thing we've got to do is- "

"Pray," Wanda interrupted. "First and last and all the while in between, you got to pray."

Henrietta smiled. Sometimes, our prayers are chants or songs or ecstatic cries of lovemaking or poems or quiet energies inside us. Henrietta was going to sing a lullaby to wake the whole world up. Some would call it rabble-rousing. Others would simply call it prayer.

CHAPTER FIFTEEN

·····

The Citizen of the Earth

Hank crested over the ridge onto a rocky quartzite outcropping and threw his arms open to the blueness of the sky. A hallelujah howl whooped from him and echoed off the slopes. The wind tossed its joy from the fluffy brilliant clouds to the thick green density of the forest down below, tussling Hank's orange-auburn hair along the way. His breath was heaving in his chest and the blood was pulsing in his veins: he was a citizen of the Earth and he was free!

"Free at last! Free at last!" he shouted to the wind. He chanted with the echoes as they doubled up his voice. Gone were the latent feelings of being a second-class citizen. No longer did he feel pushed down, shoved over, run out, or unwelcome in his own home. No longer could people consider him a half-rank American, a poor nobody from nowhere Appalachia. He was a noble citizen of the Earth!

He was born on Earth and he would die on Earth. His every waking moment would be spent on Earth. His body would lie against it while he slept. His feet would traverse it as he walked. His lungs would breathe its air and his mouth would drink its water and no one could convince him otherwise. He was not an American! He was not an American! He was not an American!

His joy in liberation propelled him into leaping. A wild, goat-like, writhing dance erupted from him. No longer was he bound by the standards of a culture he despised. No longer was he measured by the capitalist-consumer system and found lacking in every form. No longer did he have to give two shits and a pancake about American values, education, or beliefs. He was free!

"FREE!" the cry shot out of him and stretched across the valley to skim the opposite ridge where No Man's Holler lay. Until the night of the revolutionary table, Hank had not known he was enslaved to his notion of himself as an American. All his life, for generations, his people had told each other they were American. The conquest of the continent was theirs to glory in. The riches of new money were theirs to lust after. The power of the greatest superpower in the world was theirs to boast about.

But Hank found vicarious experience to be as sour as a crab apple. Hank had always been that little boy who had to be in the thick of things; the adolescent that dove headfirst into the center of the pranks; the young man who rallied the troops and led the battle charges and breathed life into every party.

When people called America *the greatest nation on earth* and stuffed the word full of apple pies, corn-on-the-cob, Statues of Liberty and stars and stripes; Hank didn't know what the hell they meant. His America had dirt on its collar and shit on its boots. It had a black eye, a broken tooth, a string of loves shattered by alcohol and drugs, a suicide, a miscarriage, and a hungry belly. It was down and out and short on luck and looking for some work. Hank's America tucked its narrow-minded head into its ass and stuck to its guns as dogmatically as a Southern fire-and-brimstone church.

Then again, Hank's America was broad and leafy green. It was densely wooded; if not by the old growth forests, then by the second and third generation trees that held the promise of age and girth. His America was as generously expansive as a ridge top view and as fecund and lush as the composting carpet of leaves and earthworms on the forest floor. His America cried out in lonely birdsong mating calls. His America still wished on falling stars and caught them in its mountainsides from time to time.

That commercial, patriotic, flag-waving, red, white, and blue, gas-guzzling America sneered at Hank's America. It hissed its hillbillies into backwoods submission. It beat them up for coal. It cheated them, ignored them, loaned them to the devil and then refused to take them back. Hank was sick of America. He was weary of the nation's reputation. He was tired of disliking himself, his country, and his brotherhood of citizens.

No more! Hank grinned to the sunshine that beamed down on him. He bowed to the clouds that paraded by. He nodded to the hawk, the maples, the rocks, and the grasses that shared this Earth with him. No longer fettered by a troubling national identity, Hank sat on the outcropping between sky and land and basked in a newfound sense of belonging.

This is my home, he thought, stretching north and south and east and west, further and further until it wrapped around the curving horizons in all directions and met again, right here, in him. Of course, he wondered, what does a citizen of the

Earth do when people have sliced the world up between them like a patchwork quilt? He had no papers to prove his citizenry. Why would the Earth cut down her trees to prove the obvious? He was breathing his belongingness. It was when humans drew imaginary lines and called them international boundaries that documents had to be issued to prove nationalities existed. How would the world deal with a man who had no country, but belonged to the entire Earth?

Hank had no answers yet, so he let the question go blowing on the wind to sail around the globe and brush up against the minds of greater thinkers than he. Perhaps, one day, the wind would return with an answer and whisper it in his ear.

For now, he reveled in the secrecy of his new identity. He was a spy in the heart of a nation he no longer subscribed to. He shuddered at the precarious position he was in. He thought about the others; Patrick, Wanda, Ford, Louisa, and Henrietta, who had also received the welcome of the Earth, but still retained their American citizenships. Not him. Tonight he would burn his birth certificate and social security card. He had no passport to incinerate. He wanted no connection to this country. He wanted no part of the tarnish that it put on its citizens' souls. He wanted freedom. He wanted to belong to Earth, not to the history of men who came to this continent and ravaged it and all the peoples of it.

Three nights ago, around that revolutionary table, he had laid his sins before the Earth; from the coal that fueled his electricity, to the polluting car he drove, to the anthills he had kicked as a kid. He confessed his and all his ancestors' earlier complicities in the violent, destructive, and unjust actions done through history. He told her all he knew of mankind's sins against her and took personal responsibility. He was ready to do penance, if he must.

But the Earth had forgiven him like Jesus was said to do. She pardoned him on one condition: that he would live a life of consciousness and try to redress whatever wrongs he could. He was saved in her forgiveness and born again today.

Hank had climbed the ridge in awe. He could not remember his earliest days of life just after his mother had birthed him. An awful theft of memory had robbed him of those first sensations of the world: the first touch of cold and warmth, the alien brush of air on skin, the sharpness of sounds no longer muffled by the amniotic sac. Those were gone with the thief of time, but today, born again and fiercely guarding his new impressions of life, Hank's eyes exploded from the depth of greenery all around him. It was as if he had never known the meaning of green before. Now, as light and leaf made chlorophyll love to each other, and an infinite rainbow of chartreuse and pine splayed across his retinas, he realized mindless assumptions had been crippling his experience of life. Green is not green! It is a living phenomenon like breath, curling in and out of shade and sunlight, growing within the cellular walls of plants, visiting the eyes of humans. Today, born again to sound and color, freshly awed by the creation all around him, Hank had climbed the ridge humbled by his privilege to walk among it all.

The emotions inside him throbbed against his veins and sinews until he felt the explosion of his body loomed imminent. He shot out onto the ridge with a slingshot shout of *Hallelujah!*

and the echoes bounced around the hills. He released the intensity of sensation through whoops and wild dances. He let the ecstasy of blue skies and birdcalls tumble through him. He inhaled the out-breath of the trees and tasted their perfumes upon his tongue. He hurled the piney thrill that tickled in his blood around in circles. He ground the pulsing energy of rotting leaves beneath his feet until he could dance no more.

Everything subsided into abiding calm. He lay back against the sun-warmed rocks. The ants crept across him, tickling the hairs that shot out of the freckles on his arms. He thanked all the gods and goddesses he knew for the gift of life today. No longer was he an American, torn between heathen, atheist, or Christian, science or spirituality. He no longer had to sneak the world religions out from library shelves to study on the sly, speaking to no one in these hollows about his true beliefs. The gods and goddesses of all the Earth were an enormous pantheon stretched above, below, and all around him in his home. He had to know the powerful forces in the divided landscape that human beings claimed. He now belonged to all of them as he traversed this one undivided Earth.

Allah, Brahma, Jehovah, Odun
Gaia, Yemaya, Shakti, Shiva,
God, Zeus, Neptune, Poseidon,
Great Spirit, Indra, Buddha, Tao

He chanted all the names he knew and extended courteous invitations to those whom he had yet to meet. He humbly honored each of them. He told them that he was a citizen of the Earth. He asked for their blessings as one who must respect them all.

You've forgotten one, the many strands of divinity informed him.

I'm sure I've forgotten many, he replied.

No, this one is important for you to know.

Who is it? he asked.

You.

The majesty and mystery of all that was divine threw its force into Hank's chest and pinned him to the rocks. He felt his back melt from the intensity of searing stone. His spine merged with the ridgeline. His limbs rooted into the ground like trees.

The Creator creates the Created
who in turn creates the Creator.

He had no idea who spoke such thoughts. He had no concept of himself as separate from the spreading expanse of mountains and rock and sky and cloud. For an eternally long moment, he pushed up trees and swallowed worms and slipped over himself in fluffy patches, absorbed the sun and cooled in shadow. He drew spring water from soil into root, eroded his hard stones into dust, and composted a thick carpet of leaves.

When the stunning force of divinity backed off, he wiggled his toes and blinked his eyes like a newborn experimenting with his body. He peeled his spine up off the rocks and waited for the surging sense of separation. It didn't come. He stood. Sunlight pressed his front. Shade supported him behind. He took a step and all of Earth rose up to embrace him as he moved. The Earth was before him, behind him, above and below, inside his lungs, his blood, his cells, his nerves, his thoughts. He turned to look back where he had lain. No marks, no searing outline of his body, no blood, but Hank knew beyond a shred of doubt that the Earth had just rebirthed him. She had pulled him in and annihilated all concept of his separateness. He had no body but the Earth. All the Earth was one with him.

Perhaps this is how the gods who come back to the world of men feel, Hank thought, like Vishnu born as Ram, or God in Christ. Hank felt he was, and was not, a man. Or, perhaps, he had just now become a true man, cognoscente of the embrace of Earth.

On the tip of the opposite ridge, he spied another figure looking out and thought it might be Henrietta. A thought struck him that perhaps he was not the only one conscious of his divinity. Perhaps, Henrietta knew something of it, too.

Hank looked out along the ridgelines he had walked since birth. It seemed the forces of the world swirled around it in a great struggle to decide the fate of humanity. His life, entwined with the mountains as thickly as the forest's roots, was an epic still in the making, the ending undecided. He shrugged. He wouldn't know until the story finished and all the plot lines had been revealed. Until then, he was just a god in hiding, born into human form.

Hank squinted at the tree line and Henrietta. He thought of Tyrell locked in his lonely jail cell and shook his head; only in this country do people lock up gods. Hank snorted. Henrietta would probably laugh at the idea that she and Tyrell were some celestial couple separated for but an eye blink of their eternal lives.

But only we know the secret symbols of the great epics of

our lives. Henrietta would not have laughed. She would have told Hank that every person contains the magic and the mysteries of gods. When we forget to worship and honor the divinity in all . . . when we hit a god or starve them or sneer at them or lock them out of sight, we have failed not only the bonds of human kindness, but our responsibility as a divine family, born into such humble human forms.

CHAPTER SIXTEEN

. . . . .

Tipping Point

Jack woke to find a cold, vacant indent where his wife usually slept. He could hear her in the bathroom getting ready for work. He pulled the covers over his head. Another round of arguing had sent them to bed late last night; lips sealed against each other, backs stiffly separated. The buzz of Sarah's electric toothbrush grew fainter as she went to wake up Allie. Jack sighed and swung himself upright.

"Look who decided to get up," Sarah said under her breath when she returned. "I thought you were going on permanent vacation."

Jack didn't answer. He'd stayed home for three days in a row, telling his secretary he was sick and ignoring the boss' phone calls as he tried to sort out what to do. Every day, Sarah's looks shot out blacker and blacker while she muttered snide comments under her breath. He winced as Sarah threw her toothbrush down in the bathroom and started attacking the snarls in her hair.

"Sarah-"

"I don't have time to argue this morning. I've got to drop Allie off at school and get to work." She slammed her hairbrush on the counter and stalked out of the bathroom, muttering, "Someone has to take care of this family." She pulled on her work suit and tried to button her pants around the swell of her pregnancy. The button popped off and Sarah stood there with her head hanging down, holding the waist of her trousers, and feeling helpless.

Jack surrendered. He couldn't quit his job. Not now, not with Sarah six months pregnant, trying to hold down her own job. *She* should be the one quitting. Her hands shook slightly on the pants. Beneath the veil of her hair, he could see her biting her bottom lip. Jack sighed and stood up.

"I'll take Allie to school on the way to work."

"I thought you weren't going," she said.

"I-" he hesitated as his convictions wavered. "Look, I'll keep working while I look for a new job, alright?" He pushed her hair back from her face and tilted it up to look at him. "Don't worry so much, Sarah."

"Alright," she murmured.

"There's a new pair of slacks in the laundry room that should fit," he told her.

"I'll get them," she replied and turned toward the door. "Jack?" she said. "Thanks."

"Sure."

She left. He moved wearily to the bathroom to shave. Jack rubbed the four-day stubble and lathered up. The hairs pulled against the blade.

"Damn," he swore as he nicked his jawbone.

He blotted the blood. Some things, like shaving and living a life of conviction, had to be a daily practice. You couldn't just shave off an overgrown beard full of tangled principles, he reasoned. You had to trim them back first, a little bit at a time.

He'd keep working his old job, but he wouldn't let them kill Henrietta Owens. There were other ways. Besides, hadn't John Henry told him not to quit something he hadn't finished right? He would see this Henrietta Owens thing through and then resign. He dressed quickly and went downstairs, avoiding further reflections on the subject.

"You cut yourself," Sarah mentioned.

"Yeah," he said, "a little blood sacrifice in the line of family duty." It was meant as a joke, but neither of them smiled. The remark cut a little too close to truth.

"You ready, Allie?" Jack called. He kissed Sarah goodbye and scooted their daughter out the door. Allie rode in silence until Jack grew worried and asked,

"You alright, Allie? You're awfully quiet this morning."

"Yeah, Dad. I'm just thinking."

"About what?"

"Convictions."

"Yours, mine, or your mother's?"

"Anybody's. What's a conviction?"

"Aside from a prison sentence, it's a matter of principle," he told her and launched into a lecture on the subject. He rambled on about morality as they passed stoplights and shopping malls. He was just getting up to full steam on the example of John Henry when Allie screeched,

"Dad! You missed the school!"

He swung the car around and pulled up to the entrance of Allie's private school, nursing a suspicion that she had been as oblivious to his lecture as he was to the impressive facade of Greelington Academy. Allie hopped out and waved as she tore up the granite steps, calling back,

"Bye, Dad!"

"Bye, Allie!"

Jack reluctantly turned the car in the direction of the office and merged onto the freeway. The traffic grew more congested as he approached the city. He had nearly ground to a complete standstill when his cellphone rang. He dug it out of his pocket.

"Hello? Right now? On national radio? Alright, I'll turn it on. Thanks, Schwartz."

Henrietta was on the radio.

Jack tuned to the station as the traffic crawled. The static receded and the radio host's voice crackled into clarity.

*   *   *

"Welcome back to National Public Radio, folks. You're listening to the Morning Rush, a daily talk show devoted to jolting you awake like a strong cup of coffee. Today we've got Ms. Henrietta Owens and son in the studio, and though I doubt the little guy's gonna say much, his mamma's here to talk about mountaintop removal and climate change."

"Let's be clear," she said in voice as crisp as morning sunlight, "this isn't about keeping mountains looking pretty. Ending mountaintop removal is about keeping humanity alive."

Henrietta didn't hide the intensity from her voice. She unleashed it on the listener, stark and passionate. All night, she had lain awake as the pitch black pressed up against her wide-open eyes. Outside her cabin, the animals treaded cautiously through the dark. Twigs cracked. Small growls shot out and then subsided. Jerome lay in her arms, a tiny bundle of life, hardly much more than a patch of warmth and breath. The blackness was absolute. No moon, no lights; nothing. Time hung in suspense. No clocks ticked. No stars trekked across the sky. At one point, Henrietta guessed it was close to dawn, but the moments crept by so slowly, she thought it might never come. She stared into an eternal darkness that would not pass until she answered her question:

What was she going to tell those people tomorrow?

She was lying awake on the eve of human extinction, staring wide-eyed at a blackness that had no end. If she could not wake her fellow citizens up, the darkness of extinction would engulf them forever. No laughter. No sunrise. No songs. Nothing. The dawn would never come to caress a human face again.

What could she say to these people?

Henrietta breathed and tried to listen. Her heartbeat battered in her chest like a great fist pounding at the door of answers. She had promised to sing a song to awaken humanity, and though the melody pulsed inside her, she had yet to learn the words. She closed her eyes, but the thin slip of her eyelids could not split the impenetrable dark. A vast and lonely sorrow welled up within her. She yearned for a murmur of humanity to break the fierce silence.

Jerome sighed.

Dawn pushed back against the blackness. Her son emerged from the sightless womb of night, a curve of head, a tiny curling fist, a pucker of a mouth. A yawn trembled across his face. His hand unfurled. His eyes opened.

Henrietta knew exactly what to say.

*   *   *

"Life is precious, beyond all else, and we are about to lose it." Her voice cut across the airwaves into Jack Dalton's car. His eyes flicked down to the photo stuck in the crack of the radio console. Allie was leaping midair into a swimming pool as Jack held out his arms to catch her. Sarah's thumb covered one corner of the photograph. He could almost hear their happy shrieks of laughter.

"Each and every person in the country has got to make a choice. Since the dawn of creation, we have been handed life from father and mother to child in an unbroken chain. The question is: are you the person who destroys that link and ends human existence on Earth?"

Jack jolted up from the photo.

"No-" he answered. Then he shook his head in disgust. "Environmental scare tactics. No one person causes extinction."

Still, though, the concern about human extinction remained. Jack fingered the steering wheel uncomfortably. As the cars around him idled, frozen bumper to bumper, he imagined the vines creeping over the highways, the skyline crumbling, buzzards circling; the planet, vast and lonely, spinning through the void of space without a single human on it.

A jackhammer truncated the vision as it burst into action next to his car. Jack flinched. The reverberations shook his car as he inched past the construction site. Jack gritted his teeth and sighed when the hammering finally subsided.

Henrietta's sigh echoed his as it across crackled over the radio.

"We are standing by the deathbed of our culture," she said.

"You mean our species," the radio host corrected.

"No," Henrietta assured him. "The death of our species is only a distinct possibility. The end of our way of life is certain."

"Well, that's real comforting," the host joked.

"I think so," Henrietta answered. "I think we can do a lot better than what we've got now."

She paused and in that dead air space Jack heard the echoes of a thousand years of history's unintended, unresolved consequences; black holes of shame that everyone avoids, genocides we bury because we don't know what else to do, corruption we tolerate because to rout it out would kill us, injustices piled as high as mountain ranges, poisons and lies spread under a poker face of truth, atomic meltdowns that could happen any second while we burn the evacuation plans- because there is no evacuating Tokyo, New York, London, Los Angeles, or the Earth.

"Our culture has got a terminal illness," Henrietta said, "a lifestyle disease caused by over-consumption. It can't go on much longer and it won't," Henrietta diagnosed, pulling no punches and telling her listeners the truth.

The radio carried the message across the country. In Denver, a cancer patient stared out the hospital window where suburbs and strip malls sprawled like tumors across the foothills of the Rockies. In a rural church, the pastor gazed out the window of his office, where the soil grew dusty and barren from overuse. In Manhattan, a Wall Street stockbroker paused in the midst of flashing screens and fanatic greed. In the humid warmth of Florida, a diabetic's swollen legs throbbed inside his wheelchair. Over-consumption was rotting him from the inside out. He recognized the same symptoms in his country.

The radio reached them all, stretching across the diverse landscapes of our country, joining the lonely, the lively, the disheartened, and the enthusiastic with a generous spirit of equanimity. The host of the Morning Rush informed the Central and Mountain Time Zone listeners who had just tuned in,

"I'm here with Henrietta Owens, mother and activist, who is talking to us about mountaintop removal."

"Actually," Henrietta answered, "I'm talking about a national crisis on every level." Her voice plunged them into the baptismal waters of awareness, stunning and startling, but hopefully saving them all at the same time.

"Mountaintop removal is the symptom of a disease called: *if-I-can't-see-it-I-don't-care*. It's endemic and devastating. We don't care about melting icecaps and rising sea levels. We don't care about heat waves and floods. We don't care about bombs exploding people. We don't care about sweatshops overseas. We don't care about our abusive criminal justice system. We don't care about the gross inequities in our economic system."

The radio host asked her what she advocated. As his car eased out of the traffic jam, Jack Dalton turned up the dial. The radio host tuned out, preparing for the usual non-answers, platitudes, and his commercial break. Henrietta, however, had an answer ready and waiting,

"Care."

The word clicked like a light bulb in the listeners' minds.

"We need to treat ourselves like a national crisis," she said. "We are one. If our personal lives were in as much pain and turmoil as our country, we'd all be sedated and locked away." She choked, because it's true and we are. Her silence echoed onto airwaves and penetrated the ears of listeners across the nation.

"Everything we love is at stake," Henrietta said passionately. "We've got to accept that there can be no more *life as usual*. We need to live *life unusual*, and get ready for the adventure of a lifetime!"

"It sounds like the trumpeting of a battle cry," the comfortable tenor of the talk show host chuckled.

"Not a battle, but a call to action," Henrietta said. "We've got to make change our national pastime and hold protests more regularly than weekend parties," Henrietta urged. "There's a dedicated and hardworking crowd that's been actively trying to address the problems in our country for years and we've got to join them. We have to . . . it's our life!" Henrietta emphasized the last word, trying to imprint the preciousness of existence onto the listeners' minds.

"If I could," she continued, "I'd reach out and shake every person in this country and say; stop listening to the TV tell you about America the beautiful . . . get up and *be* America the beautiful. *Make* America beautiful. We got energy sources to clean up and skies to clear out and mountaintops to restore. And more than that; we've got a whole new way of life just waiting to be born!"

"Like a sick man getting a new lease on life?" the host said.

"Yes, and that's the good news. We got a chance to remake ourselves and our whole society, to throw out the old, and bring in something better!"

"We're starting to sound like radio evangelists, here," the radio host laughed.

"Good," Henrietta answered emphatically. "We're in a dark night of the soul. But as you said, we got a second chance at life today."

"Saved and born again?" the radio host inserted skeptically.

"Not saved. We definitely ain't saved yet," Henrietta chuckled, "but we're born again each day from the darkest of nights, and I believe that if our country can rouse itself to greet the dawn that's coming, we'll not only make it through some tough times, but we'll come flying out the other side into a world we can hardly even imagine!"

Henrietta smiled down at the child who had brought her that message last night, emerging into life with vigor and enthusiasm. In the cramped radio station, she chased Jerome's inquisitive fingers away from knobs and buttons. Then she sighed. We won't get through the night without some real hard work and tough truth, though, and it's time to say it. The radio host drew in a breath to bring the short interview to a close, but Henrietta exhaled first,

"I want to tell a story about our country that may not be fun to hear."

The announcer started to say, "We don't have time-"

"We never do," Henrietta interrupted flatly, "but this is the time to say it . . . and the time to hear it. I want to thank the listeners for not turning away." She sent the announcer a beseeching look. He pulled his inner courage out of hiding, turned off the announcements, and filed the selected music back onto the shelf.

"Alright, go on," he said.

"Thank you," Henrietta replied. "And thank you for caring enough to take the time to listen."

In a house in Illinois, the microwave beeped *ready*, but the ramen noodles stayed on the counter. In South Dakota, a truck idled by its destination, waiting for Henrietta to continue. In an office in New York, a secretary silenced the ringing phone. One by one, Americans began to carve out a minute here and there to listen.

"There are three hundred million true stories about this nation. There are poor folks in poisoned hollers in Appalachia. There are wealthy lakeside mansions and seven car garages. There are hard working teachers and secretaries and steel workers and executives. There are beat officers and accidental lawbreakers and hardened criminals and old ladies scraping by on social security and mortgage failures and family farms with cattle grazing on them. There are taxis screeching to a halt and airplanes taking off and long haul truckers driving fifty-five on the freeway while kids in sports cars zoom past them. There are people riding horses and buggies and children wobbling on their bicycles. There are so many true stories about this country. But between them all, there's one that strikes me truest."

There's truth and then there's truth. Henrietta began to unpack the one that hurts the most.

*　　　*　　　*

Jack Dalton screeched his car around a corner as he fumbled for his cellphone. He slammed on the brakes at a stoplight. Henrietta said,

"It's our job to get this country off coal and all the other fossil fuels. The carbon emission are gonna spike global warming up high enough to kill us all. And I don't mean someday. I mean now! We got to pull the plug on them and then do a whole lot more."

Jack hit the gas and called the station manager.

"People can't possibly believe what she's saying, can they?"

A voice that sounded like dark coffee slurped through thick whiskers replied,

"I don't know if they believe her, but they're *listening*."

Jack hung up and turned the radio up as he drove past construction downtown.

"If somebody in your family got sick," Henrietta was saying, "you wouldn't be throwing a wild party in the other room, would you? If your little daughter couldn't afford to see the doctor, you wouldn't be buying a shiny new car, would you?"

"No, of course not," Jack found himself answering with Allie on his mind.

"Our human family is in some serious trouble. Every mother, father, son, daughter, sister, brother, and second cousin is in danger right now. And as a family, we got to come together and help each other out."

In the parking garage, the valet services were blaring Henrietta's voice out the office window. Jack had to shout to be heard as Henrietta said,

"If we want a better life, we got to redefine better. It ain't gonna be about money, comforts, gadgets. We got to invest our money in our neighbors and communities. And we got to insist the richest people in this country do it too. We got to remember that money is meant for taking care of our communities, not just ourselves. There's enough money in this country to take care of everybody twice over. But we got to change a lot of things, because a few rich people in this country own most of the wealth and the rest of us are beating each other up for their pocket change."

Jack asked the absent-minded valet who took his keys,

"Do you think that's true?"

The man looked at him like he was from Mars.

"Mister, of course it's true. Otherwise I'd be driving your fancy car instead of parking it."

The bicycle couriers outside the office building chatted on their radiophones,

"She said we got to turn our backs on politicians unless they start tackling climate change head on. She says we don't need leaders who don't *care* about us."

"Do you think that's true?" Jack asked one of them.

"Dude, of course it is. There hasn't been a candidate on the ballot who cared a rat's ass about me since before I was born." He flexed his tattooed legs and zipped off to outrun traffic on his bicycle.

Jack climbed the office steps and spun through the revolving door. He followed the cleaning women into the elevator instead of waiting for the next one. The smell of bleach curled his nose hairs. One of the women whispered,

"She said Americans have to humble down and start doing

things they don't like so the whole world has a chance to survive."

"I hope they do it," her companion returned in a whisper. Jack flicked his eyes at her. Hispanic. Probably an illegal immigrant. Jack shifted resentfully. Americans weren't the only ones who had to change, he grumbled silently.

The first woman shook her head. Her yellow gloves and cleaning supplies rattled in her bucket.

"That Owens woman said that they're scared of all the work it's going to take to change."

"Hah! They're scared to *care*, that's what. They always have been."

They stepped off at the third floor. Jack didn't need to ask them; do you think that's true?

Every floor carried its tidbit of the national equation. The phone company salesman from the fourth floor knew the media was intentionally censoring climate change from the news reports. The stockbroker on the fifth floor knew the finances were rigged in favor of fossil fuels. The sixth floor charity knew that cancers were triggered by environmental toxins. The social services that shared their office suite were tracking the connections between environmental upheavals and economic instability. The seventh floor software gurus were modeling climate change projections while the political party on the eighth floor denied global warming's whole existence. The ninth floor bankers were putting pressure on the politicians to protect the oil and gas industry and the tenth floor's answer to the question was,

"Of course it's all true. But who cares? There's nothing we

can do."

Subject closed. Elevator door shut. End of conversation. Jack shuddered. The capacity to change seemed to correlate with an increasing lack of caring. Well, thought Jack, that's how it is. Business requires a certain lack of compassion. Get tough. Get smart. Get ahead. Play hardball. Slam the opposition. Undercut the competition. How? With sweatshops, prison labor, media blackouts, insider trading, government subsidies, bribes, coercion, political clout; the list of possibilities was endless. And if you don't use them, your opponent will. Jack closed his eyes and leaned against the elevator wall.

"Is it true?" he sighed. How did the lack of caring spread so rampantly? When had it become a terminal societal disease threatening to slide us past the point of no recovery? There were no doctors in all the eleven stories of this building. No priests. Not even therapists. Jack was alone with his thoughts.

The elevator reached the eleventh floor. Jack froze. The doors slid open and waited patiently, but he couldn't move. For twenty years, he had fed his family through the machinations of Standard Coal, but Henrietta's voice now rang in his ears,

"This isn't about keeping the mountains looking pretty. Ending mountaintop removal is about keeping humanity alive. The carbon emissions coming out of coal are gonna spike global warming up high enough to kill us all."

"It's true," Jack murmured. He read the company reports, the scientific studies, the climate change statistics. He wasn't a politician or a CEO. He was a lawyer. He knew where the lines of truth and half-truth lay. He couldn't live in lies.

If he stepped off onto the eleventh floor, Jack would be working toward the extinction of mankind.

The doors slid shut and he plummeted. Jack leaned on the wall while his life, his notions, and his world heaved and tossed with vertigo. Other businessmen and women got on and off, shooting curious glances at his pale and sweaty face. Jack remained in place, eyes fixed on the lit-up numbers counting down the floors to the lobby. His mind raced frantically. The star on the elevator panel shined. *Bing.*

John Henry stepped into the elevator.

Jack groaned and rolled his eyes heavenward. Just what he needed . . . a sure sign of insanity coming to kick him when he was down. John Henry said nothing. He leaned next to Jack with the quiet energy of one who had come to bear witness. He laid a companionable hand on Jack's shoulder.

The weightless gesture was lost on Jack. He stared through the open doors. A layered scene of humanity piled up. Secretaries scurried past. Couriers dropped off packages. The revolving doors sucked people in and out. A homeless man begged behind them.

It's a whole world of people just like me, Jack thought, going about their daily business as we hurtle toward disaster.

Jack retracted his senses into the box of elevator music. He pulled its confines over him like a child pulls the covers across his head and waits for the monsters in the closet to disappear. The doors slid shut and waited for a command. His mind throbbed. A snide little voice jabbed inside him.

Push the button, Jack. Which floor will you get off on? Which layer of this madness? One through ten, they'll suck you in. You can spread communication lines across the country and refuse to say what's going on. You can campaign against your own survival. You can mine the coal to kill us all. Which floor Jack? Push the button.

Jack spread his fingers across his face.

John Henry pointed to the button and spoke softly,

"Don't quit something you ain't finished right."

Jack peered out through his fingers and met the steady, brown-eyed gaze of the other man. John Henry looked up at tall Jack Dalton with firm insistence. Jack's insides squirmed. John Henry refused to look away. He was testing the mettle of Jack Dalton. *Be a man*, his eyes seemed to say. Don't wallow in this indecision. You know what's right. Jack swallowed hard. He looked down and shook his head. One hand slid off his face. He reached out reluctantly.

Bing.

Eleventh floor. Going up. Questions pounded through Jack as they rose. His eyes watched the lights climb up the floor numbers one by one.

One: Is it true? . . . Yes.

Two: Do you care? . . . Yes.

Three: What are you going to do? . . . I don't know.

Four: Can you keep doing what you have been? . . . No.

Five: Can you quit? . . . Yes/No.

Six: Why not? . . . Sarah, the baby, Allie, our life.

Seven: Are you afraid? . . . Yes.

Eight: What are you going to do? . . .

Nine: What are you going to do? . . .

Ten: What are you going to- *Bing.*

Time ran out. The door slid open. John Henry vanished. Reluctantly, Jack walked out of the elevator. As he crossed the office lobby, the mathematics of social equations computed in the sound of his footsteps, laying out the progression that brought him to this moment:

Human Extinction = Climate Change

equals

Carbon Emissions = Fossil Fuels

equals

Coal = Profits

equals

Standard Coal = Mountaintop Removal

equals

Environmental Devastation = Loopholes in Protection Acts

equals

Corporate Politics = Political Corruption

equals

Unjust Laws = Wealth Inequities

equals

Economic Oppression = Increased Crime Rates

equals

Incarceration = Henrietta's Family

equals

Mother with a Child Photo = Front Page News

equals

National Attention = Problems for the Coal Company

equals

Jack.

What are you going to do?

His footsteps dragged along the carpet, through the rows of cubicles, past the diligently bowed heads. Beneath the longest line in social mathematics was one common denominator: lack of caring. Jack boiled it into a sticky note equation:

$$\frac{\text{Jack}}{\text{Lack of Caring}} = \text{the extinction of mankind}$$

I don't want this equation on my desk! He rebelled and threw his mental notes away. It wasn't correct, anyway. Each person could write their own version of the equation. Sarah divided by lack of caring equaled the extinction of mankind. Thomas Shipley, his boss, divided by lack of caring . . . seven billion individuals split by their lack of caring equated to the extinction of their species.

He heard someone listening to Henrietta on a webcast and looked into the cubicles as he walked toward his office. He wondered what the other coal employees thought of Henrietta Owens. They must know what she was saying was true . . . didn't they?

"It's total frog-swallop!" Thomas Shipley roared, penetrating the entire eleventh floor. "Turn that off! If I hear another webcast of that woman, I'll fire every last one of you!"

Jack mildly thought that might be a violation of the first amendment. Then again, there was probably a loophole. He closed his office door on the boss' abject denial of the truth. He sighed and looked around at the business he had served for twenty years. Climate change was signaling lights out for coal. Either coal or humans or both were about to become extinct. An entire way of life was changing.

Jack walked to the windows and stared out at the intersections in the streets below. There was no easy solution. Henrietta, herself, had said it: there could be no more life as usual. Those shiny cars constantly churning out emissions as they commuted hours every day . . . the semi-trucks that shipped food and products all over the continent . . . those thick electrical lines stretching from the city streets to the coal-fired electrical plant miles away . . . all of this would have to be reevaluated. The glistening, pristine offices of Standard Coal would be used for other purposes. Henrietta was advocating for nothing less than a massive social revolution.

Jack sat down at his desk and stared at the mahogany surface. What was he supposed to do? He snatched up a paper and threw it at the wastebasket in frustration. Henrietta's photo sailed across the room. He shot out from his chair to retrieve it. He spread it out and pinned it on his bulletin board. Her eyes glared at him. He blinked and walked across the room. Her eyes stared at him. He scratched his hair and turned his back to her. Her eyes bore holes into his head. He spun around.

What are you going to do, Jack Dalton?

The antiquated clock above him ticked in an audible reminder that the seconds, minutes, hours, *days* were passing while he stood confused in the middle of his life. Henrietta's photo eyes began to smile. Jack kept the pact their gazes made.

He found himself wishing they could sit down and have a conversation. She blinked. Or maybe he did. But either way, the feeling of connection broke and Jack found himself alone.

He scowled at the photo. Every word she said was true . . . and people knew it. She could level out the playing fields and put the tops back onto mountains. She could tear apart the social fabric and stitch it into another pattern. She could pull the plug on fossil fuels. She was the most dangerous woman in the world. Standard Coal could not -would not- let her continue. Not with the nation tuning in. Not with the people glued to her channel. Not with the office staff listening on webcast. She would destroy them all. All eleven stories and the entire city with its skyscrapers. Henrietta Owens was a social terrorist in a hijacked plane, fueled by the necessity of change, hurtling toward him with a vengeance.

Jack Dalton crossed his arms and bowed his head. His blood was pulsing in his ears. All around him, the question hammered,

What are you going to do?

*   *   *

The late afternoon sun poured in the windows. The time of day where life holds still arrived. The elusive lull, as likely to slip by unnoticed as to catch one in its languor, suspended Jack inside its blessing. He stood in a statue of a pose, holding his fist to his lips in thought. When Schwartz entered the office, he thought his boss was praying.

177

"Sorry to interrupt-"

Jack twisted out of reverie. Schwartz caught the flash of an unguarded expression whip off Jack's face, replaced by the familiar lines and drawn lips. The bloodhound man sniffed. He snuffled up the scents and signals of the office's secrets. He noted a hint of uncertainty in Jack. Very interesting.

"You wanted to see me, sir?"

"Sit down, Schwartz. Please."

Schwartz' ears pricked up. Since when did Jack Dalton say *please* to him, Walter Schwartz?

"What's the rumble, Schwartz?" Jack asked, almost reluctant to know.

"Movement's growing," Schwartz affirmed.

"So soon? She just spoke this morning on the radio."

"She's been busy. Her organizers are jumping on this opportunity. They've managed to snare half a dozen newspaper interviews via phone. That *Motherhood Today* article is still circulating like crazy. They pumped out a couple of online articles, interviews, etc. They got that television interview airing and a few more spots lined up for next week. Every time she talks, they're getting a direct increase in volunteers and donations."

Jack frowned with such displeasure that Schwartz hesitated.

"What else?" Jack demanded.

"It isn't just the anti-coal folks."

"Oh?"

"Polls indicate all the environmental movements are picking up steam."

"Oh." Jack scowled at the other man. "What is it about her

that's getting to people?"

Schwartz gave him a startled look.

"Isn't it obvious?" he huffed. "She's a mother with a baby talking about the future of the world."

"Humph." Jack rubbed his temples.

"Sir?" Schwartz began, reluctantly.

"What?"

"She's gonna be a real problem." Every bloodhound hair of his was standing on end. He could feel it brewing. "You gotta do something about her, sir. Now."

Jack steeple his long fingers together. Schwartz slouched in his overcoat. The two men sat in silence for a long time. The afternoon quiet continued to pool around them. Jack felt eerily out of time, surrounded by a sense of dangerous repose while a freight train of tough decisions hurtled toward him. His eyes pierced Schwartz suddenly.

"Anything else?"

Schwartz squirmed and Jack knew something was really bothering the man.

"Spit it out, Schwartz."

"For chrissake, why do kids like her get involved in things like this?" Schwartz exploded.

"She is not a kid," Jack said sternly. "She's a calculating, manipulative woman. She's getting employed for this activist work."

Schwartz's drooping brown eyes regarded him steadily.

"Alright then, boss. Just . . . just go easy on her, will ya?"

"Get out of here, Schwartz. You're getting soft," Jack scoffed. Schwartz looked hurt for a moment, then rose.

"Maybe. But maybe it's time-" he broke off.

"Time for what?"

"Never mind, boss. Never mind. She'll be on the radio again at five-thirty."

The man left. Jack leaned back in his chair, unsettled. Schwartz? Solid, dependable Schwartz who didn't bat an eye at anything? Surely she couldn't be getting to him, too?

He was still mulling on this forty minutes later when his secretary popped her head in the door.

"I'm off. Need anything before I go?"

Jack shook his head. She left. He glanced at the clock. He flung the rolling chair across the carpet and turned the radio on.

"-Larry Prince here, host of Appalachia Talks, covering a mountain range of information all the way from Katahdin up in Maine to Springer Mountain down in Georgia, now bringing you the lady of the hour, Henrietta Owens. Welcome to the studio, Ms. Owens."

"Thank you, Larry," Henrietta answered, "and thanks to your board, too. I know it was a controversial decision for them to have me on the air."

Damn right it was, Jack fumed. We pay them to keep anti-coal talk to a minimum.

"For all you listeners out there, let me give you a visual."

Jack groaned. This was a Larry Prince special, describing his guests' appearance. The man was a crowd-pleaser. Women loved his show.

"Henrietta's a lovely young woman and her little boy here, Jerome, why, you ladies out there would be cooing and fussing in a heartbeat. Ah, look at that smile. Knows when he's being talked about, doesn't he?"

"Yes," Henrietta answered with the pride of motherhood in her tone. Jack remembered Sarah's delight in every wave of Allie's toddler hands and his own obsessive wonderment with his child. He shifted in his chair, unsettled to find this kinship with Henrietta. *Man ain't nothing but a man*, he thought. Everybody loves their babies.

"Henrietta -may I call you Henrietta?"

"Sure."

"Now, you aren't from these parts, and I'm sure many of my listeners are wondering . . . how come you're standing up for our mountains?"

Jack scowled. The locals ought to be wondering why she's attacking the major source of employment in the region, he grumbled.

"When I first moved here, I was dead-set against getting involved in this mountaintop removal thing. My mamma taught me to keep my nose on my own face and don't go screwing around in other people's business."

"That's fair enough advice," Larry chuckled. "My mamma told me, if you're gonna be nosy, find out the whole story and then tell everybody else. That's why I'm on radio."

"Me too. See, I saw one of those mines on a trip through West Virginia and it hit me in the gut. We know, instinctively, when something is just plain wrong. Then, later, I moved here and found out I couldn't drink the water. The neighbors told me to be careful about how I feed my son. And someone else took me up over the ridge to see the mine itself. Larry, I looked at that gaping hole and I thought, shoot, this isn't just my business. This is the world's business."

"In many ways, Henrietta, in many ways. Coal's a major issue. Major source of energy, employment, commerce, export. It's also a major source of carbon emissions and, according to most scientists, a major cause of climate change."

"Yes, and that's when keeping my nose on my own face ceased to be an effective strategy for staying safe."

"What did your mamma say when you told her that?"

Henrietta burst into laughter.

"Oh lord, she wasn't pleased at all."

"Well, it's kind of like signing up to be a soldier without the prestige or the salary."

"Mmm-hmm. She was real worried about me. Still is." Henrietta paused as another ripple of laughter ran through her. "She's always worried about me. It's one of a mamma's jobs. And that's what got me involved in this."

In his office, Jack could hear the sucker-punch of Henrietta Owens coming. He buried his face in his hands.

"I'm a mother and my baby, Jerome, he has got the most beautiful smile in the whole world. From his toes to his ears, every little bit of him is beyond precious. You mothers out there know exactly what I mean," Henrietta said.

"And the fathers, too," Larry added.

"I have nightmares," Henrietta said quietly. "They come from over that ridge. They come from the days when the tap water runs red. They come from knowing my baby is breathing in coal dust every day, and the ice caps are melting, and the planet's heating up. In those dreams, this little baby's screaming like we never want to hear a child scream. I dream he's starving, crawling on his belly, lips cracked, begging for water. His children are dying before they're born. Families are screaming, trying to survive tsunamis, famines, and hurricanes.

"I wake up shaking and gasping for air, and I can't believe my baby's still so small and safe and sleeping. The forest is standing quiet all around me. Dawn's coming up. The birds start singing. Then the explosions start."

"The what?"

"The explosions. They are blasting away the mountains, Mr. Prince. It's like a warzone out there. Most of this country can't hear it, but we do. We live with the nightmares that our whole society is creating. " She paused to let that sink in. Then she continued,

"The people fighting mountaintop removal are trying to hold those nightmares at bay. They're like soldiers, you know? Brave and peaceful warriors. They don't look away from the terrors that we're facing. They speak up and endure scorn from the rest of us. I'm just one mother out of billions of mothers, and let me tell you, I don't want to be in this struggle more than any other mother. I want to curl up in a safe little house, with my baby sleeping peaceful and growing up strong. But if I don't stand up now, nobody's babies will get that chance. Not mine. Not yours. Not anybody's."

A deep silence followed her words. Jack felt spooked, shook up. The images of her night terrors were needling into him. He could see Allie crying. The new baby was a bundle of skin and bones in his arms. He threw himself back from the desk and paced to clear those images away.

"Environmentalist brainwash!" he cried. "Goddamn shock

talk to scare everyone. That's far in the future. We're not talking about our children here."

The radio stoically endured his rant. The little green lights glowed brighter as the shadows grew in the room. Children or children's children? What difference did it truly make? That day of small bodies wailing would come. They would be as tender and vulnerable as the ones alive today. Their cries would echo their predecessors. They would stare back through history with accusatory eyes and wonder; *why didn't our great-great-grandfather prevent this? Didn't he care?*

Jack kicked a wall.

"Get out!" he yelled to the images in his mind. They fled. He breathed heavily.

"So," Larry was continuing, "I hear there's a major protest ramping up, am I right?"

"Well, it's not a protest, exactly," Henrietta answered thoughtfully. "It's a multi-city rally. We're calling in our heroes."

"The heroes of the mountains?"

"The heroes of humanity. There's a story that needs to be told and we're all a part of it. Mankind is in an epic struggle for survival," Henrietta's voice turned hot with passion and excitement. "It's the greatest battle that's ever been fought and it's not about killing other people . . . it's about keeping each other alive. This gathering is to tell that story, not just with the mountaintop removal protestors, but with everyone."

"The other eco-activists who are fighting oil, gas, etcetera?"

"Everyone," Henrietta said unequivocally. "Moms and dads and kids, and people who never thought about the Earth at all.

The story is for all of us who live in this time. It is our myth, our great legend, the story that our ancestors will tell of us around the campfire."

"If there are ancestors."

"Exactly. We are gathering to tell the story of the Great Turning, when the people of the world turned away from a society based on extraction, greed, and accumulation, and made unbelievable efforts to change to a sustainable way of life that leads to generations of descendants who will be around to tell our story."

"Sounds inspiring," Larry commented.

"Wanna come?"

Larry chuckled, but didn't answer.

"That's a personal invitation, Larry. You're a good guy," Henrietta said. "You've got kids. You care about people. You've got honest eyes."

"I do?"

"Yes. For all you listeners out there," Henrietta said, "I don't know if your host has ever described himself, but he's the kind of guy you know you can trust. It's not just in his voice. He's got short reddish-blonde hair-"

"Kinda going white, to be honest," Larry put in.

"-and the lines around his face are full of laughter."

"Why, thank you, Henrietta."

"You're welcome. If you do come to hear the story, bring your family. I'd like to meet them."

"I'd like my kids to hear it," Larry said thoughtfully. "And I'd like them to know I was part of -what did you call it?"

"The Great Turning," Henrietta said. "There is something

else I'd like to mention."

"Alright, go ahead."

"I was sent up here with a message today."

"Haven't you been delivering one this whole time?" Larry chuckled.

"Well, yes," Henrietta said with a touch of laughter, "but today I'm carrying a special message from the heroes on the front line of birth and death, the folks who have been trying to hold the threshold of survival steady for the whole planet. It's a message from them, to all the rest of us."

"Alright," joked Larry. "Lay it on me. I'm ready."

"No," Henrietta's voice replied softly, "I don't think you are. None of us are ready for this."

"Try me," Larry bragged. "What do they want to say?"

In his office, Jack felt his shoulders tensing as if expecting a punch. He almost reached out to turn off the radio.

"Help us."

Jack shivered. The languor of sunshine was gone. The cool chill of its departure raked his back. The urgency of sunset crept in. His hairs were standing up on his arms.

"Help us," Henrietta repeated, passing on the plea. "We are losing ground. Everyday, our defensive lines are crumbling. We cannot hold back what's coming any longer. Not without you. We need you. We need your help."

Jack heard the desperation of people who challenged encroaching darkness, often in lonely, heroic actions. He heard the despair of a movement that was struggling even as it grew. Beyond his office, the cubicles were emptying, the staff closing files, turning off lights, shutting everything down, and going home. The cry of people whose work was never done echoed in Henrietta's voice.

"Help us. We are calling in all of the brave people who are ready to stand in defense of Earth and all her creatures. We are calling in the sleeping heroes who have been awakening. We need you. Now. There is no time to waste. Leave your uncertainties, your fears, and your hesitation. You may feel unprepared, but come anyway."

Jack thought of the office workers driving home. He wondered if any of them would answer the call.

"This is the story that no one is telling," Henrietta said. "A great struggle for survival is going on. Those who are fighting for our future are laughed at. The heroes of humanity are scorned. If we survive, that's all gonna change. But if we don't survive, no amount of ridicule is gonna matter. So come. Come help us. Come."

Three times she said *come* and three times, Jack jolted in his chair. He gripped his desk. The message was obviously for someone else. Other workers who had second thoughts about their jobs, or politicians, students, activist-types.

Do not get caught in her sentimentality, Jack ordered himself. There are seven billion people on this planet to protect mountains and trees. He told himself to think of all the coal company employees who depended on him for survival. They depend on her for survival, too, his mind traitorously informed him. Jack reached to turn off the radio. Henrietta's voice stopped him.

"You."

"Me?" Jack responded.

"Yes. You. You know who you are. You are the hero I need. Placed in the exact right spot with the knowledge and power to help us all."

She's just talking to air, Jack thought angrily.

"I know you are listening."

Oh, yeah? How?

"You don't want to be my hero."

Jack jumped. She's just making this up, he rationalized, but the goose bumps were climbing his arms.

"You want things to be cut and dry, simple, like the old days. You want things to be like they were."

Jack's heart was pounding.

"I'm sorry."

A lump choked his throat.

"But it will never be the same as it was. You know that."

Larry Prince coughed discretely and then gently cut in,

"Henrietta, I am so glad you came in today, but we are out of time. I would give you all the time in the world, if only I could convince my board to do so.

"Then do it. You're a hero too, you know. We all are. Hidden in our very ordinariness is our heroism."

Hidden in our very ordinariness is our heroism. The line echoed in Jack.

Larry thanked Henrietta for coming on the show and delivering her message.

"We wish you the best of luck. And Henrietta-" Larry Prince paused. "I wish I was that hero you last called for. Whoever it is, I hope he comes forward. We need heroes in high places."

"No, Larry, we need heroes in all places," Henrietta replied. "There are three hundred million American heroes, each one just waiting to be called."

Her words shot out over the airwaves, traveling over the hills and mountains of the East Coast. She tracked them down in the hollows and slopes, the farmlands and coastal towns. She called them from their cozy suburbs and apartments. She had to plunge their heads in a bucket of truth and bring them out gaspingly sober. Henrietta needed a nation of heroes . . .

Jack Dalton knew he could not turn away.

CHAPTER SEVENTEEN

· · · · ·

The Great Turning

"Hey, Mom, you missed the exit!" Allie squealed.

"No, honey, we're not going to the recital hall. We're going up to Crawley's Slope," Sarah answered.

"Really? How come?"

Sarah hesitated, biting her lower lip in an effort to find the right words. She'd vacillated all day about doing this. If Jack found out after all their arguments about Henrietta Owens and her insistence on him returning to work . . . Sarah didn't finish the thought. He had been so pleasant this past week, like the old days. A little distracted, maybe, but that was to be expected.

"Remember on the radio, when Henrietta Owens said they were going to tell a story?"

"Uh-huh."

"We're going to hear them tell it."

Allie's eyes widened. She sat up straighter in the passenger seat. They were on an adventure. An illicit, secret adventure. One Dad didn't know about. No wonder Mom let her wear blue jeans. Sheesh, she should have guessed. Mom never took her to hear concert music in anything short of a skirt and tights.

"Hey, Mom, can we get fast food?"

"No, your dinner is in the back. It's sandwiches from the deli."

Allie made a face. Just like Mom to plan ahead and veto junk food. Maybe though . . . she snuck a look at her mom's somber expression. Never mind. Mom wasn't in an ice-cream-for-dessert sort of mood. Her fingernails were drumming nervously on the steering wheel, and she kept sweeping her blonde hair behind her ears only to pull it back out a moment later.

"Allie, uh, you can't tell Dad about this," Sarah said hesitantly.

"I know." Sheesh, hadn't she been tiptoeing around landmines called Henrietta Owens for three weeks now? Last weekend when she had thoughtlessly asked if they could go hiking in the mountains, Dad had roared,

"No! Absolutely not!"

-and stalked out of the room. Poor Dad.

"How come we couldn't have just heard it on TV?" Allie asked.

"Your father," Sarah answered shortly.

Oopsy, Allie realized, Mom must be really annoyed at Dad if she was calling him, *your father.*

"But Dad's probably going to watch it on TV," Allie pointed out. "He watches everything Henrietta Owens does."

"He has to, honey, for work."

"But how come we can't watch it with him?"

"I-" Sarah fumbled for the words, "I thought we should be there in person. And I'm sure your father wouldn't want to go."

"Oh." Allie rode along quietly for a moment, thinking

about cameras and television and wondering what the story would be like and too bad Dad couldn't be there with them and-

"Hey, Mom, we could wave to Dad on the cameras!"

"*Allison Dalton!*"

"Uh, just kidding, Mom."

Allie shut up and rode in silence so that Mom wouldn't change her mind and turn around. Allie watched the suburbs give way to the rural routes and enjoyed the swishing motions of the winding roads.

"Maybe he won't watch it, anyway," Sarah said out loud, nervously voicing her thoughts. "It's mostly other people talking tonight. Henrietta might not say anything. And they probably won't be airing this live. Even so, we should try not to get on the camera, Allie. Someone from Jack's office might see us."

"Maybe they'll be there, too," Allie offered.

Sarah gave her an exasperated look.

"What?" Allie defended herself, "Just because you work for the coal company doesn't mean you don't care about the earth. Look at Dad."

"What about your father?"

"Well, he cares. He just doesn't know what to do."

"Your father's job is very important, honey. It feeds you, clothes you, keeps the roof over our head."

"He could get a different job," Allie said optimistically.

"The economy's really bad right now," Sarah responded.

"So he can't get a job?"

"Well, I'm sure Jack could get a job. He's very good at what

he does." Sarah sighed and turned into Crawley's Slope. "Look, sweetie, let's not talk about your father right now, alright?"

"Okay."

As they pulled into the Grange Hall parking lot, Sarah made a quick survey of the vehicles. There were a lot of people here. Judging from the cars, they probably wouldn't see any of Jack's associates. Sarah shut off the engine and sat still for a moment, both relieved and saddened by that observation. They should be here, she thought. Everyone should.

When the phrase *The Great Turning* came rolling off the radio, she hadn't believed it. She hadn't heard those words in years and then there was Henrietta's gentle voice inviting them all to come hear the story. God, it was as familiar to Sarah as a bedtime story. The mere mention of it had walloped Sarah with such strong memories of her college days and activism work that she had sat down in her office, overwhelmed.

Where does the time go? Here was Allie, eleven, pushing open the car door with impatience, itching to run into the Grange Hall, with not even a clue of what The Great Turning was all about.

"Allie! Don't go anywhere!" Sarah yelled. The parking lot was full of swiveling vehicles. *Don't go anywhere!* The phrase echoed in Sarah. Just hold still and stay a little girl for a minute while your mom catches up. Sarah fumbled for her purse, turned off her cellphone, craned awkwardly around to make sure Allie had obeyed, tried to squeeze her belly past the steering wheel, and -dammit! She dropped the keys.

"Hurry up, Mom!"

"I'm coming. Don't go anywhere," Sarah ordered as she scrabbled in the dirt for the keys. Don't run off while I try to explain things I should have told you years and years ago. Things I should never have forgotten, but did. Sarah sighed as she took Allie's hand. Well, they were here, weren't they? No use regretting the past.

They made their way through the cars to the brightly lit hall. Sarah nudged Allie up the steps suddenly feeling for the first time since leaving the house that she had made the right decision. No matter what Jack thought, it was important for Allie to be here. She has to hear the story, Sarah thought, so she'll understand what Jack and I are dealing with.

A punch of excited voices hit them. Allie's eyes flew open at the hall of strangers. The people spoke animatedly to each other, waved at friends, and wound their way to the brown wooden folding chairs that looked as old as the Grange.

"This way, honey." Sarah took Allie by the hand, grateful that, for once, Allie didn't seem inclined to run off and make mischief. Sarah felt conspicuous, as if at any moment someone would shout, *there's Jack Dalton's wife!* and throw her out. Sarah thought about picking seats in the very back corner, but Allie was too short to sit behind ten rows of adults.

Allie watched the other kids. Some were definitely locals. They were too rambunctious and daring to have been hauled over here for the first time. Others, like Allie, stuck close to their parents' sides and tried to behave themselves. Allie smiled at a pack of strawberry blonde kids ranging from teenage to toddler.

"Larry?" their mother called to an almost white-haired man.

"There's a bunch of seats over there." The mother roped in the littlest ones and the whole family moved across the hall.

"Here, Allie." Sarah slid into a chair and gave Allie the aisle seat so she could look down it to the events in the center. Sarah rubbed her lower back. This new baby sure was growing fast. She hoped no one would need to squeeze by.

"Hey, Mom! Look! It's Louisa!" Allie hopped up and Sarah grabbed the back of her tee shirt just in time.

"Shit," Sarah swore as she caught sight of the dark haired woman. Oh Jesus, she should have figured. All this time worrying about Jack finding out and it never occurred to her that she might run into Louisa. Sarah stared at her old friend, remembering the bitter words with which Jack had driven her activist friend away. Sarah sighed. Of course Louisa would be here. This was her work.

"Allie, sit down," Sarah commanded. "Sit down!"

Allie obeyed, confused.

"We'll say hello afterwards, Allie. Louisa's busy getting ready to speak."

And she was. The thin, dark haired woman held up her hands for silence. The room quieted.

"Thank you all for coming, for answering Henrietta's call, our call. We're so honored to have this room packed full tonight. And we have some wonderful news! Our friends in D.C., New York, Vermont, Pennsylvania, Tennessee, Maryland, Maine, North Carolina, and many others have sent word that their halls are as crowded as ours. It is rumored that the groups in the western time zones will also have standing room only by the time their meetings begin. We are grateful to our friends from public television and radio for broadcasting this gathering tonight for those who could not come in person. And I must express a deep gratitude to Henrietta Owens for spreading the word about these meetings."

The crowd clapped and cheered. Allie leaned to look down the aisle.

"Mom, look! There she is!"

Henrietta waved briefly to everyone from her seat in the circle. Jerome was in the lap of the black woman next to her. Allie thought Henrietta might get up and talk, but it was Louisa who kept speaking. That was fine with Allie. She didn't know what Mom's old friend Louisa was doing here, but she wished she could go give her a hug. Mom must have guessed her thoughts because she hooked a finger through Allie's belt loop.

"Stay put," Sarah commanded. The last thing she needed was Allie running up there and causing a commotion. Louisa didn't know they were there and Sarah half-hoped they could keep it that way. Still . . . Sarah greedily fixed her eyes on Louisa. It'd been so long . . .

Someone dimmed the overhead lights and turned up the wall sconces. Decorative white Christmas lights looped in a canopy to the central peak of the hall. A lone fiddler stepped out into the middle of the circle and began to play.

"Tonight is a memorable night," Louisa said as the fiddle slowly stroked the strings. "In halls like this, both smaller and larger, all over the country, people like us are telling this same story to groups of people, like you, who have come seeking a message of hope and direction in the face of grave challenges."

The fiddler turned in a yearning circle. His passion shone on his cheeks. His eyes would close in breathless humility and then fly open again as his chest arched heavenward.

"This is the story of the Great Turning," Louisa told them. "We tell it because it is the story of our time and without it we feel lost and confused, unsure of what we're doing here on this troubled Earth right now."

Allie leaned into the aisle, keeping the fiddler in view. He hit a low, dissonant chord. A baby let out a cry. A mother shushed it. The fiddler pulled another shuddering stroke across the fiddle. He followed with a series of short jabs that rasped like bare branches scraping against a window.

"We have come because we are frightened," Louisa continued, pacing in a ring around the fiddler. "Even the most courageous of us have fears about the uncertainty of our future. But we have also come because we know that we can no longer look away."

Allie watched the fiddler straighten his spine. His eyes stared at something looming in the distance. His bow quivered with the trembling of his heart, but he stood firm, determined to face what lay before him. Louisa drew near and paused by his shoulder.

"I call upon those guardians who have stood vigil while this nation slept. They have come from all corners of our continent, carrying tidings of our friends and of the challenges we face."

Allie saw figures moving forward, seven, no, eight. One brushed past her as he walked down Allie's aisle. They came to the first row of seats and stopped. In the glow of the canopy of lights, Allie could see their faces. They're so ordinary, she thought. A pot-bellied man with a red face and plaid shirt huffed out,

"Greetings from Pennsylvania, New York, and the Marcellus Shale region, where we seek to end hydraulic fracking."

A wiry, long haired lady stepped forward.

"Greetings from the arid deserts of the Southwest," she said, "where water grows ever scarcer as global warming heats up the planet."

"I bring greetings from the North and the Tar Sands where we are trying our best to stop oil and gas pipelines," a thick Canadian accent said. Allie craned to see who spoke, but couldn't tell.

"I bring solidarity from small farmers in midst of the corporatized Heartland," a heavy-featured woman with kind smile said.

"And I come from the troubled Gulf of Mexico," a darker man with weary shoulders drawled out.

"I come from California with a whole range of tidings from people up and down the coast," said another woman.

One by one, each stepped forward, in sneakers and reading glasses, cut-off shorts and baseball caps, looking as ordinary as the folks next door. And yet, Allie thought, Louisa had honored them as guardians.

"Mom?" Allie whispered, leaning against Sarah in the dim light. "This is big, isn't it?"

Sarah looked around at the gathering. Two hundred, three hundred people, maybe. Even with groups scattered across the continent, even including the larger networks that had sent the representatives . . .

"No, honey," she said. "Not really, not compared to the three hundred million other Americans out there."

"But, Mom, it's important, isn't it?"

"Yes, Allie, it is."

Allie sat back satisfied. If it were important, the grown-ups would do something about it. Sarah watched her wistfully, wishing she were an eleven-year old girl who still believed that adults made the right decisions and knew all the answers. Louisa spoke, addressing those who came forward and those who sat listening,

"We live in uncertain times. We face an unpredictable climate shift that will most certainly change our lives, only we do not know exactly how."

The fiddle flooded the hall with a quivering tremble of sound. Sarah swallowed hard. She hated this part of the story. Truth. Sheer, raw, uncertain truth. She wrapped her arms around the new baby in her belly and rocked a little. She glanced at Allie. Her feet were wrapped around the chair legs. One hand clung to the back of her seat. She was leaning so far into the aisle she was likely to fall at any moment. Sarah put one hand firmly on the wooden chair to prevent Allie's inevitable tumble. The fiddle shivered. Allie echoed it. A smile grew across her face and Sarah could see a gleam in her eyes.

My God! Sarah thought. She's not scared at all. Sarah scanned the other faces in the room. Anticipation and anxiety. Excitement and trepidation. The fiddler was wrenching honest emotions from where they hid inside the people. The cautious wore their worries on their expressions, but some, like Allie, were leaning forward in their seats, answering the looming questions with inquisitive courage.

Allie's foot slipped. She tipped. Sarah instinctively grabbed her shirt and hauled her upright. Allie sent her an apologetic look that didn't fool Sarah for an instant. Two seconds later, Allie was leaning even further into the aisle. She was just like Jack, Sarah thought. Fearless. Ready and eager to jump into the thick of the action. Whenever she told Allie to use some common sense, Jack would inevitably pipe up.

"We need her uncommon sense. 'Common sense, by definition, is already prevalent enough in the world'," he would state, scratching his head to remember the source of the quote.

Sarah smiled at the memory. She shifted on the wooden chair. The fiddler built the tremor of his playing to a crescendo. A roaring filled Sarah as the reverberations of his strokes echoed off the ceiling and flooded the room, the people, and drove every rational thought from their minds as the sounds inundated them with the visceral yearning of their own hearts.

Then suddenly, the fiddler ceased. Sarah hung suspended in the silence, hardly breathing. The fiddler stood without moving, slightly to one side of the center. Louisa came forward.

"In times to come, humans -if there are any humans at all- will be living in a way radically different from us now. The nature of this way of life is unknown. They may be living in massive turmoil. They may be living in relative ease and peace. In either case, our actions now determine their future."

Louisa paused and bowed her head, solemn beneath the responsibility of her choices and actions. Then she lifted her head and took a deep breath.

"In the times to come, surely our great-great-grandchildren will speak of us. If they live in a dangerous, poisoned world, they may curse us, or scorn the ignorance of our ways."

Sarah shuddered at that thought. Louisa continued,

"However, if our descendants live in peace, even if they still face many challenges, they will certainly speak of this time, now, and they will give it a name: *The Time of the Great Turning*."

They will give it a name because *we* have given it that name, Sarah thought. We will not leave this in the hands of judgmental historians whose hearts are not beating in the here and now with us. A small smile formed across her face. Louisa spoke again,

"As we have said, it is uncertain if there will always be humans on this planet," she admitted sadly. Then her expression rose and she added, "But one thing is certain, if there are, then those children are wanting to come into this world as strongly as the sun wants to rise."

Sarah looked down at her new baby. Yes, she thought, yes. Every day it grows, kicks, and beats its heart.

"In the times to come, our descendants will ask: what was it like for you? In those times when your way of life was crumbling, what did you turn to for strength?"

Sarah blinked. What did we turn to? Well, each-

"Each other."

Sarah jumped as the woman from the Heartland voiced her thoughts.

"Hope," an older, stocky man added.

"And this story," said the thin woman from the desert.

"Tell it then," Louisa urged the representatives, "for we have come to hear it."

The fiddler sprang to life again, bending out of his stillness, lifting his instrument, and stroking long across the strings.

Allie watched the guardians as they straightened up their spines and shifted their feet. She studied these people from every corner of the country who stood up to guard life and the future of human beings.

"We live in the time of the Great Turning," the stout man from Pennsylvania began, "when the systems of the past no longer serve us."

Allie could feel his baritone pulsing through the floorboards. He boomed out a list of problems like the pounding of deep tympani drums.

"Greed. Over-consumption. Extractive mining practices. Fossil fuels. Pollution."

Each word jolted through those who sat listening. When he finished, the guardian from California spoke next, her voice as steady and rich as a firm clarinet.

"More and more, however, people are realizing it's not working. People like you. And like me. We feel it in our bones. Despair and depression are rampant in our country. We are told to medicate it, but perhaps we have every reason to be depressed. Perhaps our despair comes from a sense of foreboding that life as we know it cannot continue."

Sarah felt her lips quiver and pressed them firmly together. There were things being voiced that she rarely dared to say, even in the privacy of her own thoughts. She didn't like this fearful feeling that was slipping out now. She blinked ferociously at the canopy of little lights. The darkness that now encompassed the Grange Hall pressed against the back of her neck. The air felt clogged and thick. Sarah rubbed her arms. All this talk of pollution left her feeling grimy.

Sarah slumped against the chair. It's hopeless, she thought. Look at those people up there. Their faces were yellowed from the light. They looked as exhausted and battered as the earth itself. Sarah wanted to scream at the people as they called out lists of mountains falling, forests burning, lakes vanishing, and ice caps melting. She wanted to throw her hands over her ears, grab Allie, and leave all this behind.

You can't leave, something in her warned. There is nowhere you can go. Look at Allie. Look at her sitting upright in her chair, eyes wide and solemn. Borrow her courage. What was it Louisa said? *We have come because we can no longer look away.*

She couldn't hold them back. One tear after another slid down her cheeks. She didn't bother to wipe them away. The fiddler was now bowed under grief, the violin weeping as if it had wept a thousand times before. He took the sorrow from the room into himself, collected the tears before they fell, pulled the sadness from them, through him, into the voice of the fiddle's sighs and sobs. Just when Sarah thought she could take no more, Louisa spoke,

"Where there is despair, there is also hope."

Sarah wiped her eyes. Yes, she agreed. Because we feel, we act.

"Life as we know it will not continue . . . because it cannot.

Already, it is changing. We live in the time of the Great Turning, and while we have spoken of where we have been, we have not told the story of what we are moving toward."

Louisa gestured. Allie saw the guardians put away their tears. The pot-bellied man blew his nose loudly and a few laughs trickled out. Allie watched the room straighten up, thirsty for hope. The weary man from the Gulf stepped forward, his shoulders straightening as he spoke,

"Even as all seems hopeless, we are moving toward sustainable societies. As the need grows, so do the solutions. It is a desperate, uncomfortable race, but the truth is, we are running it. The finish line may feel far away, but we are headed toward it and picking up speed."

The Californian woman chimed in, her tone piping with enthusiasm,

"Think of all that has been done already! Recycling programs, the resurgence in commuter rail development, universities opening departments of environmental sciences."

"Classroom gardens!" someone called out from the listeners.

"Electric cars!" another person added.

"Solar and wind technologies!" a third voice shot out from the darkness.

One example led to another. Each person had an idea, an experience, something uplifting to share. The fiddler could not contain himself. He leapt into the circle with enthusiastic strains. His body whirled and folded. The notes soared and dove as people called out,

"Green financing!"

"Emphasis on local economies."

"Regional water conservation programs!"

"Young farmer programs and farmers' markets."

Sarah thought it was like striking matches one by one to ward off the darkness of a long, cold night, but she couldn't stop her growing smile. We'll see the sunrise yet, she thought, one flaring match at a time. The fiddle rang out a triumphant note and Louisa held her hands up.

"There is much to celebrate and much to be done. The outcome of this time is uncertain, but-"

"It's an adventure!" Allie called out enthusiastically.

Allie clamped her hands over her mouth. Sarah glared. The heads swiveled her direction. Louisa smiled and peered into the dimly lit listeners.

"Yes," she answered the child's voice, though she could not see who it was. "It is the adventure of a lifetime. Our lifetime. Henrietta called for heroes . . . and here you are!"

She gestured to the room. Allie snuck a look at Henrietta, Louisa, the guardians. Heroes are so ordinary looking, she thought. It's like seeing St. George or Robin Hood in blue jeans and sneakers.

"So, tell us what to do!" a man's voice called out.

"Yeah! We're ready," another young man declared.

"Send me your dragons!" a third daredevil said with bravado. People laughed. His companions clapped him on the back, all wearing wide grins. Louisa turned toward the speaker.

"I can't send the dragons to you. You must seek them out yourself. You must go home and challenge them in your workplaces, your home environments, your daily lives, and your political choices."

"Whoa, that's a lot for one guy," the voice protested.

"Just do one thing," the guardian from the north suggested.

"Then another," the Gulf guardian drawled.

"And then another," laughed the woman from California.

"Tell them about the ways in which they can help," Louisa encouraged the guardians.

"There are three aspects to the Great Turning," began the thin woman from the desert.

"One: holding actions," the Canadian said firmly. "These stop the slide of environmental degradation, such as protesting pipelines and the coal export ports, like we're doing in the North and on the Pacific Coast."

"But these alone are not enough," the woman from America's Heartland warned. "We must also create new systems to replace what is not working. Our local farmers' markets and organic farming are examples of this."

The excited voice of the Californian woman came tumbling out, "And hand-in-hand with that comes a re-education of our ways of thinking and ingrained beliefs. This is happening not only in schools, but also in workplaces, spiritual centers, community action groups, and cooperative societies."

"We must learn to see life differently," Louisa put in. "And it can be done. It is being done right now. Right here. Tonight." Louisa looked around the room. The guardians who worked so hard seemed lighter now, less weary. Beyond them, the people listened, alert, eager to lend their hands. The fiddler played a hope-filled melody, an aria of the possible. It was time. Louisa addressed the guardians,

"To those who have come from the far corners of the

continent, I ask you, what can we offer you and your friends?"

"We need to know that someone is listening," the Pennsylvanian said.

"They are," Louisa assured him, indicating the room.

"We need to know we're not alone," said the woman from the vast desert regions.

"You are not," the guardians answered her.

A strong young man with a head full of red hair stepped forward. Allie tried to remember what region he was from. He hadn't spoken much tonight.

"I need to know . . . "

Allie grinned. His voice gave him away. He was from here, from West Virginia, from the mountains. Just like her.

"I need to know," he repeated, "who will join hands to help me?"

"I will!" Allie cried out.

The crowd startled at the young voice calling out in its midst. Before Sarah could grab her, Allie darted up the aisle and shot across the circle to the redheaded man. She boldly took his outstretched hand.

"I'll help you!"

"You're just a kid," he laughed.

"I won't always be. I'll grow," she promised. "Tell him, Louisa. I can help."

Louisa's eyes flew open. Her mind placed the familiar little girl. She scanned the crowd and her eyes found Sarah's. A bemused laugh rippled through them both.

"Yes," Louisa said. "All of us can help, from the smallest to the mightiest. One day," Louisa told her, "one day, you will look back on tonight and proudly tell your grandchildren; *I was there. I was a part of the Great Turning.* It wasn't always easy, but-"

"It was fun!" Allie blurted out enthusiastically. The adults laughed. The kids hooted. Cheering broke out. The fiddle broke out into racing melodies. People began clapping along.

"*This*, my friends," Louisa cried, "is the story of the Great Turning!"

The fiddler strummed the bowstrings as if his very fiber would fly apart. The sound exploded from the instrument. Suddenly, a second impromptu fiddler joined the first. Someone notched up the lights, illuminating the startled and smiling expressions of the crowd. Greetings were called out. Folding chairs were flung back against the walls.

Oh lord, Louisa thought, they're going to dance. She'd seen it happen so many times; the fiddles started racing, the people clapping their hands, the kids linking arms to whirl together. Once they got going, they'd dance the night away. She saw Hank slip away from the circle to rile up the youngsters.

Well, that's as it should be, she thought. She looked down at the girl holding her hand. My, but she had grown!

"Hi, Allie."

"Hi, Louisa," Allie replied shyly. "Louisa? You told me that story before, didn't you?"

"Mmm-hmm, but that was a long time ago. I didn't think you'd remember," Louisa answered.

"I didn't. But then tonight, I did."

Louisa hugged this kid who had once been like a daughter

to her. With her face buried in Louisa's shirt, Allie couldn't see the older woman's eyes grow wet and shiny. *She remembered. Allie remembered the Great Turning.* The daughter of Jack and Sarah Dalton -a girl who shouldn't have been at this meeting at all- had remembered the story and ran up to join hands with Hank Crawley to stand up for the Earth. Louisa couldn't believe it.

The first lines of dancers were forming up and down the hall. Voices bounced off the ceiling. Louisa felt that maybe there really was a chance. A little girl she had told a bedtime story to long ago, remembered. Louisa squeezed the child who had somehow grown so tall.

"Come on, kid, let's go find your mom."

CHAPTER EIGHTEEN
· · · · ·
Treadmills

Jack began to run. Each night, he climbed onto the treadmill and raced. Sarah commented as Jack grew stronger. He didn't care. The shedding weight and strengthening limbs were side effects of thinking. The pounding rhythm of his strides and the raw rasp within his throat paid justice to the pressures of his days.

Resistance to the coal company grew daily. Henrietta Owens rang alarm clocks in slumbering souls across the nation. The rallies were gaining in steam, strength, and number. Even Allie knew the phrase *The Great Turning*, though she had been evasive about where she had learned it. Jack shrugged it off as one of her classmates. He couldn't turn on the radio these days without hearing Henrietta or someone talking about Henrietta.

The Captain told him to put every option on the table: threats, bribes, coercion, murder, kidnapping, illness, imprisonment, exile, defaming, co-option. One by one, Jack set aside the gentler persuasions. He hardened his heart and ran the analysis of the crueler methods. From nine to five, they fanned out on the glass-covered mahogany of his desk. He kept his notes and files in his briefcase and carried them back and forth to work each day.

At night, he exploded across the treadmill. He groaned his

frustration as his chest throbbed and ached. He pushed for stamina, bemoaning the years that had slid him into sloppiness. Running coursed the blood back through his veins, stimulated nerves inside his mind, quickened, awakened and enlivened him.

One day, the treadmill could not keep up. It heaved in surrender and whined to a standstill. Jack stepped off and went running through the neighborhood. After all this time spinning his wheels in place, Jack shot across the suburbs that sat on top of forgotten farmers' fields. He sensed the ghosts of back-lot burials. He heard faint echoes of native people underneath the trails that had been bulldozed, tarred, and renamed 'Feather Lane' and 'Cherokee Drive'. Beneath the carefully constructed roads, the older pathways still murmured as he ran. He heard the hammer of distant places and other times, the sound of tracks being laid, stages set, and tunnels blasted.

Some nights, John Henry kept pace beside him. John's breath made no sound. His footsteps didn't mark the earth. His body passed like a whisper of wind through the night. They didn't speak. When Jack grew weary, John would pick up the pace to urge him on. Jack met the ghost's challenge stride for stride. Finally, in front of Jack's house, they would finish. Illuminated by the streetlight, Jack would wipe the sweat from his brow. John Henry would wait. Then their hands would rise in a gesture of farewell. The ghost would walk down the darkened street and vanish. Jack, breathing hard, was left alone in the streetlight.

CHAPTER NINETEEN

. . . . .

Primetime Gladiator

"Three minutes, Ms. Owens."

"Thank you," she told the station hand.

"Oh, you're very welcome!" the girl gasped out like a desert traveler thirsty for a draught of kindness. Henrietta watched the girl's retreating back straighten until a stress-laden voice hollered and she crunched back into a knot.

Henrietta grimaced. It had been a long week of interviews since the night Louisa had facilitated the story of the Great Turning. They got easier every time, but Henrietta had learned that every newspaper, radio, and television was a different world. Some were friendly and welcoming, but others were as uncomfortable as a too-tight pair of blue jeans.

"Hurry up," she whispered to Jerome. He nursed slowly in rebellion and twiddled with the buttons on her blouse. "Stop that," she said and moved his hand away. He grabbed her finger in a silent, *don't be nervous, Ma*. He smiled through his milk. "Finish up or I'm gonna have to cut you off," she warned him. Nervousness leaked into her body. He made a face and finished nursing. She buttoned up her blouse and straightened in the mirror. It reflected back her worries. Except for those, she looked alright, Henrietta acknowledged.

Fashion had never been her friend. It dragged its standards

through her hair, sneered at her clothes, and laughed at her shoes. Nothing ever seemed to please it. The girl called Henrietta had once tried to squeeze and straighten and simmer down her curves and curls. She tried to fit the mold. It didn't work. Her mother nagged her from Ohio, sent her money for new clothes, and told her, "Don't spend it on the rent. You've got to look nice, you know." Henrietta sighed. One's rent and personal appearance held equally non-negotiable positions in her landlord and her mother, respectively.

"Looking nice gets you places like a decent running car," her mother claimed, but Henrietta hadn't had the time or money to fool around with either.

There is something that happens, though, when the woods shelter you beneath the stars and crickets chorus possibilities and welcome your heart into their song; when a ravaged mountain bares no judgments; when rocks have no eyes to care about the color of your skin; when birds outnumber flocks of people; and your days pass quietly in a tiny place tucked against a mountainside, where age and rot remind you of your eye blink of a lifetime. All things shall pass and so will you. Here, your soul has room to breathe a little. It creeps out of hiding and people start to see it.

"Henrietta," they'd exclaim, "you look nice! You done something to your hair?"

"Nothing. Just let it be, for once."

It proudly curled into its lineage of continents. The hills etched their strength into her limbs. Color raced into her cheeks like long lost friends. The stars came down to chuckle in her eyes. When the media called Henrietta from the mountains, the mountains stayed inside her. Their beauty echoed in her smile; their devastation in her sorrow. Henrietta let the TV people do their make-up and styling work -but not too much.

"I can't look too fancy," she'd protest against the onslaught, "not with Jerome here, reminding everybody what humans really look like."

They kindly offered to put a little 'shine' on him.

"No, thank you," she declined, "his soul is shining out already."

She watched the stylists at their work, appreciating the ones that looked real close and then did very little. Those artists saw the soul come shining out in all its beauty. They simply made sure the fabrications of the stage and screen would not destroy it. They adjusted for the glare of lights, brought out the eyes so that those laughing stars would reach the viewer, and then left well enough alone. They knew better than to conceal a shining soul. It has no secrets left to hide. It has no awkwardness to cover up. Unabashed and unadorned, a human soul contains the majesty of mountains.

"Are you ready, Ms. Owens?"

"Is it time?"

Henrietta was and was not ready, but time propelled her forward nonetheless. She followed the station hand. Jerome clung to her. His eyes flitted from cable to camera, peering out at the dark shapes of the studio audience and the waiting set with its bright facade of coziness. Henrietta chose a chair. She jiggled Jerome on her knee. He scowled. *Stop that, Mamma!* Her nervousness kept gnawing her. Her arm hairs refused to lie supine. The pin-prickles creep-crawled along her back, up and down like an anxious march of ants.

The fox, the bear, the wolf, the mouse; all animals struck by these same symptoms will freeze within their places, sniff the air, and take the pulse of premonition. Man, however, with his claims of elevated evolution, denies such subtle intuitions. He blunders on where other animals wisely fear to tread.

Henrietta's prickles had started when the station called the organizers. She shushed the creepy-crawling feelings down as Louisa and Patrick told her the importance of Jane Simon's primetime talk show.

"Yes, but she's so scathing," was Henrietta's comment.

"Yeah," Hank acknowledged, "but that's why everybody watches her."

Henrietta thought of the barbaric days of Roman gladiators who skewered beasts and murdered slaves. Evolution is not guaranteed to move us upward to become better human beings; only onward, come what may.

Jane Simon barreled onto the set, a gladiator in heels and a shiny, short cut dress. Henrietta switched Jerome to the other arm and held out her hand.

"I'm-"

"You're in my seat."

So much for courtesy, Henrietta thought. But from whom to whom, did she mean? She rose and offered the hostess her seat. The other chair tried to suck her backwards into an unsightly slouch. Henrietta extracted herself from its clutches and perched untrustingly on its edge. Jane Simon flicked her platinum hair and arranged her long waxed legs. Henrietta swore the hostess' chair was tailored for such a purpose. Jerome hid his face as the stage lights swiveled toward him. Henrietta squinted at the glare and caught the lighting guy waving. She smiled. He winked. She had a friend. The light was shuttered off her eyes. *Thank you*, she mouthed. Jerome peeked up out of hiding and tried out his newfound gurgling sound. Jane Simon frowned.

"Is he going to make that racket through the whole show?" She eyed him with such distaste that Henrietta couldn't hold back the edge in her reply,

"Ms. Simon, he's a baby. He might decide to scream." Consternation contorted Jane Simon's expression. Henrietta relented. "He's usually very well behaved," she said.

Jane refused to be amused or reassured. She swung her sharp and pointed nose out toward the crew.

"Are we ready yet?"

"Ready," the call came back. Silence hit the set.

Three . . . Two . . . One . . . Theme music rolled. The show went live. The APPLAUSE sign glowed green. The audience obeyed. It faded. They stopped. Jane Simon smiled to the country,

"Good evening, Americans! Welcome to the Jane Simon Show -that's me!" She preened and purred as the APPLAUSE sign commanded its appropriate response. It faded. So did the clapping. Jane beamed.

"I'm here with Henrietta Owens."

(No sign, no clapping)

"Tell me, Ms. Owens, how does stardom suit you?"

Henrietta, caught disengaging Jerome's hand from her hair,

looked up surprised. Sincerity shot out of her,

"Am I a star?" She laughed, but her butterfly warnings were on high alert. Jane's face had frozen its expression. She showed her teeth in what is sometimes called a smile.

"I suppose not. Stars usually have to *work* for the title." She smirked the catty-sexy grin that drove the ratings up a notch and sneered, "I've never met a star on welfare." Jane fluttered her mascara lashes. Henrietta's butterflies shuddered. Jane looked at her manicured nails. Standard Coal had offered her the icing on the cake of bribes to *cream* this woman . . . and she intended to. Everyone expected it. Jane Simon held the championship title in the arena of primetime gladiators. The viewers loved to watch pure viciousness look so pretty.

Henrietta's hackles sprang to life. The laughing heavens in her eyes turned white with heat. *You didn't come to pick a fight,* she told herself, *simmer down.* Out loud she said,

"I guess you still don't know a welfare star." Henrietta took advantage of Jane's frowning silence to thank the sponsors of the mountaintop removal protests and all the soccer moms and yoga buddies and girlfriends across the nation who had felt the urge to help a fellow mother. Henrietta didn't mention that when the funds came unexpectedly in her name, welfare had cut her off. She didn't mention the substantial gap between the welfare income cut-off and the amount that was really needed to pay the bills. Henrietta just thanked the donors and leaped across that chasm . . . for now.

"Tssk, tssk," Jane shook her head, "from charity to charity."

Across the nation, viewers tssk-tssk-ed with her. Charity and donations were considered un-American. Everyone should support oneself. Every man for himself. Every woman, too. And all children thrown into this dog-eat-dog philosophy. Survival of the fittest. Improve the human race. Those without a salary shouldn't even reproduce. We need ruthless businessmen in our blood. No welfare imbeciles. No lazy handout takers. Across the nation, savage thoughts came out to cheer their inner devil on.

As for the gladiator in heels, she did not consider bribes to be a handout. Bribes aren't a sinful flaw when they look so good in American genes, right? Besides, a bribe is not the same as a welfare check. There's a difference when you already have a million dollars in the bank. And inheriting your wealth, your education, your society, your job, and your connections is not at all like getting a few dollars from the government . . . even if you didn't work for that money either.

Jane Simon sneered at Henrietta with the condescendence of one who has only known hunger through voluntary weight-loss plans. She snuck appraising looks at Henrietta's slimness and wondered who her personal trainer was. If Henrietta could have read her thoughts, she would have answered, "Hunger, Jane, and hauling drinkable water up and down a mountain." But their thoughts and perspectives and understandings were worlds and worlds apart. Jane 'tssk-tssk-ed' at Henrietta's survival and Henrietta stared back at her, wondering what crawled up this woman in the night that made her act like she had cockroaches in her heart.

"I'm employed by an environmental non-profit, Ms. Simon."

"Yes, a charity," she yawned. "You know, if those charities

would offer a real product of value to the American people, they'd be making a profit. We'd be paying them instead of giving handouts to their boards."

"I agree," Henrietta said. Jane shot out her famous, 'oh-do-you-now' eyebrow raise and wondered; how stupid *was* this colored woman, anyway? Henrietta took a breath and prepared to face the gladiator. The stands of spectators leaned in to catch the blow-by-blow.

"You agree," Jane Simon smirked, "that we shouldn't be giving hand-outs to those who will not work?"

"Mmm-hmm, like government subsidies for oil, corn, and warfare that are going into the pockets of executives and presidents of banks."

"That's not what I am referring to."

The battle began. The first blows were exchanged. Henrietta carried her baby in her arms. Such is the case; poor soldiers for the human heart have no place to put their children safely. They don't carry them into the battlefields; the generals drop the bombs right on their lives. They take up arms to survive the madness all around them. Henrietta prayed they would survive.

"Subsidies for highway projects aren't any different than funding the Women, Infants, and Children program," Henrietta pointed out. The self-righteous certainty flickered briefly in Jane Simon's face. Henrietta dodged another blow by saying quickly,

"We've put the weight of taxes into war, oil, industry, and greed. Non-profits are just trying to rebalance the ship. We've gotta shift the money in our country into ending hunger and poverty; supporting healthcare and education; and protecting our environment. You ever been on a ship, Ms. Simon?" Henrietta didn't wait for the answer about private yachts and cruise lines, but said, "Any child knows we gotta keep the boat in balance. Can't put all the weight on one side and expect to stay upright."

Jane frowned. "It's not that simple."

But it was. The accumulated convolutions of congressional reasoning fell apart before the simplicity of taking care of one another.

"The tragedy of charity," Henrietta pointed out, "is that we all wish it weren't necessary in the first place. Like you said, don't we wish we could just buy an end to poverty? But we can't. We gotta fix the roots that grow the brambles of injustice. It's gonna take hard work, though. Folks spend a lot of time judging the poor for lacking work ethic, but no matter how hard the lowest class works, they're never gonna get as rich as the wealthiest in this country. The hard work has also got to come from the people that already have paid vacations, healthcare, and triple digit salaries. Our politicians and businessmen are gonna have to work harder at making economic and social justice. Only then is the need for charity gonna go away."

Henrietta shifted Jerome from her tired arm. Jane took advantage and pulled out a convenient never-failing tactic.

"Surely, Ms. Owens, you're not suggesting that we become," she let the silent drumroll thunder, " . . . *socialists!*"

There was no BOO & HISS sign, but the audience responded instantly. Jerome squirmed as if trying to crawl away. Henrietta didn't blame him. She held him close and tried to send a soothing message through her heartbeat.

"Socialists don't have a monopoly on human kindness," she answered softly, "and if capitalists ignore all forms of ethics, then, yeah, I'd rather be a socialist than sell my conscience to the devil."

Jane was quick in her attack.

"How capitalist of you to *sell* your conscience. As a good *socialist*," she smeared the word with scorn, "shouldn't you *give* it away?"

"No, Ms. Simon," Henrietta stated clearly, "socialists, capitalists, and communists alike need to *use* their consciences to feed the hungry, educate the people, wage peace instead of war, and keep our air and water clean."

Jane hid her scowl from the camera. She couldn't attack a holy high ground . . . at least not with pious Christians watching. First, you had to sell them on the concept of crusades, masking over 'invade and conquer' with words like 'convert and save', and never tell the truth of rape and pillage, genocide and famine. Jane leaned back in her chair and circled for an opening in the conversation. The baby caught her eye. Waving at his mother's pounding heart (he could hear the anxious butterflies flapping), he caught her blouse in his tiny fist.

"Look at the little tyke," Jane Simon cooed (she was an actress, after all). "He must take after his daddy, grabbing at a pretty lady."

The blow came out of nowhere. Henrietta staggered. The sign flashed LAUGH. The audience obeyed. Henrietta turned her gaze toward the darkened shapes . . . and Jane Simon grabbed her baby.

"Ah-ah-ah, you have to wait until you're older," she teased him.

LAUGH the sign said. Henrietta couldn't breathe. The instincts of the mother bear were raging in her body. She watched Jane's viper nails splay around Jerome's sides. Jane was hissing in a singsong,

"You're going to have to wait until you're married."

LAUGH. The sign said. Jane's scorn stung Henrietta like a sword's edge.

"Don't be like your daddy or you'll end up just like him, in-"

"That's enough." Henrietta blocked Jane's final word. She truncated the LAUGH sign. She held her hands out for her baby. The unspoken word *prison* hung between them both. Jane put Jerome on her lap and waved his hand at his worried mamma.

On the sidelines, Jane's director waved beseechingly at her: *too far Jane! The ratings!!!! Give the baby back!*

She ignored him. Blood was in her eyes. She'd walked in on the warpath. Victory hung on standby. The director tried to motion for an early commercial break, but Jane started singing,

"Rock-a-bye baby, in the treetop."

She began to toss him up and down in the age-old game.

"When the breeze blows, the cradle will rock," she cooed.

Jerome stared at the viper, mesmerized. Henrietta's heart jerked up and down with every toss. Her eyes watched the red nails that splayed out, not knowing which she feared the most: that they'd slip or that they'd stab. Jane stood up and tossed him higher.

"When the bough breaks," Jane sang.

The lullaby song made Henrietta's hackles start clanging like alarm bells.

" . . . the cradle will fall," Jane tossed him up, "and down will come-"

She dropped him.

Henrietta died and dived and caught him, horrified. Her heart hammered. Her mind rattled out rationalizations; Jane didn't mean to, it was an accident. Henrietta looked up from her crouching shock and turned to stone. There was no mistaking the sneer the camera angles couldn't catch. Henrietta stood. Jane looked away. The great actress mustered up some faux concern.

"Oopsy," she tittered, "I guess I'm not very good with children."

LAUGH the sign ordered, but no one did. Discomfort choked the humor from them all.

"No," Henrietta told her flatly, "you're not."

Thousands of mothers sent outraged emails to the network. Henrietta never knew it. The lighting guy gave Jane Simon an unflattering chin glare. Henrietta didn't notice. The director had a raging fit in the silence of the sidelines. Henrietta only knew that every person in that room had stood by silently doing nothing -NOTHING- as a woman dropped her baby on live television.

She knew with gripping clarity they'd do nothing when the schoolboys beat up her son. Nothing when the police abused him. Nothing when convictions stripped away his hopes.

Nothing when politicians robbed him of his rights or banks stole his wages or drugs took his mind. They would murder him by doing nothing.

The mass graves that dot our planet are miniscule when measured against the properly buried citizens who have done nothing. How can they rest in peace, or sleep in peace while still alive, when they stand by doing nothing as atrocities pass by like scenery on the roadside? A hundred thousand years of history's babies have been dropped into mass graves and the cruelly cooing murderers are but specks of dust compared to the mountain ranges of people who stood by doing nothing.

Henrietta drew a breath laden with the last breaths of all those who came before us. Their dying words gathered in her chest. The director signaled for an immediate commercial break. The technician held a one-man strike and kept the cameras rolling. Henrietta blazed the frozen studio with the fire in her eyes. Viewers in homes across the nation turned to stone, petrified with the feeling that *they* had let that baby fall. She spoke,

"I hope nothing fragile is ever in your hands; not a baby, not a life, nothing." Her disappointed fury shattered all the frozen listeners into bits. They cracked beneath the weight of failing her. They did not know they saw themselves, their babies, and their mothers, all in Henrietta.

Jane felt her inner signals flashing DANGER! She signaled for that commercial break like a dictator putting on a parade: distraction . . . NOW! The director lunged for his disobedient technician. The lighting guy stuck out his foot. Henrietta turned and burned a hole into Jane Simon. Jane felt a desert fire scorch her inside and sear her out. She burned red and blistered in the blaze that raged in Henrietta. Forget any notion of stars and stardom, Henrietta crackled with the burning intensity of the sun.

"The earth -our world-" the sun struggled for words in human language, "it's my baby in your hands. You're tossing up my baby -our baby- all of us."

Henrietta shuddered. Suddenly, sorrow eclipsed the anger of the sun. The viewers watched the shadow fall upon the baby, who whimpered in his mother's arms.

"Please," she whispered and the one word eroded them like water as her sorrow welled up within their cracks, "please . . . don't let our baby fall."

They felt it then: fragility. Theirs, hers, the Earth's, and the baby's as he hugged against his mother. In homes across the nation, mothers saw his eyes and tried to put a finger on the familiarity of the boy's expression. They'd seen it in their children. What was it? The grandmothers stared in dawning understanding: the children now are born with worry in their eyes.

"We can't let this baby fall," Henrietta repeated, "not this one. Not this time."

The lighting guy plunged them into blackout. The audience erupted. The APPLAUSE sign flicked on belatedly. The audio engineer did his best to strum the nation's syndicated heartstrings. Henrietta walked off in the blackout. Walked toward the green glowing EXIT sign. Walked through the night of the human soul. She walked without ever looking back.

CHAPTER TWENTY

. . . . .

Cowboy Astronauts

" . . . He's got the little bitty babies in His hands!
He's got the whole world in His hands!"

The closing song of the Jane Simon Show rang out. Jack and Sarah sat together on the couch, stunned. Jack blinked in disbelief at the audacity of the audio engineer's musical selection. Sarah's hands wrapped around the growing globe of her pregnancy. Her mouth hung open in an 'o'. Jack said,

"She's unbelievable."

There are rare instances, Jack conceded to himself, when a meteor hits the earth's atmosphere at exactly the right angle, and its shooting flair just keeps streaking across the sky. It flies on and on, leaving its shiny trail lingering on the horizon as eyes and hands point upward. Henrietta seemed to be one of these stars.

"It needed to be said and she said it," Jack shook his head at Henrietta's daring. Sarah looked at him with tears in her eyes and stammered,

"If it was our baby-" she couldn't finish the sentence.

Jack clicked off the commercial.

"What would Jane Simon be doing tossing you?" He glanced at Sarah's teary face and stroked the baby still safely

227

tucked inside her. "Don't worry, I'd catch you," he said.

His words sounded hollow, though he had meant them. His thoughts were packed with conundrums revolving around the problem of Henrietta Owens. He wondered how many corporate boardrooms were evaluating the threat of Henrietta's social message? How many American couches held similar conversations at this moment? How many news stations were calling to get her on the air? He and Sarah sat on the couch together, miles apart in thought. The inches between their bodies stretched across a family rift. Each held a tension toward the other, a physical form of unspoken grudges from their earlier arguments.

Sarah rubbed her bulging belly and wouldn't look at him while she spoke.

"Jack . . . I was thinking . . . I've been thinking . . . you may have been . . . well . . . you were right."

Jack blinked.

"I was?" Suspecting that he was about to come tumbling down from this tenuous throne of bewildered righteousness, he asked, "Um . . . what am I right about?"

"We have to stand up for our beliefs. We have to live a life of principle no matter what the cost. I mean there's Henrietta Owens who's got nothing -nothing! And is she playing it safe just to get by? No. She's risking life and limb and child to tell us that we have to take risks now to avert the inevitable disaster of our extinction."

Passion flushed into Sarah's cheeks. It took Jack back to the day they met; back when he was a Harvard MBA and she was a counter-culture radical who wore those thick-rimmed glasses that were so fashionable among the avant-garde. Her hair was in her eyes and Howard Zinn's *A People's History of the United States* in her hand.

Sparks flew. Jack had never had such an exhilarating top-of-his-lungs argument in his life. They spent four hours in the courtyard, skipping class to interject one more point on . . . he can't even remember what now. Politics? Social injustice? Corporate corruption? Something insignificant in comparison to the glinting blue eyes and dancing face surrounded by that meadow gold sheaf of hair. Not that he'd ignored her words. Oh no. Memory tries to romanticize the past, but he clearly remembered her stinging scorn and the fire she flashed in her lightning quick rebuttals of his arguments. He also remembered stoning her points with the boulders of the business world. The bricks of Harvard trembled. The ivy shivered on the vines. They parted ways with hearts and minds of one accord: each held the championship title for the most arrogant, conceited, self-righteous know-it-all the other had ever met.

She called him to apologize. He asked her if she wanted to go on a date. She refused and hung up on him. Jack's prayers and persistence paid off; the next semester, they shared a political science seminar. Jack wisely kept his mouth shut and nodded along with everything she said. After three weeks of watching her slash the great debaters of the class into tiny pieces, he eventually screwed up the courage to ask her to dinner again. This time, she accepted.

All these years later, Jack found himself showering her with a gaze of pure affection as she resurrected the passions of her youthful convictions, glowing with intensity and maturing pregnancy, as if the weight of cars and jobs and mortgages and five-year plans could all be annihilated in a single instant of illumination. And they can. Everything accumulated through our lives is shed at death, right down to our flaps of skin and stored up mucus and memories and fears. No one knows the journeys we depart on when we leave all our baggage on our deathbed. And very few dare to throw it all away at the halfway point of life with a shrug, thinking only; why did I wait so long?

From her earlier years of faith in freedom, when Sarah had owned a typewriter, a suitcase, and a ten-speed bicycle, she had slowly put on tons of suburban baggage; clothes, make-up, shoes, couches, comforters, feather mattresses, cars, computers, televisions, treadmills. She tied herself to imaginary roots by planting landscapes and remodeling kitchens and delving into home improvement projects. All the while, she felt herself drifting from her moorings like an empty boat at night, away from all her beliefs and loved ones, without any real sense of home.

Home is where the heart is, Sarah. Where is yours?

Here, she thought, and placed her hand upon her chest. All the other baggage piles up around you like shipments on a wharf. It comes. It goes. Even loved ones can drift off. Little girls grow up and sail away on their own adventures. Babes in wombs emerge to float in baskets through the rushes of the river of life. Even the man who bound himself to you with rings and vows and swore to orbit around the earth with you can disappear. Look at him. He sits far away on the couch. He smiles, but does it reach his eyes? Is he moving away from you? Or you from him? You're like two untethered astronauts drifting in the empty void of space.

Sarah's heart began to hammer. Since the night she had taken Allie to the story of the Great Turning, Sarah had felt the pressing force of change. Night after night, she'd tossed and turned in the throes of uncertainty. Tonight, Jack had turned on the TV to watch Henrietta's interview, and Sarah had sat down beside him, twisting her fingers nervously. She found herself praying that courage and guidance would come from Henrietta's words. She watched anxiously for an opening to this conversation, a moment in which to spill the secrets in her heart. She looked at Jack. Now! The moment was now. If she didn't reach out, they'd drift even further apart.

Sarah felt the wild workings of her heart. In desperation, she gathered her love up like a rope. With a rancher's flick of wrist, she threw her thoughts out into words, and prayed that she could lasso Jack.

"We have to do what we believe is right, Jack. How can we bring this new baby into a world that we know our lifestyle is destroying? How can we raise Allie up to believe *this*," and she gestured to the living room, the dining room, appliances, computers, two car garage, the family room, the guest bedroom, the baby's room, the mudroom, the second freezer, the playground swing set in the backyard, the dinosaur sized houses up and down the block, the highways, the rush hours, the commuters, the urban sprawl, the ravaged mountains, the shaved off forests, the blackened streams, the drought-ridden deserts, the forest fires, the melting ice caps, the warming oceans, the thinning atmosphere . . .

"How can we raise our children up to believe *this* is all okay? It's not okay! It's not!" she cried. Their house was suffocating her. She pushed panic down as it attacked. After all these years of endless worrying, she finally threw down the hammer of her heart and said, *ENOUGH!*

"I don't know how we do it, Jack, but we have to make a change; for Allie, for our baby, for us, for everyone. I don't know how.   Doesn't anyone have an owner's manual for instructions on shifting gears? Is anyone even looking for the manual? Even families like us, who have the means to change our lifestyles . . . we aren't even trying to do a single thing!"

An amazed and loving cowboy reeled her in.

"Whoa, whoa, Sarah, calm down. I'm with you here."

"You are?"

"Right here," Jack assured her.

"Jack," Sarah said as she wiped her face, "I'm sorry about what I said. You know, about being a man and going to work and all that. I was scared, Jack. And, I -I didn't react very well. But I've thinking . . . if you want to quit right now it's okay. We'll figure it all out somehow."

"Of course we will," Jack said confidently. From A to Z, from here to there, from now to then, they could plot a course of family action. Jack knew they could. He and Sarah had orbited this earth and spun around the sun a score of times together. They'd just pulled back from the terrifying gulf of drifting, lost, through outer space. It didn't matter that their too-large house was just a buffer against the void of unanswered questions. Their hands were linked again. Jack's heart was racing with excitement. He could leave Standard Coal and move on to cleaner horizons. He could find work that helped this world! Already he was drafting up his resignation. He could turn it in on Monday.

"Sarah?" he said. "It . . . well . . . it might be a little bumpy. We have to be realistic about things like money, Allie's education, the new baby," he trailed off as Sarah's smile sent them both back to the memory of Allie's unexpected arrival. Like an asteroid's collision, everything went topsy-turvy for a while. Sarah chuckled as she reminded him,

"I think our little Allie-gator is up for adventures anytime."

Jack snorted. That was true. If life threatened to stagnate with boredom, Allie set out to shake things up. Roller skates skidded down the basement stairs. Science projects exploded in the kitchen sink. She had even sent a battering ram shiver-me-timbering through the patio window once.

"I wonder if she'd like to farm," Jack mused.

"Oh Jack, don't be dramatic about post-apocalyptic utopian societies," Sarah began. Then she realized he wasn't joking. "Oh, uh, well, that would be an adventure." She started forming prayers for a gentler transition then shook her head. Screw it! They'd been born of pioneers and immigrants, the cast-offs of stagnant societies. They would join the cultural pioneers of the twenty-first century, not to conquer territory, but to reclaim the wasteland of their consumer culture and turn it back into fertile ground. A great adventure of social transformation was exactly what they -and their country- needed. The more radical the better! The quicker it came, the wilder it loomed; the more the spirit surged to meet it. Come on America, Sarah thought, let's meet this climate change challenge in a showdown. Global warming's already counting out the paces: one, two, three . . .

Jack and Sarah sat together on the couch, two cowboy-astronauts ready to blast off of this American suburban landscape into a frontier of change. Already the backdrop of home and place was fading. Already, thrill lit up their eyes. Their courage sprung to life like a dandelion of the soul. It poked its indomitable golden head up between the sidewalk cracks and beckoned like a symbol of revolution. The dandelion insurrection of suburban lawns had finally begun.

Jack and Sarah basked in thought until the unexpected asteroid called Allie crawled over the back of the couch.

"Dad?" She stretched out on the crocodile couch spine.

"Yes, Allie-gator?" Jack welcomed her into his and Sarah's closeness. Sarah smiled. He hadn't called his daughter that old nickname in a long time.

"I have to do a project for school about my two biggest heroes," Allie said.

"Mmm-hmm," he murmured. The problem called Henrietta Owens resurfaced in his mind, calling in all of the heroes. Allie continued,

"I was going to do it on John Henry."

Jack smiled. Excellent choice.

"Who's the other one?" he asked.

"Well, uh . . . I wasn't going to tell you in case you didn't like it."

"Spit it out." He steeled himself, hoping this wasn't headed where he was thinking. Please don't say Henriett-

"You."

Jack blinked. Lately, his life seemed to hit him with more unexpected asteroids than the Milky Way.

"Me?"

"I asked Mom. She said it was okay. She said you'd be an unexpected hero."

Sarah smiled at Jack's expression. She'd actually said there wouldn't be a more *unsuspecting* hero. But there's truth and then there's truth. We pick the one we like the most.

CHAPTER TWENTY-ONE

. . . . .

The S.O.S. Family

The prison officials decided to slide a wall of glass between them. Celebrity status separated Henrietta and Tyrell under the auspices of security. For whom or what? No one seemed to know. The only real threat, Henrietta sighed, were the guards with guns.

Tyrell's hands and forehead pressed up against the glass. A line of sorrow curved an S through both he and Henrietta's spines. His: an elongated standing S. Henrietta's: a sitting slumped down one. Two people bending to the letter of the system, weighed down by the way that sorrow strikes. Between them on the narrow counter perched their baby 'o', a prayer of opportunity for bending S's. Their bodies screamed an S.O.S., but there was no one but stony guards to read the Morse code of their lives.

"I'm done. I'm not doing any more interviews." Henrietta's voice struck dully at the words. Tyrell searched her downturned face for any sign of light or spark of heat. Nothing. The fire of her anger had long since died. He looked for her ever-burning streak of stubbornness, an orange ember he could always hold a scrap of kindling to and spark her back to life.

"Come on, Henri-"

"She *dropped* him, Tyrell. She looked me in the eyes and

dropped him."

Jerome slapped his palms against the glass. Tyrell tapped his fingers to meet the baby's.

"Henri, it wasn't very far. He would have bounced-"

"What?!" Henrietta's S curve of sorrow un-sprung her into standing. Tyrell jumped back. Gotta watch out when you're playing with fire, he thought. He cocked his head.

"Come on, you know I'm only teasing-" he tried to say. Henrietta glared furiously at him, wrapping her arms protectively around Jerome.

"Tyrell-" she choked. A thousand resentments burned and lodged inside her throat. There they stuck, a whole year's worth of *how could you's?* and *you weren't there's* and *don't tell me how to raise my son's!* Our son, she amended. She tried to swallow the thickness of the bitter words and spit them in his face, but she couldn't. They hurt too much. They pulled the corners of her mouth down and flooded up her eyes.

"Aw, Henri-"

Despite knowing the solidity of glass, Tyrell's hands leaped on faith to touch his family. Faith betrayed him with the cold repulsion of his warmth, but he kept his hand of truce up on the glass. Henrietta matched his palm with hers. They didn't move, and in their patience they felt their bodies' warmth meet through the wall. She leaned her forehead on the glass. Tyrell kissed it.

The guard harrumphed. Guards frowned on convicts kissing glass. Tyrell's jaw twitched. Glass, bars, walls, laws; a hundred obstacles between him and everything he loved. Sometimes, he thought these visits were allowed simply to ensure the inmates' good behavior. He turned back to Henrietta.

"Come on, Henri. It's going to work out alright. You just gotta trust."

"Tyrell, I don't trust anything these days," she sighed wearily.

"Is that true?" he asked.

"No," she sighed. She rallied for a scrap of hope. "I trust the sun is gonna rise. I trust Jerome is gonna love me. And I trust you."

"Why?" he asked. "Why do you trust me? I can't do anything to help you from in here." He gestured to the prison.

"You do what you can and you apologize for what you can't and you love me, Tyrell."

He smiled in gratitude for her faith.

"I trust you, too," he said.

"What is trust anyway?" she mused, staring off at concrete walls.

"Trust is a streak in the night of possibilities," Tyrell answered. "It's like a shooting star of a promise that might come true."

Henrietta laughed at him, "How'd you come up with such an idea?"

"I don't know. I thought about it."

Tyrell watched Jerome tug at Henrietta's belt and sighed. He had become a billionaire of time and he spent most of it on thought. His days oozed slowly by in muddy ponds of thought. He worked out and thought. He lay awake and thought. He pushed around the unappealing food and thought. He thought of his son and Henrietta until longing clenched him in the gut. Then he peeled back the clinging hand of yearning, finger by finger.

When night released his spirit to travel where it willed, he drifted in and out of thinking and dreaming. With darkness all around him, possibilities spread like galaxies and nebulae. He searched the dreamscapes that opened in him and found Henrietta dreaming, too. She dreamed he dreamed of her dream . . . and he had.

His days were filled with guards, so the night became his guardian. Here, he could cast the conniving minister called despair out of his inner realms. He built a fortress of trust up against the mounting injustices of his life.

A woman he loved.

A child.

A home.

A hope.

A life.

All shot through the heart one day, when he went to get a pen.

"What did you need a pen for?" the prosecutor had asked.

"My wife wanted one," he'd answered.

"You don't have a wife."

No, according to their records, he didn't. According to their accounting he had nothing: no money, no savings, no equity, no education, no insurance, no wife. And, according to their calculations, that added up to motivation for robbery.

Or so they thought.

He was a prince of all things immeasurable . . . what need

had he for robbery? He had the nourishment of love and the solace of the stars. He had contentment and joy overflowing his accounts. What more did a man ever need? You can't measure the nighttime sky. You cannot weigh its vastness. You cannot count the innumerable asteroids and Milky Ways that spread across the soul.

"Henri . . . " he said. The glass between them muffled his subtle tones of love. She looked up.

"Yeah, Tyrell?"

How old were those two lovers? Twenty-five, seventy, fifteen? Numbers and years struggled to hold their logic when confronted with those too-old, too-young eyes.

"I'm proud of you," he said.

Suddenly, time lost its grip. The too-old, too-young phenomenon reflected in them both and when their eyes met, time surrendered the stranglehold that propels our whole world forward. The ordered march of seconds-minutes-hours-days fell out of step. Like soldiers touching home soil, the ecstasy of release broke time into a thousand shooting fireworks flung like stars across the heavens.

Tyrell used the trick like magic up his sleeve. It fractured the lie of linear time into zigzags and spirals that went flying in seven directions all at once. With one look, Tyrell could sweep aside the weight of worry, sorrow, stress, and fear.

Henrietta, too, had ways to break the spells our world insists on casting. Before the days of glass and bars and separations built of concrete, she'd snuggle up and challenge him,

"Tell me where I stop and you begin."

His fingers would trace the lines and contours of their

touching skin, but love would start and lines would blur, and *he* and *she* would end. One day above their growing baby, she whispered, "*Now* tell me where you end." Never, nowhere, he had replied, and all their parents', parents' ancestors funneled through the present in the single point of the mother's womb, the empty place where all of life begins.

Time threw its hands up around these two and gave up all efforts to represent its true nature to other humans. You can't perceive time's magnitude with eyes and three dimensions. It will only show itself to lovers who won't confine it into lines. It will reveal its vastness to those who will break themselves apart to join it.

Time blessed them with this eternity of a moment, but neither Tyrell nor Henrietta knew the secret incantation that could part a wall of glass. Their hands rested on it, separated and lonely. Their baby placed his hands upon his mother's belly. His face screwed up, listening for the words of spells that can break through the barriers we begin to learn at birth.

Here's a hint, child: it's not a language. The way to pass through *that* and *thou* predates the use of words.

Jerome leaned against his mother, trying to remember the secrets he had known before his birth. Every day, his memory of them faded. By the time he could speak in words, he would have no recollection of the journey that brought his soul to earth through the portal of his mother. Henrietta would never know the reason he had come to join her family just as his father was torn away from them.

Can't you see, Mamma? he was saying silently. *I came to keep you company through this. I came to wake you up in the morning with my smile and to inspire you to song when your heart is breaking. I came because it was time for me to come. I could not wait another day. If I had, I would never have met my father even through a wall of glass. I would not have his eyes. I would not be here carrying half his genes outside of prison bars and delivering him hope that life is waiting beyond the concrete walls.*

But life wasn't waiting. It was racing by as Jerome stretched his vocal cords toward words and lost all memory of what he meant to say.

The guard cleared his throat (so as not to startle them) and then barked out, "Ten minutes," (which did) and then he stuffed all other expressions of compassion, guilt, and curiosity back within him. He was the keeper of the marching ranks of time, the guardian of well-ordered society. Had he known what secret weapons passed between the lovers' eyes or how close this little S.O.S. family was to walking through a solid wall, he would have handcuffed them immediately. Instead, he merely dragged time back into line, reinforced the notion of the wall of glass, and let them know that he -and his kind- were in charge of prisons of all sorts.

Henrietta knew this. She knew the prison never stopped. She knew the barbed wire wrapped around our courts of law and circled the heads of elected lawmakers. It wrapped its barbed wire crown of thorns around everything in our good Christian nation. There were fences round the schools, the lawns, the playgrounds; prisons in our lack of options, our dwindling rights, and mounting fears. Our only hope of freedom is to convince the guards to let us touch a little longer and love a little more.

"You heard that? Ten minutes," the guard warned them.

Time grumbled back into its place. Henrietta picked up Jerome. Tyrell continued where he had left off,

"I'm proud of you. No matter what you decide to do. I'm proud of all you've done. We all are."

"We? Who's we?" Henrietta asked.

Tyrell realized how far apart they were. His world of *we* had no immediate translation in her language.

"The men here. We watch you on television. Sometimes we hear the radio, too."

Tyrell thought of the day he'd wandered into the common room to find a pack of men nodding at every word his not-yet-wife was saying, sometimes breaking out in cheers more loudly than they did during the sports games.

"What is this?" he had asked the closest man.

"Shhhh."

The TV host had finished babbling. The camera focused in for Henrietta's response.

"Mountaintop removal is just one symptom of our national disease of not caring. Hunger, poverty, wealth inequities are all part of it. If your child goes to bed stuffed full, you've robbed the extra from another child who can't sleep because she's hungry. And it's not a question of charity . . . it's a nation-wide system of injustice."

Hooting erupted. Tyrell rubbed his eyes. What was Henrietta doing on TV? The room silenced as she continued,

"Right down our entire economic system we gotta trim off the fat of wealth with the same passion that we put into our personal appearances. We need a weight-loss plan, a healthy one, for the fattest pocketbooks in our country. Because you know what? It's going to kill them and all of us. We're one nation -one body- a whole body indivisible. And just as an over-growth of cancer is gonna weaken every other cell until the body dies, a mass of wealth among the very few is gonna destroy the vitality of us all."

"You tell them, girl!" shouted the man to Tyrell's left. His buddy leaned back and praised,

"Damn, she's sma-art!" he whistled the word into two syllables. Finally, someone remembered Tyrell's question,

"This is the third time we've caught this girl. We're scanning the listings to find out when she's on again. You won't believe the stuff she's saying. Just this little woman, name of Henri-"

Tyrell cut in, "I know. Henrietta Owens. That's my son up there in her arms."

Suddenly, Block 4 had a hero. Not an impersonal, long-ago folktale hero; not a hero of the masses that you only saw on television; not a hero who worked for a common good that did not quite include your situation. Oh no! She was *their* hero, the patron saint of Block 4. Her man was standing next to them. Her man was one of them.

It became a prison obsession. Everyone was chewing on Henrietta's words. Fights broke out over philosophic differences and nuances of the applications of her comments. Tyrell almost laughed. If the men in Washington in suits of gray would engage in these discussions, there wouldn't be so many men in prison arguing them in orange.

Tyrell occupied a special place on the altar of their saint. Despite his sadness that he could do so little, he was cast in the role of best supporting actor. They passed details of Henrietta's visits mouth-to-mouth until Tyrell heard the stories seventeenth hand and shook his head in disbelief. They worshipped her and him, and, most of all, their love. They prayed to all their other saints to have a love like that. They tried to figure out how to tell their wives, their babies, their families, *I'm sorry* and *I love you.*

Tyrell knew Henrietta wasn't a saint. She was a wonderful, incredible, courageous woman, but he also read those letters where she lay awake at night with worries all around and no one else but paper, pen, and thoughts of him to hold them off. He listened to her tell him about the times Jerome got sick or they got stranded without a ride. He gave her all he could. He squeezed support and strength and love through satellites and wires and the postal service and glass walls. Still he couldn't give her all he wanted. It pushed in him like a flood against a dam.

When she was caught by that photographer, fired from the cannon of the media, and shot across the attention of the nation, Tyrell had prayed for her. He prayed she wouldn't crash or get shot down by national security. He prayed that by some miracle she'd learn to fly.

But where could she fly to? Tyrell dreamed of Henrietta flying with Jerome, searching, searching, searching for a place to land, a safe place to come back down to earth. But our planet is filled with planes and ships and cars and satellites and cellphones. We can't escape the madness that washes over it.

The world has shrunk, crisscrossed by global connections that pull continental causes and effects tightly onto collision courses.

As he struggled to awaken from his dreaming, Tyrell would call out in sleep for the aid of angels. Henrietta was tired and falling and there was no safe place for her to land. "Come, catch her!" he would shout into the inky blackness. No one came and she tumbled like a shooting star as his voice echoed back, "Catch her!" and he dove, reaching, reaching, reaching-

"I wouldn't blame you if you packed up Jerome and went back to Ohio," he said gently as they sat divided by the wall of glass. She had done so much already, risked so much. He'd lunged with Henrietta on that primetime Jane Simon Show. He'd shot across the prison common room as that woman dropped his son. The guards jumped at the explosion of the usually calm Tyrell. His fellow inmates held him back from pounding in their only TV. No one said a word. Silence reigned in this room like every other in America. When Henrietta implicated all of them for letting her baby fall, Tyrell had dropped to his knees, destroyed.

He hadn't been there. He hadn't caught their baby. He hadn't. He couldn't.

That's when the jail convicted him and made a prisoner from a man. At night he dreamed unceasingly; he couldn't catch his falling family. Jail had thrown its shackles on his soul.

S.O.S. their bodies cried.

Save Our Ship, the guard eavesdropped.

No, no, dear guardian of time, your military logic has translated dots and dashes wrong.

S.O.S. means Save Our Souls. The ship is already sinking.

They sat rocking on this sinking ship. Tyrell told her quietly of how he watched all her interviews on TV. He touched the glass.

"I get to see you both that way," he said. She tapped it back,

"If they made this place a reality TV show, then I could watch you, too."

"They'd never do that in a jail."

"Too boring."

"No, too real."

Their eyes exchanged the timeless look of *we can't talk about it here*. The guardian of time looked at his watch and missed the secret message that they passed.

"Five minutes," he warned them. The price of wasted moments tripled. Tyrell hastened,

"Henri, if you did change your mind and kept doing the interviews . . . it would mean a lot. The guys in here, they've got nothing. Nobody cares what happens to us, what got us in here in the first place, or how we're going to stay out once we're released. Somebody has to say all the things you are. And we've got to make them listen."

He tried to grab her eyes to make time shatter long enough to explain his use of pronouns. *They* meant *we*, *us* meant *me*, and *the guys in here* included *him*. She was looking at the baby, growing so fast, so caught in time, such a victim of the forward march. The guard signaled for them to say goodbye. Tyrell plunged his heart through metaphors and imagination and reached for hers.

"Henrietta? If you did the shows, I'd get to see you more."

He found the secret language that traveled through the walls and touched her heart. The baby stared at his father, trying to decipher the workings of the spell.

"Time's up," the guard announced.

"Waaaaaaaiiiiiit!" the baby wailed.

"Shhh," his mother nudged him.

"I love you," his father said.

"I love you, too," his mother called as the guard motioned toward the door. The baby wailed again, trying to form the words to join the conversation; *I love you!*

Shhh, child, here's a secret: Daddy knows you love him. The cry of love predates the words of every human language in the world.

CHAPTER TWENTY-TWO

·····

The Efforts of An Appalachian Pugilist

Louisa begged her, "Every time you turn down an interview, an acre falls to the bulldozers."

Patrick reasoned with her, "We'll make precautions, stipulations, contracts."

Wanda volunteered herself as bodyguard, "I'd have knocked that woman's head off."

In the end, it was Hank who did the trick.

"Aw, screw 'em Henrietta, the whole national kit and caboodle. Say so long mountains, so long Earth, so long!" he teased the baby, "Say so long, Jerome . . . Dad will see you when you visit." Jerome laughed at Hank's expressions. He didn't understand a word of what Hank was implying.

Henrietta did. Beneath his self-mocking Appalachian demeanor, she recognized the bitter blue inside his eyes. Another chance drowned in the shithouse. Oh well, they'd keep on protesting like they always had. Nothing would change. The mountains would be leveled. Subdivisions would be raised. Everyone would toast progress and gulp down water in plastic bottles until there wasn't a drop left to drink. If global warming didn't kill them all, Tyrell would see his baby in ten years.

Tyrell would miss Jerome's toothless grin, though. He'd

miss the first steps, the first words. Ten years of firsts down the hole with everything else precious on the earth. So what? Hank steeled himself against the rising bitterness in his blood. Nothing ever changed.

An Appalachian boy and a black girl from the city locked eyes. Their biographies were trashed with broken promises and dreams. Their resumes read: survival. Their futures screamed out: uncertain. Hard determination etched lines into their faces. Stubbornness sparked the tenacious fuel that kept them going.

The gnarled branches of Hank's family tree were said to have been shined with luck. The family spent many late nights with empty stomachs and homemade moonshine, regaling each other beneath the stars, recounting close calls, near death encounters, and scrapes that should have scrapped them, but still the Crawley's came out on top. Or at least survived. Some luck, Hank scoffed, we get knocked down and get back up like a bunch of idiotic boxers who can't seem to get enough. Black eyes and broken noses were a family trait by now.

Aye, the Irish can sing their ballads and play them on the fiddle. Sad enough to break your heart, they are, but the Irish wouldn't know. They were born into such tough luck they had to die to stay alive . . . but even then the devil wouldn't take them . . . he just threw them back to life again.

Such is the luck of the Irish.

Hank was a battered, punched-up pugilist who simply had no concept of lying down. He'd fought the fights both good and bad as they crossed along his path. He learned to climb adversity like hollow slopes. He invented curses thick as trees.

He leapt or lumbered as he pleased. He met the dark eyes of Henrietta with the blue steel of his own.

Hank fought for the end of mountaintop removal with gritty determination. Coal was not a mineral to Hank, not fuel, a company, or a person. It was a force of supernatural persuasion, as devious as the devil. It charmed housewives with electrical convenience. It drove men mad with hints of riches. It destroyed the mountains that sat above it like a black demon breaking loose from Hell. It flew on air and poisoned lungs. It leached toxins everywhere and made monsters out of men.

But every now and then, this scrappy, red-haired survivor saw a chance at heaven open up. Once, he had drunken too much moonshine and a fight had laid him out. St. Peter's Gate swung open. He rose to enter. A fist knocked him back to earth. Another time, he thought he caught a glimpse of God working on a plan to bring his heaven down to earth. He sent his proposal before the U.S. Congress. It would take some sacrifices, God warned, and the politicians began to gripe. God rolled up his blueprints and flew back to heaven in a huff.

And that was that.

Then along came Henrietta Owens with an unwritten citizens' petition: we, the people, would like to have that bit of heaven here on earth.

The priests of coal screamed, "Sacrilege!"

Hank spat at those devil's servants.

The politicians cried, "Socialists!"

Hank put his fists together.

The coal company bribed a primetime gladiator.

Hank wouldn't let them win without a fight.

"Yep," he said to Henrietta, "Poor Tyrell. Of all of us, he's the one that loses."

It was a low blow and he knew it. Henrietta felt truth hit her gut.

Henri, she remembered Tyrell saying, *if you did keep doing interviews, it would mean a lot. I would get to see you then.*

"And good luck sleeping," Hank added a second blow to the first, "as you stand by and do nothing."

Henrietta glared defensively as he threw those words back in her face. His third blow struck came from that night around the revolutionary table,

"Never mind that you're the one who said, we risk dying just to live."

That seemed so childish to her now. How could she risk Jerome? How could she bear to brush him up with death again? How could she urge other mothers to take that chance as well? It wasn't worth it. She looked out at the sagging ridgelines, the scars of grey, the vanishing hills and forests. Her breath caught on coal dust even now. Jerome and all of history's latest batch of children were already breathing in their graves.

"Come on, Henrietta . . ." Hank pleaded. He had this one life to live and he had to give it all he got. "We're walking dead unless we try to live." He looked down at her weakest point. She felt the punch before he threw it.

"You can't save Jerome's life by trying to play it safe."

Something in her howled. Resentment burned her. Hank had ripped her last illusion down. In her cabin kitchen, she put her head down on her arm and started crying. Choking, frantic, gasping, angry, heartbroken, betrayed tears sobbed out of her.

There was no safe place that she could run to, no fall-out shelters, no secret islands. She could not build a fortress around her family. She could not believe in the buttresses of wealth or the buffer zone of power or the treaties of humanity's highest virtues. The entire world was a splitting ice flow in the spring. She could not run for higher ground. She could only leap over the most dangerous spots and try to catch her breath at a momentarily stable point.

And it wasn't just her. The ice flow was full of people and families just like hers. A Noah's Arc worth of Earth's flora and fauna were also striving to find a space. Meanwhile, at the far end, a handful of powerful idiots were drilling, mining, bombing, burning, and combusting the ice flows apart. Determination returned and grounded her. Certainty stuck her feet to slippery ice. There was no way out but through.

Hank held out his hand, a pact between two survivors who just had to keep on living, a lifeline in a lifetime in the ocean of despair. She took it. In two days, she was back on the air.

CHAPTER TWENTY-THREE

. . . . .

Odelle Jordan, Tightrope Walker

Henrietta waited for the ants to march across her back. Nothing. Her arm hairs lay flat and calm. She sniffed the air for premonitions. Nothing. She walked onto the set.

This time, the hostess beamed a golden smile, showered her with courtesy, complimented her on Jerome, and offered her a choice of seats.

"Ms. Owens, it's an honor and a pleasure to have you here with us today."

"Thank you." Jerome was fussy, squirming. Her hostess offered him a teething ring. Henrietta almost cried. Kindness and consideration should not be so rare in our culture, she thought.

"I have to admit," her hostess confided, "as my viewers already know, I'm brimming full of questions." She'd waited weeks to meet the famous Henrietta Owens. She'd thought Jane Simon had wrecked her chances. Ms. Owen's staff told her she was no longer giving interviews. (Ms. Owens staff was Wanda, who answered the phone whenever she felt like it.) Then, out of the blue, Henrietta returned the call.

"Please, if it is possible, I would like to come on the show."

Was it possible? If Odelle Jordan wanted a bridge to be built to China, her staff got out the maps. If Odelle asked for

radio connections to the moon, they fired up the rockets. If
Odelle wished to interview Dr. Martin Luther King Jr., her
staff prepared the séances to raise him from the dead. Odelle
was careful what she wished for. She asked Henrietta Owens if
she could fly up to New York this week.

For twenty years, Odelle Jordan had traversed the delicate
tightrope of the mainstream media as the network ringmaster
bellowed from below,

"Ladies and Gentlemen! Come see the greatest wonder in
the world: Mademoiselle Odelle Jordan, an African American,
descended from the Congo, great-great-great-grandchild of
escapees of enslavement, a living survivor of generations of cruel
oppression! Come see her thrive in the jungle of corporate
media, rising all the way to the top! Eh, heh," the Ringmaster
paused while Odelle Jordan seethed to be sensationalized
through stereotype, "Well, ah, not *all* the way to the top. Heh,
heh." The Ringmaster stroked his mustache and patted his
round little belly, confident in *his* arena, *his* big top, and *his*
ownership of everything.

Where would you be without your laboring Chinese
acrobats who bend over backwards and don't eat very much?
Odelle questioned silently. Or our Hispanics who set up the
tents and chairs and clean the stadium and fix the equipment
and then are treated like clowns the moment they step into the
arena? The Strong Man, the Fat Lady, and the Ones Who
Collect The Money are the only Anglo-Americans in this
circus. The freak-show is imported until it's out of style and
then shipped back to whatever country we can't pronounce
when a new hopeful batch of freaks arrive. And the blacks?

Odelle sighed. We're doing whatever we can simply to survive. Selling peanuts, managing the sideshows, chauffeuring the clown car, shoveling the elephant and donkey shit.

"And, Ladies and Gentlemen!" the Ringmaster cried, then dropped his voice to a conspiratorial whisper that could be heard across the stands, "Furthermore! Our tightrope master, black as night, sultry as the setting sun, is for the first time in the modern media arena . . . drumroll, please!" The spotlights swung . . . the Ringmaster drew in breath . . .

" . . . a woman!"

The music blared with pre-recorded cheering and the audience joined in. No one wondered why gender was the highlight of the show. They all assumed, like peanuts and cotton candy, that some things belonged in the three-ring circus, while others, like healthy snacks and moms, should stay at home. A woman who crossed into the spotlights was like bringing homework to the show . . . but sexier. Odelle Jordan tugged the bottoms of her sequined red-hot lace-trimmed bathing suit and stepped out onto the platform. From her narrow niche she waved. Her toes hung over the edges of her allocated platform: household issues, women's style, home improvements, and cooking.

Ah, but over the years, she'd learned . . . once she stepped onto the live wire there was little they could do to stop her. In fact, her swaying into women's rights filled everyone with delighted dread. A sudden direction change into social issues thrilled the spectators to no end. And, though every heart choked in their throats and beat in syncopation with the drumroll, when she back-flipped into politics the crowd would gasp and roar! When they could not get enough of her and kept returning to the circus, the Ringmaster grudgingly let her run her own act, choose her costumes, her music, her tricks . . . as long as everyone paid for their tickets and kept applauding.

Still, danger limited her options. She walked a tightrope between two abysses. On her left, deep, dark, and bottomless, were all the things that needed to be said . . . and on her right was the sharp and rocky chasm of the things that *could* be said. For twenty years she had paced the thin wire stretched between them.

No one walks the tightrope like a black woman, Odelle Jordan thought. No one else is trained by sheer necessity. She'd learned to juggle knives and swallow fire while a child in this circus. She'd done her share of sleights of hands and contortion acts. She'd been the target for the drunken sharpshooters. She'd been the ballerina on horseback, the stunt-girl on the elephant. She'd put her head in the tiger's mouth and withstood the lion's roar, but her truly greatest feat in all these years was keeping one toe-tip on survival. Odelle advocated for wider ropes, safety nets, and insurance, but the Ringmaster had refused them all.

"You're a tightrope walker," he thundered, "what do you need those for?"

"I'm just a person. I could fall. If it was your wife-"

"Heh. My wife's not crazy. Heh-heh!"

"Your wife has other options. Some of us must do insane acts to stay alive."

Around and around and around they'd fight in an on-going sideshow off the air. Odelle always worried about the future tightrope walkers, the young girls following in her footsteps; who, without her decades of experience, could wobble, miss a step, and fall. The Ringmaster worried about keeping up his profits. The thrills and constant danger raked in the customers. He didn't care about the expense of replacing acts. Day after day, Odelle would try to use the weight of her position to make him change until he'd finally lose his patience and yell,

"This is MY circus, MY big top, MY tent!!! If you don't like it . . . GET OUT!"

(Welcome to America, the Greatest Three Ring Big Top Circus in the World!)

Then Odelle Jordan saw Henrietta's photo on the magazine. Twenty years ago, this young woman's face had been her own, full of defiance, honesty, trust, suspicion, sorrow, and beauty all comingling. This was the young girl who came to take her place, Odelle realized. This was the next girl who ran the risk of falling to her death. This was the next woman who would wow the crowds and make them gasp and clap and scream. Odelle burned to get her on the show. She built a bonfire in her personnel.

"Forget the bridge to China. Forget text-messages to the moon. Get me Henrietta Owens!" Odelle Jordan, tightrope walker extraordinaire, had met her match. Out of devastated mountains and the shambles of a shattered life, Henrietta Owens somehow seemed to fly. She soared in and out of those great abysses of what-needed-to-be-said and the things-that-could-be-said without any sign of fear. Odelle, the tightrope walker without a safety net, longed to know this woman's secret. When the cameras rolled, she started there.

"So, Ms. Owens, you've been challenging the greatest issues of our country more courageously than a foreign war correspondent embedded in the trenches . . . what's your secret?"

Henrietta smiled, "I have no secrets. Secrets weigh you down and chain your soul to lies."

Ahh, the tightrope walker thought, that's the first step in learning how to fly. She leaned on the table like an old friend and commented,

"Honesty takes courage. I guess that's why so few people use it."

Henrietta laughed. She liked this Odelle Jordan.

"We got a real problem with honesty in our country, don't we?" Henrietta said. "We don't want to hear it and we don't want to speak it."

"That's for sure," Odelle and all her viewers relaxed into the camaraderie of the two women. "Can you imagine our politicians saying; well folks, we got a real climate change situation here and I think I'm gonna need your help."

The backflip was smooth and polished after all these years. Odelle made it look easy to address politics around the kitchen table. Henrietta suddenly realized that here was one person in the media who seemed ready to dive right in. She agreed,

"I'd like to hear a politician say that. It'd be nice to be truly included in the decision-makings of our country."

Odelle suggested, "I think our politicians are scared of us."

Henrietta set the squirming Jerome down at her feet,

"Well, that's foolish. If they're representing us, what are they afraid of?"

Odelle's chuckle shook her elbows off the table,

"That's the problem. They know they aren't doing the job we're paying them to do."

Henrietta rose and scooped Jerome up as he embarked on a great exploration of the set. The scene was so familiar to the viewers: mothers, babies, old friends, and kitchens. Henrietta bounced Jerome as she walked back, saying,

"If we worked at our jobs like they do, we'd get fired."

"Honey, if we needed a convoluted impeachment process to be fired, we'd all still be employed."

"With benefits," Henrietta grinned.

"And healthcare," Odelle added.

"Not to mention pension plans."

The women rolled their eyes. If elected officials were paid like average Joes, we'd have a different country on our hands. If average Joes were paid like politicians, well, we wouldn't have much to complain about in our kitchens with our friends. Henrietta paused and studied Odelle's patient, listening face. She thought the time had come to trust and said,

"I'd like to mention something that's been on my mind."

The tightrope walker gave her full attention.

"All this time I've been talking about the mountains, there's been a whole lot of gossip going on about where I work or don't work . . . as if a person's worth is measured in a paycheck." She bent her head and smiled at her baby, "What do you think, Jerome? You don't pay me to be your mamma. Does that mean I'm worth nothing?" His spreading smile spoke wordless volumes. Henrietta laughed and pinched his cheek. Odelle leaned across the table to mention,

"I think some people feel welfare is a drain upon our tax dollars."

Henrietta's snort jumped out before she could stop it.

"War's a bigger drain than welfare will ever be," she stated. "*All* the mothers in this country could go on welfare and it wouldn't add up to what we spend killing other mothers' babies . . . and our own."

Henrietta and Odelle both looked at Jerome as if suddenly seeing him blown apart. Henrietta broke the silence with a sigh,

"Yes, people are real concerned about me being on welfare. That'd be a very kind thing, if they were actually concerned about me . . ." her voice trailed off, but her expression finished the sentence *but they're not.*

"People have heard a lot of stories about mothers who keep having babies to get the welfare money to spend on drugs," Odelle said carefully.

"Yes, and some of those stories are true. But the rest of the men and women on welfare are like me. They've had some hard knocks in life. They're trying to get out of poverty, debt, maybe they're leaving abusive spouses, or facing addictions and illnesses, or trying to raise kids single handedly for whatever reasons. Welfare is a way of caring for people until they're in the position to take care of themselves. I think it's real sad that we look down on it so much."

"Maybe that disease of lack of caring is eating at our hearts," Odelle mentioned. Henrietta nodded,

"That's unfortunate, because if we're gonna keep this planet habitable for humans, we gonna have to *care* like never before."

Odelle sighed, "There's just so much to care about. I think we get tired of caring for all the problems in the world."

"That ain't gonna make them go away," Henrietta said frankly. She searched Odelle's face for a moment, and then decided the time had come to speak out.

"I've said all along that we're suffering from the disease of if-I-can't-see-it-I-don't-care and I've mentioned a number of aspects; the environment, wealth, health, but there's one more that's personal to me."

Henrietta found her hands shaking. It was easy to talk about justice for the mountains. They weren't her mountains. Ultimately, she knew she could leave them and move back to the city. But in those mountains was Tyrell. The prison that held him, held her. The mountains were a symbol to Henrietta of a whole range of unjust practices that tore apart the nation. She couldn't put them on her altar; they were too large for any altar but the Earth. So she moved to West Virginia and set her life upon the shoulders of those mountains. She became a symbol of the mountaintops, but beneath them lay another vein of problems. Henrietta took a deep breath and spoke out about the injustice that had hurt her most of all.

"There are over two million men and women in prison in this country. That's the highest incarceration rate in the world and most of those inmates are minorities. It ain't skin color that makes them criminals. It's prejudice."

She stopped for a moment. A hundred bitter accusations sat within her throat. She wanted to fling them arrow-like into the audience, pierce the listeners with her barbs of blame, but she knew her fury could never shoot through the vastness of the problem. Sadness took anger's place within her.

"No man was born to be a convict," Henrietta said softly, looking at her son and thinking of his father. Her thoughts raced through the arrest, the trial, the conviction, and the infuriating injustices she had seen through it all. She set her jaw and continued,

"There's only one thing that's gonna keep people from becoming criminals; not laws, police officers, imprisonment, or fines."

"What's that?" Odelle asked.

"Justice."

Across the nation, eager viewers choked. Justice?

"Justice keeps men out of prison," Henrietta said firmly. "Economic, social, racial, and educational justice."

In a jail room in West Virginia, Tyrell was surrounded by the heavy tension of a whole room hanging on her words. In the studio in New York, Odelle replied,

"Some of those convicts have done serious crimes."

"Yes," Henrietta agreed, "but some of them have done nothing at all. And all of them need our care and consideration. I believe crime is an indication of the way our society has failed its people, not the other way around. If you want to keep a man from doing wrong," Henrietta said, "don't throw him in a jail, cross your fingers and look the other way. That strategy never cooked a pot of beans. It won't keep crime down on our streets. We have to *care* for people."

In the jail in Appalachia, the men broke out in cheers. In New York, mutterings started in the audience. Odelle, ever the graceful tightrope walker, voiced them.

"Well, we all must make personal choices to stay out of trouble."

"Yes, ma'am," Henrietta acknowledged, "and we all must make personal and societal choices to keep other folks out of trouble, too." The suggestion implicated all of them; housewives, workers, lawyers, doctors, judges, police . . . everyone.

"We gotta be building opportunity and hope instead of jails," Henrietta said. "We've got serious worldwide climate issues and we're gonna need strong and healthy people that can work together to resolve them. And that means we've got to work on all levels of society to fix the problems that strip away people's options, incomes, homes, and families."

Miles away, the men in orange nodded approvingly, while the rest of the nation winced. Once again, the tightrope walker attempted a tricky balance.

"There are many who have been deeply hurt by the wrongs committed by others," Odelle pointed out.

Henrietta sighed. She knew. As much as anyone, she knew. This was the hardest part, where it gets hot and close and personal; where preachers have to practice, and walkers must walk their talk.

"There's this thing called forgiveness," Henrietta began. "It's like honesty. We got a problem with it. No one wants to give it, but we all expect to get it."

She thought of all the ways in which our country needed to change and all the people who would have to forgive each other if we were to accomplish all those changes. Henrietta, just like everyone else, had a list of the people who had wronged her.

She sighed,

"In the end, we got to take a leap of faith and forgive the other person." She shifted Jerome onto her other hip. "There are politicians and coal executives who are gonna have to do a complete turnaround for us to get out of this climate change mess. And you know what?"

"What?"

"There's no sense in locking some of our most brilliant businessmen up in jail. We're gonna need to forgive them, put their skills to good use, and move forward, together. "

"As long as they really are working for us," Odelle hesitated.

"We're in crisis," Henrietta pointed out. "We're gonna have to leap and pray. Forgiveness is real rough work, but we need it in order to move forward. I could say that to Jane Simon. Lord, I don't think what she did was right. But I'd rather forgive her now and see her start helping people instead of hurting them."

That last comment tripped the audience's buttons. They didn't want to forgive the evil gladiator. They wanted her to suffer. They wanted to lynch her in their emails, slander her across the kitchen table, and stone her for her viciousness. Eyes for eyes and teeth for teeth, the gladiator, herself, had trained them in such bloodlust.

But here was Henrietta Owens saying that wouldn't do. Saying punishments and prisons didn't change a thing. Saying justice began right here, right now, inside of her.

Odelle felt the rumblings in the audience. They had come for a good, safe, thrilling time, where no one would get hurt. This conversation was hitting too close to home. They wanted their money back.

Poised upon her tightrope without a safety net, Odelle hesitated. Every balanced step she took was merely dancing to the Ringmaster's tune. Every neatly executed backflip put a profit in his pocket, but didn't collect a penny for her safety nets. Yet, here was Henrietta Owens, plummeting toward the ground, daring to fall to the depths of the things that no one else was courageous enough to say, flying when everyone expected her to fall.

Henrietta looked up and met her gaze. The young mother's eyes burned with the suggestion; leap off that tightrope, Odelle, come on, you could truly fly . . .

Odelle glanced around. Sure, she'd be a real stellar act. Why, she could probably buy her own darn circus and put the safety nets under everyone. Her head reeled with possibilities. Viewers would go crazy for a blaze of scorching honesty in the primetime field of lies. If she could take them through both the darkest pits and the most exalted heights of this nation . . . Odelle's heart raced. Then she shuddered. What if she couldn't really fly? Henrietta hovered, waiting. Odelle balanced, uncertain. Then the tightrope walking woman breathed deep and prepared for a tricky set of turns.

"We've been talking about the differences between punishment and justice," Odelle summarized, bringing the audience's attention back. "We've got a lot of punishment and not much prevention, and where's the justice in that? It seems that Henrietta's saying we have to start to make the change in here."

She pointed to her heart and made it personal. She showed

them the nice pink platform, their own arenas of personal growth and families, the place from which she always started. Her viewers followed her with trust. If she would try it first, then maybe the nation would follow her into the realms that had no safety nets.

"I know I've got folks to forgive in my own life. My father's deceased now, but for years I didn't wish him a merry Christmas because he left us. I never sent him a Happy Birthday card, although I got them every year. Today, I'd like to take a little stab at that hard old thing we call forgiveness. Though we're still a couple of weeks away, I'd like to take this opportunity to say," she turned and looked directly at the camera, "Happy Father's Day, Dad."

The secret language of the heart cut through the camera lenses and TV screens and veils of life and death and even up to St. Peter's Gate to send that message to his soul.

Henrietta's baby began to cry.

He had felt the secret language and incantations happening. He, too, had many messages he wished to send his father. He yearned for words to speak them. Henrietta shushed him, surprised.

"He hardly ever cries," she apologized.

"Maybe he wants to wish his daddy happy Father's Day," Odelle suggested, knowing the man must be watching somewhere. Henrietta's face turned stony. In a jail hundreds of miles away Tyrell's heart clenched in his chest. He could see the sorrow push against the barriers of her eyes. She shook her head and answered softly,

"Ain't gonna be a happy day for us."

Henrietta's honesty cut Odelle's heart. Jerome wailed louder and hearts across the nation ached. Odelle stroked the baby's head,

"Come now, don't cry."

"Why not? He's got plenty to cry about. We all got plenty."

Henrietta spoke truth and only truth. In an Appalachian prison, faces grew into stony dams of unshed tears. It was not going to be a happy Father's Day for them. One crying baby multiplied into two million prisoners' own babies, children, wives, and families. A child who didn't know the word called grief cried out the flood inside them all.

The studio audience and the household listeners watched that baby wail and wondered how long the crying would continue. There were enough reasons for a thousand years. And when the past's sorrows had been wrung out, the future loomed full of woeful floodwaters. Ms. Odelle Jordan, tightrope walker, felt her line grow slick and wet. She felt she could no longer travel on that tightrope. The weight of all that must be said unbalanced her.

"I hate to hear a child cry," she said, "shhh, shhh."

"Odelle," Henrietta answered, "if we can't listen to this one baby crying . . . how are we gonna face the sorrow of our entire world?"

Odelle Jordan crouched into her soul. The drumroll flared a final time. Twin spotlights of integrity and compassion illuminated her. The Tightrope Walking Woman, Wonder of the Modern World, without knowing if she would fly or fall, leapt off the rope and said,

"Listen, viewers. This child's cry is the tip of the iceberg of what is killing us all. Behind his cry, you can hear seven billion other voices just like his -mine and yours and everyone that we love. Next week, we start listening to these cries and seeing what we can do to soothe them. Thank you and goodnight."

The Ringmaster tried to sue her. She walked out. The audience followed. Tightrope Walking Woman had leaped and learned to fly.

CHAPTER TWENTY-FOUR

· · · · ·

The Jungle of the Beasts

Jack was free. The realization struck him as he drove to work with his resignation in his briefcase. A smile curled across his face and his long fingers drummed the steering wheel.

Twenty years ago, he had sunk his teeth into the savage adventure of his job and relished the chance to play hard and fast. His daughter thought he worked in an office doing nothing? Hah! In truth, he walked the jungle of man's ferociousness. He ran with tigers, lions, and saber-toothed types of men. They were hierarchical and growly, quick to fight and domineering.

Jack had never lost sight of his frailty around them. They flashed claws and wealth. Power rippled their sleek coats. Jack, though quick and clever, wore only a man's bare skin beneath his tough facades. He built a frightening reputation among the ranks of businessmen, but underneath it all, he knew the softness of his flesh. He was a human hunter in the territory of beasts. He merely wished to cross their jungle and emerge out the other side unscathed.

For twenty years, Jack had watched his bosses and associates warily. In board meetings and corporate offices, Jack saw men who were no longer hunter, gatherer, or agrarian. Bread and meat were secondary to their craving for control. They drank the draught of power. They repelled empathy with great distaste. They found little nourishment in love.

Like a twilight hunter as the beasts came out, Jack moved with increasing caution as the years slid them into a savage darkness. His associates erased the bonds of brotherhood and broke connections with their origins. They turned blind eyes and deaf ears to the suffering their actions caused. The plight of the common man no longer bothered them. At times, it seemed they were not human anymore.

As a young man, convinced of his invincibility, Jack strode into the corporate jungle and learned to work for beasts. Back then he had been cocky, proud, and confident of his ability to keep his humanness intact. But now, Jack wondered if he was changing like the others. After all, he was the hunter for the beasts. He built the legal snares. His contracts flushed the birds from bushes, corralled the bison for easy slaughter, and set the traps for the unions, subcontractors, politicians, and bankers.

He tried to close his heart dispassionately, but, at night, eyes glared from the darkness of his dreams. Dead eyes. Accusing, tortured, starving, suffering eyes. The eyes of every person he had ever screwed to turn a percentage of a profit.

He would wake drenched in sweat. Quickly, he would clamp down on his conscience. He would go to work with the cold rationality of a scientist who, regrettably, must mutilate a thousand laboratory mice to serve humanity's need for knowledge. He summoned up the professional dispassion of a federally employed torturer, who, unfortunately, must do this gruesome work to save his country. He rallied the fortitude of a butcher in a slaughterhouse, who told himself that meat is necessary for the survival of humanity. Jack did not allow the screams and pleas and heaped up carcasses to touch him.

Or so he thought.

Like the torturer worshipping in church on Sunday, something in Jack whispered *mea culpa* and prayed for forgiveness of his actions. He knew his sins. They all knew. The cold-blooded butcher in the pool of animal blood surrounded by the screams of creatures in their death throws; the objective laboratory scientist disposing of mutilated mouse carcasses; the business-like torturer reducing men to whimpering flesh; and Jack. They all knew. No matter how deep they buried their compassion, it lurked in them like a time bomb waiting to go off. Jack had prayed that he would make it to retirement or death before compassion resurrected in his chest and crucified him with guilt. He had suppressed his feelings with more viciousness than he had ever directed at the anti-coal protesters. He put silk suits on his limbs and steel armor on his heart and went to work.

Today, however, he would be free of all that madness. Jack strode up the office steps and nodded cheerfully to the guard. He held the elevator door for the woman racing across the lobby. He stepped out of the elevator onto the eleventh floor with his resignation in his briefcase and his words to tender it in his throat-

"Dalton!!" the Captain roared. "Get in here!"

Jack threw his secretary a quick look. Alarm blanched Cathy's face. She shrugged. Jack followed Thomas Shipley, CEO of Standard Coal, into his office.

"I just got a call from Joe up in Washington," the boss said. "Pressure's mounting up there to address climate change."

"They can address it for a hundred years without doing anything," Jack replied carefully as he shut the office door behind him.

"There's a new crop on Capitol Hill this year," the Captain snarled, "green energy guys."

"Agitating, as usual," Jack shrugged. Good time to get out of here, he thought. His resignation was burning in his briefcase. He waited for his opening, alert beneath his outward casualness. The Captain wasn't reassured,

"Joe says the President's cooking up some legislation to switch energy subsidies to solar."

"Maybe we should put some solar panels on top of the stripped out mines," Jack joked. The Captain glared at him.

"Public Relations is working double-time, Jack," Shipley warned him in a low tone, "trying to put out the Henrietta Owens fire."

Jack glanced at a stack of publications on the Captain's desk: Henrietta Owens calling out the coal company, Henrietta Owens and the growing environmental movement, Henrietta Owens shaking hands with various politicians at a climate change conference in Washington last week, and, on top of it all, the disturbing quarterly report. The Captain snatched them up furiously and flung them back down on the desk. He stalked around the desk and ordered in a snarl,

"I want you to get that woman in your office. Make the terms precisely clear. I want her mouth shut or we will silence her once and for all. Do you understand?"

Jack stood still as stone. His words of resignation floundered in his throat. His blue eyes steadily met the Captain's furious gaze.

"Yes. I understand."

He would strike a deal with Henrietta Owens or she would end up dead.

CHAPTER TWENTY-FIVE

· · · · ·

Coal Under Pressure

Jack sent out a tightly worded invitation: *Ten o'clock. Tomorrow.* She sent back a short answer: *I'll be there.* No one else was on the invite. No coal executives, no organizers.

Jack rose before dawn and slipped into his gray suit. He drove to work in the eerie quiet of the city before it awakens. In his office, Jack stared dully out the skyscraper window, watching the world shift tiredly from gray to hazy reds.

He cracked the stiffness in his neck and tensed up his resolve. That girl would leave here silent. He would make sure of it. He snorted softly and wondered if Henrietta Owens would realize that he was trying to save her life.

But for what? he thought. Jack kicked gently at the carpet with his shiny shoes. She'd live. He'd live. The coal company would live. They'd all live another day on the countdown to extinction.

We're on the front lines of life and death, Jack thought grimly. The battlefield is all around us. He stared at the haze curling around the financial district. No one's getting out of this one alive, no matter what goes on today.

The sun hit the satellite dishes on top of the skyscrapers. Light scraped the rooftops and raked its fingers down the buildings' sides. Everything seemed weary today, dingily resisting sunrise's rosy efforts.

"John?" he heard his voice call. In broad daylight, with his secretary due to arrive at any moment, Jack pleaded with a dead man, "John? You know I have no choice. You know I have to do this." Jack's world was imploding inward. He clung to the desk. The room grew hazy in his eyes. He called out one more time,

"John?"

A hand grabbed his collar and threw him to the ground. The dust of men and tracks and tunnels choked him. Chains and iron filled his ears with clinks and thuds. Heavy beams of wood fell to the dirt. Gravel scraped against a hundred shovels. Jack glanced around at the sepia-toned swirl of stripes and swinging hammers. Steep mountain hillsides rose up on either side. He was drowning in a vision of the early railroad builders. John Henry stood above him. The hand that had thrown him down now pointed to an iron spike. John frowned against the sun. The air stilled in a silent challenge.

"Pick up the spike," John ordered. Jack felt his life was lying on the line. The other men watched from lidded eyes. Jack scrambled to his feet and hefted up the heavy pin.

"There," John Henry commanded. Jack set it in its place.

WHA-BAMM!

Everything exploded. Jack was sprawled upon the earth, hands stinging and ears ringing. John inspected the spike. He nodded once.

"Good. Again."

Jack obeyed. John boomed out one instruction,

"Watch your hands!"

The hammer swung. Jack yelped. The spike fell.

WHA-THUMP.

"No good," John spat. The spike lay bent and smashed. That would have been my hands, Jack thought. John reprimanded him,

"You let go too early. Again."

John Henry thrust the third spike in its place, grabbed Jack's hands and placed them. He swung up. Jack held his ground. The hammer flashed. Jack waited. It kissed the top of steel. Jack-

WHA-BAMM!

-let go just in time.

"Good," John praised him. "You see? It's all in the timing. You have to hold on just long enough." His eyes pinned Jack's and secrets passed between them. "Do you understand?" Jack nodded. "Good." John's chuckle grew. "We'll make a shaker of you yet."

Jack looked at the steel plunged into the rock. The men who held the pins bore the title *shakers.* Jack looked down at his hands and thought; good term . . . all you want to do is shake, but you're too afraid to move.

"I'd rather swing the hammer," Jack muttered. John's laugh swung out low and slow as he looked appraisingly at Jack.

"Maybe so," the steel-driver chuckled. "Maybe so."

Then he vanished. The dust, the spikes, the mountains, the railroad all disappeared as well. Jack's office was frozen in stillness. No one else had arrived at work. The morning sun streaked between the skyscrapers, but Jack's office remained in shadow. He sat down at his desk, heavy with the thought: *you have to hold on just long enough.*

*   *   *

Hours later, Jack gasped out of thought like a pearl diver resurfacing. He shook the reflective waters out of his hair and rubbed his face. He glanced at his watch. Nine fifty-five. Henrietta Owens was probably riding eleven stories up in the gold shining elevator and walking into the offices of Standard Coal . . . right . . . now. He looked out the glass panel through the offices. They were elegant and high-tempered. They had no room for nonsense and metaphor. Voices clipped on phones. Carpets soaked up conversations into appropriately murmuring hums. His secretary tapped politely and opened the door.

"Ms. Owens is here, sir," she informed him.

"Thank you, Cathy. Send her in."

Jack collected himself behind his desk. He laced his fingers together and perched his elbows on the armrests of his chair. He felt the habitual suit of armor clanking up around his soul. Gray steel hardened around his heart. His synapses started crackling like Olympic athletes warming up.

Jack began a rapid-fire assessment the moment she walked in the door. He coolly dispelled the glamour of the media with the truth that stood before him. She's young. Black. Good-looking enough. Strong lines. Poor. Jeans, belt, tucked-in blouse, flat shoes, short hair wiry on her scalp, a purse, no jewelry.

"Good morning, Mr. Dalton," she said.

Jack noted the courtesy. Noted that she did not say 'sir'. Noted that her civility was firm and proud and had the undertone of one who considered anything less than courtesy beneath her.

"Please, sit down. Where is your son?" Jack thought she brought him everywhere, like her purse, her heart, her soul. She looked at him and blinked.

"With a babysitter."

"You'll carry him into protests, but not into my office, huh?" Henrietta stared back, unsmiling.

"A baby crying in the middle of a protest ain't gonna keep that protest from carrying on. If you want to carry on a conversation in the quiet of your office . . . it better be about this protest, not my son." Her voice firmly put all things in their places. Jack smiled. There was her mettle; quick, sharp and protective of her child. He decided to test it and asked pryingly,

"How old are you, Ms. Owens?" He waited for a stinging retort, ready to measure up her prickliness. Her laughter leaped out to surprise him.

"Too old to look so young, and younger than I feel!"

Jack noted the wryness in her humor and the fearlessness that blasted through the open door of honesty. Interesting. He pried again,

"Where you from, Ms. Owens? You didn't grow up in this area, as I recall."

Her laughter stilled. Humor faded. Door shut.

"No. Ohio. But I live here now. How about you?"

"I grew up in New York City," he answered.

"Mmm. Gets cold up there. Can freeze your heart if you let it."

"Come, come, Ms. Owens, there are plenty of cold Southern hearts too."

She pursed her lips and shook her head, "No, now that's a little different. You ever take a dead hunk of meat from the freezer and let it sit on a hot kitchen counter too long?" She waited for his eyes to meet hers, pulling him into the question. "You know what happens?" She paused until Jack shook his head. "It rots." She let the allegory hang with the patience of a spider until Jack felt maggots crawling up his skin. She continued, "It's hard to heal a rotten heart. A cold one though? That just needs a little warmth."

He felt her checking the vital signs and status of his heart. He noticed his pulse kicked up a notch and quickly ordered it to cease and desist. He picked up a pen and held it briefly before placing it back down. He looked her in the eyes.

"Why are you here?" He laid out some bait.

"You wanted to see me." She sniffed it.

"I invited you to come speak with me," he tantalized, "because I believe there is something you wanted to say . . . "

Her breath paused a hanging beat. He enticed it,

" . . . about the mountains?"

She sensed a trap and pulled back quick.

"I think you know what we've got to say about those mountains. I think you know what people want-"

"Coal." He snapped her in the one-word trap. "They want coal, Ms. Owens, like a baby wants milk and tugs at mamma's breast. This country cries out for coal's convenient energy. You know what that's like, Ms. Owens, don't you? The plaintive cry? The knowledge that, without you, that baby's going to die? Your son-"

"-is at the baby-sitter's. Don't bring him in the room," she warned him clearly.

"I'm only calling on your understanding. We've got a nation full of people who need coal like mamma's milk."

She hooted and leaned back chuckling,

"We got a nation full of people that need to be weaned, that's what." An easy laugh slipped out while she shook her head. Henrietta looked at Jack with humor dancing in her eyes.

Jack froze. Across the desk, this *girl* in jeans and blouse, short hair and strong lines raised the hairs up on his arms. She could have spit that comment out like smoking poison and watched him jump away. Instead, she laughed, and suddenly you could not cast her as the villain in your story. Her laugh erased all lines drawn in the sand and walked through solid walls and dared to hold a festival in the middle of a battlefield.

For a man in Jack's position, it was more dangerous than guns. *Those* you could take away. Guns kept the enemy lines drawn clearly. Guns guaranteed the war games would continue. Jack could deal with guns and wars and lines. There were always victors. He always won.

Her dark eyes gazed clearly at him with unwavering conviction. She knew. Jack Dalton was not her enemy.

"Ms. Owens," he began. "Your position is tenuous."

"What position?" she replied. "Standard Coal ain't hired me to speak up for what's right."

"You could be paid to remain silent," Jack hinted.

"Like you?" She met his gaze firmly.

"I am a lawyer, Ms. Owens, I receive an honest salary to negotiate for the coal company."

"Ain't nothing honest about lying to yourself," she murmured softly.

"Ms. Owens, my employment is not the subject of today's meeting."

"Should be. You're the one who can do something about mountaintop removal. You receive an honest salary negotiating how to kill us all through climate change. *Your* position is tenuous, Mr. Dalton. All I'm doing is sitting in your office at your invitation."

"All you're doing is threatening the entire coal industry. You can't expect to be welcomed with open arms."

"Why not? Their babies are breathing coal dust just like mine."

"That's not how they see it," Jack snapped.

"How do they see it?" Henrietta asked, pinning him with her eyes. She wanted honesty. Well, he'd deliver.

"They don't see it," Jack said.

"Are they blind? Or just hiding their heads under the pillow?"

"Neither. They don't want to see it, so they don't."

Henrietta gave him a scornful look.

"They got their heads under the pillow," she decided. Then she shrugged, "Climate change is gonna whack their asses right along with everybody else's. And they got bigger assets," she joked.

"They, unlike you, have the power and ability to protect

their assets," Jack informed her harshly, "which is why you're in my office today."

Henrietta laughed, unworried.

"I'm threatening their assets? That's the best news I've heard all week."

"Ms. Owens, if you understood the position you are in-"

"What's that, Jack Dalton?" she cut off his hint.

"I'd wager you've got a few assets that are dear to you, Henrietta Owens. Quite a few." Jack froze her with his unflinching eyes. He drew no quarter. He gave her a dose of her own scathing honesty. "Your life . . . your son's life . . . your mother's life."

Henrietta's face went impassive. Jack drew a mask of impenetrability over his own. They searched each other for weak points. Nothing. Without blinking, she said softly,

"I don't think you ought to be threatening me."

"I'm not. I'm warning you."

"What do you expect me to do?"

"Go on vacation," Jack suggested. "Quit doing interviews."

Henrietta leaned back in her chair. She turned her head and looked out the window. Her lips pressed firmly together and her arms crossed her chest. Jack stayed like stone. He could see thoughts racing behind her eyes. He let her think, but he also didn't budge. She knew he was watching her. He kept the pressure of scrutiny on. Without looking at him, she said,

"Do you know what happens to coal under pressure?"

"I'm aware," he replied.

"Diamonds," she answered anyway, gazing out the window as if she could see something glinting on the horizon. "Don't push me, Jack Dalton, or you'll end up dealing with the hardest substance in the world."

She said it sadly though, and her focus on the skyline took on a tone of longing, as if she were saying farewell to a hundred thousand facets of life itself. She turned back to Jack.

"I promise you this," she said, ringing with certainty, her body tensed and leaning forward, "if you harm me or my baby, you will never -*never*- come out of this unscathed."

Jack clenched down on the shiver that ran up his spine. She spoke again, utter surety lacing her tone,

"There's a resurrection of the human heart going on in this country," she warned him, "and there ain't nothing you can do to stop it. Now, I ain't got my sights set on martyrdom, but if you try to crucify me or my baby, the hearts of this nation are gonna rise up against you and everything you represent."

Jack knew beyond a doubt that there was nothing he could say to alter Henrietta's course. She saw the sweeping movements of this nation as clearly as he. The coal company represented a seawall of enormous proportions, but walls could not turn back the strongest tides. They crumbled. The swells churned over them. Henrietta sensed the tide was turning; even if she was swept under it, the wave of change was racing forward.

Still . . .

"Just be quiet for a little while," Jack suggested softly.

"No."

"One week, that's all."

"No."

"They will come after you."

"It won't matter," Henrietta said.

"To your son it will."

"Exactly."

Henrietta's hands were on the desk. She rose. He followed suit. They stood as mirrors of each other's postures. In her eyes, Jack saw the moment that would one day come, when our children look back on us and judge us for our actions. Her son was John Henry's son, and all the children of our fallen heroes who asked; did their parents die for nothing? Her eyes were John Henry's eyes answering; *Jack Dalton, it all depends on you.*

"What do you want?" Jack asked sharply.

"I want your help," she told him, simply. "I want you to switch this company's policies. I want you to shift corporate focus and lean on your politicians. I want you to end mountaintop removal and get this company producing renewable energy."

Jack blinked.

"I could sooner turn the Titanic," he replied.

She laughed again, her mahogany skin stretching into creases as her eyes pinned his. "I've just run up from the boiler room. You already hit the iceberg. Coal's over. All I'm asking you to do is get this company -and our country- off this ship."

Then it was Jack's turn to laugh because there was nothing else to say. They couldn't -wouldn't- do it. Never in a million years. Not even to save their lives. They were ostriches with their heads stuck in the sand as the ocean flooded up around them. They were dinosaurs complacently munching breakfast while an asteroid hurtled toward them. They were capitalist American businessmen who refused to believe they were causing climate change.

Henrietta frowned at his levity.

"Extinction is not particularly funny," she said.

"No," Jack agreed, "it's the worst calamity mankind will ever face."

"Then why are you laughing?" she asked him.

"Because there's nothing to laugh about and-"

"-that's when you need to laugh the most," she finished.

Their eyes met in a moment of understanding that startled them both. Jack broke her gaze and turned to his desk. He picked up the pen again and tapped it three times on the ink blotter before admitting with regret,

"I'm sorry, Ms. Owens. I'm afraid there's nothing I can do to help you."

"Oh, I'm certain there's plenty you *can* do to help us. You simply won't do it."

"I'm sorry," he repeated, sincerely.

"You should be."

She stood silently for a moment and let her words sink in. The quiet hung around them and a subtle hum rose up from the city down below. Both wondered if this might be the sink or swim moment of the human species. The tragedy of failure loomed. Neither wanted to accept it. Henrietta looked at Jack and thought he looked old. Jack looked at Henrietta and shook his head at her youth. Henrietta seemed to catch a flash of his thoughts for she sighed and studied her hands. When she looked up, a shudder snapped through Jack. Something in her coal-dark eyes bespoke the millenniums of plate tectonics and galaxy formations and weighed his choices on the scale of eons.

"There's a little list in the world of heroes and villains," she said quietly. "A lot of people have got you on the villains' side, but not me. You're right in the middle. I thought maybe if I came and met you face to face, you might understand the scorecard of the universe. No man should be written down as a villain unless he understands he had a chance, and always has a chance, to be a hero. So . . . now you know."

She turned toward the door and he stepped out from behind the desk, not believing what he was hearing. Not the meaning of the words -that he knew. It was her tone of graciousness that stunned him, like she was throwing *him* a lifeline.

"You came all the way here to tell me that?" Jack folded his arms across his chest with the glinting cityscape stretched behind him in the window.

"Yes," she said.

And that was it. They were done. Henrietta hitched her purse strap higher on her narrow shoulder. She stepped away from his desk and turned back. Her eyes lingered on his family's photos and suddenly widened. She nodded toward them,

"That your daughter?"

"Yes."

Henrietta smiled.

"Nice kid. Real nice kid." She struggled to hold back laughter, remembering the girl who'd run forward on the night of the Great Turning. Henrietta looked back up and told him,

"You got a family just like me. Remember, that family's gonna have a family too, someday, and you're not gonna be here to look after them. Don't leave your daughter's babies in a mess they can't survive. I wouldn't wish that on anyone."

She meant it too, Jack realized. He walked her out the office door and shook her hand. Then, he closed the door and wondered why he felt like he'd been run over by a freight train and pounded through with solid steel.

CHAPTER TWENTY-SIX

. . . . .

Tyrell's Pen

The door shut and Henrietta lost her temper. She stormed through the rows of cubicles. Papers blew from desks. Computer screens blipped a brief electronic hiccup. She was tempted to kick the office door, but the secretary scurried past and held it open as if expecting such a farewell gesture from an angry black mother. Receptionists are good at putting labels on things, Henrietta fumed. Filing and categorizing is what they're paid to do.

"Thank you," Henrietta said as civilly as she could manage. The receptionist dropped her sticky-note description. Henrietta kept on walking.

She resisted the temptation to slam the elevator open. It slid back and forth with mechanical control. Henrietta seethed until the fifth floor, where she slid her fury back within her as two businessmen took an early lunch. Five *bings* of suspended silence passed. Three lives hung on hold until they reached the ground. The men walked out without a memory of the woman in the corner. They took a taxi to their luncheon, loudly spewing memo phrases of "budget crises" and "cutting public spending". They had never waited for a city bus.

The bus was late and old and crowded. Henrietta hadn't

cooled off at all. She had just had her life, her mamma's life, and her baby's life threatened. She had gotten an offer to keep them all safe and she'd refused it. Was she out of her mind? Her mamma's warning screamed,

"Ain't nobody messing around out there . . . They will roll their bulldozers over you . . ."

"Stop that," she whispered to her face that was now hiding in her hands. She lifted up her head and assumed the armored mask women wear to protect a raw and hurting heart. What had she just done? Beneath her unblinking frown, hope and truth waged a battle for her heart. Like a good American reporter, she tried to suppress the news of all-out warfare, but bitterness twisted over her expression as the city bus carried her further from the sky-rise offices of Standard Coal. She stared out the window as she retraced the chain of events that had led her to this moment.

There was that photographer who had pinned a bull's eye on her forehead. But then, there was Hank dragging her to that protest with Jerome in her arms. But she was the one who had decided to move to West Virginia. Why? Well, Tyrell was in prison there.

Henrietta sighed. Before that, there were memories of the two of them, young and in love, without a thought toward the future of even themselves, let alone humanity. How long ago was that? Two years. Not even two years.

Henrietta stared at her own reflection in the window. She traced the lines of her face, cool and hard in the windowpane. Oh, Henrietta, she moaned to herself, if you had only known back then on that starry night up in the mountains. That's where this all began.

She leaned her head against the glass and thought of the last time she'd seen Tyrell, leaning against the glass in prison. There was no warmth slowly reaching through to meet her now. Henrietta tucked her knees up to her chin. The bus idled at a light. When she so yearned for him beside her, Tyrell was stuck in prison, paying ten years for allegedly robbing a grocery store.

*   *   *

"Henrietta, love," Tyrell had said, "let's go see the stars." Just like that, with the freedom that she loved him for, they had climbed into their beat-up survivor of a car and left the sweltering summer of the city behind them in the sunset. He didn't take a map. He took the eastbound routes out of Ohio and followed the signs for the National Forest. Night swung its canopy over them as they crossed the border into West Virginia. The road narrowed and started curling around itself. The trees bowed over them, dark shapes against the darker sky. Clouds and full moons graciously cooperated by staying far away and the stars streaked like a river over the road. An unexpected field opened to their left and Tyrell pulled off onto the shoulder.

"Come on," he told the skeptical Henrietta. She slid her toes through her flip-flops and he twined his fingers through hers. "City-girl," he teased. He stretched the barbed wire of the fence apart and slid between.

"Tyrell! This ain't our property."

"Of course it is. It's government property. We, the people,

own it."

"Then who are they keeping out with that barbed wire? Canadians?"

"No, silly, they're keeping the cows in." He held his hand through the fence and she reluctantly followed.

"Cows? You want me to watch the stars with a bunch of cows? Probably gonna lay down in some cow dung," she grumbled, feeling her way through the grass with the tip of her flip-flop. The darkness pressed up against them. Tyrell pulled her close to him.

"Look up!" he breathed. She tipped her head back against his throat. He tilted back his chin and laid it on her curls. The stream of milky pinprick lights glinted and whispered at them. The mysteries of the heavens illuminated in silver ink, an inverted tattoo on the black skin of the sky. The jewel mine of the galaxies stretched above them, and its beauty stole Henrietta's breath away. She trembled beneath them. Age and distance and scientific explanations of the speed of light were erased from the chalkboard of the nighttime sky. Myth and mystery scrawled their poetic handwriting across the cosmos. The verses hummed and echoed in their human bodies.

"It's the love-song of the whole universe, Tyrell," Henrietta sighed, "I wish we could write it down."

He stroked her arms. The love-song of the universe is as infinite as the stars. Two lovers spend their whole lives singing variations on its melody. The warmth of two bodies in a sea of dew-dripping grass was the verse they sang through that night. In the morning, sun stroked them as they woke. The tall grasses were rolled down around them and they were soaked with dew and loving. Henrietta scratched ruefully at her bug bites.

"Mosquitos robbed my blood."

"Can't blame them," Tyrell laughed. "They'll die in sweet ecstasy, telling their buddies they've sipped from a goddess."

"We better get outta this field before those blood-thirsty worshippers come back then!" She pulled Tyrell to his feet.

"Maybe we should just stay. We could live on raspberries and moonbeams," he joked.

"Easy for you to say. Ain't no hordes of mosquitos after your god-head."

"Nope. I'm not so sweet as you." He kissed her to inflame the jealousies of mosquitos.

In the end, a bull chased them out of that field, suspicious and ornery. Henrietta lunged through the fence the minute he bellowed out from the other end of the meadow, but Tyrell took his time, teasing and hollering back at the bull.

"Tyrell! Get out of there, you fool!" Henrietta yelled at him. Then the bull charged and Tyrell came racing across the field, taking the fence in a flying leap while the bull skidded to a stop and Henrietta dove behind the car. She scolded him all the way down to the gas station for his craziness, but she didn't mean any of it and he knew it. He jogged elatedly to the grocery store across the street while she filled the car at the gas station.

"I'll get us some breakfast!" he yelled.

"I thought you were gonna live on raspberries and moonbeams!" she called back.

"Sweet love, write down the love-song of the universe and

I'll eat nothing but its nectar for a thousand years."

"Get me a pen then!" she laughed at him.

He loped into the store. Two minutes later, a second black man entered. Ten minutes after that, cop cars surrounded the market. The robber went out the loading dock. Tyrell came out the front doors in handcuffs.

*   *   *

The memory ached in Henrietta as the city bus rolled into the downtown terminal. She wove through the throngs of people and climbed onto the regional bus that went through the rural routes and up to No Man's Holler. The rumbling dinosaur of transportation pulled away from the station, chugging through the low-income areas of the city.

Henrietta's lips curled into a grim smile as she watched the skyscrapers shrink in stature. The news reports had called her an unwed mother. I have a husband, Henrietta thought, we just didn't have a chance to marry. After his conviction, Tyrell told her to sell the engagement rings. *Pay your rent and feed Jerome,* he wrote, *you know it doesn't change our hearts.* Henrietta sold the car, then the computer, then the TV, and finally, when the lights went off, she sold the rings to bring back electricity to her apartment.

I'm working now, he wrote her from the prison. *They've got programs. I make pens and office supplies. Half my wages go to the court debts. The other half I'll send to you. It isn't much. I'm sorry.*

They paid him twenty-three cents an hour.

As the bus shot out of the city, an image from Jack Dalton's office hit Henrietta between the eyes. She started laughing. Humor is so intimate, so personal. It knows us so completely, gets close in ways a lover only dreams of. A woman across the aisle frowned; what did that girl have to laugh about? Nothing, Henrietta thought, nothing . . . but that's when you're gonna need to laugh the most.

In his fingers, Jack Dalton had been twirling a pen Tyrell had made.

CHAPTER TWENTY-SEVEN

. . . . .

The Hammer

That night, it seemed the whole world slept except for Jack. Upstairs, Sarah and Allie traveled through the dreamscapes while their bodies slumbered above his head. The kitchen light rubbed raw against his tired eyes. The microwave clock glared an ugly black and red eleven fifty-one. Jack wearily told himself to go to bed. Tomorrow he had to put on his suit and tie, go to work, and deal with the problem called Henrietta Owens.

But Henrietta Owens was not the problem. Getting rid of her was just a band-aid on a festering wound. Once Henrietta Owens was gone, someone else would appear to threaten the vital statistics of the coal company's profits, and the same patterns of life and death would play out all over again. The entire system had to change to stop the real root of the problem called Henrietta Owens.

Jack laughed at the irony. It would take a well-placed corporate bomb to catalyze the series of reactions necessary to transform business, politics, and culture all at once, but the people who knew exactly where to place the bomb would never do it. They had too much invested to move against the spider web agreements of the power elite. Yet, could an activist ever understand the intricacies of the high-level business world?

Jack ran his hands through his wheat-stubble hair. He

sighed and rubbed his aching eyes. He wearily got to his feet and turned toward the stairs to the bedroom.

Then, it hit him. A crazy notion started racing through his mind. He shook his head in disbelief.

"No. Yes. It might work. I need -no, I can't do that," Jack raved madly, pacing back and forth on the hardwood kitchen floor. He skidded to a halt as a thought struck him. He frowned and discarded it. He resumed pacing. The thought returned, insistent. Jack paused, uncertain. He crossed the room and hesitated. He lifted up the phone and froze. Finally, he dialed an old, old number from the basement of his memory. The clock flipped to midnight.

Brrrinng . . . she wouldn't be awake.

Brrrinng . . . but somehow he felt she was.

Brrrinng . . . he looked out the kitchen window.

Brrrinng . . . the moon was full. She'd be awake.

"Hello?" her voice answered through the dark.

"Louisa?" he replied. He sternly told his pulsing blood to quiet down.

Silence. Then, reluctantly, she spoke his name.

"Jack Dalton?"

A quarter century of animosity and rocky friendship sprung up out of the graveyards of the past, shaking off the dirt of six years of bitter silence. He could hear the distance grow between the receiver and her ear.

"Don't hang up!" His voice hurdled over hesitation by sheer necessity. She made no answer, but he heard her breath and knew he had a fraction of a chance.

"Sarah's alright, isn't she?" Louisa's words slid out

reluctantly, surrounded by the quagmire of lost friendship and the broken glass of blame. Jack could almost see the shards pointing at him.

"She's fine. She's pregnant with our second child."

"Congratulations," Louisa said. Jack winced at the strange tone in her voice. He remembered the stern convictions of Sarah's environmentalist roommate who couldn't stand her best friend's love for a *businessman*. He remembered, even now, the venom of scorn Louisa had laced him with. He remembered the years of Sarah's diplomatic negotiations that left her exhausted, in tears, and having to decide between her husband and her best friend. It had been a long time since he or Sarah had socialized with Louisa, which was just as well, since he knew from company reports that she had become active in fighting mountaintop removal.

"How are you?" the polite question slipped out stupidly from him.

"Fine."

He could tell she didn't want to talk to him.

"Why are you calling me at midnight?" she asked.

"I need some help."

"Go call your lawyer," she told him coolly, "or your accountant or your CEO buddies or your personal politicians or your paid police or god-knows-who you keep in your deck of power playing cards."

"They don't understand this."

"Call your therapist."

This wasn't going well. Still, Jack persevered with determination. Things could be worse, she-

She hung up.

Jack's exasperation exploded. He swore and shook his head. He set the phone down and started to redial her number.

Brrr-

He answered halfway through the first ring.

"Louisa?"

"Who else calls at midnight?"

"Why did you call me back?"

"I've got some things to say to you."

Oh god, he thought, and steeled himself for her tirade as the dam of silence burst. She let loose years' worth of unspoken criticisms. She hammered him with every personal, political, and professionally unkind, insensitive, and unconscious act he'd ever done. It stung him more than ever before. He counted how many times he found himself agreeing with her scathing indictments. He caught himself nodding along with her terrible assessments of his character. He truncated defensiveness mid-heartbeat and listened as he watched the microwave clock turn its digital numbers over, one by one. At twelve twenty-two, she stopped.

"Are you still there?"

"Barely. I'm half-dead, I think."

"Good. What's the other half doing?"

"Uh," Jack winced in a moment of truth, "agreeing with you." He took a little comfort in the stunned silence on the other end. Then her distrust sprang back into action.

"What did you call me for?"

"I told you, I need some help. I need a general systems theorist -and not just a half-rate one," he interjected before she could tell him to go hire one. He needed the most intelligent one he knew. He tried not to tinge his honesty with bitterness. He swallowed the sting of regret. "I'm at a crux, Louisa."

"You sure are, buddy," she spat the word out with no endearment in her term. "If you're finally figuring out the bastardly things *you* have been doing to the rest of humanity, I doubt you'll ever sleep at night again."

He sighed, "Louisa, for someone who preaches compassion and loving-kindness, you sure can be a bitch." He could hear her muffled squeak of outrage. He shook his head at the old dynamics that flared up between them. "I'm sorry. I shouldn't have said that."

"Why not? It was true," she admitted, but she didn't apologize for her earlier words. "You ever hear of tough love?"

"Is that what you've been giving me all these years?"

"No, that was intense dislike for corrupting Sarah under the auspices of love."

"But I do love Sarah."

"I know . . . I know," and he heard her halfway forgiveness come creeping out of hiding. "Jack, I'm giving you a dose of tough love because you deserve it."

"Yeah, I've been a dick."

"No, you've only been half a dick. The other half of you is heart-felt, sincere, noble, and truly cares about people. That's what deserves some tough love."

"I'm at my mid-life crisis, Louisa. There's a hope I'll swing toward improvement."

"Yeah," she sighed, "there's always that hope. I guess that's why I called you back. What do you need help with?"

"It has to be completely confidential."

"Does this project have anything to do with Henrietta Owens?"

Jack answered carefully, "Of course it has to do with Henrietta . . . and everyone else; you, Sarah, Allie-"

"Allie's getting tall," Louisa commented.

"You've seen her?!" Jack blurted out.

Silence.

"Louisa . . . " Jack growled.

"I saw her the other night with Sarah. She didn't tell you?"

Jack said nothing.

"Sarah brought Allie to one of our events," Louisa confessed.

"That would explain why Henrietta Owens recognized my daughter's photo in my office," Jack muttered.

"Henrietta was in your office!?"

Jack cleared his throat, "She didn't tell you?"

"She had to fly up to New York for another interview."

Well, Jack certainly wasn't going to tell Louisa the contents of their meeting.

"Look, Louisa, let's stay on topic and not walk into any interpersonal landmines. You talk to Henrietta and I'll talk to Sarah, and no hard feelings about being left out of the loop, alright?"

She was silent.

"Louisa, think of the position I'm in. Don't you see?"

She did. She saw the possibilities. Jack Dalton, chief lawyer and negotiator for Standard Coal, was calling on her aid. If he understood the need for radical social change, he could tip the entire scale of things.

A shudder ran through Louisa. She didn't want to trust him. He'd done so many things that made her blood boil in her veins. There was no telling what he wanted from this interaction, nor what his application of her knowledge could lead to. It was like the invention of dynamite. He could blast away countless lives or he could build a whole new civilization. Slowly, with much trepidation, Louisa said,

"I won't tell anyone about this phone call . . . but I also might hang up on you."

"Deal." He could tell she liked neither his word choice nor his tone, but he continued talking anyway, choosing words now as carefully as a swat team diffusing a bomb. "I'm working on a project that has major ramifications, to say the least, and I have a couple of questions about causes and effects that I hope you can answer."

"Continue," she said, listening as he talked softly in the silence of the late hours. She stared out at the moon that had kept her awake as it sailed across the midnight sky. Her mind was stretching with his words over vast networks of interactions of entire nations, continents, and the whole world. She was running her mental fingers down the lines of interconnection, feeling the tension of the web, and seeking out the threads that he was missing. All at once, a realization startled her.

"You know, Jack, you actually understand systems theory."

"I did study it along with you, remember?"

"It's a practice, Jack, a way of looking at the world, not a course in college."

She softened the bite that always wanted to creep in and nip at him. He had made more progress than she had ever thought he would. When he went directly to Standard Coal from Harvard, she told Sarah he had sold his soul to the devil.

"They'll ruin him," she had warned her friend, "all the sweetness and gentleness you see in him? How long do you think that'll last? They're cutthroats. One day, he'll bring that attitude into the house and butcher you."

Well, she might have been wrong, Louisa admitted to herself. The concept Jack was outlining required a healthy dose of compassion to perceive. You can't see the interconnections that string this world together if your heart is lacking love. Even an iota of compassion will show you that you're not alone. A short nod at your kinship with other beings generates a kindly feeling toward them. From connection to compassion to connection, around and around, the cycle of understanding grows. As long as we don't cut off our hearts, the inner workings of the universe illuminate before us. Louisa shivered as a wild concept struck her.

"Jack? Did you ever think that the Earth, herself, might be calling you?" She heard his silence on the other end, awkward and uncomfortable with the idea. Louisa let the moment pass. She knew him. He would mull it over at a later date, in the safety and privacy of solitude. She finished answering his questions. Then, with tremendous reservations, she went one step further.

"Jack? There's something else I could tell you. I've worked with top-level environmentalists, social theorists, political people . . . hundreds -no, thousands of them over the years. There's an idea that I think can help you, but if I tell you this, I need you to promise-"

He cut her off, "I can't promise anything, Louisa. You know that."

A hot sigh of frustration escaped her. She knew it. Jack Dalton never made promises. He was a lawyer. He had even told Sarah bluntly that the vows they exchanged in church were meaningless in a court of law and insisted on a prenuptial agreement. He was such a dick sometimes, Louisa thought.

"Look, Jack," she hissed, "if I tell you this concept and you use it against humanity, you will be written down as the blackest of villains, the cruelest of criminals, the most wicked of child murderers, a turncoat of unspeakable proportions-"

"Louisa, I get it," he sighed impatiently.

"No, Jack, you don't," she snapped. "I'm going to tell you how we could actually save the human species from extinction and if you use this information for anything but that effort, I will personally call you out before an international tribunal for the murders of seven billion people and the infinite number of future generations that might have lived!"

"Won't the international tribunal be dead too? And me? And you?" Jack's logic slipped out before he could stop it.

"Jack!" she screamed into the phone.

"Louisa, why do you always have to be so goddamn dramatic about the fate of the Earth?" he complained as he rubbed his ear.

"There is nothing, *nothing*, more worthy of one's passion, Jack. Without the Earth and all of her life-support, we are dead as dust," she raged at him.

"Alright, alright, but, Louisa, it's not entirely *my* fault if the

Earth goes to global warming hell."

"It will be once I tell you this."

Silence. Jack stared at the tiled floor and weighed her words carefully. Louisa never bluffed. She never lied. She might get passionate and outraged, but she meant every word she ever spoke. If she said she had an idea that could save the world . . . she did. And she knew Jack could implement it in the halls and offices where it would detonate a cataclysm of reactions. Suddenly, all his earlier plans seemed trite and small. Stopping Henrietta Owens. Transitioning his family. Saving his soul. Nothing seemed to matter in the face of this.

Jack looked down at his limbs. Small tremors ran up and down his body like a series of internal earthquakes. Fear touched his heart. He felt small compared to the opportunity before him. Weak, in light of the strength he thought might be necessary.

Suddenly, John Henry appeared before him with his hammer in his hand. The black man crackled with furious intensity. Jack recoiled slightly as John Henry lifted up his hammer. He almost dropped the phone and ran. Then he realized John wasn't raising the tool to smite him, but to offer it to Jack.

"Your turn to fight the steam drills, Jack," John said. His eyes were burning with challenge. "My steel driving days have long since gone. Your turn, Jack, your turn."

Jack looked at the strongest man he had ever seen. John Henry pulsed with muscle, but even he had not been strong enough to stop the onslaught of a steam drill culture. What can I, with my chicken bones, do? Jack thought.

"Jack?" Louisa's voice called out. "Are you there?"

"Yes," he answered. *Barely.*

"Take the hammer, Jack," John Henry told him.

Jack said nothing and made no move.

"Jack?" Louisa asked again.

Silence.

"Pick up the hammer, Jack," John Henry commanded.

"I'm still on the line, Jack," Louisa said.

Everything is on the line, Jack thought.

"Take it," John offered one last time.

"Alright, Jack, I don't have to tell you," Louisa whispered, sadly.

Jack reached out suddenly and took the hammer.

"No, wait Louisa. Tell me."

He accepted his fate. John Henry nodded once and disappeared. It was Louisa's turn to tremble.

"Alright," she began, "I hope you understand the trust I'm trying to muster for you, Jack. If you betray this concept, you will be blacklisted as the biggest turncoat in history -and I will be right behind you on that list." Louisa shuddered to think of the uncountable confidences of her colleagues she was about to deliver into the hands of a mortal enemy of the environmental movement. We don't have time for enemies, she thought, we've got to trust each other. She took a breath and began to explain how to use the principles of interconnectedness to flip a cascading ripple of transformation through society.

Jack listened in complete silence and crackling sharp attention until she finished. He asked for a few points of clarification. Then they said good morning and goodbye, for the sun was pushing at night's blackness and both of them had work.

"Tell Sarah I say hello," Louisa urged him.

"I'll talk to you later," Jack said.

They hung up.

Jack rubbed his eyes and felt wrung out inside. He was drenched in perspiration. He'd have to shower before he went to work. He fired up the coffeemaker. The aroma was steaming from the pot as Sarah came groggily downstairs in her bathrobe.

"Were you up all night?"

"Yes," he said. He didn't tell her about the phone call with Louisa. He glanced at the clock. The workday loomed in front of him. He poured her a cup of coffee and then ran up the stairs two at a time to throw himself in the shower. Louisa's trust chaffed him. The knowledge she had handed him boiled in his blood. She had given him a little silver key to everything. He now knew exactly how to destroy the threat of Henrietta Owens. Hot water stung him with the prickles of his conscience. The hiss of the showerhead whispered, *you promised, you promised!* Jack grunted. He had promised nothing. The steam bathed his red and aching eyes. He washed away the memories of any half-truths or lies he might have said. He toweled off and slid into his work attire. He firmly left the hammer of last night's conversation behind him as he drove to work.

That day, news reached the office that the unions had finally moved in support of Henrietta. Labor issues were now socio-economic-environmental issues. The boss spat and howled. Jack simply told him,

"Don't worry. The unions are exactly where I want them."

"You've got a deal with Henrietta Owens?"

"Close. It's very close," Jack said. "I need more time."

"How much?"

Jack shrugged. Thomas Shipley didn't push it. He knew these things were delicate.

"I can't force it," Jack replied. "Everything must be in place."

"And the unions?"

"The bigger the monster, the harder it falls," Jack quoted the old adage, smiling to win the Captain's confidence.

The boss smiled too, all teeth. Twenty years with the legendary Jack Dalton had taught him to trust the man. Jack had never failed them. Never.

Jack was carefully laying his greatest trap, setting it piece by piece, but everything depended on Henrietta. So he watched her, waiting.

Rivera Sun

CHAPTER TWENTY-EIGHT

· · · · ·

Arellia's Premonition

"Henrietta? It's your mamma. Look, I don't know where you are, but for god's sake call me back. I've gotten some more signs. I don't like them. Not at all. Henrietta? I don't mean *call me back when it's convenient.* I mean call me *now.* Do you hear? And I'm going to call you back every half hour until I get ahold of you. I do not like these signs. Not at all."

CHAPTER TWENTY-NINE

. . . . .

An Allie-gator's Heroes

"Allie?! Let's go!" Sarah held the door open. Allie hustled through. Jack flinched as she dove into the backseat of the car.

"There goes her dress," Sarah moaned.

"It's fine." Jack kissed her and helped her swing her swollen belly in.

"It's gonna be a boy," Allie claimed. Jack didn't argue. It could be nice to have another guy around here.

"You look tired, Jack. Is everything alright at work?"

"Fine."

"You didn't come to bed last night," Sarah put a hand worriedly on his arm.

"I know. Sorry. There's a lot going on at the office." Jack keyed the ignition. Sarah straightened her hair. Allie mussed it up teasingly. Sarah scolded her as they pulled out of the driveway.

Jack tried not to resent the necessity of attending the Greelington Academy Awards Ceremony. With the coal company breathing death threats down Henrietta's neck, he didn't have time to sit around applauding boring speeches and academic awards. Apparently, however, Allie had been selected to read one of her essays as the opening speech. Sarah kept getting misty-eyed and refused to let Jack look at it. Jack

317

vaguely remembered assignments on heroes, John Henry, and himself. He looked in the rearview mirror.

"Are you nervous Allie-gator?" Jack asked.

"Nope, not a bit."

He glanced back to see if she was fibbing. Nope, not a bit. Nervousness and Allie didn't seem to mix. She'll make a good lawyer . . . or skydiver, Jack thought.

At the school, Jack politely shook hands with the other parents and tried to think of some way to step outside to continue making phone calls. Sarah glued her hand to his arm and shot him a warning look, so Jack played the game of 'nod & greet', and tried to maintain his half of the conversations as Sarah complimented kids, dresses, and the weather. Jack wondered if the little miniatures of their parents wearing blouses, ties, and patent leather shoes, rebelled like Allie on ordinary school days.

Jack smiled at the complicated negotiation that was their daughter. A protracted Sarah-Allie battle over apparel for the evening had settled in a treaty of a yellow polka-dotted dress. Jack could easily spot their yellow rebel as she scooted through the crowd of parents to find her friends. Sarah tugged his elbow toward their table. Heels clicked. Watches glinted. Seats settled.

Jack fingered the cream and linen program as he sat at a little cafe table with a royal purple tablecloth under frosted glass. I'm paying for all this, he realized. Is it really necessary for Allie's education? A server interrupted his thoughts.

"Coffee, sir? Or wine?"

Jack began to lean toward eschewing private school

excessiveness. Then he thought of handguns in the hallways, tired teachers, brimming classrooms. Not every school is like that, he told himself, determined to balance such sensationalized stories carefully.

"The problem with our schools," he remembered Henrietta saying on a recent radio program, "is that we're running away from them." She'd said it was our approach to all our problems. "We need some cultural and moral courage. We have to care."

No one wants to sacrifice his or her own kid, Jack thought grimly, not if they have other options.

The principal took the podium. Words washed over Jack. Polite applause followed. Then Jack's yellow spotted alligator took the stage. Sarah squeezed his hand. Allie clutched her essay. She crossed her eyes and waved to them. Parents laughed. Sarah groaned. Jack smiled. Allie cleared her high-pitched pipes,

"This is an essay about my two heroes. It was an assignment, otherwise, I wouldn't have thought much about it."

Chuckles followed her precocious honesty.

"I think a hero is someone who stands his or her ground on behalf of humanity," she read.

Excellent premise, Jack thought. Allie continued,

"A hero can be any of us. For example, my dad could be a hero."

Could be . . . like it wasn't guaranteed. Good girl, Jack approved, that's exactly how it works. There are no guarantees that any of us will do the right thing at the right moment. He thought of the situations brewing at his office and shuddered.

"My dad was a hero for me once, when I fell into a river and almost drowned. But now I think he's got a harder hero's task because there's a whole planet full of people drowning in the river and he has to choose which ones to jump in and save. There's this woman on television, Henrietta Owens, who keeps asking us all to be heroes. It's like our whole planet has swung off its course and we all got to push together to get ourselves back in orbit. Except, we don't have a place to stand and shove from. One half the planet has to push and the other side has to jump and we have to do this by taking turns because the earth is spinning."

Jack wondered who else was dizzy from the analogy.

"It's got to be like a ripple of cooperation running around the earth," Allie explained. "But that's a lot of people. A lot of people like my dad who worry that saving somebody else's kid is going to hurt his own. That's where my other hero comes in, this guy called John Henry."

Allie shuffled her papers and looked up,

"One day, I heard my dad saying to my mom that he had to stand up for what is right, like John Henry did the day he faced the steam drill. And my mom told him to think about the wife and child John Henry left behind when he died, even if he was a hero for humanity."

Jack and Sarah exchanged looks. Neither knew their eleven-year old had overheard them, but kids hear all their parents' arguments, even the muffled ones behind closed doors, or the silent ones in slammed down coffee cups.

Up on the stage, Allie continued,

"Well, I thought about it. I'd miss my dad if he broke his heart beating a steam drill. But I'd also miss my dad if he broke his heart doing something that wasn't right. And then I thought, what if my dad wasn't like John Henry? What if he was just some thin little guy working on the railroad who needed someone strong to stand up for him? I'd want John Henry to stand up for my dad. And I'd want my dad to stand up for others even if he might die trying."

Allie frowned and added, "But I'd like it best of all if my dad stood up for humanity and didn't die."

The blaze of eleven-year old sincerity hit a vein of laughter in the room. Jack wistfully wondered if heroes ever survived their real life battles. Allie kept speaking,

"But what I'd like worst of all is what really happened to John Henry. Imagine if my dad died making a stand for everybody and no one changed a bit. 'Cause that's what happened to John Henry. I read about it in the library. We laid the tracks of progress down over his grave and just kept on using steam drills."

Jack wondered if Allie understood the power of her pronouns. A simple switch to "*They*, that's what *they* did," would erase all historical culpability from the room and relegate responsibility to the long-dead figures of the past. But *we*? *We* brought John Henry back to life and invited his presence to join the ceremony. Jack could see John Henry's spirit towering over the assembly. The silent figure demanded answers: why had no one honored his efforts through their actions? Why was he considered an American hero if the steam drills of progress continued to replace the livelihoods of men and women with no concern for their survival?

Progress, huh? Jack snorted in his seat. There is no *progress* while children go to bed hungry in a first world country. Our towering heights of *progress* are not greater than the pits of our fellow brothers' and sisters' suffering. We cannot take one step forward on the path of progress until everyone is with us. And if our forward march destroys our land, our water, and our air, where is our *progress* leading us but straight to living hell?

Jack's face drew into grim lines. All around him, he saw this academic hall of wealth and progress lined with the bones of the poor, the chains of the convicted, and the sweat of the laborers enslaved through generations. Their blood stained the purple silks that graced the tables. The toils of their children served the wine and staffed the kitchen while his daughter proudly gave her speech. John Henry stood above her, evoked by her sincerity and hope, but on either side, John's fellow convicts ringed the auditorium with their chains.

Every day is judgment day, Jack thought. A jury of seven billion souls condemns us. They deliver verdicts on the selfish, thoughtless cruelties that have become our way of life. They are watching us from ghettos, barrios, prisons, mental institutions, rehab centers, churches, schools, and trenches. They stretch for generations back through history and they span out into our children's children's children, too. We will not be found 'not guilty'. Not one of us is innocent. There is no plea of insanity for our everyday way of life.

I have to get us out of this, Jack thought. I have to break the dream that shrouds this waking nightmare. I can't allow Allie to grow up believing in liberty and justice for all, while an unseen host of people die and suffer to pay the price for our pretty platitudes.

His thoughts glowered darker than the auditorium and pinned to his little yellow girl trying to shine up there on the stage. The horde of other parents sat dim and motionless around him like lighthouses blackened out on the bitterest of nights. Every soul should be a beacon, he thought. Regret flooded him. I've wasted half my life obscuring everything in soot and coal dust, he rued. I've shuttered lamps that should have kept men off the rocky shoals of pain and suffering. I kept my own conscience dimmed for so many years.

Well, not anymore. He knew how to polish, clean, scrub, and relight a burnt out wick. He returned his attention to the stage. He would show his candle-yellow daughter how to keep one's soul shining in the darkest times.

"We all know the tune of John Henry's ballad," Allie was saying, but she stopped to hum it, just in case, "but do we know the meaning?" Her eyes searched the darkened audience to find her father. "My dad does," she said.

I do? Jack thought.

"He told me John Henry is a hero not because he lived or died or won or lost, but because he stood up to the steam drills of his time. Well, today the steam drills of our time are walloping us real bad. They're poisoning the air, the water, the land, and they're forcing the planet into climate change. And it's going to take all of us acting as heroes, like Henrietta Owens says, to face those steam drills with the hammers of our human hearts."

The audience shifted uncomfortably. Allie looked up, filled with eagerness.

"We can do it, though!" she encouraged them. "My dad

323

gave me this lecture on steam drills once -well, more like a million times," she rolled her eyes and the audience laughed. "And even though Dad thought I wasn't listening, I remember what he said. He told me: when the steam drill pounds down a nine-foot shaft of hate, we gotta drive in fourteen feet of love. When the steam drill throttles greed full-force, we got to pull ahead of all its smoke and grit to see the effect it has on humanity. When we have fear drilling inside us, we gotta remember that we can always use the double hammers of hope and courage to beat it. That's what my dad said and that's why he's my hero. Thanks!"

Allie hopped off the podium, shook the beaming principal's hand, and ran through the rows of clapping parents to find her own.

Jack couldn't speak. How many lectures do fathers give their daughters and assume they aren't listening to a word? How many times had she yawned through all his rants and rambles? For months he'd been asking her questions about this apparition called John Henry, and for months she'd been rattling off answers without paying too much attention. But Allie had plucked the lighthouse lessons from him after all. He squeezed the yellow polka-dotted alligator that climbed into his lap. He hugged her until her fifth grade sense of dignity returned and she slid into her own chair.

"Thank you, Allie. I- I don't know what to say."

She grinned her wide smile.

"No, thank *you*, Dad. All those John Henry lectures made this essay the easiest homework assignment I ever had." Then she collapsed into giggles until Sarah made her sit still. Sarah smirked at Jack. The unspoken, *see dear, I was right* gleamed in her eyes. He didn't argue. She was right. There never was a more *unsuspecting* hero.

The lists of honors flashed by unnoticed. Jack didn't hear a word. Allie's essay had just made *his* assignment the hardest one he'd ever had.

CHAPTER THIRTY

. . . . .

The Trap

The next day, he arrested Henrietta Owens.

The nation screamed in outrage.

His boss screamed in triumph.

Jack's wife screamed in disbelief.

Henrietta's mother screamed in horror.

Louisa screamed in betrayal.

Henrietta heard only her baby's screaming as he howled through the airport. The flight home from New York City had rolled her through the wringer. Jerome howled from the air pressure changes and drove all the sweetness of a successful set of interviews from Henrietta's mind. Henrietta tried to soothe him and apologized to the accusing eyes in all directions. The airline stewardesses said nothing helpful except, "he's too young for air flights, ma'am." Finally, a Hispanic woman paused on her way to the restroom.

"Sometimes nursing helps. The niños swallow and it helps their ears." She spoke gently to Jerome in Spanish, who lowered his screams to cries and eventually was convinced to nurse and finally to sleep . . . until they circled for the landing.

He wailed now as Henrietta tried to walk up the off-ramp faster. The travelers in front of her plodded on. You'd think a screaming infant would speed them up, Henrietta thought testily. If Wanda wasn't waiting for her, she'd just stop right here and nurse him. Instead, she gritted her teeth and stoically continued. Just past the security checkpoint, with Wanda beaming and reaching out to hug her, a group of officers surrounded her.

"Ma'am, you're under arrest."

"Very funny." She thought it was a joke, a stunt they played on parents who hauled howling children through the airport. Wanda waved her hands and motioned frantically to their badges. They aren't airport security, she mouthed; it's the police! Wanda edged in closer. Jerome stopped crying and reached for his favorite friend. Henrietta let Wanda take him. The police grabbed her arms.

"Wait! What are you arresting me for?"

She didn't get an answer. They rattled off her Miranda Rights. She knew her rights, dammit; they had to have a cause for her arrest!

"Why are you arresting me? Or don't you know?"

Heads turned. Baggage claimers stared.

"Wanda!" Henrietta hollered, "Call my mamma, she'll help you with Jerome. Call Hank and Patrick and Louisa!"

The officers pushed Wanda backwards as she yelled in return,

"Honey, I'm gonna call your *lawyer!!!!*"

"I don't have one!"

"You're gonna now!" Wanda trumpeted out her promises to take care of Jerome, get her out by midnight, and find out what was going on. People tripped on escalators, staring. Airport security looked on, inscrutable. Worried parents pulled

328

their children quickly past. Once again, a teeming mass of people watched a violation of the law and did nothing.

*   *   *

She was locked into a private cell. Her head throbbed. Her body ached. She sank onto the little bed and took in concrete, iron bars, and not much else. At least she had no other company. Privacy and silence were something to be thankful for. She counted blessings.

One . . . I'm alive . . . *breathe.*

Two . . . my baby boy is fine . . . *breathe.*

Three . . . I didn't get arr-

She forgot to breathe. Panic swam like agitated schools of fish inside her and leaped into unformed sentences and questions.

How long?

How come?

It wasn't legal-

How would her baby fall asleep tonight?

Breathe!

Three . . . Wanda will get that baby sleeping . . . *breathe.*

Four . . . my mamma will come and help take care of him for however long I'm here oh my god it could be years they'll never let me out Jerome will be an orphan both parents still alive and stuck in prisons-

Breathe!

Five . . . Patrick and Louisa will get a lawyer . . . *breathe.*

"Ms. Owens?"

She jumped. Her calm flew out the iron bars.

"Y-yes?"

"There's a lawyer here to see you," the guard announced. That was fast, she thought.

Jack Dalton entered. Her patience snapped in half.

"You ain't my lawyer and I'm not talking to you." She crossed her arms and glared as he sat on the stool outside the bars. He'd lost weight, she noticed. The indulgence of excess had been trimmed off him. He looked fresh, somehow, like an old fallow field that had been plowed up for planting. Something calm and quiet sat there with him. Humility, she named it, but then thought that must be wrong. Her frown forced itself back across her face.

"You don't have to talk to me," he said. "I'm sorry this had to happen." He brought his apologetic eyes up to the hot coals of Henrietta's.

"Did you do this?" she asked. He nodded, once. She couldn't read the sentences in the lines of his face. She tried to spell out guilt or maliciousness, but he remained inscrutable.

"How long are you gonna keep me here?" She tried to hold civility intact, but her fury was rebelling.

"You'll be released to attend a special meeting next Wednesday with the Standard Coal executives," he told her. He hadn't answered her question, she noticed, and next Wednesday was next week.

"Five days? You're gonna keep me here for five days?"

"It's a very important meeting. Standard Coal is interested in resolving this mountaintop removal question once and for all."

She didn't like the sound of that. Coal companies only closed doors on subjects when it locked their opposition out.

"Someone needs to tell the organizers."

"No. We only want to speak with you."

"I can't sign anything or make promises for anybody," Henrietta protested as he pulled a thick document from his briefcase and passed it through the bars.

"This is the draft of the agreement you'll be signing, Ms. Owens," he said firmly, as if she had no other options.

"Is that a threat?" she snapped.

"No. It's an invitation," Jack said, his face remaining tightly guarded.

"This is completely illegal," she argued. She gestured to the surroundings, looking young and lost in her tee shirt and blue jeans. Jack remembered she was only twenty-five and just as quickly threw away chronological calculations of her age. He shrugged.

"I am sorry, Ms. Owens. I didn't have much choice."

She scoured his face with truth-seeking eyes and found no apologies or further explanations.

"Why not?" she asked.

"Negotiations go much better when all parties are alive," he stated simply and refused to expand or reassure the shiver that snapped through her.

"This country's going to tar and feather you," she warned him.

"Maybe. Maybe not."

A cocky grin spread across his face. He ran thin fingers through his stubble hair. His wedding band mowed down a streak like a haying machine. Henrietta bit down the bile of resentment that burned her throat. Even the indents of her engagement to Tyrell had vanished from her hand. Jack Dalton would go home tonight to his wife, his child, his bed, with his wedding band on his finger. Who knows how long she or her child would cry before they fell asleep tonight? His cold eyes held no sympathy as he passed the document through the bars.

"You can't expect me to sign this," she told him flatly.

"You haven't looked at it. Don't judge a contract by its cover." His confidence annoyed her. She glanced inside and scanned the legalese. She stopped. Her eyes widened. She flipped the page. Her eyes grew bigger still.

Their expressions held an arms race as his smirk matched her widening eyes width for width. She said,

"Is this for real?!"

"As real as it gets," Jack replied. "I suggest you read that document very carefully, Ms. Owens. Your life is in your hands."

He left. Henrietta sat stunned and all alone in a concrete cell. No way out. No other options. Nothing.

*   *   *

The arrest of Henrietta Owens touched the drought-crisped indignation that stretched across America. The empty promises of campaigning politicians to free her exploded pent-up gas tanks of frustration. The sudden perception of the people's eroded rights caused an avalanche of outrage.

"You can't arrest somebody for speaking truth!" the nation

roared. In their lingo, *somebody* was *her*, *you* was *them*, and *truth* was *what Henrietta Owens said.* Pronouns passed the blame and pointed fingers and in the hysteria hardly anyone realized *she* translated somehow into *we*, the people, the working class, the average Joes, the welfare moms, the unwed daughters, the poor girls, the waitresses, the bus drivers, the soccer moms, the convicts, the spokeswomen, the secretaries . . .

"*We* means all of us," Henrietta had told them once. "Rich and poor, black and white." But that nuance eluded understanding as the tempers kept on rising. *We* stopped short of full potential, crouched in terms of *most of us*; the unions (not the employers), the policemen (not the lawbreakers), the prisoners (not the cops), the soccer moms (not the super-wealthy). *We* certainly did not include whoever had ordered Henrietta's arrest.

Who was that? The chief of police?

No, no, he's just following the mayor . . .

who is following the coal company's lawyer . . .

who says it's all perfectly legal . . .

according to the laws . . .

passed by the elected leaders . . .

chosen by . . . drumroll please . . .

We, the people!

Like a wave of blame hitting the furthest shore, the accusations and excuses came crashing back . . .

Corruption! The people never wanted those leaders!

Coercion! The politicians had to pass those laws!

Precedence! The judicial branch had to uphold them!

Duty! The policemen were sworn to enforce them!

People snapped. Up and down the circuit of democracy loose wires frayed and caught on fire. The smoldering and frantic soldering stung the eyes of everyone.

"This is a nightmare," said the chief of police.

"This is a nightmare," echoed the governor.

"This is a nightmare," moaned the coal company.

"This is a nightmare," screamed the people.

It has always been a nightmare and *we* have always been the ones creating it. Only now, we are waking up. The people took to the streets. Petitions went flying across the country. The prisoners in Block 4 quietly went on strike. They left their food on the altar of their saint and went hungry in protesting prayer. The union workers soon joined them, fasting from work instead of food. The media kept eating both, feeding news of resistance to the voracious ears of listeners.

Jack watched it all and waited. The boss paced his office and straightened his tie and tried not to show his mounting nervousness. Thomas Shipley told himself reassuring stories of Jack Dalton's cleverness and cunning. He had never let them down before. He would not let them down now.

Hank, Patrick, and Louisa slammed into action, organizing a massive rally on the steps of the eleven-story office building. The news shot through the networks like a silver bullet. The bus drivers' union drove folks in from all around the country. The envisioned stroller moms appeared. The police held emergency strategy meetings -they couldn't tear gas moms with strollers! The mayor whipped out a permit for the rally. The coal company's lawyer told him to. He smiled at the mayor's questions. Jack had his reasons. His trap stretched itself through every city, network, home, and person.

By Wednesday morning, all was ready.

CHAPTER THIRTY-ONE

· · · · ·

The Whole World Waits

The trouble with shooting stars is that they burn out. Henrietta spent five silent days in jail and hour-by-hour she shrank closer to her core. They had allowed her one phone call on the first day. She called her mother. When the connection sent her straight to voicemail, Henrietta realized exactly where Arellia was. Not at home in Ohio, the land of immaculate urban cellphone coverage, but tucked in No Man's Holler, where reception was a standing joke and nothing else.

"Hi, Mamma, it's me. I'm fine. I'll be here until Wednesday, when I'm supposed to go to a meeting with the coal company. Tell Louisa to get everybody she can into the streets that morning. It's important. Take care of Jerome. Oh, and call Tyrell, would you? He probably doesn't know I'm here."

(He knew. Everybody knew.)

"Thanks, Mamma. I love you. I'm fine."

She hung up feeling like an idiot. She should have called a lawyer or told her mother to. She didn't think of it, only important things: *I'm fine. I love you. Take care of my baby.*

When the guards returned her to the cell, she sank the sockets of her eyes wearily onto the palms of her hands. The clang of closing doors filled her ears. Conversations around the revolutionary table floated back: *"Can't we have some fun?"* *"Got to risk dying just to live."*

Henrietta pictured her mother arriving at the cabin door and seeing her daughter's altar arranged upon the windowsill. She saw her mother with her ever-present purse and heels, the earrings that matched her bracelets and her hair straightened firmly and coiled against the dark skin of her neck. Two lighter lines where age folded secrets into skin stretched to circle her neck like the silver necklace that hung there with them.

Henrietta pictured her urban mother now standing in the woodland grandeur of floor-to-ceiling foliage. She would see the mix of browns and greens, the floorboards dappled with sun, and the gray-brown columns of tree trunks reaching upward. She would hear the unfurling canopy of whispers over her head and feel the stirring of the fanning breezes. The dogwood outside the kitchen window would offer a bouquet of white flowers to welcome her. The wisteria climbing up the porch might rush a single cluster into blossoming. Her notary public mind would stamp *approval, disapproval, pending* onto Henrietta's tumbled nest of bedding without a bedframe, the ancient armoire that, like the table, would outlive the crumbling cabin, and the yellow lace curtains in the windows. Henrietta imagined her mother's eyes falling on the revolutionary table, her knowing creased hand touching it and asking silent questions about its complicity in these events. Arellia would understand the wildness of the wood. The veteran midwife of birth and death would recognize the stain of blood. She would wonder if the table's nature brought forth life or hastened death.

Arellia would hook her purse on the back of the chair,

slowly pull off her suit jacket and tuck the loosened waistline of her blouse back into her skirt.

Henrietta imagined a shadow falling across the doorway for a moment before it entered. Henrietta's civil, regal, tucked-in mother would be confronted with the overflowing, booming, colorful presence of Wanda.

"That's my father's birth stain, there, that you had your hand on," Wanda would say, always one to be spitting out truth before any sort of introduction. Arellia would look at the table for a while and then ask,

"Was it an easy birth?"

"It was never easy to push my father around," Wanda would chuckle.

"Thank you for caring for my grandson and daughter," Arellia would announce unexpectedly, truth before introductions. "And not just now, but since she came here."

"Oh, you're mighty welcome," Wanda would beam, crossing the cabin and depositing Jerome into Arellia's arms. Wanda would watch them curl around the little boy, distrustful of this city-woman's heels and matching skirt and jacket. Finally she'd harrumph and put her own backwoods stamp of approval on the notary public grandmother.

"I'm Wanda Nelson."

"Arellia Owens."

Truth before the introductions laid a strong foundation for a friendship. Arellia, too, had sized up the other woman, taking note of her own snobbery toward backwoods folk as she had watched Wanda standing in the doorway with her grandson.

In her lonely jail cell, Henrietta quit her imagining and

silenced the sob that wanted to escape. She clamped her jaw shut and gritted her teeth. She did not permit herself any more imaginings until late that night. Then she lay sleepless on the bed and thought about how Wanda and her mamma would rock her baby into slumber.

* * *

Thanks, Mamma. I love you. I'm fine.

Arellia listened to the cellphone message three times in the parking lot of Crawley's Market. Then she went into the grocery store and slowed her frantic heartbeat with produce section price calculations. She weighed her apples in the hanging scale and tried to keep her mind on fifth-grade math, but her worry overwhelmed her. Ordered rows of waxy fruit sat crisply at attention as Arellia's mind raced circles around the situation.

How could they arrest Henrietta?

When would they release her?

Would they ever let her out?

Stop that nonsense, Arellia ordered herself. She shook her head to clear away the questions. She pushed her cart forward through the stacks of fruits. Then she froze dead still in front of a cheerful stand of imported bananas. The questions were not nonsense. They were real. Very, very, deadly real.

In between the red, green, and yellow apples of the Crawley's Market, Arellia Owens dropped down upon her knees.

"Ma'am? Are you alright?" the produce clerk inquired.

"Oh, I'm fine," she snapped. "Just peachy. Rosy as a little red apple. Can I peel you a grape?" The clerk drew back as she spit the words out. "No, I'm not fine. I'm praying. Now go away."

The awkward fellow in his uniform kept standing there, glancing nervously around.

"Um, ma'am, there is a church down the street."

"This country has got a freedom of speech and a freedom of religion, which means that I can spend all day chastising you for denying me a chance to worship in front of your fruits." The young man gulped and looked for backup. Arellia told him, "I won't be but two minutes and then I'll continue with my shopping peacefully. Now go away."

The clerk shrugged and went back to stacking potatoes. He was paid to arrange vegetables, not to deny shoppers their constitutional rights.

Arellia bared her soul before the waxed and shiny apple altar. Her rubber matted prayer rug bit into her kneecaps. No more fervent devotion has ever been displayed, not under the Vatican's vaulted ceiling, nor at the cathedral of Notre Dame, nor in any of the holiest of shrines and mosques and temples throughout the world. Her prayer was to the puzzled shoppers all around her, to the suspicious clerk, and the oblivious corporate officers. Her prayer was to the truck drivers, their wives, the farmers, the bank tellers, the stockbrokers, the bicycle couriers, the street beggars, the oil tycoons, the middlemen, and the entire nation that went about their daily lives while her daughter who had only dared to speak the truth was locked up in a jail.

"Please, please, please," she begged, "do not drop my daughter into the pit of your forgetfulness. Do not make my child yet another somber bone in the jumbles of your mass grave. Do not kill her with your lack of caring. Demand her release. Do whatever it takes. Please. Please. Please."

Her elbows leaned heavily on the cold produce case railing. The misters hissed a warning. The artificial showers sprinkled holy water on her. She rose. Her fingers flicked away what felt like a fly on her arm. A little produce sticker took a leap from arm to thumb and clung to her. Arellia looked down. It was red and round, with a single word: TRUST. Arellia tucked it in her purse and continued shopping.

*   *   *

Henrietta had no signs or symbols or little stickers to offer her a single scrap of trust. She had five long days, Jack's contract to read, and questions that had no answers. Her body searched frantically for her baby's heartbeat, the constant counter-rhythm to her own. Her milk longed for his need and asked aching questions about the purposes of life. Her hands sent off the message of warmth and love, but heard no response. She pulled in tightly to her core. No energy flung out in anger. No blazes wasted in frustration.

Her streak across the nation's eye seemed to have winked out. But, hidden where they could not see her, Henrietta still hurled and burned on her collision course with the Earth, hotter than ever before. In another cell, in a different West Virginian jail, so close the irony would ache them if they knew, Tyrell slept as fitfully as Henrietta. He dreamt dreams made sharp by hunger's edge. In them, he was plunging furiously toward Henrietta, arms outstretched, reaching, reaching . . .

She struggled out of dreams with hands that searched the sheets for her loved ones. Cold cotton met her fingertips. Slumber faded. She woke to an iron understanding of where she was, where Tyrell was, where their baby was. Geography and mileage meant nothing. *Separate* is a single word that covers all distances that aren't *together.* For the first time since her arrest, Henrietta wept. She howled out a misery that echoed off the concrete walls. Across the country, fasting convicts felt the howl reverberate within them. Their demand was simple: free her. Underneath it roared their own request: let us go! Let us go!

Not just from jails. Not just from orange suits and iron bars. Let us out of places of no escape; of poverty and ghettos, no hope alleys, no-out neighborhoods. Release us from the threat of climate change, pollution, cancers, fear. The list was too long for strikers to demand, so they simplified: let her go.

She'd done nothing wrong, like some of them. Nothing that she didn't have to, like most of them. Nothing that she wasn't driven to by circumstance and situation, like all of them. She'd taken the only options handed to them all:

One . . . fight back . . .

Two . . . make a desperate lunge for your survival, or . . .

Three . . . perish in a system that leaves no hope.

Welcome to the Prison System of America. All citizens are inmates. Money can buy you privileges. Skin color works against you. We have strict rules about love and sex, but we won't tell you what they are. Whether born here, naturalized through immigration, or caught illegally, you have three options:

One: steam drill your enemies into the ground.

Two: pant desperately on the treadmill to stay alive.

Three: let go of all the rules and shoot across the sky.

Warning: you may crash.

Henrietta's howl stopped. She pulled it to her core. Her breasts stopped leaking longing. She pulled the nurturance of human life back into her. She snatched up every stray thought and worry and fed it to her inner fire. Her final plummet was arcing across the sky. Everything became fuel to keep her last, tiny, propelling ember burning. The ground replaced the landscape of the heavens. Henrietta looked fiercely for a decent place to land. She read and reread Jack Dalton's contract. It was like it was a picnic blanket held out to catch her. He claimed the loops and weaving lines would be strong enough to catch the world, but she sensed traps. She sensed the possibility that he might drop it, drop her, drop everyone. She sensed the utter lunacy of holding out a picnic blanket to catch an out-of-orbit world. Laughter ricocheted off the jail cell walls. She searched her soul for a scrap of trust. She scoured her landscape for other options. She pulled in tightly to the confines of her core.

By Wednesday morning, she was ready.

CHAPTER THIRTY-TWO

. . . . .

Steam Drills vs. the People

Jack watched the subtleties of war stack up around the conference room. Corporate officers placed themselves as strategically as battleships. Blockades of water pitchers were placed . . . just so. Intimidation tactics were deployed in a missing pen, a broken rolling chair, no place to plug one's laptop. The room was navigated as precisely as a battlefield. At ten a.m., the light would blaze through the eastern floor-to-ceiling windows. Henrietta would enter blinded. Her waiting opponents would be inscrutable backlit silhouettes. They'd seat her where she couldn't see; where the air conditioner left a gap; and where the floor sloped ever so slightly downward.

Jack knew the landscape of the conference room intimately. Over the years, every curve and nuance had been stroked by his affection and appreciation. The architects had understood the art of conference rooms. They used the beauty of its swooping lines and the elegant parade of windows to conceal its grim-edged purpose. This was war. This room was the battleship of conquerors, a top-class death machine under the command of contracts men. The boss strode around it as the Captain. Jack ran it as the engineer.

Eleven stories down, the streets were thronged with the

tops of heads. Faceless, voiceless, unreal and . . .

"Unbelievable," Thomas Shipley exclaimed to his corporate officers, staring at the people demonstrating down below. "Those ingrates! My fuel got every last one of them here today."

No one in the corporate boardroom argued. If not by coal, then by oil. If not by oil, then by natural gas. If not gas, then by solar, wind, or nuclear. And if not by those, then by the fuel of misery left in the wake of progress. They owned them all, politely, modestly, and prudently assuming different corporate faces. They went through all the motions of competition, passing profits from right hand into left. Juggling, it's called when clowns attempt it. However, no one laughs when the ringmaster pulls such tricks.

Jack wondered about the masses far below, shouting and chanting to make their voices heard. No amount of them would stir this tower's innards. Not one of them would stand where he was now.

Except for Henrietta. Jack smiled. It was a long way up from accidental protesting to high-ranking negotiations. No one can fathom such a leap. No one breached the battleship unless invited by the Captain. Then the environmental, social, and political justice types found themselves facing Jack Dalton at the helm of the conference room maneuvers. Thomas Shipley, the Captain, gave out the orders. Jack knew his duty: win.

Five 'til ten. They expected her to be prompt. A police escort ensured it. Jack glanced around the room. He watched the men pad to their places. He stood silent as they folded their hands upon the table. They glanced uneasily around and asked Jack one more time,

"You're sure of this?"

"Of course he's sure," another retorted.

"What's there to lose?"

"She has no one to represent her."

"We made sure of that."

"Hah! The entire ACLU jumped to champion her."

"It's only the best lawyers that count, anyway."

"Danworth wouldn't do it."

"Shelby and Sterns accepted bribes."

"Willis was unfortunately detained."

"And who would stand against Jack Dalton?"

"No one."

Laughter broke through the men. Pens flicked and fingers twitched. Baleful eyes stared at the clock. The door opened. Henrietta entered with . . .

No one.

She wore the white silk-linen suit that Jack had sent. Wore it like a flag of truce. Jack read the secret message: trust. The suit blazed against the morning sun, reflecting back the glare. Hands rubbed at eyes. In the winking and squinting, no one caught Jack quickly moving,

"Ms. Owens, here."

He gestured for her to sit, not in the creaky, slightly canted downward, sloping, blinded broken rolling chair, but in his own position. No one saw exactly how it happened. Startled strategists glanced around. They slid back and swiveled to keep her in their sight. Jack smiled. The sun now had her back. It blazed defensively, straight into all the other eyes, and hid her expressions in its shadow. The tables had been turned. Jack knew they would soon spin faster. The Captain tried to grab the wheel and assume command,

"Ms. Owens, let's not waste any time. You've read the contract?"

"Your copies are out of date." She swept their contracts off the table, removing them like a layer of leaves laid over Jack's trap. She threw the new contracts down in a stack. Jack's secretary, following his orders, had handed them to her as she walked in the door. The men reached out suspiciously. The Captain crossed his arms and smirked.

"You need a lawyer to be changing contracts."

"I have one."

"Where is he? He didn't come with you?"

"I didn't bring him. He-"

"Who is it?" tittered a sharp-toothed man. "Your baby?"

A hammer rang against Jack's heart. His memory flashed to other meetings where they had plotted infanticide around this table, ripped the mother's image in half, and snarled of tear gas strategies. An entire deck of memory cards spanning twenty years of brutal jungle images fanned across his mind. Dams that broke and washed whole towns down mountain slopes. Poison leaking underground to god-knows-where. Dust that sliced men's lungs apart. Tap water that lit on fire. Forced relocations. A list of carefully planned 'accidents'.

"Where is the little boy?" the man persisted. "I thought you brought him everywhere."

Henrietta held her shard of trust, the last piece of broken

glass from the windows of her life. It stung her to hold it in her hand, but she had no other choice. She said,

"I only bring him where he's invited. He's not my lawyer. Now, we have work to do."

"Not without your lawyer present," the Captain gleamed. It was such a convenient excuse to deflate the ballooning crowd below and send them home while the meeting was rescheduled for a less convenient time.

"I didn't say he wasn't present. I said, I didn't bring him in the room." Henrietta crossed the fingers of her soul. Her heart pounded, the collision of her shooting star slammed up within a second's time. Hands were reaching, ears were screaming . . .

In a prison an hour northward, her husband-not-yet-married struggled against the bonds of time and space. Dreams bound his sleeping body as it poured a thundershower of sweaty efforts into his sheets. He struggled for release so he could fly to where his love was falling. *Catch her!* He pleaded with the angels who could walk in ivory towers and sit with men who claimed God's power. *Catch her!* He struggled against despair and helplessness. He sent out the Morse code of the heart: *Save Our Souls! S.O.S. Catch her!*

An angel heard. He turned and plunged toward the meeting of Henrietta's falling star. He hurtled at such blinding speed that the feathers seared off his wings. Then the wings themselves dissolved. He pulled his limbs into his chest. The heat of travel scorched the burning ball. He streaked across the sky's horizon like a comet foretelling civilization's fall.

The angel hit the earth. It shook. He uncurled. His wings were gone. His white skin was burned into the common ancestors' color. He shook his charcoal blackness once . . . and started running with a speed that scraped his blackness back to white.

In his dream, Tyrell sent him all his strength, his breath, and his love for Henrietta. There were no dams to hold it back, no narrow funnels of wires, words, and letters. Everything he yearned to send her coursed through the open state of dreaming. The angel sprinted like a fallen Hermes, no wings, no magic shoes, just a messenger with a priceless package to deliver. His legs pounded through a field of grass, a wide savannah of the soul. Laughter pealed in freedom's tone. His hands, so full of the dreamer's love and strength, reached for the falling woman . . .

. . . and caught her.

"I am Ms. Owens lawyer," the angel said. Jack's heart pounded in his chest. His blood raced marathons within him. Despite their ears, the corporate officers could not believe it. They looked at the door to see who had entered and spoken.

No one.

"Is this a joke?" the Captain laughed.

No, Jack thought, this is the moment John Henry said to wait for. In Jack's hands he held the hammer and the spike of the steely situation that pinned them all. For weeks the hammer had been slowly raising, hanging, and now Jack calmly lifted up his hands . . .

. . . and let his resignation fall.

It struck the table with a sledgehammer's force; with the weight of history behind it; with the sparks of uncompromising debts come due.

"Sirs, you now have my resignation. And *this*," he pointed to the new-forged contract, "is the document you will be signing."

He met the Captain with his challenge: I will fight your steam drill, Captain. I will knock that steel on down.

"This a commitment to action, gentlemen, legally binding, enforceable by law. The people will sign, the leaders will sign, and you will, too. We've stalled in traffic long enough while the emissions of our lifestyle threaten to kill us. It's time for us to move forward, all together."

The contract Jack had written had been drafted millenniums ago. The terms and prices were as reasonable as falling rain and gentle winds, rustling trees and running springs. The binding articles were man's survival, an alliance forged with all of Earth. Man would survive *with* the Earth, or else they would vanish from its face. The contract was non-negotiable. The terms were coming due.

"This contract is the legal commitment to drastically change our way of life. The first page, as you'll see, is a general agreement to take action on climate change. The rest of the document details the specific actions each person can take. In section fourteen, it states that if you, as executives of Standard Coal, agree to shift into clean energy, the whole society will help you do it. However, gentlemen, if you don't, the document empowers the nation to move against you. The people will boycott coal. The politicians will close loopholes on pollution and outlaw fossil fuels. The media will lambast you."

"I don't see the signatures of any of those people," the boss growled.

"No," Jack said calmly, "but you will." The most ruthless contract lawyer on the East Coast locked eyes with his former boss. He felt the weight of steam drills being rolled up against him. He bristled with the challenge and began.

Jack swung the weight of John Henry's hammer with the force of Henrietta's truths. He pounded out the basic contract. The steam drill executives resisted every point. He hammered down carbon emissions. They fought against fixing watersheds. He drilled the crucial aspects of transitional energy programs. They protested that restoring mountains was pushing things too far. They had the force of systems, cogs, wheels, motors, steam, connections, and societal momentum. Jack had his hands and heart, and not much else. He pitted his strength against the steam drill madness and prepared to fight to death.

"As you'll see," Jack informed them, "I have signed this document. Sections twelve, fourteen, and seventy-five now legally commit me to the professional actions I am taking here today."

"You've lost it, Dalton," Thomas Shipley exclaimed. "You're nuts. This is professional suicide."

Jack's face was grim as he answered,

"That, sir, is preferable to the collective suicide of the human species."

"Nonsense!" Shipley protested.

"If it is not suicide we are facing, then it is genocide," Jack warned him. "And I swear that I will call you before an international tribunal to answer for crimes against humanity. Continuing to extract and process coal is actively leading toward the deaths of untold numbers of human beings."

Thomas Shipley locked eyes with Jack Dalton. For twenty years they had worked intimately together. Each knew the other man's blustering and bluffing. He knew Jack Dalton would make good that promise.

"This world that sails around the sun will sink," Jack told him, "unless we chart a different course. You are the captain of the ship. If you don't steer us out of danger, I, and all the crew, will mutiny."

He gestured to the streets below, where the threat already formed. People had heard the cries of the S.O.S. family. They were ready to take command.

"Call security," the Captain growled.

"I wouldn't, if I were you," Henrietta warned him. "I would listen to Jack Dalton very, very carefully."

"Why should I listen to the ravings of a madman?" Shipley hissed, infuriated that she dared to threaten him.

"Because there are three hundred million more of them in this country. And seven billion of them worldwide."

"They'll never sign," Shipley argued.

"Yes they will," Henrietta answered. "I already asked them to."

Every head swung toward her.

Henrietta crossed her fingers and prayed that Jack's document was whipping across the country even as she spoke, gathering steam and speed. *Please,* she prayed, *let this be a nation of heroes. Please!*

Earlier that morning, as she climbed the office steps, Henrietta had caught sight of a familiar face among the surging crowds.

"Wanda?!" Henrietta cried, then suddenly saw Patrick, Louisa, Hank, her mamma and . . .

"Jerome!"

The magnetic force of motherhood pulled her toward her son. The police escort seized her. The crowd roared. Arellia flashed premonitions of jailbreaks. Jerome howled. Henrietta spoke softly to the guards and they loosened their grip. She asked for a bullhorn and pulled Jack's contract from her coat pocket. The many strands of shouting blended into a single chant:

Set her free! Set her free! Set her free!

Henrietta started laughing. Surprised, the crowd slowly came to silence.

"Set me free?" she asked them. "Free to go where?"

The crowd shifted uncomfortably.

"We are facing a death sentence," she said. "This whole Earth is nothing more than our prison." Henrietta shuddered as she looked out at the throng of people. "If we don't change our way of life, we are all walking in our graves."

The banners stilled. No one moved.

Henrietta showed no trace of laughter now. She blazed with serious intensity as she raised Jack Dalton's contract and told them,

"In my hand, I hold a remarkable document. It calls on us to change our way of life. It calls on us to take action to protect this Earth. It calls on us to care."

The silence had grown absolute. Henrietta sent the crowd a measuring look.

"This is the moment of truth," she said. "Do you care

enough to do yourself what our politicians and leaders are not courageous enough to do? Will you boycott coal? Embargo oil? Forgo dirty energy until they deliver cleaner options? That is what this agreement calls for! Do you care enough about this world, your family, and yourself to sign up for this revolution?"

Henrietta paused and found that she was shaking. One way or another, the time had come to choose. She drew a breath and demanded that they answer.

"Tell me! Do you *care* enough to change?"

A spattering of voices cried out. Henrietta repeated,

"Tell me! Do you care?"

"Yes!" the reply shot back, a hundred voices strong.

"Do . . . you . . . care!?" Henrietta demanded of every last soul before her.

Thousands of throats opened in readiness. The swelling crowd pushed against police barriers, riot gear, fear and danger, thirsty for the dropping rain of change, roaring out their wordless affirmation. They had come out marching in the streets to proclaim the depth of caring this woman had awakened. They were publically demonstrating that this was no ordinary workday in America. Life as usual could not continue on its devastating path. Henrietta smiled and then continued,

"This document requires individual responsibility. It must be signed by you and for you alone. You cannot force your neighbors to do it. The president cannot make you sign."

Henrietta waved Jack's document above her head,

"But this simple commitment to action, held in the hearts of schoolteachers and senators alike, has more power than any decree of Congress! For when each of you," she gestured to the entire crowd, "and each of these policemen," she nodded to them, "and the coal company executives upstairs all decide that the future of humanity is worth more than any amount of money, power, or prestige," Henrietta paused to draw in breath, " . . . then nothing in the world can stop this revolution!"

The crowd broke into cheering. In the sidelines, Louisa bowed her head in gratitude. This concept had kicked around in so many lonely, longing hearts and minds. Finally, it had cut through all time and space to burst from nowhere like a field of wildflowers in the spring. Thank you, Jack, she silently cried, thank you. Louisa leaned toward a certain redheaded citizen of the Earth and whispered,

"Remember when you asked me if you could ratify the Kyoto Protocol for yourself?"

"Yeah," Hank mumbled, "I wanted to know what a guy could do when the country was falling short of the mark."

"Well, here you go. This is your chance."

Hank threw a startled glance at Louisa. Her brimming grin told him all he needed to know. He let out an ear-splitting whoop, grabbed a bullhorn, and leapt up on a streetlight. He shimmied up it with muscles bunching full of enthusiasm. His legs pinned him halfway up it. One hand gripped the streetlight's gray trunk. The other pulled the bullhorn from his teeth. He hollered out,

"No more waiting for politicians! No more waiting for laws! The time is now! The change is you! Look around!" He gestured with the bullhorn to the teeming mass of people. From one end to the other, they wrapped around and through the city streets. "You are the fuel that runs this country! Your hearts! Your actions! And why?"

He paused in the sunshine that streamed between the skyscrapers. He trembled in his gripping streetlight perch as the Earth sent her strongest breath to fill his lungs.

"You are America!"

The roar was deafening. The secret citizen of the Earth had given them back their country. He placed blame, responsibility, power, unity, and action solely in their hands. He awakened in them the visceral understanding that nothing could stop them from ensuring their own futures; *the time was now, the place was here, the change was them!*

Hank slid down the streetlight and wound back through the crowd, pummeled by the hands that pounded him on the back. On the steps of the office building, Henrietta beamed at the people's reaction. She raised her bullhorn. Time was pulsing toward the meeting and there was one last thing to say,

"In a few moments, I've got to ask a group of men to sign this document . . . but how can I ask them to sign if we won't? We need to hold ourselves to the same standards of awareness, responsibility, and action. I am going to sign this agreement," Henrietta told them, "and if you care, I urge you to sign it, too."

She flung the papers toward the front line. Hank shot up with a startling leap and snatched them from the air. Louisa smoothed the pages. Henrietta could see her mother's tears. Jerome reached out for her as she was forced to turn away. She prayed the document could make a difference as time ordered her on its forward march.

Upstairs, she told the group of men, "I explained to the people that it was a contract, legally binding, enforceable by law.

357

The time to change is here. The agreement merely holds us to what we know is true."

They gave her a look beyond disbelief. She shrugged. Hope slips in where logic fears to tread. Maybe no one would dare to sign it. But how could they dare *not* to?

"H-holy shit!" one of the executives shouted, staring at his computer. He stammered out, "I just searched for *contract-coal-henrietta owens*, and it came right up. They put it on the internet!"

Henrietta clapped her hands across her grin, but she could not hide her cheering eyes. Below them, the people had turned the thronging streets into a massive communal office. Cellphones buzzed and rang and shot out messages as the people chanted, over and over again:

"The time is here! The place is now! The change is us!
Sign it! Share it! Send it! Shout it!"

The people sent the contract through alliances that stretched across the country. Louisa sent messages to all her colleagues, highlighting the sections that were inspired by their work. The leaders of every major environmental, social, and political justice movement gave their endorsements. Odelle Jordan received a text message. In fifteen minutes, the document was primetime talk. The media pounced. The internet buzzed. The people signed. Commentators swore the country's politics had suddenly changed direction. Ambitious legislators howled at their interns until they got a copy. The contract swept up the chain of command gathering signatures by the second.

"How many have signed?" the Captain snarled out.

"One million, two hundred and thirty-eight thousand."

"What?!!! There must be some mistake!"

"No, no mistake. The number's up to one million, four hundred, and twenty-five . . . twenty-nine . . . forty. Five hundred and -holy smokes!!!!"

"What?!!" they all roared as the man's jaw dropped, speechless. Someone grabbed the laptop.

"The President just signed it."

Jack felt the urge to howl in delight. Instead, he simply shut the laptop and said with a wicked gleam,

"You know the saying, gentlemen: lead, follow, or get out of the way." His eyes bore holes into each of them. They choked. They swore. Steam hissed out of their ears. He had them trapped. They knew it. The will of the people surrounded them on every side.

"Gentlemen," Jack continued, "it seems the country is no longer waiting for your signatures. I suggest you sign this document for your own sakes. The world is turning toward a new direction. You don't want to be left behind." He turned to Henrietta and said, "Let's go. Our work is done."

Henrietta rose, elated and weary. She followed Jack and then she stopped and laughed.

"Hold on."

She turned back toward the table, reminiscent of her shining entrance. She smiled at a familiar object on the table and pulled a copy of the contract toward her.

"We gotta lead by our own example, " she said.

And with Tyrell's pen, she signed it.

CHAPTER THIRTY-THREE

. . . . .

An Old Ballad Crooned Low and Slow

When a meteor hurtles across the sky, fingers point and pulses quicken. It streaks across the night, searing an imprint of its path upon the eyes. Then it vanishes. Somewhere, it falls. Its collision absorbs into the Earth. Tiny tremors make their way through strata of solid rock. Ripples echo throughout the world. The meteor finally rests.

Henrietta rocked Jerome. Her porch slanted comfortably in all directions. The evening sang harmony to the old song that she hummed. The rocker creaked along with the beat and the forest gulped up the sound. The meeting with the coal company receded into memory as the summer raced by.

There were changes, some slower than an old pick-up truck chugging up the hollow slopes, others growing faster than her baby boy. Like raindrops ionizing in the atmosphere, everything was crackling fresh with energy, but the force of the storm had yet to break. The mountaintops still choked the valleys and the prisoners still crowned the flattened spaces waiting for change and justice to reach in and unlock hope.

Henrietta could feel it coming though.

"Did you hear, baby boy of mine?" she asked her drowsy child. "There's another baby who's joined us in the world." The birds were hushing in the trees. "Jack and Sarah had their son. They named him Henry . . . after me."

She smiled. Jack was blazing like a shooting star these days. No, steadier, she thought. Jack was blazing trails of social contracts, building paths for folks to follow, like a railroad toward their future.

Henrietta counted Jack in her list of blessings. He'd caught the falling meteor and brought it safely down to earth. Back in June, a week after the meeting, he had introduced her to his family: Allie, whom she knew already, and Sarah, bulging with their new one. Henrietta then took a leap of faith, and invited Jack to meet Tyrell. At the prison, Tyrell had shaken Jack's hand and stared.

"I had a dream about an angel's hands," he started to say.

But then Tyrell turned and not only his hands shook, but his whole self, too. With the weight of legalese and notoriety, Jack Dalton had leaned his power on the prison supervisor and won back Tyrell's right to hold his family in his arms. Jack stood discretely to the side and found that the reunion of the two lovers left him shaking. They were too young to be so old, too old to feel so young.

Hadn't it gone the other way around? Jack thought.

Ah, but the barriers that held things in their proper order had just dissolved. Eyes, hands, bodies met. Time threw the bonds of a minute into the madness of eternity. No bars, no glass, no walls, just Henrietta's spell that made one forget all notions of *he* and *she* until no lines existed any more. Don't tell the guards, but the prison walls just vanished. If only for a moment where all words fail, Tyrell was free. Jerome hung within the embrace of his parents and heard the language of the heart.

Tyrell poured forth all the words that had been censored from postcard apologies and chin-up phone calls. "Five years until parole, what's that?" he proclaimed to Henrietta. Jack, standing unobtrusive by the door, made a mental promise to himself that it wouldn't take that long. Tyrell told Henrietta how fast it'd go. Her touch revived their future. A kiss returned their dreams. Their embrace restored a rush of hope.

Henrietta couldn't speak. Her eyes were full, her skin flushed, her heart flooded to the brim. He believed all the things he'd come so bitterly close to losing faith in. He believed in an end to jails and prisons of all sorts. He believed that justice would one day come. He'd seen a falling star and made a wish. You couldn't see the suit of orange for the brightness of his eyes. His soul was shining with his faith. It blinded out all concrete, bars, guards, and locks. His words replanted their devastated lives with new-growth forests, young woods of promises for future generations. He held his love and told her,

"We're gonna make it, Henrietta. We'll make it out the other side of this."

It was the word *we* that caught Jack's attention. It reeled him in and made him bold enough to offer his assistance to the little family. They could reopen his case and appeal to a higher court, Jack said. It was the word *we,* later on, that welcomed Sarah, too, when Jack told her about the meeting in the jail. It was that *we* that set Sarah's heart on fire and gave her the courage to call Henrietta.

"There's a good chance we can get Tyrell out of there," Sarah had said, her belly pregnant with growing promises of new life.

"I've got time until the baby comes," she said, "and then I've still got time, just less of it for a little while." Sarah gathered up the legal documents and Jack got the court case moving through the bureaucracy. Then the baby had arrived and things slowed down a little.

But that's how change comes, Henrietta thought as she rocked on her porch. Change comes rushing along in big gushes followed by slower periods. But not to worry, behind the winds and gathering clouds was always rain. It would come.

The far-off lightning flashed. Thunder cracked belatedly. It seemed the whole country was ripe for a storm of change. Some folks were hiding in the bushes or burrowing in their dens, but others were out there riding the crosswinds and gusty updrafts. Odelle Jordan was one such courageous flier. She plunged her network into investigations, making change and ethics a primetime focus for the nation.

"This is reality TV," she told her viewers. "Don't blink or look away."

By turns, her shows were inspirational, sensational, horrific, and unbelievable. She carried awareness like a beacon through the dark night of the nation's soul.

"Someone has to lead," she told the people, "and that someone is every single one of us. We can start with our household decisions. Let's hit corporate corruption where it counts." She struck the corporate pocketbooks by sealing up the purse strings of the nation.

On the heels of the Purse String Strike, as it later came to be known, Louisa masterminded a ten-day blackout. The nation went camping in their homes. Business ground to a screeching halt. Power stalled in the IV drip lines of the country. We want ethics in our energy, the people cried! One blackout followed another until they rolled across the country in the storm clouds of protest.

The changes rumbled tonight with the thunder along the ridge. There were motions, movements, and pressures mounting. The rain would be here quicker than they knew it. Change would have them scrambling to get the drying clothes inside, the doors shut, the car windows rolled up. Henrietta thought a little rain would be real nice. She would listen to it on the porch, wrapped up in a blanket with Jerome. She felt the winds blow, hot and heavy, then sweetly cool.

It would come. The change would come. The summer had sprung into full bloom all around her. Yellow dandelions occupied every lawn. Even here, beneath the dense canopy of trees, a patch pushed up against her porch. One grayed and tufted orb of seeds begged for some winds to carry them. Henrietta smiled and hung her wishes on its quivering strands. Then the gusty breeze arrived and shook the seeds, rippled the grasses, and rumbled in the leaves. The trees flipped their silver underbellies back and forth.

Henrietta sang an old song to her baby, sang it far too slow. The trees were sucking up her sounds, nursing like her baby. She crooned the ballad like a lullaby, long and low and soft. It sounded like gentle pattering of rain a-coming, a far-off humming thunder.

She sang,

365

"Every Monday morning,
when the bluebirds begin to sing,
you can hear . . ."

She paused to listen to the closing in of wind and rumbles, smiling softly at the scent of the storm. The song throbbed in her heart and slid out from between her lips,

". . . you can hear John Henry half a mile away,
you can hear John Henry's hammering,
Lord, Lord,
you can hear John Henry's hammer ring!"

. . . and so it begins.

Steam Drills, Treadmills, and Shooting Stars

COMPENDIUM

&

A New Dedication

I dedicate this section to you, our heroes.
For in this world of beating hearts and lifetimes,
many of us will never meet,
but I know in my soul we are companions,
no matter how far apart on earth we stand,
for one thing is clear, forever and for always,
our actions march hand-in-hand.

–Rivera Sun

The Compendium

In the back of this novel, I have included a collection of documents that influenced the creation of this story. It begins with a short statement that inspired Jack Dalton's contract, followed by the Ballad of John Henry. I have included more information about *The Great Turning*, which was developed by Joanna Macy as part of The Work That Reconnects. I have included The Earth Charter because it is a revolutionary document. I have reprinted The Universal Declaration of Human Rights because not many Americans even know it exists, which is unfortunate, since Eleanor Roosevelt was instrumental in its creation. All of these are fascinating documents to read and study. And, finally, there is a little information about me, an excerpt from my next novel, and most importantly, my expression of gratitude to all the people who brought this book to you. Enjoy and share with friends, please.

A Note On
The Statement of an Interconnected & Self-Governing People:

One day, I got involved with a group of gifted people who proposed the concept of individual adoption of common principles as the only method of meaningful change. They proposed key words that described some commonly held values of a global society. I then crafted those words into the following statement. This statement served as a core inspiration for Jack Dalton's social contract.

I would like to note that the use of the word "corporate" is intentional. In the United States, corporations are considered people, and while the wisdom of such an approach is dubious, the effects are significant. Corporations are powerful entities in our world, and, since humans are responsible for creating them, we must now address how to ensure that their actions are beneficial, not detrimental, for the whole of creation.

The term "ethereal" is also included in the list of beings that affect our world. While scientists would like to dismiss them, gods, goddesses, spirits, etc. certainly influence the actions of the humans who believe in them, and must therefore be included in this summary of interconnected forces.

For a few years now, I have pondered the deeper implications of this simple statement, and have found that living in accordance with its principles has profoundly altered my life, worldview, and inner being. Simple as it appears on the surface, these words have the power to forge a new concept of how humans and all other beings live together on this planet.

Statement of an Interconnected & Self-Governing People

"We address this statement to our selves, taking conscious and aware responsibility for the knowledge that all beings are created interconnected, and that each, whether they be human, animal, plant, or mineral, corporate or ethereal, affects the existence of the whole as they secure the inalienable needs of all beings for their own forms of food, shelter, and rest.

"Seeing that the strength, happiness, and survival of our own being is interconnected with all others, we commit ourselves to uphold the supreme ethics of compassion, respect, love, and mutual consent in all of our interactions, and to work on an individual, societal, and global level on behalf of the organic unity of all creation.

"Such self-governance, held with consensus through the whole of humanity, and used as the basis of all personal, societal, civil, business, and international relationships, naturally forms a global society bestowing equal right of life, liberty, and pursuit of happiness to all."

The Ballad of John Henry

Note: These lyrics are very similar to the ones used by many of our well-known folksingers. However, there are hundreds of variations of the song. John Henry, himself, is a matter of historical debate. Although most accounts agree that he actually did live, race a steam drill, and die around 1870, there are many ideas about where that event took place, as well as other stories about his legendary life.

The captain said to John Henry
"Gonna bring that steam drill 'round.
Gonna bring that steam drill out on the job.
Gonna whop that steel on down. Down, Down.
Whop that steel on down."

John Henry said to his captain,
"A man ain't nothin' but a man,
But before I let your steam drill beat me down,
I'd die with a hammer in my hand. Lord, Lord.
Yes, I'll die with a hammer in my hand."

John Henry said to his shaker,
"Shaker, why don't you sing?
I'm throwin' thirty pounds from my hips on down.
Just listen to that cold steel ring. Lord, Lord.
Listen to that cold steel ring."

The man that invented the stream drill
Thought he was mighty fine,
But John Henry made fourteen feet;
The steam drill only made nine. Lord, Lord.
The steam drill only made nine.

John Henry hammered in the mountain
His hammer was striking fire.
But he worked so hard, he broke his poor heart.
He laid down his hammer and he died. Lord, Lord.
He laid down his hammer and he died.

John Henry had a little woman.
Her name was Polly Ann.
John Henry took sick and went to his bed.
Polly Ann drove steel like a man. Lord, Lord.
Polly Ann drove steel like a man.

John Henry had a little baby.
You could hold him in the palm of your hand.
The last words I heard that poor boy say,
"My daddy was steel-driving man. Lord, Lord.
My daddy was a steel-driving man."

Well, every Monday morning
When the bluebirds begin to sing.
You can hear John Henry a mile or more.
You can hear John Henry's hammering, Lord, Lord.
You can hear John Henry's hammer ring

Notes On The Great Turning

The Great Turning has been a source of inspiration to me for several years. In 2010, I attended a workshop with Joanna Macy and Kristen Masters, and experienced first-hand the strength of what they call *The Work That Reconnects.* Joanna Macy has published a number of brilliant books that I highly recommend reading. Her work seeks to open us to the effects of environmental and nuclear problems on our inner and outer beings. It also gives us stories and knowledge for moving forward, and the tools for change that are becoming increasingly necessary for our society.

I chose to include the Great Turning in this novel as a way to share Joanna Macy's work and honor it. I use elements of several aspects of the Work That Reconnects, including the story of the Great Turning, the Council of All Beings, Deep Time, and Deep Ecology. The experience of the Great Turning that Sarah and Allie Dalton have is a variation on the themes of the Work That Reconnects. It attempts to give you a glimpse of the effect and empowerment of the actual workshops. If you have the opportunity, make sure you attend one!

You can find more information about all of this on Joanna's website:

www.joannamacy.net

The Great Turning

*from The Work That Reconnects
developed by Joanna Macy and associates*

The Great Turning is a name for the essential adventure of our time: the shift from the industrial growth society to a life-sustaining civilization. The ecological and social crises we face are inflamed by an economic system dependent on accelerating growth. This self-destructing political economy sets its goals and measures its performance in terms of ever-increasing corporate profits--in other words by how fast materials can be extracted from Earth and turned into consumer products, weapons, and waste. A revolution is underway because people are realizing that our needs can be met without destroying our world. We have the technical knowledge, the communication tools, and material resources to grow enough food, ensure clean air and water, and meet rational energy needs. Future generations, if there is a livable world for them, will look back at the epochal transition we are making to a life-sustaining society. And they may well call this the time of the Great Turning. It is happening now. Whether or not it is recognized by corporate-controlled media, the Great Turning is a reality. Although we cannot know yet if it will take hold in time for humans and other complex life forms to survive, we can know that it is under way. And it is gaining momentum, through the actions of countless individuals and groups around the world. To see this as the larger context of our lives clears our vision and summons our courage.

The Three Dimensions of the Great Turning

1. Actions to slow the damage to Earth and its beings

Perhaps the most visible dimension of the Great Turning, these activities include all the political, legislative, and legal work required to reduce the destruction, as well as direct actions--blockades, boycotts, civil disobedience, and other forms of refusal. A few examples:

> Documenting and the ecological and health effects of the Industrial Growth Society;
> Lobbying or protesting against the World Trade

Organization and the international trade agreements that endanger ecosystems and undermine social and economic justice;

Blowing the whistle on illegal and unethical corporate practices;

Blockading and conducting vigils at places of ecological destruction, such as old-growth forests under threat of clear-cutting or at nuclear dumping grounds.

Work of this kind buys time. It saves some lives, and some ecosystems, species, and cultures, as well as some of the gene pool, for the sustainable society to come. But it is insufficient to bring that society about.

2. Analysis of structural causes and the creation of structural alternatives

The second dimension of the Great Turning is equally crucial. To free ourselves and our planet from the damage being inflicted by the Industrial Growth Society, we must understand its dynamics. What are the tacit agreements that create obscene wealth for a few, while progressively impoverishing the rest of humanity? What interlocking causes indenture us to an insatiable economy that uses our Earth as supply house and sewer? It is not a pretty picture, and it takes courage and confidence in our own common sense to look at it with realism; but we are demystifying the workings of the global economy. When we see how this system operates, we are less tempted to demonize the politicians and corporate CEOs who are in bondage to it. And for all the apparent might of the Industrial Growth Society, we can also see its fragility--how dependent it is on our obedience, and how doomed it is to devour itself. In addition to learning how the present system works, we are also creating structural alternatives. In countless localities, like green shoots pushing up through the rubble, new social and economic arrangements are sprouting. Not waiting for our national or state politicos to catch up with us, we are banding together, taking action in our own communities. Flowing from our creativity and collaboration on behalf of life, these actions may look marginal, but they hold the seeds for the future.

Some of the initiatives in this dimension:

- Teach-ins and study groups on the Industrial Growth Society; - Strategies and programs for nonviolent, citizen-based defense; - Reduction of reliance on fossil and nuclear fuels and conversion to renewable energy sources; - Collaborative living arrangements such as co-housing and eco-villages; - Community gardens, consumer cooperatives, community-supported agriculture, watershed restoration, local currencies...

3. Shift in Consciousness These structural alternatives cannot take root and survive without deeply ingrained values to sustain them. They must mirror what we want and how we relate to Earth and each other. They require, in other words, a profound shift in our perception of reality--and that shift is happening now, both as cognitive revolution and spiritual awakening. The insights and experiences that enable us to make this shift are accelerating, and they take many forms. They arise as grief for our world, giving the lie to old paradigm notions of rugged individualism, the essential separateness of the self. They arise as glad response to breakthroughs in scientific thought, as reductionism and materialism give way to evidence of a living universe. And they arise in the resurgence of wisdom traditions, reminding us again that our world is a sacred whole, worthy of adoration and service. The many forms and ingredients of this dimension include:

- general living systems theory; - deep ecology and the deep, long-range ecology movement; - Creation Spirituality and Liberation Theology; - Engaged Buddhism and similar currents in other traditions; - the resurgence of shamanic traditions; - ecofeminism; - ecopsychology; - the simple living movement.

The realizations we make in the third dimension of the Great Turning save us from succumbing to either panic or paralysis. They help us resist the temptation to stick our heads in the sand, or to turn on each other, for scapegoats on whom to vent our fear and rage.

More information can be found at:
www.joannamacy.net

The Earth Charter

(from the Earth Charter website)

The Earth Charter is a declaration of fundamental ethical principles for building a just, sustainable and peaceful global society in the 21st century. It seeks to inspire in all people a new sense of global interdependence and shared responsibility for the well-being of the whole human family, the greater community of life, and future generations. It is a vision of hope and a call to action.

The Earth Charter is centrally concerned with the transition to sustainable ways of living and sustainable human development. Ecological integrity is one major theme. However, the Earth Charter recognizes that the goals of ecological protection, the eradication of poverty, equitable economic development, respect for human rights, democracy, and peace are interdependent and indivisible. It provides, therefore, a new, inclusive, integrated ethical framework to guide the transition to a sustainable future.

The Earth Charter is a product of a decade-long, worldwide, cross cultural dialogue on common goals and shared values. The Earth Charter project began as a United Nations initiative, but it was carried forward and completed by a global civil society initiative. The Earth Charter was finalized and then launched as a people's charter in 2000 by the Earth Charter Commission, an independent international entity.

The drafting of the Earth Charter involved the most inclusive and participatory process ever associated with the creation of an international declaration. This process is the primary source of its legitimacy as a guiding ethical framework. The legitimacy of the document has been further enhanced by its endorsement by over 4,500 organizations, including many governments and international organizations.

In the light of this legitimacy, an increasing number of international lawyers recognize that the Earth Charter is acquiring the status of a soft law document. Soft law documents like the Universal Declaration of Human Rights are considered to be morally, but not legally, binding on state governments that agree to endorse and adopt them, and they often form the basis for the development of hard law.

At a time when major changes in how we think and live are urgently needed, the Earth Charter challenges us to examine our values and to choose a better way. At a time when international partnership is increasingly necessary, the Earth Charter encourages us to search for common ground in the midst of our diversity and to embrace a new global ethic that is shared by an ever-growing number of people throughout the world. At a time when education for sustainable development has become essential, the Earth Charter provides a very valuable educational instrument.

Please also visit www.earthcharterinaction.org

The Earth Charter

Preamble

We stand at a critical moment in Earth's history, a time when humanity must choose its future. As the world becomes increasingly interdependent and fragile, the future at once holds great peril and great promise. To move forward we must recognize that in the midst of a magnificent diversity of cultures and life forms we are one human family and one Earth community with a common destiny. We must join together to bring forth a sustainable global society founded on respect for nature, universal human rights, economic justice, and a culture of peace. Toward this end, it is imperative that we, the peoples of Earth, declare our responsibility to one another, to the greater community of life, and to future generations.

Earth, Our Home

Humanity is part of a vast evolving universe. Earth, our home, is alive with a unique community of life. The forces of nature make existence a demanding and uncertain adventure, but Earth has provided the conditions essential to life's evolution. The resilience of the community of life and the well-being of humanity depend upon preserving a healthy biosphere with all its ecological systems, a rich variety of plants and animals, fertile soils, pure waters, and clean air. The global environment with its finite resources is a common concern of all peoples. The protection of Earth's vitality, diversity, and beauty is a sacred trust.

The Global Situation

The dominant patterns of production and consumption are causing environmental devastation, the depletion of resources, and a massive extinction of species. Communities are being undermined. The benefits of development are not shared equitably and the gap between rich and poor is widening. Injustice, poverty, ignorance, and violent conflict are widespread and the cause of great suffering. An unprecedented rise in human population has overburdened ecological and social systems. The foundations of global security are threatened. These trends are perilous—but not inevitable.

The Challenges Ahead

The choice is ours: form a global partnership to care for Earth and one another or risk the destruction of ourselves and the diversity of life. Fundamental changes are needed in our values, institutions, and ways of living. We must realize that when basic needs have been met, human development is primarily about being more, not having more. We have the knowledge and technology to provide for all and to reduce our impacts on the environment. The emergence of a global civil society is creating new opportunities to build a democratic and humane world. Our environmental, economic, political, social, and spiritual challenges are interconnected, and together we can forge inclusive solutions.

Universal Responsibility

To realize these aspirations, we must decide to live with a sense of universal responsibility, identifying ourselves with the whole Earth community as well as our local communities. We are at once citizens of different nations and of one world in which the local and global are linked. Everyone shares responsibility for the present and future well-being of the human family and the larger living world. The spirit of human solidarity and kinship with all life is strengthened when we live with reverence for the mystery of being, gratitude for the gift of life, and humility regarding the human place in nature.

We urgently need a shared vision of basic values to provide an ethical foundation for the emerging world community. Therefore, together in hope we affirm the following interdependent principles for a sustainable way of life as a common standard by which the conduct of all individuals, organizations, businesses, governments, and transnational institutions is to be guided and assessed.

Principles

I. RESPECT AND CARE FOR THE COMMUNITY OF LIFE

1. Respect Earth and life in all its diversity. a. Recognize that all beings are interdependent and every form of life has value regardless of its worth to human beings. b. Affirm faith in the inherent dignity of all human beings and in the intellectual, artistic, ethical, and spiritual potential of humanity.

2. Care for the community of life with understanding, compassion, and love. a. Accept that with the right to own, manage, and use natural resources comes the duty to prevent environmental harm and to protect the rights of people. b. Affirm that with increased freedom, knowledge, and power comes increased responsibility to promote the common good.

3. Build democratic societies that are just, participatory, sustainable, and peaceful. a. Ensure that communities at all levels guarantee human rights and fundamental freedoms and provide everyone an opportunity to realize his or her full potential. b. Promote social and economic justice, enabling all to achieve a secure and meaningful livelihood that is ecologically responsible.

4. Secure Earth's bounty and beauty for present and future generations. a. Recognize that the freedom of action of each generation is qualified by the needs of future generations. b. Transmit to future generations values, traditions, and institutions that support the long-term flourishing of Earth's human and ecological communities.

In order to fulfill these four broad commitments, it is necessary to:

II. ECOLOGICAL INTEGRITY

5. Protect and restore the integrity of Earth's ecological systems, with special concern for biological diversity and the natural processes that sustain life.

a. Adopt at all levels sustainable development plans and regulations that make environmental conservation and rehabilitation integral to all development initiatives. b. Establish and safeguard viable nature and biosphere reserves, including wild lands and marine areas, to protect Earth's life support systems, maintain biodiversity, and preserve our natural heritage. c. Promote the recovery of endangered species and ecosystems. d. Control and eradicate non-native or genetically modified organisms harmful to native species and the environment, and prevent introduction of such harmful organisms. e. Manage the use of renewable resources such as water, soil, forest products, and marine life in ways that do not exceed rates of regeneration and that protect the health of ecosystems. f. Manage the extraction and use of non-renewable resources such as minerals and fossil fuels in ways that minimize depletion and cause no serious environmental damage.

6. **Prevent harm as the best method of environmental protection and, when knowledge is limited, apply a precautionary approach.** a. Take action to avoid the possibility of serious or irreversible environmental harm even when scientific knowledge is incomplete or inconclusive. b. Place the burden of proof on those who argue that a proposed activity will not cause significant harm, and make the responsible parties liable for environmental harm. c. Ensure that decision-making addresses the cumulative, long-term, indirect, long distance, and global consequences of human activities. d. Prevent pollution of any part of the environment and allow no build-up of radioactive, toxic, or other hazardous substances. e. Avoid military activities damaging to the environment.

7. **Adopt patterns of production, consumption, and reproduction that safeguard Earth's regenerative capacities, human rights, and community well-being.** a. Reduce, reuse, and recycle the materials used in production and consumption systems, and ensure that residual waste can be assimilated by ecological systems. b. Act with restraint and efficiency when using energy, and rely increasingly on renewable energy sources such as solar and wind. c. Promote the development, adoption, and equitable transfer of environmentally sound technologies. d. Internalize the full environmental and social costs of goods and services in the selling price, and enable consumers to identify products that meet the highest social and environmental standards. e. Ensure universal access to health care that fosters reproductive health and responsible reproduction. f. Adopt lifestyles that emphasize the quality of life and material

sufficiency in a finite world.

8. Advance the study of ecological sustainability and promote the open exchange and wide application of the knowledge acquired. a. Support international scientific and technical cooperation on sustainability, with special attention to the needs of developing nations. b. Recognize and preserve the traditional knowledge and spiritual wisdom in all cultures that contribute to environmental protection and human well-being. c. Ensure that information of vital importance to human health and environmental protection, including genetic information, remains available in the public domain.

III. SOCIAL AND ECONOMIC JUSTICE

9. Eradicate poverty as an ethical, social, and environmental imperative. a. Guarantee the right to potable water, clean air, food security, uncontaminated soil, shelter, and safe sanitation, allocating the national and international resources required. b. Empower every human being with the education and resources to secure a sustainable livelihood, and provide social security and safety nets for those who are unable to support themselves. c. Recognize the ignored, protect the vulnerable, serve those who suffer, and enable them to develop their capacities and to pursue their aspirations.

10. Ensure that economic activities and institutions at all levels promote human development in an equitable and sustainable manner. a. Promote the equitable distribution of wealth within nations and among nations. b. Enhance the intellectual, financial, technical, and social resources of developing nations, and relieve them of onerous international debt. c. Ensure that all trade supports sustainable resource use, environmental protection, and progressive labor standards. . Require multinational corporations and international financial organizations to act transparently in the public good, and hold them accountable for the consequences of their activities.

11. Affirm gender equality and equity as prerequisites to sustainable development and ensure universal access to education, health care, and economic opportunity. a. Secure the human rights of women and girls and end all violence against them. b. Promote the active participation of women in all aspects of economic, political, civil, social, and cultural life as full and equal partners, decision makers, leaders, and beneficiaries. c. Strengthen families and ensure the safety and loving nurture of all family members.

12. Uphold the right of all, without discrimination, to a natural and social environment supportive of human dignity, bodily health, and spiritual well-being, with special attention to the rights of indigenous peoples and minorities. a. Eliminate discrimination in all its forms, such as that based on race, color, sex, sexual orientation, religion, language, and national, ethnic or social origin. b. Affirm the right of indigenous peoples to their spirituality, knowledge, lands and resources and to their related practice of sustainable livelihoods. c. Honor and support the young people of our communities, enabling them to fulfill their essential role in creating sustainable societies. d. Protect and restore outstanding places of cultural and spiritual significance.

IV. DEMOCRACY, NONVIOLENCE, AND PEACE

13. Strengthen democratic institutions at all levels, and provide transparency and accountability in governance, inclusive participation in decision making, and access to justice. a. Uphold the right of everyone to receive clear and timely information on environmental matters and all development plans and activities which are likely to affect them or in which they have an interest. b. Support local, regional and global civil society, and promote the meaningful participation of all interested individuals and organizations in decision-making. c. Protect the rights to freedom of opinion, expression, peaceful assembly, association, and dissent. d. Institute effective and efficient access to administrative and independent judicial procedures, including remedies and redress for environmental harm and the threat of such harm. e. Eliminate corruption in all public and private institutions. f. Strengthen local communities, enabling them to care for their environments, and assign environmental responsibilities to the levels of government where they can be carried out most effectively.

14. Integrate into formal education and life-long learning the knowledge, values, and skills needed for a sustainable way of life. a. Provide all, especially children and youth, with educational opportunities that empower them to contribute actively to sustainable development. b. Promote the contribution of the arts and humanities as well as the sciences in sustainability education. c. Enhance the role of the mass media in raising awareness of ecological and social challenges. d. Recognize the importance of moral and spiritual education for sustainable living.

15. Treat all living beings with respect and consideration. a. Prevent cruelty to animals kept in human societies and protect them from suffering. b. Protect wild animals from methods of hunting, trapping, and fishing that cause extreme, prolonged, or avoidable suffering. c. Avoid or eliminate to the full extent possible the taking or destruction of non-targeted species.

16. Promote a culture of tolerance, nonviolence, and peace. a. Encourage and support mutual understanding, solidarity, and cooperation among all peoples and within and among nations. b. Implement comprehensive strategies to prevent violent conflict and use collaborative problem solving to manage and resolve environmental conflicts and other disputes. c. Demilitarize national security systems to the level of a non-provocative defense posture, and convert military resources to peaceful purposes, including ecological restoration. d. Eliminate nuclear, biological, and toxic weapons and other weapons of mass destruction. e. Ensure that the use of orbital and outer space supports environmental protection and peace. f. Recognize that peace is the wholeness created by right relationships with oneself, other persons, other cultures, other life, Earth, and the larger whole of which all are a part.

The Way Forward

As never before in history, common destiny beckons us to seek a new beginning. Such renewal is the promise of these Earth Charter principles. To fulfill this promise, we must commit ourselves to adopt and promote the values and objectives of the Charter.

This requires a change of mind and heart. It requires a new sense of global interdependence and universal responsibility. We must imaginatively develop and apply the vision of a sustainable way of life locally, nationally, regionally, and globally. Our cultural diversity is a precious heritage and different cultures will find their own distinctive ways to realize the vision. We must deepen and expand the global dialogue that generated the Earth Charter, for we have much to learn from the ongoing collaborative search for truth and wisdom.

Life often involves tensions between important values. This can mean difficult choices. However, we must find ways to harmonize diversity with unity, the exercise of freedom with the common good, short-term objectives with long-term goals. Every individual, family, organization, and community has a vital role to play. The arts, sciences, religions, educational institutions, media, businesses, nongovernmental organizations, and governments are all called to offer creative leadership. The partnership of government, civil society, and business is essential for effective governance.

In order to build a sustainable global community, the nations of the world must renew their commitment to the United Nations, fulfill their obligations under existing international agreements, and support the implementation of Earth Charter principles with an international legally binding instrument on environment and development. Let ours be a time remembered for the awakening of a new reverence for life, the firm resolve to achieve sustainability, the quickening of the struggle for justice and peace, and the joyful celebration of life.

A Note On The Universal Declaration of Human Rights

The Universal Declaration of Human Rights was created by the United Nations directly after World War II. It was ratified by the United Nations in 1948. It is the first expression of the rights all humans are inherently entitled to, and several subsequent covenants and international treaties have arisen from it. Although the United States has signed the declaration, and also the International Covenant on Social, Economic, and Cultural Rights, our Congress has yet to ratify the covenants, making them ineffective on a legal basis.

It is my belief that citizens of the United States should know the rights that the global community believes all persons are entitled to, regardless of what our congressmen and women seem to think. I encourage you all to read not only this declaration, but to also seek out the covenants that arise from it, and learn the complicated and slightly shameful response of our government to these noble principles.

More information can be found at www.un.org

Universal Declaration of Human Rights

PREAMBLE

Whereas recognition of the inherent dignity and of the equal and inalienable rights of all members of the human family is the foundation of freedom, justice and peace in the world,

Whereas disregard and contempt for human rights have resulted in barbarous acts which have outraged the conscience of mankind, and the advent of a world in which human beings shall enjoy freedom of speech and belief and freedom from fear and want has been proclaimed as the highest aspiration of the common people,

Whereas it is essential, if man is not to be compelled to have recourse, as a last resort, to rebellion against tyranny and oppression, that human rights should be protected by the rule of law,

Whereas it is essential to promote the development of friendly relations between nations,

Whereas the peoples of the United Nations have in the Charter reaffirmed their faith in fundamental human rights, in the dignity and worth of the human person and in the equal rights of men and women and have determined to promote social progress and better standards of life in larger freedom,

Whereas Member States have pledged themselves to achieve, in co-operation with the United Nations, the promotion of universal respect for and observance of human rights and fundamental freedoms,

Whereas a common understanding of these rights and freedoms is of the greatest importance for the full realization of this pledge,

Now, Therefore THE GENERAL ASSEMBLY proclaims

THIS UNIVERSAL DECLARATION OF HUMAN
RIGHTS as a common standard of achievement for all peoples
and all nations, to the end that every individual and every organ
of society, keeping this Declaration constantly in mind, shall
strive by teaching and education to promote respect for these
rights and freedoms and by progressive measures, national and
international, to secure their universal and effective recognition
and observance, both among the peoples of Member States
themselves and among the peoples of territories under their
jurisdiction.

Article 1.

All human beings are born free and equal in
dignity and rights. They are endowed with reason and
conscience and should act toward one another in a spirit
of brotherhood.

Article 2.

Everyone is entitled to all the rights and
freedoms set forth in this Declaration, without
distinction of any kind, such as race, colour, sex,
language, religion, political or other opinion, national or
social origin, property, birth or other status.
Furthermore, no distinction shall be made on the basis
of the political, jurisdictional or international status of
the country or territory to which a person belongs,
whether it be independent, trust, non-self-governing or
under any other limitation of sovereignty.

Article 3.

Everyone has the right to life, liberty and
security of person.

Article 4.

No one shall be held in slavery or servitude;

slavery and the slave trade shall be prohibited in all their forms.

Article 5.

No one shall be subjected to torture or to cruel, inhuman or degrading treatment or punishment.

Article 6.

Everyone has the right to recognition everywhere as a person before the law.

Article 7.

All are equal before the law and are entitled without any discrimination to equal protection of the law. All are entitled to equal protection against any discrimination in violation of this Declaration and against any incitement to such discrimination.

Article 8.

Everyone has the right to an effective remedy by the competent national tribunals for acts violating the fundamental rights granted him by the constitution or by law.

Article 9.

No one shall be subjected to arbitrary arrest, detention or exile.

Article 10.

Everyone is entitled in full equality to a fair and public hearing by an independent and impartial tribunal, in the determination of his rights and obligations and of any criminal charge against him.

Article 11.

(1) Everyone charged with a penal offence has the right to be presumed innocent until proved guilty according to law in a public trial at which he has had all the guarantees necessary for his defense.

(2) No one shall be held guilty of any penal offence on account of any act or omission which did not constitute a penal offence, under national or international law, at the time when it was committed. Nor shall a heavier penalty be imposed than the one that was applicable at the time the penal offence was committed.

Article 12.

No one shall be subjected to arbitrary interference with his privacy, family, home or correspondence, nor to attacks upon his honor and reputation. Everyone has the right to the protection of the law against such interference or attacks.

Article 13.

(1) Everyone has the right to freedom of movement and residence within the borders of each state.

(2) Everyone has the right to leave any country, including his own, and to return to his country.

Article 14.

(1) Everyone has the right to seek and to enjoy in other countries asylum from persecution.

(2) This right may not be invoked in the case of prosecutions genuinely arising from non-political crimes or from acts contrary to the purposes and principles of the United Nations.

Article 15.

(1) Everyone has the right to a nationality.

(2) No one shall be arbitrarily deprived of his nationality nor denied the right to change his nationality.

Article 16.

(1) Men and women of full age, without any limitation due to race, nationality or religion, have the right to marry and to found a family. They are entitled to equal rights as to marriage, during marriage and at its dissolution.

(2) Marriage shall be entered into only with the free and full consent of the intending spouses.

(3) The family is the natural and fundamental group unit of society and is entitled to protection by society and the State.

Article 17.

(1) Everyone has the right to own property alone as well as in association with others.

(2) No one shall be arbitrarily deprived of his property.

Article 18.

Everyone has the right to freedom of thought, conscience and religion; this right includes freedom to change his religion or belief, and freedom, either alone or in community with others and in public or private, to manifest his religion or belief in teaching, practice, worship and observance.

Article 19.

Everyone has the right to freedom of opinion and expression; this right includes freedom to hold opinions without interference and to seek, receive and impart information and ideas through any media and regardless of frontiers.

Article 20.

(1) Everyone has the right to freedom of peaceful assembly and association.
(2) No one may be compelled to belong to an association.

Article 21.

(1) Everyone has the right to take part in the government of his country, directly or through freely chosen representatives.
(2) Everyone has the right of equal access to public service in his country.
(3) The will of the people shall be the basis of the authority of government; this will shall be expressed in periodic and genuine elections which shall be by universal and equal suffrage and shall be held by secret vote or by equivalent free voting procedures.

Article 22.

      Everyone, as a member of society, has the right to social security and is entitled to realization, through national effort and international co-operation and in accordance with the organization and resources of each State, of the economic, social and cultural rights indispensable for his dignity and the free development of his personality.

Article 23.

      (1) Everyone has the right to work, to free choice of employment, to just and favourable conditions of work and to protection against unemployment.

      (2) Everyone, without any discrimination, has the right to equal pay for equal work.

      (3) Everyone who works has the right to just and favourable remuneration ensuring for himself and his family an existence worthy of human dignity, and supplemented, if necessary, by other means of social protection.

      (4) Everyone has the right to form and to join trade unions for the protection of his interests.

Article 24.

      Everyone has the right to rest and leisure, including reasonable limitation of working hours and periodic holidays with pay.

Article 25.

      (1) Everyone has the right to a standard of living adequate for the health and well-being of himself and of his family, including food, clothing, housing and medical care and necessary social services, and the right to security in the event of unemployment, sickness, disability, widowhood, old age or other lack of

livelihood in circumstances beyond his control.

(2) Motherhood and childhood are entitled to special care and assistance. All children, whether born in or out of wedlock, shall enjoy the same social protection.

Article 26.

(1) Everyone has the right to education. Education shall be free, at least in the elementary and fundamental stages. Elementary education shall be compulsory. Technical and professional education shall be made generally available and higher education shall be equally accessible to all on the basis of merit.

(2) Education shall be directed to the full development of the human personality and to the strengthening of respect for human rights and fundamental freedoms. It shall promote understanding, tolerance and friendship among all nations, racial or religious groups, and shall further the activities of the United Nations for the maintenance of peace.

(3) Parents have a prior right to choose the kind of education that shall be given to their children.

Article 27.

(1) Everyone has the right freely to participate in the cultural life of the community, to enjoy the arts and to share in scientific advancement and its benefits.

(2) Everyone has the right to the protection of the moral and material interests resulting from any scientific, literary or artistic production of which he is the author.

Article 28.

Everyone is entitled to a social and international order in which the rights and freedoms set forth in this Declaration can be fully realized.

Article 29.

    (1) Everyone has duties to the community in which alone the free and full development of his personality is possible.

    (2) In the exercise of his rights and freedoms, everyone shall be subject only to such limitations as are determined by law solely for the purpose of securing due recognition and respect for the rights and freedoms of others and of meeting the just requirements of morality, public order and the general welfare in a democratic society.

    (3) These rights and freedoms may in no case be exercised contrary to the purposes and principles of the United Nations.

Article 30.

    Nothing in this Declaration may be interpreted as implying for any State, group or person any right to engage in any activity or to perform any act aimed at the destruction of any of the rights and freedoms set forth herein.

Special Thanks

(For me, writing a book is never a lonely effort.)

The following dedicated their love, support, proof-reading, inspiration, and/or feedback to the creation of this novel: Marada Cook, Leah Cook, Skylar Cook, Land Cook, Delores Cook, Ted Cook, Kate Simonds, Annie Kelley, Laurel Thomsen, Laurie and Joe Garner, Rita O'Connell, Jillian Michel, Lindsay Simonds, George Sherman, Sarah Vekasi, Joanna Macy, Karen Lane, April Green, Claire Paul, Kathleen Dudley, and many more.

Dariel Garner, my dedicated and patient partner, deserves a very special thank you for unending editorial suggestions offered to this sometimes extremely unreceptive author. Thank you for all the meals you cooked, laundry that got washed, and countless other ways in which you have supported me in the writing of this book. It would have been a whole different story without you!

I would also like to thank the organic growers of Taos Pueblo for the incredible vegetables that nourished the writer of this book; Jenny Bird who built the beautiful earthship house that shelters my partner and I; the wild and rapidly changing publishing industry that got this book to the readers' hands; and, of course, the Earth that creates and sustains us all.

The Dandelion Insurrection
a novel
by Rivera Sun

"So . . . the Dandelion Insurrection?"

As soon as he asked, he wished he hadn't. The moonlit rapture fled from Zadie's face. She looked up at the iron bridge, her expression full of shadows.

"Lines, Charlie, they're putting down lines to divide people. Do you know where you're standing?"

"On a freezing bridge between the U.S. and Canada."

She shook her head and pointed down. A white line gleamed on the metal. He was straddling the border, one foot on each side.

"Watch this," Zadie said. She pushed off the rail and spun around in the moonlight, her cream coat winging out in all directions. Her footsteps clanged as her heels twirled across the white line, mocking the international border.

"Come on, Charlie, dance!"

He stood up awkwardly, "Uh, I can't really dance-"

"The moon doesn't care, and neither do I." She grabbed his hands and whirled him faster and faster until they stumbled and clung to each other for balance.

"I'm dizzy," she giggled, muffling her laughter in his coat.

"Me too," he confessed.

"Where are we?" she asked.

"On a bridge, stupid."

"In Canada?"

"No, America -wait, shoot, I don't know," he realized. "Where's the line?"

Zadie threw her fingers over his eyes, "You can't feel it, can you?"

"Well, it has to be here somewhere. Jesus, your fingers are like icicles on my eyes." He pulled them away and stuck them against his chest.

"That's better," she sighed. "Now, where were we?"

"Somewhere between the U.S. and Canada," he said.

"No, we were talking about the Dandelion Insurrection." Zadie brought her lips next to Charlie's ear. "The Dandelion Insurrection is two people on a border, spinning until they don't know which country they're in."

"Huh?"

"The Dandelion Insurrection is putting on a clown nose as you go through customs at dawn."

"This doesn't make sense."

"The Dandelion Insurrection *is* not making sense."

"Zadie," he sighed.

"The Dandelion Insurrection is an out-cropping of golden humanity. It's an indomitable spirit that refuses to be rounded up. It's the wild seeds of rebellion blowing onto the well-ordered lawns of society."

"Is that a metaphor?"

"Yes and no. The Dandelion Insurrection is both imagined and real; metaphoric and practical-"

"-and cryptic," Charlie complained.

"Not really," she grinned. "Not when you get to know it better."

"Will I?" he asked.

"Undoubtedly."

Zadie Byrd Gray threw her arms up in the moonlight. Her laughter bounced delightedly against the looming trusses of the bridge and rang out on all sides of the border.

"Watch out world!" she shouted. "The Dandelion Insurrection is here!"

The Dandelion Insurrection is the second full-length novel from actress/author, Rivera Sun. Zadie Bryd Gray, aerialist, traveler, and renegade teams up with Charlie Rider, reporter and reluctant poet, in a spirited revolt against the growing police state. Their wild adventure, fanning the flames of human kindness, takes them from a tiny French-Acadian border town in Maine across the diverse American continent, encountering the most uplifting and inspiring stories of humanity along the way.

Scheduled to be released in 2013. Follow the progress at . . .
Email: info@risingsundancetheater.com
Facebook: Rivera Sun
Blog: www.risingsundancetheater.com/wpblog/
Website: www.risingsundancetheater.com

Also, don't miss Rivera Sun's other books:
The Imagine-a-nation of Lala Child
Freedom Stories: volume one

About the Author

Rivera Sun has red hair, a twin sister, and a fondness for esoteric mystics. She went to Bennington College to study writing as a Harcourt Scholar and graduated with a degree in dance. She founded the nationally touring Rising Sun Dance & Theater company in 2010, which performs a series of plays, *The Freedom Stories of Lala*, written by Rivera. She lives in an earthship house in New Mexico, where she grows tomatoes, bakes sourdough bread, and writes poetry, plays, and novels on the side. Rivera has been an aerial dancer, a bike messenger, and a gung-fu style tea server. Everything else about her - except her writing- is perfectly ordinary.

Rivera Sun also loves hearing from her readers.
Email: info@risingsundancetheater.com
Facebook: Rivera Sun
Blog: www.risingsundancetheater.com/wpblog/
Website: www.risingsundancetheater.com

CPSIA information can be obtained
at www.ICGtesting.com
Printed in the USA
LVOW10*2321070517
533655LV00019B/627/P